# POLARIS RISING

# POLARIS RISING

A NOVEL

## JESSIE MIHALIK

HARPER Voyager

*An Imprint of* HarperCollins *Publishers*

POLARIS RISING. Copyright © 2019 by Jessie Mihalik. All rights reserved. Printed in the United States of America. No part of this book may be used or reproduced in any manner whatsoever without written permission except in the case of brief quotations embodied in critical articles and reviews. For information, address HarperCollins Publishers, 195 Broadway, New York, NY 10007.

HarperCollins books may be purchased for educational, business, or sales promotional use. For information, please email the Special Markets Department at SPsales@harpercollins.com.

Harper Voyager and design are trademarks of HarperCollins Publishers LLC.

FIRST EDITION

*Designed by Paula Russell Szafranski*

Library of Congress Cataloging-in-Publication Data has been applied for.

ISBN 978-0-06-280238-5

19 20 21 22 23 LSC 10 9 8 7 6 5 4 3 2 1

*To Dustin, who made it all possible.*
*I love you so much.*

# ACKNOWLEDGMENTS

A story only requires an author, but a book requires a team. I'd like to thank the following people who helped turn my story into a book.

Thanks to my agent, Sarah E. Younger, who believed in Ada and Loch's story when it was just a blurb and a beginning. Thanks for your tireless work and for patiently answering a million newbie questions!

I am deeply grateful to my editor, Tessa Woodward, for her expert guidance and editorial advice. Thank you for helping me deliver the best story possible! I'd also like to thank assistant editor Elle Keck and the rest of the team at Harper Voyager for their help.

Thanks to Lisa Silverman, the copyeditor responsible for eradicating the pesky typos I missed.

My heartfelt gratitude to Ilona and Andrew Gordon for their invaluable help and advice as I navigate the strange new world of being a published author.

Thanks to Whitney Bates, Patrick Ferguson, and Tracy Smith for reading the early drafts of the story, offering feedback, and generally listening to me whine.

And finally, my deepest love and appreciation to my husband, Dustin, who encouraged me to pursue my dream of writing even when I didn't always believe in myself. You have no idea how much your support means to me. I love you!

# CHAPTER 1

T he steel toe of my boot slammed into the blond merc's knee with a satisfying crunch. He went down with a curse, but the two men holding my arms didn't release me, even as I struggled in their grasp. The blow had been more luck than skill, but it was enough to make the fourth mercenary pause before trying to grab my legs again.

I planted my feet and pushed back as hard as I could. The men behind me barely budged. I was a decently strong woman, but they each outweighed me by fifty or more pounds and the physics just weren't on my side. My self-defense tutor had warned me that one day I would regret slacking off in lessons—turns out, she was right.

"Stop fighting, you little bitch, or I'll stun you again," the blond warned. He climbed to his feet and waved his stunstick as if I needed a visual reminder. He wasn't the ship's captain, so he must be the mercenary commander. He was young for commander, but mercs weren't known to have long lives.

The ship's captain stood back while the merc crew tried to

wrestle me farther into the ship. The skin around his left eye was fiercely red. He'd have a shiner by tomorrow, thanks to me. That blow had been more skill than luck, but not enough to save me.

The captain was a handsome man, older, with dark hair that was gray at the temples. He looked like a gentleman, not a bounty hunter, and that had allowed him to get close enough to grab me. The rest of his crew was standard-issue mercenary: big, mean, and calculating. As soon as I'd caught sight of them, I'd known that I'd made a mistake.

I hoped it wouldn't be my last.

I fought on, determined. As long as the ship was still docked, I had a chance. I could escape and disappear into the crowds of the space station until I could find another ship. I was good at hiding.

The blond lost his patience. Before I could kick him away, he hit me with the stunstick. I screamed as my body lit up in agony. The mercs dropped me. My head hit the metal deck and pain blazed bright before dulling to a low throb. The world went dark and floaty.

"John, what are you doing? Don't hurt her!" the captain shouted. "If she shows up with so much as a bruise, von Hasenberg will kill the lot of us."

"Where do ya want her?" one of the other men asked.

"She can stay in my—" the captain started, but the blond, presumably John, cut him off.

"Put her in with Loch. That'll teach the little hellion a lesson. It's not like he's using the space anyway."

The crew laughed uneasily. Whoever Loch was, he made them nervous, and it took a lot to rattle a merc crew. Yay for me.

I tried to struggle as they picked me up by my arms and legs, but my muscles weren't responding, thanks to the blow to the head. And the nanobots in my blood that should have been repairing any tissue damage were also susceptible to the stunstick. They'd recover in a few minutes, but until then I had to wait for natural healing.

Nanobots, or nanos, were available to anyone who could afford the exorbitant price tag. I'd been injected with them as a newborn.

A door squeaked open and the men cursed quietly as they tried to maneuver me through the opening.

"Put her on the bed," the captain said. "Carefully."

"Why, Gerald, you shouldn't have," a deep voice rumbled from within the room.

"I didn't," the captain snapped. "She's worth three times what you are, Loch, so you don't want to make me choose which of you to keep," he continued. "Keep your comments to yourself or I'll purge you. Same thing happens if you even look at her sideways."

One of the men grumbled something too low to catch.

"She give you that eye?" Loch asked. "Did you try to get some on the side and she took offense?"

"Stun him," the captain said flatly.

The electric hiss of a stunstick was followed by a grunt. I'd never heard anyone get stunned without screaming; it didn't seem possible.

I cracked my eyes open a tiny bit. The light panel on the ceiling glowed softly. Were there supposed to be two of them?

"She's coming to," one of the men warned.

I squinted, trying to get my vision to clear, and when that

didn't work, I closed my eyes and willed the nanos to work faster. They weren't affected by my desire for speed, sadly, so I resigned myself to wait.

"Everyone out. Pull up the separator and leave it up. Let's see how the little princess likes her new palace," John said.

The faint ozone smell of an active energy field reached my nose. Booted footsteps exited the room, then the door creaked closed and locked with a metallic *thunk*.

I wiggled my fingers and toes. It was a start.

"You alive?" Loch asked.

"Mostly," I slurred. "They stunned me then dropped me headfirst onto the deck. I'll live."

"Where are we?"

"Station orbiting Theta Sagittarii Dwarf One," I said. I sat up and closed my eyes against the light-headedness. In addition to my throbbing head, I was sore from being hit with a stunstick twice in an hour. Overall, it could've been worse, but not by much.

"Damn," he muttered. I was with him there. I didn't know why he was concerned, but I knew that we were just two short jumps away from the gate that would deliver us directly to Earth. That only gave me a little over a week—in open space no less—to escape.

I cracked my eyes open. I sat on a narrow cot with a thin mattress and no sheets or blankets. A quick glance confirmed I was in a standard holding cell on a Yamado frigate—only the Yamados etched their House symbol, a crane, on every door.

Far more interesting than the Yamado door was the man sharing the cell with me. Even through the slight distortion of the blue energy barrier, I saw that deeply bronzed flesh

4

wrapped his heavily muscled frame. Broad shoulders tapered to a narrow waist with rippling abs. Defined arms and muscled legs completed the picture.

It was only after I'd stared for a solid five seconds that I realized why I was seeing quite so much of him: he had been stripped down to only a skintight pair of black boxer briefs.

I jerked my gaze up to his face and blinked in surprise when I met luminescent eyes. But when I met his eyes a second time, they were brown. Ocular augments existed, but as far as I knew, they permanently altered your eyes. It could've been a trick of the light, but it was worth watching.

His gaze was sharp and direct. Several weeks' worth of dark beard shadowed his jaw. His hair was the same length and I wondered if he normally kept his head shaved. The scruffiness made it hard to tell his exact age, but he was probably a few years older than my twenty-three.

"Like what you see?" he asked with a smirk.

"Yes," I said after a few more seconds of frank appraisal. Surprise flashed across his face, but why would I lie? He was beautifully built. He was perhaps not conventionally handsome but he had a deep, primal appeal. One glance and you knew that this was a man who could take care of problems. Add that deep, gravelly voice and he was temptation incarnate.

Now that I wasn't mesmerized by the amount of flesh on display, I saw that he was chained to the wall behind him from both ankles and wrists. The chains disappeared into the wall and their length could be adjusted. Right now, they were short enough that he couldn't sit comfortably. Whoever he was, the mercs weren't taking any chances with him.

I stood and wavered as sore muscles protested. Damn

stunsticks to hell. With the bed taking up more than half of the floor space, there was barely any room to walk. I knew from the schematics that the cell was a meter and a half wide by three meters long. The barrier dropped down just past the two-meter mark, leaving my unfortunate cellmate trapped in a one-and-a-half by one-meter box. He wouldn't be able to lie flat even if they released the chains enough to let him.

The barrier was blue, which should mean safe, but I'd known some people who thought it was funny to reprogram the system. I carefully reached out a finger and pressed it against the field. I didn't get shocked, so I wouldn't have to worry about avoiding it. Today was finally looking up.

"What are you doing?" Loch asked.

"Exploring."

He raised a skeptical eyebrow but didn't say anything else.

In addition to the bed, the only other features of the room were a tiny sink and, on the other side of the barrier, a toilet. The cell wasn't designed to be permanently divided the way the mercs were using it. The barrier was meant to hold the prisoner away from the door while the cell was cleaned or maintained.

"Do you know how many crew are on board?" I asked.

"At least eight, maybe nine."

A merchant ship of this size could be efficiently managed by as few as six, but the standard crew size was between eight and ten. If it was loaded out for maximum crew space, they could have up to fourteen.

The lights flickered and the floor vibrated with the subtle hum of running engines. The captain wasn't wasting any time getting under way. I moved around the room, touching the cool steel walls seemingly at random. I knew we were being watched, and I didn't want to make our audience nervous just yet.

"First time in a cell?"

"It's rather small," I said.

Loch barked out a laugh. "You get used to it. Let me guess, you're a surfacer."

Surfacers were people who grew up primarily on planets. Every day they woke up to big blue—or green or pink—skies, lots of solid ground under their feet, and plenty of room to roam.

Spacers, the people who grew up in the ships and stations floating around and between those same planets, seemed to think that surfacers had it easier. Even I knew that wasn't always the case.

"What gave me away?" I asked. I'd lived entirely on ships and stations for the last two years. I'd gotten used to the smaller spaces, but I still longed for the wide-open blue sky of my home.

His answer was interrupted by a male voice through the intercom speaker. "Stand away from the door."

I had not expected anyone so soon and this cell didn't give me much room to fight. Chains rattled behind me. I glanced back as Loch stood to his full height. At a meter eighty in boots, I was a tall woman. Loch still had me beat by at least ten centimeters. Damn. Why were the attractive ones always criminals?

The door swung inward to reveal a young man with a shaggy mop of blond hair that looked like it had never seen a brush. He held an armful of frilly fuchsia fabric and a stunstick. "Give me any trouble and I've got permission to zap you," he warned.

"Give *me* any trouble, and you'll get a boot to the teeth," I replied. "No permission required."

He almost smiled. What do you know, a merc with a sense of humor—it was like I'd found a unicorn. I'd have to blame it on his age because he looked all of sixteen.

"You're having dinner with the captain," he said. "Here's your dress." He dropped the frilly monstrosity on the bed.

"No," I said. I didn't balk because of the frills, which were horrible, or the color, which was equally horrible. I refused because it was a dress. I had no problem with dresses in general, but on a ship full of hostile men, it was smarter for everyone if I didn't go out of my way to advertise the fact that I was female.

"Umm, no to which part?" he asked hesitantly.

"I'll dine with the captain, but I'm wearing my own clothes." I had on a sturdy pair of black cargo pants, heavy black boots, and a long-sleeved black shirt. I wasn't trying to win *Monochromatic Monthly*'s best dressed award, but black was easy to find, easy to match, and generally didn't show dirt or grease stains as fast as other colors. Win, win, win.

"Uhh . . ."

I tilted my head ever so slightly and let my expression frost over. "I will dine with the captain, but I *will* be wearing my own clothes."

He ducked his head. "Yes, ma'am," he said. "Right this way."

A deep chuckle followed us out.

THE KID GRIPPED THE STUNSTICK LIKE HE EXPECTED ME to jump him at any moment. I guess word of my arrival had already spread to the rest of the crew. And, honestly, if they'd sent anyone else, I probably would've made an attempt at escape. If it came down to it, I would go through the kid if he stood between me and freedom, but it wouldn't be my first choice.

As we walked, I took in my surroundings. The captain had not spent much on interior upgrades. The walls were flat gray metal, the floor was steel grating, and the lights were few and far between. I saw at least three major wiring issues that would get them grounded if a safety officer ever bothered to do an inspection. The ship was holding up well for her age, but it was apparent that either the captain or his crew didn't truly love her.

I, however, saw plenty to love. Access panels were open or missing. The wiring issues would be an easy way to disable some key ship systems. And the layout matched the reference layout, so I could find my way around even in the dark.

The kid led me to the captain's chambers, which were exactly where I expected them to be. Yamado had been making this style ship for approximately a thousand years, give or take a few, and I was suddenly very glad that they liked to stick to tradition.

The captain's entertaining space was brightly lit, with

real wood floors, thick rugs, and antique furniture. A table that could seat sixteen dominated the middle of the room. Two place settings were laid out on the right side. The captain sat in an overstuffed chair next to a sideboard that was being used as a liquor cabinet. He rose to meet me. The skin around his left eye was already darkening.

I pulled on my public persona, affixed my politest smile to my lips, and tried not to think stabby thoughts. "Thank you for the dinner invitation, Captain."

"Of course, my dear, of course," he said. "Ada, may I call you Ada?" He continued before I had a chance to respond, "I know we got off to a bad start, but now that we are under way, I thought we could put all of that behind us. I know your father is quite eager to have you home."

"I'm sure he is," I murmured. Albrecht von Hasenberg was nothing if not thorough. When his security team couldn't find me and drag me back for my engagement party, he went above and beyond by posting an enormous bounty for my safe return. Of course, he told the news, he was devastated that I was "missing." He failed to mention that I had left of my own volition. Or that I'd been gone for two years.

"Can I get you some wine? Or perhaps brandy?" the captain asked.

"Wine would be lovely, thank you," I said. I knew where this road led. I'd been playing this game since I could talk. The captain wanted something, and he thought—rightly—that House von Hasenberg could help him get it. As patriarch of one of the three High Houses, very few people in the universe wielded more power than my father.

As the fifth of six children, I wielded no power in House

von Hasenberg at all. But the good captain didn't know that, and outside of the Consortium, my name carried its own power.

"Captain—"

"Please, call me Gerald," he interrupted as he handed me a glass of wine with a shallow bow. "Gerald Pearson, at your service."

I let a chill creep into my expression and he flushed. You did not interrupt a member of a High House if you wanted to keep breathing. By acknowledging who my father was, he'd moved me from *bounty* to *potential ally,* and now I was quickly moving to *superior.* It was his first mistake, but I didn't hold it against him. He'd never had to swim with the glittering sharks of the Consortium. I had, and I excelled at it.

I hated it, but I excelled at it.

"Gerald," I said with a dismissive little sniff, "have you already sent word to my father that I was found?"

"Of course, my lady," he said, practically tripping over himself to get back into my good graces. "I let him know as soon as I returned to the ship. I also sent along a copy of our flight plan."

*Damn.* Interstellar communication could be slow, but we were close enough to the gate that the message had probably already made it through. I would not put it past my father to send a fleet escort to meet us at the gate. My escape time just dropped to three or four days.

I sized the captain up as I toyed with my wineglass and made polite small talk. He was not a merc who had worked his way up to captain. He didn't have the hardness, the craftiness that mercenaries wore like second skins. A true merc commander would never be so easy to play.

"Shall we dine?" he asked.

"Yes, thank you," I said.

I made sure his wineglass was kept topped off and waited until the second course had been cleared away. "How can I help you, Gerald?" I asked in my warmest tone.

It took two more courses, but eventually the story came out. He was a merchant fallen on hard times, but he still had a ship. He'd partnered with the bounty hunters specifically to hunt Loch. They'd found him a few days ago, but Loch had killed two men during his capture, including the previous commander.

The mercenaries didn't respect Gerald and he was afraid they were plotting his demise. And he was just so lucky to have found me because his third cousin once removed was married to a von Hasenberg second cousin's sister-in-law and he just knew he had a great deal he could contribute to the House, considering he was almost family.

I nodded along and made all the right encouraging noises. The picture became clear. Even if I managed to overpower Gerald and take him hostage, the mercs wouldn't care. He'd already created the flight plan, so the ship would deliver us to Earth without any further input from him. It was time to end the evening.

"I should go," I said.

"You should stay," he slurred. "You can sleep in my room." He staggered to his feet.

I considered it. He was drunk enough that he'd probably be asleep as soon as he hit the bed. But I needed time to devise an escape plan and I couldn't be caught wandering around the ship. So I just had to make sure this wasn't my last dinner with the captain. I stood as well.

"Gerald, you naughty man." I laughed and lightly touched his arm. "I never sleep with a man on the first date."

He flushed and spluttered. "I didn't mean—"

The tone of the engine changed and my stomach dropped as the FTL drive engaged. We'd traveled far enough away from the station for our first jump. The lights flickered as the ship switched to auxiliary power. The hum of the engines ratcheted up and then went silent. Less than a minute later, my stomach settled and the main engines started up again. Depending on the age of the ship, it would take up to a week to recharge the FTL drive for the next jump. I had to be gone before that time was up.

"I will see you tomorrow for dinner, yes?" I asked with a coy smile.

"Yes, yes, of course, my lady. The lad'll see you back to your quarte—" He flinched. "I'm terribly sorry for your accommodations, but I'm afraid the mercs won't like it if I move you."

"It is fine. I like it; it makes me feel safe." And I was surprised to find that it was true.

THE SAME KID FROM BEFORE WAS WAITING FOR ME OUTside of the captain's door. I wondered if he stood there all the time, and if so, was he looking out for the captain's interests or the mercenaries'?

"What's your name?" I asked.

"Charles, but everyone calls me Chuck."

"Chuck, I'm Ada. Pleased to meet you." He ducked his head but didn't respond.

We returned to my cell by the same path we'd taken earlier. When we arrived, the display next to the door showed Loch still standing in the back section. He had to have been standing for hours, but he wasn't slumped or fidgeting. I made a quick decision that I hoped I wouldn't come to regret.

"The captain said to lower the barrier," I said. "So that if I need to use the facilities, they are available."

"Umm . . ." Chuck stole a glance at the control screen, but he clearly had no idea what to do.

I swept past him. "Allow me."

"I don't think—"

But I was already tapping on the screen. I lowered the separator, set the lights to stay on all night at a dim setting, and lengthened Loch's chains. He wouldn't be able to stretch out, but at least he could sit. And I would remain out of his reach.

"Easy peasy," I said. "I could teach you, if you'd like."

The kid eyed the video display with distrust, but it was easy to see that Loch remained chained. I prayed that Loch wouldn't move and give away the fact that his chains were longer, but he still stood in the same position. I wondered if he was sleeping standing up. Was that even possible?

"I don't need help from you," Chuck said. "The crew is teaching me everything I need to know." He swung the door open. "Now get in there and don't give me any trouble."

I entered the dim cell and the door slammed closed behind me. Without the energy field separating us, Loch seemed bigger, more immediate, and vastly more dangerous. *The enemy of my enemy is my friend.* I just had to keep reminding myself that we both wanted the same thing.

I tilted my head slightly toward the door, and Loch barely shook his head. I hadn't heard the kid leave, either, so I had to assume we had an audience.

"Did you miss me while I was gone?" I asked.

"No."

"Ah, that's too bad. Would you like to hear about the captain's quarters?"

"No."

I couldn't help the slightly evil edge to my smile as I began to describe, in excruciating detail, the captain's dining room. Every rug was lovingly described, as was every vase, flower, piece of furniture, and place setting.

After five minutes, Loch stepped away from the wall with a rattle of chains. "He's gone, but feel free to keep talking. I was nearly asleep."

"Did they feed you?" I asked.

He shrugged. "I ate."

I'd spent three months as part of a merc crew shortly after I left home. I'd been on my own for the first time and thought—incorrectly—that being part of a crew would help my homesickness. It wasn't a total waste, though, because I learned a great many lessons in that short time and the nomadic lifestyle helped me stay ahead of Father's security team in the crucial first months.

One of the lessons I learned was that bounty-hunting mercenaries, by and large, were ruthless and sadistic. Even the higher-tier crew I joined was not exempt. They loved to torture their captives by providing just enough food to prevent the captive from dying, but not enough to prevent constant, aching hunger. It also kept the captive weak enough to be easy to manage, so in their minds, it was a win-win.

Loch did not look weak, but according to the captain they'd only had him for a few days.

I pulled two dinner rolls wrapped in a paper napkin out of one of the pockets on my pants. After all, what was the point of pants with so many pockets if I wasn't going to use them? And if they failed to pat me down after dinner, then that was hardly my fault.

"Sadly, nothing else would transport well, so it is bread or nothing. But I'm willing to give you these two delicious rolls in exchange for your name. I know the mercs call you Loch, but I don't know if that's your first or last name or something they made up."

"You're trying to bribe me with bread?"

"Yes. Is it working? I'm Ada."

"I know who you are," Loch said.

It was my turn to be surprised. I might be a von Hasenberg, but I'd never been in the spotlight like my four elder siblings. Those four all looked like younger versions of our father, even poor Hannah and Bianca. I had the golden skin, dark hair, and blue-gray eyes of our mother. Only our youngest sister, Catarina, shared my coloring.

"And so you are . . . ?" I prompted.

"Marcus Loch," he finally replied.

"Pleased to meet you," I said. I tossed him the bread, napkin and all. We might be making polite conversation, but I had no doubt that Mr. Marcus Loch would eat me alive if I ventured too close.

Marcus Loch. The name sounded familiar. I mentally sorted through the rosters of important people in all three High Houses, trying to place him. I knew he wasn't part of House von Hasenberg. He couldn't be directly part of House Yamado or House Rockhurst, either, because he would have their name. So either he was a distant relation or an in-law, but I couldn't remember. Where had I heard that name and who had he pissed off to get such a bounty?

"Let me save you some time," he said as if reading my mind. "I'm Marcus Loch, the so-called Devil of Fornax Zero, and the man with the highest bounty in the 'verse . . . at least until you showed up."

It was only thanks to long practice that I managed to keep my expression perfectly placid. Now the chains made sense, as did the mercs' wariness. The Royal Consortium claimed that Marcus Loch had killed at least a dozen of his commanding officers and fellow soldiers during the suppression of the Fornax Rebellion. Then he disappeared.

The Consortium put out an ever-increasing bounty, but so far no bounty hunter had been able to bring him in to claim it. Rumor had it that he'd been caught six or seven times, but every time he had escaped and left nothing but a pile of bodies behind.

Marcus Loch was a deserter, a killer, and a traitor to the Consortium. And he was just the man I needed.

# CHAPTER 2

How long did it take you to perfect that mask?" Loch asked between bites of bread.

I raised one imperious eyebrow and stared down my nose at him, even though he was taller than me and across the room. After seeing the expression work so well for my mother, I'd practiced it in the mirror and wielded it without mercy. Lesser prey would flee at the merest hint of it.

So, of course, Loch grinned. "That long, huh?"

"Longer." I sat on the bed and rubbed my face. After being on all evening with the captain, I was exhausted. "Haven't had much use for it lately. I must be out of practice; you're supposed to be trembling with fear."

"It takes more than your pert little nose in the air to scare me, darlin'," he drawled, dropping the *g*. As if to emphasize his point, he stretched his arms and rolled his massive shoulders. He slid down the wall and sat. "I suppose I have you to thank for this?" He rattled the chain that bound his leg to the wall. At least now he could stretch out his legs.

"Seemed like the neighborly thing," I said.

I scooted back and wedged myself in the front corner of the cell, where the bed was pushed up against the walls. I'd slept sitting up before, and being in a corner made it easier. With the bed attached to the floor, at least I didn't have to worry about him dragging me closer.

"Afraid?"

"Smart," I countered. He grunted.

Ships and stations usually operated on Universal Standard Time, so it was the clock I was accustomed to. And right now, it was well after midnight. I needed to talk to Loch about a possible alliance, but I needed to be on point to get it right—I couldn't just steamroll over him like I'd done with the captain.

He leaned his head back against the wall and closed his eyes. All of that glorious skin and muscle was on display, which prompted a question. "Why'd they strip you?"

He cracked an eye at me. "Easier than patting me down after I kept coming up with shivs. It seems they didn't share my appreciation of a good blade. You going to talk all night?"

"Maybe. Would you like me to lull you to sleep with tales of the captain's tablecloth?"

His groan was answer enough.

I SLEPT FITFULLY THROUGH THE FIRST HALF OF THE night. I kept imagining Loch prowling closer, which would jolt me awake. But every time I checked, he sat on his side of the cell. After the fourth time, I eyed his chains, calculated the distance, and curled up on the end of the bed farthest from him. Lying down helped, and I slept better.

I awoke to the cell door banging open. "Rise and shine,

princess. Captain says you get to use the crew head." John, the blond merc who'd wrestled me into the ship, stood in the doorway. I could hear the derision in his voice when he mentioned the captain—perhaps Gerald wasn't wrong about the crew plotting his demise.

I obediently followed him down the same path I'd taken last night, but instead of turning left into the captain's quarters, we went right toward the crew quarters. More people were up and around this morning and more than one merc eyed me a little too long.

I passed another woman, but any hope of sympathy died when I met her baleful stare. She wore the dark camouflage fatigues that seemed to be the merc uniform and had her long hair braided down her back. Female mercenaries weren't rare, but they generally preferred either more gender-balanced groups or higher-tier squads; being the only woman on a ship that could spend months in space was a tough gig, especially with the men that made up most of the merc squads—cream of the crop they were not.

John stopped and pushed open the door to the crew bathroom. "You get five minutes," he said. "Then I'm coming in after you." He held up a control tablet with a lecherous grin.

I stepped into the room and bolted the door. He could use the tablet to open the lock, but I wasn't going to make it too easy for him. The room was tiny, but brightly lit and surprisingly clean. A toilet, sink, and shower were the only features. No towels or personal items were anywhere to be found. I took care of business then splashed water on my face. I'd love a shower, but there was no way I was taking my clothes off on this ship.

A glance in the mirror revealed dark under-eye circles that made my eyes appear more gray than blue. My deep brown hair stuck up in every direction. Without a brush, there was only so much I could do, so I French-braided it to contain the worst of it. My upper arms sported fading bruises from where the mercs had grabbed me.

The lock clicked open and the door swung inward. "Time's up, princess," John said. He looked disappointed that I was fully clothed and merely standing in front of the sink. It had been less than three minutes.

He pulled me out by my upper arm and made a show of dragging me back to my cell. I let him pull me along instead of ruining the show by easily pacing him. Picking my battles was a skill I'd learned the hard way while growing up, but one that I *had* eventually learned.

It took until my early teens for me to realize that banging my head against Father's will got me nowhere. Feigning compliance while ultimately working toward my own goals worked much better. All of my siblings had learned to be crafty in their own way because the other option was to become a slave to Father's will, and we were all too stubborn to let that happen.

I held my tongue—barely—as the merc shoved me into the cell. "I suggest you hug the door, princess. It's exercise time." With that parting shot, he closed and locked the door. A few seconds later, the whine of motors and distinctive sound of chain links hitting the floor echoed through the cell.

As much as I hated obeying orders, I backed up until I was leaning against the door. Loch was still an unknown and with the amount of chain spooling out, he was going to have the run of the cell. I didn't think the merc was stupid enough to actually let Loch reach me, but it would be close.

"That merc must really hate you," Loch said. He rolled to his feet in a movement so smooth it was a thing of beauty. Or it would've been, if I didn't feel like a gazelle mesmerized by a lion.

"I'm pretty sure he's the one I nailed in the knee," I said, watching Loch warily. "Then I didn't try for a shower, so he couldn't drag me out naked. I think I ruined his week."

"Do you think he's good at math?" Loch asked. He was still near his side of the cell, but he was looking at the chain coiled on the floor. "Shall we find out?"

Even knowing it was coming, the lunge was nearly too fast to see. The chains snapped taut with Loch less than a foot away. The merc had been okay at math, but he was bad at kinesiology because Loch leaned forward until his chest nearly brushed mine. Sure, his arms and legs couldn't reach me, but that didn't mean I was safe.

"My, what big teeth you have," I murmured.

"The better to eat you with, my dear," he replied without missing a beat.

I gripped the door handle behind my back, so Loch wouldn't be able to drag me farther into the cell. I rested my free hand on his chest. His flesh was warm and firm. He leaned into my hand. Up close, he was massive. It had been years since I'd felt dainty, but standing next to this wall of solid muscle, I did.

"Been a while since I was this close to a lady of a House," he said. His face was mere centimeters away.

"Don't make me stab you," I breathed. I knew the merc

was just outside, watching the video, and I didn't want him to know that I'd stolen more than bread last night. "I'd hate to leave a hole in this beautiful chest."

He chuckled and some of the pressure eased off of my hand. "Do you trust me?" he asked in the same barely audible tone.

"Not even a little bit," I said.

"But you want off this ship."

"Yes, but not in a body bag," I said.

"You drive a hard bargain, darling, but fine. Give me your knife."

"What part of 'not in a body bag' led you to believe that's even a possibility?" I hissed.

"Too late," he said.

I heard a shout from outside and in a damn rookie mistake, I stopped focusing on the immediate threat to focus on the new sound. I caught the movement out of the corner of my eye, but I was too slow. Loch pinned me against the door with his upper body and his mouth covered mine.

The kiss was hot and hard and over almost before it began. Metal screeched as the motors engaged to reel in the chains. Loch retreated across the room. I touched my lips. If he'd gone for my neck, he could've done enough damage that even my nanos might not have been able to save me. But instead he'd kissed me. Why?

Loch was pulled all the way back to the wall and the energy divider went up with a hiss. The door unlocked behind me and I stepped away to allow it to swing inward. I composed myself, then did the opposite when I heard the captain's voice.

"Are you okay, my lady?" he asked.

"I'm not sure, Gerald." I sniffled. "Everything was fine and then that man was loose and he was attacking me, and thank you *so much* for rescuing me!" I wailed and threw myself into his arms.

"There, there," he said, awkwardly patting my back. "John made a mistake, but it's all fixed now. Loch is safely behind the barrier. Why don't you lie down and rest and I'll have someone bring you breakfast?"

"Oh, thank you so much. But don't forget to feed *him*," I said with a little shudder and a tilt of my head. "I don't want him looking at me like I'm food all day."

"Of course, of course. Don't worry about a thing."

The captain left and a few minutes later the kid from the night before, Chuck, came in carrying two trays. One was laid out with bacon, eggs, and waffles. The other held a bowl of oatmeal.

Chuck glanced at me, the barrier, and me again. "Umm, can you . . . ? John must've forgotten." He set the food on the bed and backed up to the open door.

"Sure." I followed him out and stopped in front of the control panel. "Are you sure you don't want to watch what I do? Just in case you need to know how?"

Chuck didn't say anything, but he didn't look away either. I showed him how to raise and lower the separator, as well as lengthen the chains so Loch could feed himself. "Understand?"

The kid nodded and ushered me back into the cell. "Thanks," he whispered before he left.

"Making friends?" Loch asked.

"The mercs are holding the kid back. If I can help him, why wouldn't I?"

"Why does anyone from a House do anything? For personal gain."

He was not wrong, and it stung. I didn't mind helping the kid, and in other circumstances I would've done the same. But in this case, the kid was between me and freedom and if I could win him to my side, it helped me.

But it took one manipulator to spot another, and Mr. Kissy McKissyface over there wasn't off the hook. Kissing me was his own form of manipulation. I tried to win him to my side with food and conversation. He went with a more direct approach. And the hell of it was, it was working. He'd had the opportunity to hurt me, and because he didn't, I found myself more willing to trust him. I needed to be careful or I'd be outmaneuvered and left behind.

I dumped the eggs and all but one slice of bacon on top of the oatmeal. It wasn't super appetizing, but calories were calories and I doubted he'd complain about getting extra. I kept the waffles and remaining bacon slice.

"Reach out your hands as far as you can," I said. I should've put the food on his side then released the chains, but I hadn't been thinking.

He lifted his hands but made no effort to take the slack out of the chain.

"If you don't want to eat, that's cool, too." I set the bowl down and picked up my slice of bacon. God, I loved bacon. I eyed his bowl.

"Hand it over." He had stepped away from the wall and taken the slack out of the chain.

I gripped the very edge of the bowl. "No sudden moves, because if you startle me and I drop your bowl, that's tough," I warned. I passed the bowl to him without incident. He wolfed down the food. They definitely had been starving him.

"I don't suppose you'd fill this with water?" he asked, holding out the bowl. His chains weren't long enough to reach the sink. I carefully took it from him, rinsed out the residue, and handed it back full of water. He drained it. "Again?"

I saw the slack in the chain just before my hand moved into range. He was fast, but this time I was faster. I pulled back and he caught nothing but air. "I suppose that's what I get for trying to be nice," I muttered.

"Don't be that way. You know you'd do the same if the situation was reversed."

I finished my breakfast and set the tray aside. I sat cross-legged on the bed and closed my eyes. I needed to focus and plan. Meditation had never been about empty stillness for me; instead, it was when I did my best thinking.

I cleared my mind of everything except the problem: escape. This ship should have an escape vessel with a short-range FTL drive. New, modern warships with the fastest computers could jump several thousand light-years at a time. Ships like this Yamado frigate could jump several hundred, depending on how old the computers were. The escape ship could jump less than a hundred and probably closer to fifty. That plus the increased recharge time between jumps meant it could easily take a month to get back to a populated planet or station if you weren't close to a gate.

Gates were essentially giant, specialized supercomputers. They could accurately plot safe jump endpoints millions of light-years away. Gates generally operated in sets of two or more, not because it was required, but because if you jumped a million light-years and didn't have a gate to calculate your return trip, you were either stuck or you risked jumping with bad data. More than one ship had ended up in an asteroid in the early days of FTL drives.

To get a jump point, you entered the queue. Depending on the gate's age and level of activity, it could take anywhere between hours and minutes to clear the queue, because the gate could only calculate a fixed number of jump points at once. Older gates were the slowest, but they were often in deserted sectors, so it balanced out.

Gates also worked as communication hubs, because they talked to each other via faster-than-light transmissions to calculate safe jump points around other ship traffic. FTL communication required vast amounts of energy and a very precise, very expensive setup, so most 'verse communication bounced through the gates rather than being sent directly with FTL transmissions.

We were several hundred light-years from the closest gate. The escape ship should have emergency supplies for fourteen people for four weeks, assuming they hadn't been raided by the mercs. It was a glorified lifeboat, meant to hold the crew until their SOS reached a nearby ship. But for me, it was my ticket to freedom.

So, step one: verify the escape ship existed and was in working order.

Step two: convince Marcus Loch that we'd make better friends than enemies. It was hard to manipulate a manipulator, but I wasn't the daughter of a High House for nothing. One thing I had to give my parents credit for: they raised all six of their children as if we were the direct heirs. We all had the same tutors, learned the same secrets, and honed our skills in the same Consortium ballrooms.

As the fifth child, I might be nothing more than a political pawn to be auctioned off to the man with the most to offer the House for my hand in marriage, but I'd learned everything required to be a von Hasenberg. Of course, my parents didn't do it out of the kindness of their hearts—let's not be crazy. They did it because I was expected to spy on my future husband's business and personal life for them. After all, House von Hasenberg came first, even if I was sold to a man from a rival House or business.

*And Father wondered why I fled.*

I turned my thoughts back to escape. Step three: create a big enough distraction that Loch and I could make our way to the escape ship. My original thought was that *Loch* would be the distraction, but I wasn't sure I could bring myself to condone killing ten people, even if I wasn't the one pulling the trigger or holding the knife.

"You asleep, darling?"

"No," I said without opening my eyes. "And my name is Ada."

"You asleep, darling Ada?"

I cracked one eye open enough to scowl at him. "I'm rather busy plotting my escape. Did you need something?"

"You're never going to escape just by sitting there," he said.

"Of course not; I will escape through the ceiling. Or perhaps the wall, I haven't quite decided because it depends on whether I decide to trust you." I closed my eye and pretended to go back to my meditation.

"There is no way out through either of those."

I made a noncommittal sound.

"I've spent more hours in these cells than you can imagine. There are no weak points, no way out except for the door."

"If you say so," I agreed easily. I waited.

It took longer than I expected, but finally he growled, "Where?"

I opened my eyes and met his stare. "I will tell you when I trust you."

"Or you're making shit up."

I shrugged. "I could be. But I'm a von Hasenberg and this is a Yamado ship. We're competitors, you know. I know as much about Yamado and Rockhurst ships as I do about our own. Maybe more."

"How do I earn your trust?"

I smiled at the phrasing. He would've done well in a Consortium ballroom. So I gave him an honest answer in return. "Slowly," I said. "But we may not have time for that. Captain Pearson sent our flight plan to my father before our first jump. Depending on how fast my father can free up ships and where they are, he's likely to have an escort waiting for us at the gate. If he received the message extremely quickly, it's possible he'll scramble a ship to meet us here, but that's less likely."

"And I suppose Albrecht von Hasenberg won't miss the opportunity to bring in the Devil of Fornax Zero."

"Not if he knows you're on board. He'll pay your bounty out of his own pocket, just to be the one to bring you to the Consortium. And there will be no escape from his ship."

"You don't know what I'm capable of, darling Ada," he

rumbled. His voice alone was dangerous. It vibrated over my skin like a caress. And every time he called me *darling,* my heart tried to do a little flip, even though I knew it wasn't an endearment.

Yeah, I didn't know what he was capable of, but I knew that he was trouble.

# CHAPTER 3

Loch and I each spent the rest of the day lost in our own thoughts. I tried to talk to him a few times when I grew tired of thinking in circles, but he just grunted at me or answered with single syllables. Apparently the knowledge that my father's fleet was en route had goaded him into moving up his own escape attempt and he had no time for idle chatter.

I ended up with two plans, one where Loch and I worked together, and one where we were adversaries. It was a fair guess that we'd both be going for the escape ship, so I had to either reach it first or make myself indispensable to its launch.

By the time Chuck came to retrieve me for dinner, I still wasn't sure which plan was more likely to play out. I was so wrapped up in my thoughts, I didn't notice that a third person had joined us for dinner until I was already halfway into the room.

"Hello, Gerald," I said. "And I believe you are John, yes?" I asked the blond man who had dragged me back to my cell earlier. I smiled shyly. I kept the smile as he grinned lasciviously and bent to kiss the back of my hand, though I wanted nothing more than to smash a knee into his face.

His presence meant he was angling for the open commander position. He also changed the game and I subtly altered my persona. Mercs in general didn't take well to superiors and this one in particular seemed to like his women meek and afraid.

Even so, dinner was trying. John sat across from me, thank heavens, so I didn't have to ward off wandering hands. But his gaze rarely strayed above my breasts and all of his comments were so rife with innuendo that it could hardly even be called innuendo.

I kept my voice soft and my eyes down—though he never bothered to look that high—all while mentally plotting the most painful demise I could come up with. Feeding him alive to the lava worms of Centarii Delta Seven was currently in the lead.

When the proximity alarms started blaring I was in a dark enough mood to almost hope for a rogue asteroid. Or perhaps just a very carefully placed micrometeoroid that would find its way through the merc sitting across from me. I'd happily deal with the hull breach for hours if the universe would be so kind.

"*Mayport,* show me the outside cameras," the captain barked. "And silence the damn alarms."

The far wall lit up with video feeds from outside the ship. It wasn't an asteroid—it was far worse. A Rockhurst battle cruiser filled the display. The designation marked it as one of House Rockhurst's personal ships. Somehow, I didn't think they were here to pay a social call.

"Incoming communication," the ship's computer intoned.

"Answer it," the captain said before I could caution him against it or find a place to hide.

The video came up and Richard Rockhurst's face came into focus. The fourth of five Rockhurst children, he was a handsome man with the trademark Rockhurst blond hair and blue eyes. At twenty-five he was only two years older than me, but he'd been in command of one of House Rockhurst's most prominent ships for nearly six years.

The responsibility had hardened him, and the amusing young man I had played with as a child at Consortium events was nowhere to be found. Rumors of the ship's more heinous problem-solving techniques were rampant, though no one had enough proof or enough power to officially charge him with criminal conduct.

His expression didn't even flicker at my presence. He'd either known I was on board or gotten much better at hiding his thoughts. "Ah, Captain Pearson, I see the rumors are true. You have found and rescued my lovely betrothed. Hello, Lady von Hasenberg."

I decided that quibbling about semantics would do me no favors. We weren't technically betrothed, as he hadn't asked and I hadn't accepted, but it had been a long-standing assumption that one day we would be. I'd left before anything official was finalized. My escape had not improved the already strained relationship between our Houses.

I inclined my head a fraction. "Captain Rockhurst, I am glad to see you are well. As I am sure you are aware, my father has been notified about my rescue and subsequent travel plans."

"Indeed, my lady, that's why I'm here. Once he heard I was in the area, Lord von Hasenberg asked me to personally escort you home aboard the *Santa Celestia*. Of course, Captain Pearson, you will still receive the bounty for her rescue."

If my father asked a Rockhurst to so much as take out his garbage, I'd eat my own boot. But neither of the two men sharing the dining room with me sensed anything was amiss. In fact, John was practically rubbing his hands together at the thought of getting paid earlier than expected.

*What was Richard planning?*

"Shall I begin preparations for a transport shuttle?" Richard Rockhurst asked.

"Of course, my lord. I will prepare our docking bay," Gerald said.

"Thank you. And please keep Lady von Hasenberg a safe distance away. I know docking accidents are rare these days, but I won't risk my future wife."

Gerald was already nodding. "Yes, my lord, quite right. She'll be perfectly safe here in my quarters until your party arrives."

"Thank you, Captain. I will contact you once our transport shuttle is prepared." The video screen went dark.

"How did you send word to my father?" I asked. "Was it encrypted?"

Gerald looked affronted. "Of course it was. I used the high-priority merchant encryption channels."

The encryption on the merchant channels was as easy to break as wet tissue paper. All three Houses routinely monitored merchant traffic. Why, oh, why hadn't he used the diplomatic channels? At least those took some effort to crack.

"We need to jump, and we need to do it right now," I said.

"My lady, calm down. Rockhurst is going to return you to your family even quicker than I could," Gerald said. "Besides, our FTL drive won't be ready for another three days."

"Rockhurst is not on your side. He's not on my side. He's a member of a rival House who just happened to show up *in a battle cruiser* exactly where you said you were taking me on the insecure merchant channels. Because you used the merchant channels, my father will be hustling ships out here, but since they're not here yet, we're on our own."

"You're overreacting, princess," John said. "I've dealt with the Rockhursts before; you just don't want to acknowledge when you're beaten."

"The *Santa Celestia* can hold two battalions of highly trained shock troopers with room to spare. It is routinely used to clean up messes that House Rockhurst wants swept under the rug. The only reason they haven't blown us out of the sky, I'm guessing, is because they want me as a political hostage. The rest of you are collateral damage."

Now even the captain was looking at me like I was crazy. "*Mayport,* prepare the docking bay for transport shuttle arrival."

"Yes, Captain," the ship's computer replied. "Opening the docking bay port. Expected completion: ten minutes." Merchant ships didn't have landing bays, so they had to rely on older docking technology. And since a dock port was essentially a hole in the side of the ship, it was protected by heavy blast doors that had to be opened before ships could dock.

"John, why don't you go find a couple men to meet the Rockhurst team. I don't expect trouble," the captain said with a glance at me, "but it wouldn't hurt to be prepared. I'll send word when the shuttle is on its way and will meet you in the docking bay."

John looked like he wanted to protest, but he decided leaving was easier than arguing. The captain refused to listen to my warnings, so we sat in tense silence as the minutes ticked by.

"Docking port available," the computer chimed.

I clenched my hands together and sat like a statue. This would be the one exception where I would appreciate my father's interference, but the outside cameras showed the Rockhurst ship and nothing else. I had warned the captain and the mercs, so I no longer felt responsible for them. They had chosen their own path. Now I just needed to get myself off-ship as soon as possible.

It seemed like an age had passed when the computer finally said, "Incoming communication," but it had probably only been fifteen minutes.

"Accept," Gerald said.

Richard's face once again filled the screen. "We're all set over here, Captain Pearson, if you're ready for us."

"We're ready, my lord."

"Fantastic. I regret that I have to stay with the *Santa Celestia,* but I'm sending my second-in-command and my most trusted security agents to escort Lady von Hasenberg back, as well as my purser to settle our account."

"Thank you, my lord. I will go meet them in the docking bay while Lady von Hasenberg rests here in comfort."

Richard nodded curtly and the video ended.

"You won't tell him that we locked you in a cell with Loch, will you?" the captain asked hesitantly.

"No," I said. I didn't plan to tell Richard anything because I didn't plan to allow him to capture me.

Gerald looked relieved. "I'm going to lock you in, for your own safety, you understand. I'll be back with your security escort."

I nodded. Already I could see the transport shuttle breaking away from the *Santa Celestia* on the video monitor. I had precious little time to act, so I needed the captain to leave already. He finally did, locking the door behind him.

I went to the wall and slid open the cover to reveal the control panel. A password prompt greeted me, but I pulled up the hidden diagnostic panel and entered the default Yamado override codes. I didn't even blink when they worked. No one changed the default codes, because only a couple dozen people in the 'verse even knew they existed. And while Yamado changed the codes every so often to try to keep rival Houses out of their ships, older ships often weren't updated to the new codes.

I shut down several of the warning systems and unlocked the escape ship hatch. I pulled up a video of the docking bay. John and another merc lounged against the wall. The captain hadn't arrived yet. No one seemed armed.

A glance confirmed the Rockhurst transport shuttle was nearing our ship. I pulled up voice control and added myself as a captain. "*Mayport,* this is Ada von Hasenberg, authorize."

"Welcome, Captain von Hasenberg. You are authorized."

"*Mayport,* close the docking bay port."

"Unable to comply. An inbound ship has already started the docking sequence."

"*Mayport,* unlock the captain's weapon locker."

A panel to my left slid aside to reveal a neat array of weapons that looked new. I strapped on a blast-pistol holster and loaded my pockets with knives and extra energy cartridges. Finally, I slung a blast rifle over each shoulder.

The vid screen revealed that the captain had made it to the docking bay, as had the shuttle. The docking process was under way.

"*Mayport,* unlock the captain's quarters."

I heard the lock disengage. I closed the weapons locker and moved back to the control panel, weighted down by my weaponry. I wanted to see what would happen in the docking bay. My own exit depended on how Richard planned to play this.

The docking door opened and Gerald moved toward the shuttle with a smile and extended hand. A blast caught him in the chest. The two mercs didn't even have time to raise their weapons before they were cut down. A squad of eight emerged from the shuttle with military precision. They were in full combat gear, including full-face helmets.

On the control panel, I quickly requested a copy of the surveillance video be sent priority to my House account. It would be a good bargaining piece against Richard.

Now, it was time for me to go.

I exited the captain's quarters and stepped out into the hallway. The ship went dark.

"*Mayport,* switch to auxiliary power."

I got no response. The Rockhurst soldiers had taken out the lights and ship's computer, but left the life-support systems, including gravity. And they did it in less than a minute. If they had some sort of plug-in override, that would almost be worth risking certain death to retrieve.

Sometimes even I couldn't outrun my von Hasenberg genes.

Shouts erupted from the hall that led to the crew quarters as the mercs tried to figure out what was going on. I needed to move before they decided to come this way, but I was frozen in the dark.

Luminescent eyes glinted in my memory.

I headed to the holding cells, counting doors and following the schematic in my head. Once I reached what I hoped was the right door, I fumbled until I found the manual release.

"Loch?"

"Been having fun, darling?" his voice rumbled from the dark.

"A squad of eight Rockhurst soldiers just took out the captain and the power. A Rockhurst battle cruiser is pacing us off our starboard side. I'll pay you a hundred thousand credits to get me safely to a planet or station with an interstellar port and let me go. You can have the escape ship after that. I've already unlocked it, but the mercs might have the same plan at this point. You have five seconds to decide."

I was met with silence. "Marcus?"

"What are you waiting for?" he said from directly in front of me.

I froze as he lifted one of the rifles from my shoulder and pulled a pair of knives out of my pocket. Holy shit, he was loose, and I couldn't see a thing. How had he gotten out of the chains?

I fell back on my training. "So we have a deal?" I asked coolly.

"Yeah, we have a deal. Wait here," he said, pushing me just inside the cell. "If you see anyone, shoot them."

I laughed quietly. "I can't see shit," I admitted.

"I know. But I won't be carrying a light, so if anyone is, shoot first, ask questions later. I'll be back in three."

I didn't hear him leave, but I had the sense that he was gone. I pulled the pistol from the holster and flicked off the safety, grateful, for once, that my unconventional childhood had included weapons classes. I wasn't a sniper by any measure, but if someone came down the narrow hallway with a light, I'd have good odds of hitting them somewhere fatal.

Time stretched thin. Distant yells and blaster discharges echoed strangely through the ship. The docking bay was past the crew quarters. So was the escape ship. The overhead access tunnels would get us close, but the firewall between the bays and the rest of the ship meant we'd have to go through one of two main hallway hatches to reach the escape ship.

I began to wonder if Loch had left me behind. The credits I'd offered him were a fortune by any standard, but if he'd decided I'd slow him down, he could've realized that being alive was better than being rich.

A boot scuffed on the floor from the direction of the crew quarters. My heart sped up. Whoever it was didn't have a light, but Loch had not made a sound either time he moved. And I was loaded down with items that would make noise the second I shifted a centimeter. I barely breathed.

"Where are you, you little bitch?" a female voice whispered from just down the hall. If she had night vision, I was so screwed. The air shifted in front of me and a hand or arm brushed against the doorway.

"Ah—" Her quiet exclamation was cut short on a wet gurgle, followed by a soft *thump* a little farther down the hall to my left.

"Don't shoot," Loch whispered. "It's me."

I reengaged the safety and holstered the pistol. "About time," I hissed.

"Ah, sweetheart, did you think I'd leave without you?"

I didn't bother to confirm what he already knew. I tried not to think about the woman's body just down the hall. It turned out the darkness was good for one thing, at least.

"I couldn't find you any goggles, so you'll just have to trust me and follow my lead. The soldiers have three mercs pinned down in the mess hall, and for the moment they're at a standoff. We'll have to take the access tunnels to come down behind them."

I was not looking forward to crawling through the access tunnels in the dark. Even with lights they were claustrophobic. In the dark, one wrong turn could mean endless hours spent finding the correct path again. But the other option was a much longer route through potentially locked-down maintenance areas, so I swallowed my fear and focused on the next problem. "I need to rearrange my gear. I jingle loud enough for them to hear on the *Santa Celestia,*" I said.

Before I could protest, Loch rifled through my pockets, rearranging knives and ammo to his liking. It was quick and professional—his hands didn't stray. My pockets felt lighter and I wondered if I'd been left with any weapons. I checked my holster; I still had my pistol.

Loch must've been watching me. "You have your pistol and a knife in each back pocket. Your side pockets each contain an extra energy cartridge. I have both rifles and most of the rest. Good job, by the way. You'll have to tell me how you managed to raid the captain's private stash—nothing else worth having on this heap."

"I knew Captain Rockhurst wasn't coming over for tea," I said. "I thought it best to be prepared."

He chuckled and the sound wrapped around me in the dark. "How well do you know this ship's layout?"

"I found you in the dark," I said. "As long as the access tunnels still match the reference schematics, I know where to go."

"Good, you lead. The ladder is just in front of you and the hatch is open. But if I say, 'down,' you flatten yourself to the deck, no questions, understand? And wait once we get to the other side. I'll go down first. If you can lead us to the farther hatch, that would be better."

"I'll see what I can do," I muttered. I stepped forward with my arms out until I found the promised ladder. I mentally pulled up the schematic for this ship. This tunnel should lead back over the cell we were in for fifteen meters or so, then it would branch left and right. The left branch would take us over the crew quarters. The right branch led deeper into maintenance areas and then, after a few more turns, to the second bay access door.

"I'm right behind you," Loch said as I hesitated.

I wasn't sure if that was supposed to be comforting or intimidating.

# CHAPTER 4

**W**ith nothing but the map in my head, I crawled through the dark, cramped tunnels until I was sure I was lost. When Loch hissed, "Down," behind me, I flattened to the floor. I didn't know what he saw, but since I saw nothing, I deferred to his judgment.

He crawled up beside me, though he was mostly over me in the small space. "There's an open panel ahead," he whispered in my ear. "Is this our exit?"

This wasn't the first open panel we'd encountered. So far, we'd been able to cross them without incident, though not without a lot of unflattering flailing and wiggling on my part. I thought about our route. We should've dead-ended into the firewall. "Does the tunnel go left and right, but not straight?" I whispered back.

"Yes."

*Hallelujah.* I'd somehow managed to find the exact exit I was looking for. "This is it. You'll drop into a hallway that runs left and right, same as the tunnel above it. The hatch into the docking bay and escape ship bay will be directly in front of you. There's no cover in any direction."

"Stay put, and I mean it," Loch whispered. "We have a deal, and I don't want my payday getting shot. But be ready to haul ass."

"I can't see, remember? Unless you get some lights on, the only thing I'll haul ass into is a wall."

"Leave it to me. Just be ready." He crawled over me toward the access panel. For such a big man, he moved nearly silently. "Guards down the hall," he whispered after a moment. "You are just over a meter from the access panel. I want you to *very quietly* move up until you can feel the edge of it and then wait for me."

"Okay," I whispered.

I heard the faint scrape of cloth on metal and then silence. I pushed myself up onto my hands and knees and crept forward. I wasn't as silent as Loch, but I was quiet enough that I doubted anyone down the hall could hear me.

I slid my left hand forward and my fingers hit open air. I traced the edge of the opening. This was definitely the access panel. The ladder should be on the near side, but I wasn't going to risk exposing my hand to check. Now I just had to wait.

I *hated* waiting.

The silence echoed until I wasn't sure if the soft footsteps I heard were real or imaginary. I flattened myself to the floor of the access tunnel. The footsteps became clearer. Someone was approaching from the hallway to the right. Had one of the mercs made it through the maze of engine rooms?

The steps were quick—whoever it was could see. Distance was hard to judge with the way sound bounced down metal hallways, but the unknown person had to be getting close to the final turn that would dump him or her directly into the Rockhurst soldier's line of fire.

A few seconds later, the footsteps slowed, then stopped. For a brief moment, the ship seemed to hold its breath. Then the hallway erupted in blaster fire and curses.

A high-pitched scream from down the right hallway proved that at least one shot had found its target. The left hall reverberated with another round of blaster fire until it abruptly cut off with a scream.

"Oh God, oh God, oh please, oh God." The soft, moaned litany came from the right hallway. It was hard to tell with my ears ringing from the blaster fire, but it sounded like the kid, Chuck. Had he been shot? I pushed myself up, even though I knew looking would do no good. It was still dark as pitch.

Warm, wet hands gripped my wrists and pulled me head-first out of the access panel. I flailed, trying to find something to anchor my feet before I broke my neck on the floor. The hands shifted to my waist and hauled me down and forward.

I went for the knife in my back pocket.

"While I do love to watch a woman with a blade," Loch drawled as he set me on my feet, "we need to move."

"You could've warned me that it was you," I hissed.

"Now where's the fun in that?"

I huffed at him and tried to move right, only to be blocked by his arm. "I think I heard Chuck. We need to see if he's okay," I said.

"He's dead."

I paused. I could still hear the kid moaning. "It seems

your definition of *dead* and mine aren't the same," I said, trying again to push past him.

"Trust me, he's dead, he just doesn't know it yet."

"But—" A shoulder in my abdomen prevented me from continuing. Loch lifted me so that my torso hung down his back. He clamped a hand around my legs and took off at a quick jog.

I wrapped my arms around his waist to keep my upper body from flopping around. "What happened to the rifles?" I asked when I realized they should've been bashing me in the face.

"I left them in the cell," he said. "Too much trouble to hump them through the access tunnels."

Clearly, my observational skills were on point in the dark.

We lurched sideways with a loud curse from Loch. An energy bolt passed close enough that I could feel its heat. The world spun and jostled as Loch moved quickly. He stopped and dumped me off of his shoulder like a sack of potatoes. I hit hard on my left side. Pain lanced up my arm, intense enough to bring tears to my eyes.

"You said there were eight soldiers," Loch snarled in my ear.

"There were eight!"

"Now there are eleven. And three of them are between us and the ship. And no doubt calling for backup." He pulled the pistol from my holster. "Don't die." His presence faded.

"Lady von Hasenberg," an unfamiliar male voice called, "Lord Rockhurst sent us to rescue you. Are you well?"

"No, I am very much not well, you idiot," I muttered under my breath. Louder, I called back, "How do I know you are

Richard's troops and not more mercs trying to steal me for the bounty?"

"Are you alone?"

"I have no idea. My abductor dropped me here. I think he broke my arm. I cannot see anything."

A light clicked on in the distance, as bright as a dying star. I could see the door to the room outlined against the light, as well as make out the dark, bulky shapes surrounding me. My mental map had failed after Loch's dash through the cargo bays, but this looked like a storage room.

The light drew closer. I curled up and cradled my left arm. I let the tears fall down my cheeks. It wasn't really acting because my arm hurt like the devil. I didn't think it was broken, but I had no doubt that the bruising would be epic.

The light bobbed into the room. They'd sent a video drone—I could hear the low whir of its motor. I shielded my eyes as they adjusted. The blocky shapes in the room resolved themselves into storage containers. Loch had dumped me on top of a waist-high container, and I'd landed on the latch bar with my arm.

I pushed myself up with a groan. This was not how I'd planned for today to go.

The drone floated around the room. The soldiers must've been satisfied with whatever they saw on the video because a few seconds later, two big men in combat armor entered, guns first. They swept the room before coming over to me. One kept lookout while the other attempted to pick me up.

I slapped away his hands. "I have had enough of being carted around like so much baggage," I said in my iciest voice. "My legs are perfectly functional."

He backed up with a murmured "Yes, my lady."

I slid off the container and almost made a liar of myself when my left knee buckled. I fell into the soldier I'd just yelled at. *Fantastic.* My high-and-mighty, untouchable lady routine was certainly off to a good start. He held my arm until I'd regained my balance then let go without a word.

"I need a light stick," I said. "I cannot see anything."

"My lady," he started. I hit him with my mother's favorite expression. He reluctantly pulled a short light stick out of a cargo pocket and handed it to me.

I clicked it on and the room became clearer. "Thank you," I said.

With only one soldier between him and freedom, I assumed Loch was already on his way to the escape ship while I served as a distraction for these two. I had a knife, but the odds were better that I'd stab myself than do any damage to two trained—and armored—soldiers. I was a decent shot because shooting guns was fun; knife lessons were grueling, dangerous, and best avoided whenever possible.

"This is Bravo Team Lead. We have secured Lady von Hasenberg," the soldier next to me said into his mike. "We are in cargo bay six. At least one active threat. Please advise."

I couldn't hear the response through their helmets, but both soldiers nodded. "We're evacuating you to the transport shuttle, my lady. Please stay close," the team lead said.

The two soldiers shepherded me out of the room, one in front, one behind. We moved slowly as they scanned for threats. I thought up and discarded plans with blazing speed. While I would love to defeat two soldiers, who each weighed twice as much as me, in unarmed combat, I didn't think it was entirely feasible. Thanks, brain, for imagining some alternate reality where I was infinitely more capable.

But if I stepped foot on that transport shuttle, I became—at best—a political hostage. At worst, my abduction would set off the long-simmering animosity between our Houses and plunge us into war. And somewhere between the two was the possibility that Richard would insist on going through with the marriage I'd been avoiding.

No matter what happened, I became a liability, at least in the eyes of my father.

So I did the only thing I could: I ran. Thanks to the team leader I knew where we were, and the map in my head snapped back into place. The next time we came to a cross hall, I waited until the lead soldier had cleared it, then I bolted.

"Stop!" the second soldier shouted.

I ignored him. I doubted Richard had given them permission to kill me, and while I'd seen a stunstick, I hadn't seen a stun pistol, so they'd have to catch me the old-fashioned way. With them weighed down by their armor, I was faster.

The light stick cast weird shadows on the wall as I ran, but I could see and that was all that mattered. The video drone followed me. I swiped at it but missed and nearly lost my footing. I decided one problem at a time was all I could handle, and right now, distance was my friend.

Footsteps pounded behind me, closer than I would've liked. I darted left at the next hall and hoped Loch hadn't left yet. With a long straightaway in front of me, I sprinted.

I might not be infinitely capable, but I could *run*. It was a skill that came in handy more than once over the last two years. I'd chased down thieves and outrun mobs, and, in one memorable case, did both at the same time. I'd also had a few close calls with House von Hasenberg security where literal running was the only way to escape.

And nothing motivated quite like imminent capture or death.

The video drone paced me, but the footsteps fell farther and farther behind. Running blindly when there could be more soldiers lurking ahead wasn't ideal, but I was out of options. I had to get to that ship.

I turned left and ran down the short hall that would take me back to the main hallway. A right and another thirty meters or so and I'd be there. *Please let the ship be there.*

I glanced left as I turned right into the main hallway to see if the soldiers' backup had arrived yet. My body found what my peripheral vision had not—I slammed into a wall of muscle that barely gave under the impact. An arm clamped around my waist to prevent me from rebounding to the floor, and a blast pistol went off behind my head.

The video drone exploded in a shower of sparks.

Loch had already pulled me back into a run by the time my brain caught up with the fact that he hadn't left. And he was wearing clothes. He looked so much like a merc that it took me a second glance to process that it was really him.

When he pulled me into the port leading to the ship, I resisted. "We need to open the doors. The manual overrides are out here," I said, trying to pull back. It would be easier to move the moon.

"No time. We'll blast them," he said. The doors that enclosed the bay were wired with explosives that could be activated from the escape ship. But that was truly the last resort because it failed as often as it worked.

When Loch didn't stop to close the port door, I dug in my feet. "The door!"

"No time," he snarled.

I shook myself loose. "I'm making time. I won't be responsible for depressurizing half the ship. You go on."

He left me.

I cursed him silently while I pulled the heavy door closed. If we blasted the outer bay doors with this door still open, every unanchored person in the cargo bay would be ejected into space. And with the ship's power partially down, I wasn't sure the safety doors would close to protect the rest of the ship.

While I had no love for the Rockhurst soldiers, they were just obeying orders. The mercs could go to hell, but it would be nice if Captain Pearson's family could recover his ship in one piece.

I turned and ran for the escape ship. Loch was already closing the door, the bastard. I slid through the narrow opening and kept going. Once I made it to the bridge I realized the ship was already powered up and ready to fly.

Loch shouldered past me and took the captain's chair. Of course he did. His hands flew over the console with obvious skill, though, so I held my comments. Mostly.

"Stop grumbling and strap in," he said without looking up.

I dropped into the navigator's chair and clipped in. A quick look showed that we already had a destination plotted. Before I could check the stats, the outer doors blew and Loch cursed. I looked up from my console and saw that only one of the doors had blown. While the depressurization had slightly opened the other, it was going to be a tight squeeze.

Warnings started blaring as Loch's hands raced. He unclipped from his seat and moved to the rarely used manual controls.

"What are you doing?" I asked, alarmed.

"Computer won't take us out," he said. "Going to have to do it manually."

I swallowed. I knew how to fly a ship manually—all pilots did in case of emergency. But most pilots practiced just enough to pass the test and to be able to land a damaged ship in a large open field or to dock to a station with docking assist. We did not learn how to finesse an escape ship out of a partially open bay door without tearing a hole in the hull.

"Can you?" I squeaked. I cleared my throat. "Do it manually, I mean. Without killing us."

His eyes glinted as he glanced at me and his lips curved into a smoldering grin. "Don't worry. I'm good with my hands."

Heat flushed through me as I imagined those big hands on my body. *Criminal,* I reminded myself. *Killer.* He'd almost left me behind. *But he didn't,* an internal voice whispered. It sounded a lot like my neglected libido. Two years on the run didn't leave much time for fun.

While casual hookups were common in the Consortium, at least then you knew what you were getting—and you'd likely known the person for years. Hooking up for a one-night stand with a stranger wasn't usually my style, but looking at Loch, I might be willing to make an exception.

"Hold on," Loch said.

He opened the docking clamps and nudged the controls. The ship slid sideways by a meter. Proximity alarms blared faster than I could silence them.

"Touchy," he muttered.

My burgeoning confidence in his ability plummeted. Dying in space was not high on my list of ways to go. But at least my father would be pleased that I'd chosen death over capture.

"Do you want me to—"

"I got it," he said without even letting me finish.

With nothing else to do, I checked our plotted course. We were jumping to the only settled planet in range, Tau Sagittarii Dwarf Nine. The ship's computer had little information about TSD Nine. It was Yamado-controlled, which was nice with a Rockhurst on our heels. It seemed to be a mining planet.

The most interesting thing about the planet was that it was in synchronous rotation with its sun, so rather than having a typical day/night cycle, one side of the planet was always day and the other was always night.

The screech of metal on metal pulled my attention back to the window. We were nearly out of the docking bay, but our escape had not gone unnoticed. A half-dozen fighters spread out before us and a larger retrieval ship was en route from the *Santa Celestia*.

I started the pre-FTL sequence. The engine noise increased and heavy shutters covered the bridge windows. Screens flickered on, showing us the same view we'd had before, but now via video. All three Houses had tried removing the windows in various ways over the years, but those ships never sold as well as their windowed counterparts. Humans liked natural sight.

"Incoming communication," the computer chimed.

"Declined," Loch and I said at the same time.

I had no doubt that Richard already had someone hard at work on overriding our ship's system. It was much harder to do because override codes didn't work remotely, but it was possible.

Another metallic screech and we cleared the *Mayport*. Diagnostics showed that we had sustained only minor hull damage—nothing that would prevent us from jumping. It took a second for it to sink in.

"I can't believe you did that without killing us," I said. "Well done."

He grunted as he swiveled away from the manual controls. A few seconds later, alarms blared. I watched on my screen as he overrode the safety warnings and prepared to jump.

The lights flickered and my stomach dropped.

Normally I wouldn't condone jumping so close to other ships, but desperate times called for desperate measures. FTL drives required enormous amounts of energy but weren't 100 percent efficient. Some of the energy escaped at the initial jump point and caused a shock wave. For a little ship like this, the shock wave most likely didn't do any damage, even to the fighters nearby. But a large ship could easily destroy smaller ships when it jumped. It was why jumping close to a station was heavily discouraged unless you wanted to start a war or get blacklisted.

The engine steadied and the window shutters retracted,

leaving a clear view of the vast emptiness of space. And for the first time, the magnitude of what I'd done hit me. I was alone on a tiny lifeboat, in the middle of nowhere, with a man twice my size. And he was a known murderer.

Without the adrenaline driving me, fear crept in.

# CHAPTER 5

L och turned to me. "Do you want to explain why Richard Rockhurst wants you enough to board a merc ship for you?"

"No," I said. It didn't surprise me too much that he'd figured out which Rockhurst was after me—the *Santa Celestia* was distinctive to anyone who knew ships.

He grinned. "Fair enough, but you should've told me it was Richard from the beginning. You could've saved yourself a pile of credits. I would've helped you escape for free just to see the look on the bastard's face."

"You two have history?"

Loch's expression went cold and flat. "You could say that," he said. His tone did not invite further discussion and for once, I obliged. He unclipped from the manual controls and disappeared behind me. I steadied my nerves and idly played with the control panel when what I really wanted was to back up to a wall and keep him in sight. Preferably while holding a gun or two.

I heard him rooting through a container. I checked on our navigation. We were six hours out. I would love to get some sleep, but I wasn't sure if it was prudent or possible.

"I'm going to shower," Loch said.

The door to the bathroom hissed open then closed. When I didn't hear anything else for a few seconds, I risked a peek. The room was empty. I sighed out some of my anxiety.

With Loch contained, I used the time to stand up and look around. My knowledge of this ship was minimal because none of my training had included a scenario where I'd be on one. The bridge and the main room of the ship were basically the same. The back of the room had a tiny bathroom tucked in the port corner, a short hall connected to the exit, and the hatch to the lower engine level.

Each side of the room had two columns of fold-down cots mounted to the walls. The cots were stacked three high, so there was room for twelve people to sleep. When they were all folded down, a narrow aisle down the middle of the room would lead from the bridge to the back of the ship.

With the cots folded up, a bench ran the length of both sides of the room. Harness points were embedded in the underside of the lowest cots, so the survivors could be strapped in for takeoff or landing. The black harness straps stood out against the gray of the rest of the room.

After two years on bland gray stations and ships, I missed the blue and cream walls of my old bedroom. One of these days I was going to have to decide on a planet and settle down and stay put, if only so I could paint my rooms something other than metallic gray. I hadn't tried it yet because in order to completely disappear, I'd have to cut all ties to my family, including my sisters. That wasn't a step I was quite ready to take.

I was so caught up in my dreams of family and colorful walls that I missed the bathroom door opening. Movement in my peripheral vision jolted me out of my thoughts. I spun around then froze.

Loch had shaved the stubble from both his face and his head. The newly revealed skin highlighted a strong jaw, high cheekbones, and full lips. His black shirt clung to his broad shoulders and clearly outlined the flat planes of his chest. He narrowed at the waist, but still the shirt clung tenaciously, hinting at the defined abs underneath.

I loved that shirt.

His legs were encased in standard-issue merc fatigues in dark gray camouflage, and he'd found a pair of black boots. He'd looked dangerous before, but now he looked deadly. It took all of my training not to flinch and back away when he approached.

"Your turn, darling," he said. "There are extra clothes in the locker." He jerked a thumb at the vertical storage locker across from the bathroom, then gave me a once-over. "Though I don't know if there'll be anything that fits."

I was tall and slender, though I liked to think of myself as lithe rather than gangly. I had a fair bit of muscle, but nothing compared to most mercs.

"Thanks," I said. "And my name is Ada."

Loch crowded into my personal space, but I steeled my spine and refused to give ground. His slow smile did all sorts of terrible things to me. "I know your name, Ada," he murmured. It was the first time he'd said my name without the derisive, mocking lilt, and it was far more devastating than I'd imagined.

I suppressed my reaction and smoothly stepped around him. "Excellent," I said. Dodging handsy lordlings without giving offense—or getting groped—had made me something of an expert at extracting myself from these situations. "I was beginning to think you'd forgotten," I tossed over my shoulder.

When the expected response didn't come, I glanced back at him. He stared at me with intense focus. The look made me want to freeze and hide, but I continued on to the storage locker. I couldn't afford to let him know just how much he was affecting me. One hint of weakness and he'd pounce.

I dug through the locker and luckily came up with a set of men's clothes that would fit. I also grabbed a rucksack for my old clothes, since they were the only other set I had. I could do laundry once we landed.

I could feel eyes on me, but I refused to glance his way. I stepped into the bathroom and locked the door. I slumped against the tiny counter. Excess adrenaline made me shaky. I took deep breaths and listened for movement. I heard nothing but the constant low hum of the engines.

Loch could easily breach the door. Even if he couldn't just unlock it with the ship's system, which he could, he could probably knock it down. It was a flimsy illusion of safety, but one I clung to.

I wanted a shower, dammit.

I undressed quickly. I had blood smears around both wrists where Loch had grabbed me out of the access tunnel, and my left arm was bruised. My nanos would be hard at work repairing the damage, but it remained tender to the touch.

Nanobots were so expensive because they were crafted specifically for each individual's DNA. Cheaper generic versions had been tried, but since the infinitesimal robots circulated in the bloodstream, the body often saw them as foreign invaders and attacked. The results were not pretty.

The nanobots were supposed to be good for life, but I'd gotten boosters every year with the latest and greatest new versions. When I left home, the boosters stopped. I couldn't afford them on my own, so now my nanos were two years out of date. I hadn't noticed any side effects, but it made me a little paranoid. One often didn't notice the silver spoon until it was removed.

I unbraided my dark hair and ran my fingers through it. My hair hit just below my shoulder blades and was wavy enough to have a mind of its own. It had been longer when I lived at home. Cutting it had hurt, but long hair was more of a liability than an asset when you lived on stations and ships.

I wet a washcloth in the sink and stepped into the circular shower stall. A ship this small didn't have a water recycling system. I had to settle for a sonic shower, but it was better than nothing. I hit the button for the longest possible shower.

The shower screen advised me to lift my hair and close my eyes. I did both and also held my breath. Scientists swore up and down that the cleaning fluid was nontoxic, but I'd still rather not breathe it.

Warm mist ghosted over my skin from the nozzles encircling the shower. A chime indicated I could open my eyes. My skin tingled as the sonic waves agitated the cleaning fluid. I helped it along with the washcloth.

An additional round of cleaning started for my hair. A

sonic shower would never compare to a real water shower, but at least I'd lose the grimy feeling on my skin. My hair was another matter. Even with the extra cycles, it wouldn't get completely clean until I could wash it properly. Sonic showers just weren't designed for women with long hair, though they tried.

Two rinse cycles and a warm blast from the overhead dryer and I was done. I took a deep breath to prepare for anything, then opened the opaque shower door. The bathroom was empty and my clothes were exactly where I'd left them. Tension drained out of me. Showering was a risk I'd purposefully taken, but I hadn't realized just how wound up I'd been.

I pulled on the boxer briefs that were my only option for clean underwear. They were surprisingly comfortable. Sadly, there'd been no extra bras, so my dirty one went back on, followed by the black shirt and dark camo pants. I was glad to see that my shirt didn't cling as much as Loch's had. Even so, I looked like his mini-me.

A quick rifle through the bathroom cabinets produced a grooming kit with a wide-tooth comb. The shower had applied a detangler to my hair, but it didn't help much. I worked out the worst of the tangles then left it loose to finish drying.

I transferred the two knives and two extra energy cells to the pockets of my new pants, even though I didn't have a gun. Being prepared had saved me on more than one occasion. I bundled up my old clothes and shoved them in the rucksack, along with the comb—Loch wouldn't need it.

That done, I squared my shoulders and shored up my defenses before stepping out of the bathroom. Loch was sitting in the captain's chair, staring out into space. He half turned at the sound of the door but didn't speak.

I set my bag on the end of the starboard bench and then read the directions on how to lower the upper cot. It was as far in the corner as I could get on this ship, and it would give me a view of the entire room.

"The *Santa Celestia* has enough extra energy storage on board to jump again in less than twelve hours, possibly as few as six," I said. They could only do it once or twice before the energy was depleted, but those extra jumps mattered.

All three Houses were racing to get the energy requirements down and the energy storage capabilities up in our new ships, especially personal House ships. Smaller House von Hasenberg ships could jump once, jump again in six hours, and jump again in twelve hours. After that, they required two days per jump and nearly a week without jumps to fully recharge the system.

"We'll be on-planet before they make their first jump," Loch said.

"Yes, but I'd rather be off-planet again before they make their first jump," I said. "So I'm going to try to get some sleep. Once we land, there won't be time."

"So eager to be rid of me?" Loch asked. He stood and stalked toward me.

*Yes.* "No, but the faster I'm off-planet, the easier it'll be for me to hide," I said. I ignored his approach and snapped the cot into place.

He stopped close enough that I brushed up against him when I reached up to raise the safety rail. I refused to back away. I met his gaze with a flat stare of my own.

"Do you know," he said conversationally, "that you're the first person in a very long time willing to stand toe-to-toe with me without flinching or backing down? Even the mercs had more sense. It makes me want to see how far I can push you before you'll break."

That drew a dry chuckle from me. "The mercs weren't von Hasenbergs and they hadn't spent their whole life dealing with the sharks of the Consortium. I'll break, and thanks to my childhood, I know exactly when." I kept those memories tightly locked down and held his gaze. "But it won't be today."

He pushed closer until our chests touched. My nose hit him in the chin and I had to tilt my head back to meet his dark eyes. I gripped the cot's safety rail to keep from retreating. I'd gotten myself into this little pissing contest, now I had to get myself out. Preferably in one piece.

Loch's nose ghosted along my chin and down my neck. I stood stock-still as his breath heated my collarbone.

"You're afraid, but you don't let the fear rule you," Loch rumbled against my skin. My belly did a little flip that had nothing to do with fear. "You manipulate those around you to suit your will, but you risked being left behind to save a bunch of mercs and soldiers intent on capturing you. You're a puzzle, Ada von Hasenberg."

"If you're done with the intimidation routine," I said calmly while I trembled internally, "I'd like to get some sleep."

Loch threw his head back and laughed. I could feel the deep vibrations where our chests still touched. It wasn't exactly the reaction I had expected, but it did get his teeth away from my neck, so I'd call it a win.

Eventually he stopped laughing, but he took one look at my face and broke out into a chuckle again. "Don't look so put out. I wasn't laughing at you."

"Right, of course not. My mistake." I glanced away, strangely hurt.

Loch eased my face back to him with a gentle hand. His thumb traced a blazing path of fire over my jawbone. "I've never met a woman quite like you," he said.

"That's because you haven't met my sisters," I said lightly. "I have three of them and they're all just like me."

"Oh, I doubt that. I've met a fair number of Consortium ladies. None were like you. You're far more interesting than any of them."

I didn't want to be interesting. It would be better if Marcus Loch thought of me as a quick payday that he needed to protect until we reached the agreed-upon spaceport and nothing else. And when had he been exposed to Consortium ladies?

I was still contemplating the answer to that question when Loch wrapped his hands around my waist and lifted me up to the cot, nearly two meters off the floor. And he did it with complete ease.

Heat curled low and threatened to send me up in flames. I slid away from temptation and to the middle of the cot. "Thank you," I said.

"You're welcome," he said with a knowing smile. "Sweet dreams, Ada."

"Good night, Marcus."

I pulled the lightweight blanket from its storage compartment and spread it out. I laid down with my head toward the back of the ship, facing out from the wall. I could see nearly the whole room from here, including Loch sitting in the captain's chair.

Under the cover of the blanket, I slipped a sheathed knife

out of my pocket and clutched it close to my chest, like a child cuddling a teddy bear. I didn't *think* Loch would attack me in my sleep, but I was not above being prepared.

I slowed my breathing and let my eyes wander. I drifted off watching Loch gaze into space.

I AWOKE WITH A RACING HEART AND A DEATH GRIP ON the knife. I knew my dreams were dark, but they dissipated like mist in my conscious mind. The hand clamped around my forearm, however, didn't dissipate.

I jerked back and the hand slipped away.

"This is the second time you've pulled a blade on me," Loch rumbled. "I'm starting to take it personally."

My eyes popped open. A quick glance confirmed I still held the knife. It also confirmed it was sheathed. "I hardly think a sheathed knife is dangerous," I said. "Besides, you should know better than to grab a sleeping person."

"You were having a nightmare," he said.

I slid the knife back into my pocket and sat up. Grit gathered in the corners of my eyes. I rubbed my hands over my face and tried to get my brain to kick into gear. "How long was I out?"

"A little over five hours. It's almost time to clip in for entry."

Five hours shouldn't have left me this groggy. I'd kill for a cup of real coffee. Hell, I'd be happy with a cup of the synth stuff at this point. I shook myself out of caffeine dreams and climbed down the ladder set into the wall between the cots.

Every muscle protested. I must've been tense in my sleep, fighting off invisible demons. I didn't have nightmares often, but when I did, I usually went all out. I stepped down to the floor and lifted my arms overhead, stretching left then right. I folded forward and put my hands on the floor, enjoying the stretch along the backs of my legs.

After I'd put sufficient distance between me and Rockhurst, I was totally getting a massage. I figured getting captured by mercs and fleeing for my life with a murderer meant I was overdue for a little luxury. And the one true perk of being daughter of a High House was the ability to afford luxury. My House accounts might be under surveillance, but I'd funneled money into several private accounts before I escaped.

I straightened to find Loch watching me with deep brown eyes. Every so often the light would catch them just so, and they'd flash, luminescent. If one of the other Houses had achieved ocular implants of his level, this was the first I'd heard of it.

All of the implants I knew about permanently altered your eye color to milky white and glowed in even the faintest light. It made it easy to determine who could see in the dark. If implants existed that could be hidden behind normal-looking eyes, that would be a strategic advantage.

I tilted my head, studying him as he studied me. I hadn't planned for more than escaping the ship then running again. But I was tired of running, especially now that every merc in the 'verse had heard of me. I wanted a house and not to have to look over my shoulder every minute of every day.

My von Hasenberg genes kicked in—perhaps Loch was the key to that future. Father would drop my bounty if I gave him Loch. Oh, he wouldn't do it easily, but Father could be swayed with the right incentive.

I shook off the thought. Loch had helped me, even if it was just for the money. While a true von Hasenberg would have no trouble stabbing him in the back in appreciation, I tried to keep my backstabbing to a minimum.

But by the calculating look on Loch's face, I wasn't the only one contemplating a double-cross. I'd need to be vigilant once we landed. After I paid him, I needed to disappear.

I stretched one last time then dropped into the navigator's seat. Tau Sagittarii Dwarf Nine loomed large in the front window. We were approaching at the border of light and dark, so the planet looked like it was broken in half. Only a few faint lights glimmered on the dark side of the planet—a giant metropolis this was not.

"Atmospheric entry in five minutes," the computer chimed. The window shutters slid closed, leaving us with video screens. I tried not to think about how long it had been since this ship had received routine maintenance. Landing was hard on ships.

The screens showed a bleak brown planet. A line of white-capped mountains marched across the border between light and dark. No greenery or oceans broke up the monotony.

We were close enough to tap into the planet's information network. I pulled up the depressingly short wiki entry. It was dated a month ago. TSD Nine used to be a Yamado mining planet. Then the ore ran out. The miners and the diplomats moved on to the next planet, leaving behind the seedier elements that were all too happy to take over.

The wiki warned that the dark side of the planet was best avoided. Smugglers had taken over the abandoned mining shafts, and outsiders were unwelcome. Those who wandered in often went missing.

Lovely place, this planet.

The light side wasn't any better, as it was rife with mercs. Every so often they'd go bounty hunting through the smugglers' tunnels. The largest city, Gamamine, sat in perpetual twilight on the border between the two worlds.

Getting a better ship was going to be tricky. Usually I'd just book passage on the first ship off-planet, but I had a feeling the options were going to be few and far between—this wasn't exactly a booming tourist location. I could afford to buy a new ship, but throwing that much currency around after landing in an escape shuttle would raise some eyebrows.

"Atmospheric entry beginning," the computer chimed.

Loch settled into the captain's chair and clipped in. The planet filled the video screens. After time in space, it was always weird to realize that you were intentionally hurtling yourself at the ground in order to land. And that there was ground at all.

It'd been over a year since I'd set foot on a planet, because I mostly bounced around between space stations. Stations always had flights available at the last minute and weren't always the strictest about checking documentation. And the biggest stations were larger than surface cities anyway, so it was easy to get lost in the crowd.

The escape ship shivered as it decelerated. We had to slow down before we slammed into the atmosphere or we'd end up in itty-bitty pieces spread over half the planet. All of the data on my screen showed our entry was proceeding as expected, but the next ten minutes were the hardest on the ship.

A few minutes later, the telltale buffeting of atmosphere vibrated through the ship. The turbulence got worse as we descended. Thankfully these seats had shoulder harnesses. I'd landed in a subpar ship with just a lap-belt before and came out bruised for my effort.

We were on course to land at the small spaceport in Gamamine. The city was both our best chance of getting off-planet again and our best chance of getting caught. If the mercs caught wind that the two highest bounties in the 'verse had just landed in their backyard, we wouldn't have a moment's rest.

Loch's hands moved across the screen and the ship blared a warning. Before I could ask him what he'd done, the ship dropped like a rock, throwing me into the shoulder harness. Blood rushed to my head and I fought the redout that lingered on the edges of my vision.

If I didn't know better, I'd assume we were accelerating toward the ground.

Another alarm went off before Loch silenced it. The uniform brown landscape shifted into hills, valleys, and fields as we descended. We were coming in way too fast.

My hands flew over my own console as I tried to slow our descent, but he'd locked me out. "What are you doing? We can't come into the spaceport like this; they'll shoot us down." When it came to casualties, spaceports defaulted to protecting the assets already on the ground unless they had a really, *really* good reason to do otherwise.

"We're not headed to the spaceport and we're sitting ducks in the air. The faster we're on the ground, the safer we are."

"We won't be safer if we hit the ground at this speed— we'll be splattered."

He grinned at me with a flash of white teeth. "Trust me, sweetheart. I know what I'm doing."

Trust was earned, and so far, Marcus Loch had done some, but not nearly enough to earn mine. I debated trying to override the lockout on my control panel while I watched the ground hurtle closer. But trust was a two-way street and I didn't think Loch was suicidal, so I clutched the edge of the control panel and did nothing.

Giving up control of my fate was harder than I anticipated. Even though I *knew* Marcus must have a plan, doing nothing went against everything in my nature.

Proximity alarms blared to life. Loch was laser focused on the control panel. I dug my fingernails into my palms and said nothing. Distracting him would not help us land.

We were coming down in a gently rolling area gouged by deep canyons. Flat areas big enough for the ship were few and far between. As we got ever closer, I realized the canyons were both deeper and wider than I first thought.

And we were aiming directly for one.

We were nearly even with the ground at the lip of the canyon before Loch fired the thrusters to slow our descent. The ship shuddered and groaned under the strain, but Loch only cranked the thrusters higher. We were nearly at the thrust level that would be used for takeoff and still we descended deeper.

The engine whine ratcheted up a notch and our descent slowed. My screen showed our landing location to be a relatively flat spot at the bottom of the canyon, still a hundred meters away. At fifty meters, the engines screamed as Loch pushed the thrusters to their maximum output.

"Brace!" Loch shouted. I crossed my arms over my chest and pushed my head back into the headrest designed for exactly this scenario.

We achieved a survivable rate of descent just two seconds before we slammed into the ground. I felt my chair give on its pedestal, absorbing some of the impact force, but we still hit hard enough to stun me for a few seconds.

The engines shut off, leaving behind a cacophony of alarms.

I *hurt*. I wiggled my fingers and toes before moving on to my arms and legs. Nothing appeared to be broken, but my whole body felt bruised from the inside out.

"You okay?" Loch asked after he silenced the alarms.

"You crashed our only escape vehicle," I said. My voice sounded eerily calm to my own ears, like someone else was speaking.

I heard him groan and unclip from his seat. The sound of his pain did nothing to calm my temper. I unclipped my own harness with clumsy fingers. I felt heavy and slow. Only part of that was due to the crash—this planet had slightly stronger gravity than the Earth-standard most ships and stations used.

"You *crashed* our *escape vehicle,*" I said again.

"The landing was within tolerance," Loch said. "Now get moving. Anyone who saw us come down is going to come investigate and we don't want to be here when they arrive."

I locked the pain and fear and anger behind a wall of icy calm. I found my rucksack and started filling it with food rations and water from the emergency supply. Water was heavy as hell, but I'd seen no indication of surface water, so I'd only have what I carried until we reached the city. I also threw in the ship's first aid kit. It was heavy, too, but worth the weight.

A quick check of the outside temperature proved that I was underdressed. I grabbed a second set of clothes from the storage locker. They were too big, but they'd work as an extra layer. The clothes and several emergency foil blankets went into my pack. I'd kill for a heat field or two, but Captain Pearson had been too cheap to equip the escape shuttle with them.

There were no winter clothes at all in the storage locker. I put on two long-sleeved shirts and shimmied into a pair of too-big pants. A belt kept the pants up, the shirts tucked in, and the drafts out. I wrapped a final pair of pants around my head and neck like a weird scarf/hat combo. I looked ridiculous, but I hated being cold.

I was slightly gratified to see Loch was wrapping himself up in much the same way. "Ready?" he asked.

I downed a bottle of water and dropped the empty container. My pack was close to twenty pounds and not designed to carry that load. It would be uncomfortable, but it would get lighter as I went along. "Ready," I said.

Loch nodded and picked up his pack. We headed to the exit at the back of the ship. He checked the tiny embedded window then opened the door. Ice-cold wind with a slightly acrid smell blasted through the opening. It cut through my layers like I was naked. If the city was more than a few hours away, we were going to be in deep trouble.

Loch disappeared through the door without a backward glance. I followed him out into the dim light.

# CHAPTER 6

**B**rown rocks, brown soil, brown grass. Even the sky seemed vaguely brown in the twilight gloom. We'd been walking for what seemed like forever, but it was impossible to judge time because the sun hidden just behind the horizon never moved. At least it worked as a compass.

The extra gravity dragged at me, making every step a little harder than it should be. The cold bit at any exposed skin, and I couldn't feel my hands, even though I'd pulled them into my sleeves long ago. My nanos would be healing any frostbite, but unfortunately they didn't help regulate body temperature or give me any extra energy.

The sides of the canyon were steep and rocky. We were still on the canyon floor, trying to find a way up. I wasn't sure I'd be able to climb out at this point.

Loch stopped and scanned the area. I dropped my pack and dug out a bottle of water. The air here was oxygen-rich but extremely dry. I'd be out of water before the end of the day. I laughed to myself, a little loopy. The day never ended here, so technically I'd be dead before the end of the day, too.

I pulled out an emergency blanket and wrapped it around my chest and waist between layers of shirt. Even with the constant movement, I was getting dangerously cold. I fumbled with my belt but finally got it secured.

I ate an energy bar then shouldered my pack and turned to Loch. "If we don't find shelter and heat in the next two hours, I'm going to be in bad shape," I said. I hated to admit weakness, but I knew my limits. Even another two hours was going to be pushing it.

He looked me over then nodded. "We're almost there. This canyon runs next to Gamamine. We need to exit on the left, so keep an eye out for a route. I'd rather not scale the walls if we can avoid it."

"Oh, I can avoid it," I grumbled. I regretted our hasty departure from the ship. If it came down to it, I'd head back there and wait for rescue/capture. At least I'd be warm.

Loch didn't bother with a response, he just turned and walked off. If he felt the cold, he didn't show it. He moved easily, with a spare, efficient gait that was beautiful to watch. He looked like he was out for a Sunday stroll, not like he was trudging through the bitter cold in inadequate clothing.

BY THE TIME LOCH STOPPED AGAIN, I COULD BARELY feel my legs. If I didn't get warm soon, I was going to collapse.

"We'll climb here," Loch said.

I looked at the wall of the canyon he was studying. It wasn't vertical, but it was steep and rocky. The canyon floor had been climbing for an hour, so the rim of the canyon was only about fifty meters up.

It was going to be a brutal fifty meters.

I followed Loch with single-minded determination. I stared at his feet, willing my own to step in the same places, climb over the same rocks. I didn't look up; I didn't want to know how far we still had to go.

Loch pulled me up over a large rock. I tried to keep climbing, but he clamped an arm around my waist. "Stop," he whispered. "We're nearly at the top."

His arm was so warm. I turned and huddled into his chest, uncaring that I was snuggling a criminal. He was a *warm* criminal and that was all that mattered right now.

"Shit," he said. "When did you stop shivering?"

I shrugged. I didn't realize that I'd stopped. My whole focus had been on putting one foot in front of the other. "I told you I had two hours. It's been two hours. I wasn't lying. How are you so warm?"

He didn't answer. Instead, he said, "The city is surrounded by a fence, but not a good one. Stay here, I'll find a way through."

I shook my head. "If I stop moving, I'll die. If you want me to find my own way through, I will, but I can't stay here."

"Can you run?"

"If I have to and not for very long."

He pushed me away from his chest. Frigid air stole the little warmth I'd collected until I felt colder than before. "Stay here for two minutes while I do an initial recon."

"You literally have two minutes, then I'm heading for the city with or without you," I said. "Your time starts now." I started counting in my head. It kept me focused. My thoughts were slowing. I'd pushed myself too far and now I was dangerously close to making a fatal mistake.

Loch stepped a meter up the canyon then froze. He didn't even seem to be breathing. He held statue-still for thirty seconds then slowly sank down.

"There's a hidden door. Just saw a kid sneak out and head for the canyon farther down. I don't think he saw me, but we need to move. I didn't see any guards. We'll run for the fence."

I stomped my feet and promised myself the largest cup of real hot chocolate I could find. It would be an extravagant expense on a planet this isolated but worth every penny if I survived long enough to claim it.

"Okay, let's do this," I said.

Loch grabbed my wrist and pulled me up the final rise of the canyon. The fence was only about twenty-five meters away, but nothing gave us any cover. It looked like a hodgepodge of whatever the citizens had leftover rather than a true fence. Old doors and windows, pieces of plastech, and scraps of wire were all held together by welds, ropes, and prayers.

We pounded across the open space. It took all of my concentration to run. Twice I stumbled, and Loch's grip on my wrist was the only thing that kept me upright. Exhaustion clawed at me with soft, sweet fingers.

We reached the fence and Loch dropped my wrist. His hand left a band of heat on my flesh. I wanted nothing more than to curl up next to him and leech away his warmth. I shook off the images of our naked limbs entwined and followed him down the fence line.

The door was only visible once you were standing right

in front of it. A bit of rope worked as a pull and two pieces of barbed wire tied around a fence post were the hinges. This section of fence was on rocky ground, so no footprints gave away the location.

Loch opened the door, peeked through, then reached back to pull me through with him. It was immediately clear that this was not the best part of town. Trash littered the street and the plastech houses were dark and shuttered.

Cheap and easy to build, plastech houses were the first buildings to go up on any new planet. It seemed the local residents then decided to take matters into their own hands, adding levels with mud bricks and closing off alleyways with the same.

It was either very early or very late because the streets were empty. Or this section of the city had been abandoned. While that would help us hide, mercs generally didn't cede sections of the city without a reason.

Loch led us through the streets like he knew where we were going. I did my best to keep up, but the world was hazy around the edges by the time he stopped in front of a decrepit building. He paused at the door, then swung it inward and stepped inside.

The inside wasn't any warmer than the outside, but at least the walls blocked the cutting wind.

"Stay here," he said.

I blinked and he was gone. How long had I been standing here? I forced myself to walk around when I wanted nothing more than to curl into a ball and sleep. In the faint light that filtered through the filthy windows, I saw that the front rooms of the house were mostly empty. A few pieces of broken furniture proved that someone had once lived here, but they seemed to be long gone.

"Come on," Loch said. "I found a room with a heater."

I followed him deeper into the house. It was dark enough that I couldn't see what I was stepping on. He stepped into a dimly lit bedroom, complete with a tiny bed and thin bare mattress. It looked a lot like the bed in the cell on the *Mayport*. True to his word, the heater in the wall was struggling to warm the room. The overhead light panel produced enough light to see by, but it must have been set to its lowest setting.

Loch shut the door and dragged what looked like a broken dresser in front of it. My heart rate spiked and adrenaline cleared away some of the cobwebs in my mind. I'd followed him like a puppy into a room with a bed and only one exit—an exit he'd just blocked.

"Strip," he said. He started pulling off his own clothes.

Oh, hell no. I backed away. He was strong and fast and not half-frozen. Even if I could grip a knife, it wouldn't do much good. That didn't mean I was going down without a fight.

Loch glanced at me then froze. He straightened. His eyes dropped half-closed and his mouth curled into a melting grin. My heartbeat kicked up and not from fear. The man could stop traffic with a look like that.

"Ada," he drawled, "if I wanted to fuck you, I wouldn't have to lock you in to do it." He stalked across the distance that separated us while I stood frozen. "I prefer my women warm and willing. And since you are neither, you're just going to have to imagine how good it could be." He cupped my jaw with a warm hand and glided his thumb over my lips. "Now strip before you die of hypothermia. And leave your underclothes on."

By the time I'd shed clothes down to a short-sleeved shirt, bra, and boxer briefs, Loch was down to his own boxer briefs and had laid out several emergency blankets on the bed. He raised an eyebrow at my clothing but didn't say anything.

"In you go," he said, holding up the edge of a blanket. I slid across the crinkly foil blanket to the edge of the bed facing the wall. "Lights on or off?" he asked.

"On," I said. Definitely on. I needed to be able to see him.

"Okay," he said. He slid into bed behind me and the mattress dipped under his weight. I tensed and held myself still on the very edge of the bed. A warm arm around my waist dragged me back against scalding skin. He cursed the air blue. "You should've told me you were this cold."

Modesty forgotten, I pulled his arm farther around me and wiggled to get as close to him as possible. With the emergency blankets covering me from neck to feet and a large, warm body at my back, I finally felt like maybe I would survive the day.

I don't know how long I'd drifted in and out of sleep before the shivering started, but once it began, sleep was a distant memory. I shivered so hard my teeth chattered. Loch turned me over so I faced him and tucked me into his chest with my head on his arm. He wrapped both arms around my back and threw a leg over my lower body.

Hours or perhaps days later my shivers slowed down and I dropped into an exhausted sleep.

WHEN I AWOKE, I WAS ALONE IN THE BED, AND I WAS *warm*. In addition to the emergency blankets, I was covered by two long cloaks. I rolled away from the wall and every muscle protested. Apparently shivering was a full-body workout.

Marcus sat propped against the wall by the door, studying a small com tablet. "Do you want the bad news or the worse news?" he asked without looking up.

"What happened to the good news?"

"You're still alive, aren't you?" He continued without waiting for a response, "There are exactly zero commercial flights out of this shithole. Three days from now a merc ship is leaving for the nearest station, but for reasons that should be obvious, that's not our best option."

"Is that the bad or the worse? Wait, did you do a sweep of this stuff to make sure it's clean?"

"That's the bad news. And yes, I checked for bugs, all of it is clean. The worse news is that Rockhurst's team landed two hours ago. So far they don't seem to have alerted the locals to who they're searching for, but it may only be a matter of time."

"They landed the *Santa Celestia* here and no one blinked an eye?" Yamado may have left the planet to the mercs and smugglers, but that didn't mean they'd overlook a rival House landing a battle cruiser on their planet, worthless or not.

"No, they left the *Santa Celestia* in space. It's too large to land here. They're in a smaller unflagged merc ship, probably one they kept in the *Santa Celestia*'s hangar for covert planet landings."

Mercenaries weren't required to flag their ships to one of the High Houses unless they wanted to announce that they were under that House's protection, so an unflagged ship wouldn't raise any eyebrows. It was the perfect cover to land on an enemy planet, and one that House von Hasenberg had been known to use as well.

Could I buy a ship before Rockhurst's men found me? Possibly, but it wouldn't be easy. "I don't suppose you bought an extra com while you were out?" I asked. I was sorely tempted to yell at him for leaving me alone while I was sleeping, but it wasn't his job to be my babysitter. I should've woken the moment he moved. The fact that I hadn't meant I'd been in much worse shape than I'd realized.

He gestured to the floor near the top of the bed. I slid over until I could see where he was pointing. My pack sat with yesterday's clothes folded on top. On top of that was a small com tablet like the one Loch was using. It was a cheap, mass-produced model. I had a moment of silence for the top-of-the-line unit I'd left on the station where I was captured.

Thin, handheld devices made of glass and metal, coms were the glue that held the universe together. I'd felt naked for the last couple days without mine. This one was produced by a Yamado subsidiary, so it was in no way secure. I reset it, touched my right thumb and pinky finger together, then held the com up to the tiny chip embedded in my right arm.

The tablet chirped, then the screen lit up with *Welcome, Irena*. Irena was one of my middle names and Irena Hasan was a burner identity that hadn't yet been compromised. This tablet now belonged to her, along with all of her accounts that had been linked from the chip in my arm.

The tablet synced to both local and Universal Time. Because the sun never set on this planet, they had conveniently decided to stick with Universal Time. It was approaching noon. I had a feeling that my internal clock was going to have a hard time adjusting to constant twilight.

I checked my messages and found several from my older sister Bianca. I tried to keep her informed of my aliases and whereabouts, at least in general terms. In return, she let me know where House security was searching for me.

Hannah and Bianca were my two oldest sisters. Neither had married happily and they didn't want their little sister to suffer the same fate. They'd quietly cheered my escape and funneled me money on the sly.

Bianca's messages contained neither names nor specifics, but I knew everyone at home was fine just from the way they were written. However, there was an undercurrent of unease and an implicit plea for caution. That was worrisome.

I sent off a quick reply, letting her know in very oblique terms that Rockhurst was after me but that I was okay. We were both using insecure alias accounts, so there had to be a lot of reading between the lines.

I checked the news feeds and didn't find any mention of unusual Rockhurst activity. If they were willing to risk House von Hasenberg's wrath to capture me, I assumed that we were on the brink of war. Instead, it seemed like business as usual—a tense, hostile truce hidden behind a facade of friendship.

Digging deeper, I found hints of Rockhurst movement but nothing big enough to set off any alarms. Was I reading more into it than I should?

Either way, I needed to escape this planet.

The bank account I'd set up for this identity had plenty of funds to live on, but not enough to buy a ship. Even paying off Loch would be a stretch. I'd have to access my true account for additional funds, which meant I needed to have an escape plan ready or I'd get scooped up before I left the bank.

"Did they find our escape ship?" I asked. I slid out of bed and started pulling on yesterday's clothes. Muscles throughout my body protested, but I was up and moving, so I'd work out the soreness before too long.

Loch glanced up then returned his attention to his com. I guess slowly pulling on a pair of men's pants while moving like a little old lady wasn't super alluring. "I didn't see it at the spaceport," he said, "but I assume so. If they're smart, they left it in the canyon and either disabled it or put trackers on it."

So returning to the escape ship was a nonstarter. A crazy idea occurred to me. "How nice is the unflagged merc ship?" I asked.

Loch looked up with a knowing grin. "It's nice. I did a little recon earlier. I wouldn't be surprised if it had House ship internals."

That was both good and bad. If it really did have personal House Rockhurst engines and systems then it would be fast and capable. But it would also mean I would need much better and more recent information to steal it. "I need a new com," I said. "Not that I don't appreciate this one, but I need a secure model, preferably one made by House von Hasenberg."

"It'll cost you," he warned. "And put you under scrutiny."

"If I'm going to steal their ship—and I am—I need a secure channel. If you'd like to help, I'd appreciate it, but I understand if you want to take your money and run. The bank will be watched, but I'll get it for you somehow if you want hard credit chips." I sat on the edge of the bed and pulled on my socks and boots.

"I promised to get you to a planet or station with an interstellar port. This hardly qualifies."

I shrugged. "It's close enough and you helped me escape the ship, which was my main objective. It would be safer for you to disappear into the dark half of the planet. Stealing a ship from a House is frowned upon."

Loch laughed. "You're good," he said. "I can't tell if you're intentionally trying to manipulate me into helping you steal the ship or if you really think I should run."

In point of fact, I wasn't sure which I was doing, either. It would be much harder to take the ship on my own, but spending more time with Marcus Loch was dangerous in its own right.

"Either way," he said, "I'm a man of my word, and I don't think I've upheld my part of the bargain. You're stuck with me awhile longer."

I would feel better about his help—and his honor—if it didn't come with the calculating look. "Okay, thanks," I said. "First things first, I need a new com. Did you see anything that might work while you were out?"

"There are a couple options, but this town is mostly dead. This whole section is abandoned. It seems smuggler hunting isn't paying the bills like it used to. Most people have moved on to greener pastures."

A smaller town was worse for us. Getting lost in a big city was easy, but a new person in a small town always drew attention. "No one questioned where you came from?"

"The people I dealt with don't question their customers. I spent credits and that's all they cared about."

I wasn't sure that honor among thieves would hold once Rockhurst started throwing money around, but I had to hope we were long gone before Richard became that desperate.

I ate an energy bar from my food stash, drank a half liter of water, then stood and pulled one of the cloaks off of the bed. "Thanks for the cloak, too," I said. "Keep a total of what you've spent and I'll add it to your payment."

Made of a heavy black material, the cloak fell from my shoulders to my ankles. The front clasped together to keep out drafts and a deep hood both protected my head from the elements and helped to hide my face. And it was still deliciously warm thanks to the built-in heat field. No hypothermia today.

I sighed and happily snuggled deeper into the warmth. I loved this cloak to pieces, but I knew it was expensive.

Loch stood. "Consider it a gift," he said. "Or an investment, if you prefer. I have to keep you alive long enough to get paid, after all." Despite his gruff words, I thought he was pleased that I liked the cloak.

He pulled on his own cloak and his face dropped into shadow. The cloak did nothing to detract from his size, though. He looked like the kind of man who would shoot first and ask questions never. It was a good look for a mercenary planet.

"Ready?" he asked. When I nodded he continued, "There are mercs literally everywhere once we get to the main part of town. Keep your hood up and stick to me. You're dressed like them, so as long as you don't do something stupid, they won't pay any attention to you."

This wasn't my first rodeo. I had long ago perfected the walk that made me just another downtrodden worker bee who was absolutely uninteresting. It was a move that, done correctly, made you invisible in plain sight.

"Let's go get me a com."

# CHAPTER 7

**L**och opened the door then ushered me into the cold twi-light. The wind still howled through the streets, but the cloak blocked the worst of it. For the first time since we'd arrived, I was outside and not freezing. *Hallelujah.*

We walked toward sunset for ten minutes before I saw signs of life. A few buildings had lights and a shadow moved behind one of the windows. Another five minutes and we were skirting around the edge of the central commercial district, such as it was.

Enough people were on the street that we didn't stand out, but a bustling city this was not. Nearly everyone was on foot and thankfully, many were cloaked and hooded against the cold. At least our hidden faces wouldn't be cause for suspicion.

I mentally mapped our path in case Loch and I were separated. The com should be doing the same thing, but coms could be lost or stolen. As the number of people increased, I dropped back to trail along behind Loch's right shoulder.

Wearing men's clothes, cloaked, and with my hair covered, I would pass for a junior merc tagging along with his captain.

The streets got dirtier and the buildings shabbier as we kept going. Even the plastech buildings, which I had thought were basically indestructible, were worn and mudded over with clay bricks. Men with darting eyes slunk through the alleys and a few brave women shivered in high hemlines and plunging necklines.

Loch must've been gone this morning for longer than I thought. Either that or he had an innate sense that led him directly to the shadiest of shady districts.

We turned down an alley that stank of urine and worse. A lanky man several centimeters shorter than Loch detached himself from the wall and stepped into our path. He was younger than me but old enough to know better. A smirk twisted what would be a moderately handsome face into something cold and cruel.

"See here," he said, "this is my alley. And I charge a toll for its use." Another man, bigger, older, and stronger, stepped out behind us. I half turned so I faced both threats. "A hundred credits each and you can be on your way," the young man said.

"Move," Loch said. He seemed completely unconcerned.

"Oh, we've got a tough one here, Vance," the young man said to the bruiser behind us. "What do we do with tough ones?"

"We break their knees, boss," Vance said. He brandished a half-meter length of pipe in his meaty hands.

Vance would be slow but devastating if he landed a blow. The "boss" would be sneaky and underhanded but would probably break down in a true physical fight. I drew my knife and kept it hidden under the cloak. I didn't know what Loch's plan was, but I doubted he'd turn over the credits.

"Do you know what I do to young upstarts who try to shake me down for money?" Loch asked as he rolled his shoulders and cracked his neck. His tone was terrifying and I was on his side.

Unfortunately for the young upstart, Loch didn't wait for an answer. In an incredible flash of speed he spun and punched Vance in the throat, then took his pipe and swung it with sickening force at the young man's torso.

Vance went down with heaving gasps and the young man crumpled at Loch's feet. Loch picked him up by the neck. "New deal," Loch said. "I won't kill you and you'll crawl back under whatever rock you came from. Try any revenge bullshit, though, and it'll be the last thing you do. Understand?"

The young man muttered something that might have been assent.

"What was that?" Loch asked with a shake.

"I understand!"

Loch dropped him on the ground. "Let's move," he said. He stalked off, and I followed without comment.

Once I was sure we were alone, I closed the distance between us. "I'm not sure that was wise," I said. "We need to be invisible, to be overlooked. You put a target on us."

"Sweetheart," Loch drawled, "I've been running from mercs for far longer than you've been slumming it. If I want to know what fork to use at a Consortium dinner, I'll ask you. If we're dealing with mercenaries, I'll handle it."

I clenched the hilt of the knife and told myself I absolutely, positively was *not* going to bash Marcus Loch in the head with it. But I imagined it. Oh, I imagined it with great relish. One of these days I was going to take the cocky bastard down a peg or two or twenty and he was going to deserve every second of it.

THE FENCE'S SHOP WAS BEHIND AN UNMARKED DOOR IN an unmarked alley. We were let into an empty room where Marcus had a quiet conversation with an older woman. After a few minutes we were led through a series of rooms and passageways until I was positive we had left the original building.

Twenty minutes of mind-numbing twists and turns later, we entered the shop. I had a fairly good idea of where we were but wouldn't be able to confirm until we were outside.

The shop looked like any high-end boutique in the 'verse, with glass counters protecting the valuable merchandise and everything else displayed on shelves. The only difference was that everything of value was placed on cloth rolls or cloth sacks for easy grab-and-go convenience. Portability was essential when the law came to call.

A tall, slender woman with warm brown skin, long black hair, and round, rose-colored spectacles stood behind the far counter. Several guards were scattered around. Clearly the fence didn't want her own goods stolen.

I started by looking at the knives. I'd dealt with fences before and you never wanted to tip your hand too early. Most of the knives were mediocre combat blades but a nice little stiletto dagger caught my eye. My younger sister Catarina would love it.

I worked my way halfway around the room, spending time looking at things I had no intention of buying. When I got to the com units, I saw that they only had one option that was going to work for me.

The shopkeeper wandered closer, smelling blood. "Do you need a new com?" she asked. Her voice was soft and melodious. I bet she'd talked many a person into spending extra money with that voice.

"Perhaps," I said. "Do you have anything decent?"

Her lips tipped up in a small smile. "Ah, a woman," she said. "Women get discounts in my shop. I am Veronica. And to answer your question, yes, I have many decent things, but if you're looking for the best, this is it. This com just arrived yesterday."

She pulled out the exact com I knew I needed. It was a top-of-the-line House von Hasenberg model very much like the one I'd left behind on the space station. In fact, there was a chance it *was* the one I'd left behind.

"May I see it?"

"Of course," Veronica said. She pulled it out, powered it up, and handed it over. *Device locked to Maria Franco* was the only thing shown on the screen.

Well, I'll be damned.

"It seems it is locked," I said. "And therefore useless."

Veronica waved her hands. "It is a small matter to unlock it," she said.

I didn't have to fake my dubious look. If she could unlock this device then I would hire her for the House on the spot. "How much?"

"Five thousand credits," she said.

I laughed. Even new it hadn't cost that much. "I will give you two thousand if you can unlock it. Otherwise, I will give you two hundred because trying to unlock it might be an interesting challenge. But most likely it will end up a paperweight."

"You give me too little credit," she said. "Thirty-five hundred if I can unlock it in the next five minutes, otherwise seven-fifty locked."

"Three thousand unlocked or five hundred locked," I countered. "Plus, I will see what other things I might want to purchase from your lovely shop."

The fence inclined her head. "You drive a hard bargain, madam, but I accept. I will start a timer."

I glanced at my current com. This room and probably the entire compound blocked the signal, but I could still check the time. I went back to shopping. Loch remained standing by the door. Apparently he was playing silent bodyguard.

I found a bracelet and necklace, a pretty scarf, some clothes, and several other odds and ends. I pointed at the stiletto and an assistant materialized from the back to pull it from the case. A couple of anonymous hard credit chips—ridiculously marked up, naturally—rounded out my purchases.

I'd spent a fortune, but by the way Veronica was frowning at the com, she wasn't having any success. It had been well over her five-minute allotment at this point.

She sighed in defeat. "I wish you luck, madam," she said. "This com is locked more thoroughly than any I've ever seen. I feel bad selling it to you."

"No worries, I agreed to purchase it. Plus, I found all of these other lovelies to soothe my frustration when I can't unlock its secrets."

"Twelve-fifty for the lot of it," she said. It was a more than fair price, so I nodded. I tapped my right thumb and pinky finger together under the concealment of my cloak.

"Hard credits?" she asked. When I shook my head, she held out a chip reader. "Then scan here, please," she said.

I checked the total then modified it to fifteen hundred and scanned the chip embedded in my right arm. The machine beeped, I picked the correct account, and then I handed the reader back to her. "I added a little token of appreciation," I said. "I do love a woman who barters well."

Veronica smiled in acknowledgment. She produced a plain white card with a number embossed in a beautiful antique font. She leaned across the display case and tucked the card in my overshirt pocket. "If you need anything, anything at all, call me," she said. Her smile turned sultry. "Any time, day or night."

ONCE WE WERE OUTSIDE, LOCH TOOK THE LEAD. "DO not say anything, and do not return to the house," I murmured to him. "I need a secure space."

We walked for ten minutes in a direction I knew was opposite from where we'd spent the night. A few curious eyes followed us at first but soon we were once again in an abandoned part of the city.

Loch stopped outside of a seemingly random plastech building. Now that I wasn't freezing, I could see what drew him to the buildings he chose. For this one, the walls were solid and dust around the entrance showed no signs of footprints.

He picked the lock in record time and soon we were inside. The living room was right off the entry. I set the bag of items I'd bought, the card the fence had given me, the cloak, and my overshirt in a pile in the middle of the floor. It might be overkill, but I didn't think so.

"I need your cloak," I said. Loch added his cloak to the pile. Without the heat field or extra shirt, the temperature in the room was bitingly cold.

"I'll see about some heat," Loch said.

I picked up the new com, touched my right thumb to my right ring finger, and held the com up to the chip in my arm.

The highly illegal, highly specialized, highly *secret* chip in my arm.

Most people were embedded with a single identity chip at birth. I had that one, my main identity chip, in my left arm, but it was dormant most of the time. The chip in my right arm was a House von Hasenberg family specialty, though I had no doubt the other Houses had something similar. The chip could hold multiple identities and each identity could be selected by a series of finger movements.

Designed for spying, the chip also worked great for staying a step ahead of Father's trackers. Purchase a new identity with untraceable funds, and—voilà!—a clean break. The trackers would eventually find the new identities, but it took time and gave me a chance to escape.

The com unlocked. Some sneaky bastard had stolen the com from my abandoned room on the station, realized it was locked beyond hope, and sold it just in time for me to buy it. And here I thought the universe didn't love me. Granted, this was the second closest planet to the station, and the shadier of the two, but I wasn't going to look a gift horse in the mouth.

Not only was this a top-of-the-line communication device, it was also designed especially for von Hasenberg family members, though you would be hard-pressed to notice based on the design. It had a few extra features, too.

I set the com to run a self-diagnostic, and when that came back clean, I turned on scanning mode. Designed to secure a space for communication, this mode would find any trackers or bugs the fence had managed to attach to us. Most coms had some form of bug sweeping functionality, but this one was much more sensitive than standard.

The card and shirt came back clean, much to my surprise. Our cloaks were a different matter. Each had a tiny tracker attached. I used my com to connect to the trackers and reconfigure them. Whoever was monitoring the trackers just saw them go offline. I, however, could now see their locations overlaid on a map. It wasn't a standard com feature, but it proved useful enough that von Hasenberg family coms always came equipped with it.

I attached the two trackers to Loch's cloak—one high near the neck and one at the bottom edge. It wasn't that I didn't trust him . . . but I didn't trust him.

The rest of the stuff I bought was clean, including the shirt, pants, necklace, and bracelet that were all mine originally. It wasn't everything I'd left behind, but the com, necklace, and bracelet were definitely the most important bits.

I scanned myself and didn't find any new trackers. "Loch?" I called. He'd left the room to find heat but hadn't returned. When he didn't respond, I put on my overshirt and cloak. I stored the small items in a cargo pocket and then put the clothes and Loch's cloak back into the bag.

Something felt off, but I wasn't going to freak out without reason.

The entry was empty, as was the dining room on the other side of the house. A hallway led deeper into the building, much like the house we'd stayed in last night. It was dark and silent.

"Loch?" I tried again. Silence answered.

Normally when presented with a choice between going deeper into a dark, creepy abandoned building or stepping out the front door into the—admittedly low—light, I'd choose the light every time. But Loch had disappeared down this hall and while I didn't necessarily think he was in trouble, it was weird that he wasn't responding.

The flashlight built into the com wasn't great, but it cut through the darkness better than nothing. I drew my knife. If Loch was just in the bathroom, I was going to feel really silly.

An open door on my right led to the empty kitchen. My stomach grumbled, reminding me that I hadn't eaten enough to cover the calories I'd burned. I ignored it and continued deeper into the house.

The next door was closed. This would be so much easier if I had a gun, because clearing a room with a knife was a terrible idea. Still, I couldn't leave a room unexplored, not if I wanted a valid retreat option.

I stood on the hinge side of the door and reached across to the handle. It turned easily and I pushed the door open then stepped back so I was hidden by the frame. Silence. I risked a peek and the part of the room I could see was empty. I cleared the other side of the room, including behind the door.

Three more rooms proved to be empty, until only one room remained. I pushed the door open, not sure what to expect. What I did not expect, however, was another empty room.

Weak light spilled in through the frosted window, illuminating an empty utility room. A door led out to the backyard. Boot prints in the dust proved Loch—or someone—had been this way recently.

To follow or not to follow.

It had been fifteen minutes since Loch disappeared. He could be out scouting the perimeter because he expected me to take longer. Or he could've decided to double-cross me and I'd walk out into an ambush.

Only one way to find out. I turned off my flashlight, pulled up the hood of my cloak, and touched the button next to the window. The windowpane changed from frosted to clear. The backyard was a tiny brown square covered in dead grass and surrounded by a low, broken-down fence. No mob waited for me to appear.

I stood at the edge of the window and let my eyes roam over the scene. If anyone was out there hiding, unless they were trained, they would eventually fidget, and the movement would give them away.

Nothing moved, other than the grass blowing in the wind.

So where was Loch?

Just as I was going to turn away to check the front, something drew my eye to the top of the next house. I froze and focused on the area. Nothing else moved and the low light made it difficult to identify what had caught my attention.

My patience was rewarded as someone moved again, just the slightest shift, but it was enough. Friends generally didn't linger on in the shadows on top of adjacent buildings, so the only remaining question was: Who was it?

We could've picked up a random tail, a random merc squad, the boss from earlier, a tail from Veronica the fence, or the Rockhurst squad. We were collecting enemies faster than I could keep up.

I retreated to the darkened hallway. For now I would give Loch the benefit of the doubt and assume he was out scouting when the other people moved in. That meant he was either captured or holed up somewhere waiting to see what happened.

I briefly debated the merits of leaving sooner versus having better protection. I opted for better protection. Only time would tell if it was a wise choice.

The necklace and bracelet felt heavy for their size. The bracelet was a wide silver cuff and the necklace had heavy silver links connected to a round silver medallion inlaid with turquoise. Both pieces were pretty but nothing indicated they were anything more than normal jewelry.

When I'd fled home, I'd only taken a small bag of possessions. These pieces of jewelry were two of the things in that bag. On the station I hadn't had them on because I'd just popped over to the nearby shop to pick up an early dinner. Unfortunately, Captain Pearson had ruined that plan.

I performed the complicated left hand motion that activated my true identity chip. I held the necklace to the chip. Nothing happened, but that was expected. I turned the necklace over twice, then rotated the center of the medallion like I was opening a combination lock.

The center of the medallion sprang open, revealing a DNA tester. I clasped the necklace around my throat then pricked my thumb on the embedded needle. The medallion clicked closed and once again it appeared to be a normal necklace. Now it was authorized until I unclasped it.

I held the bracelet up to my real identity chip for a count of ten. It had less stringent security because it wouldn't work without the necklace being authorized. I clasped the cuff around my right wrist and deactivated my real identity chip.

Now to face whatever awaited me outside. I'd delayed long enough to put on the jewelry not only because of the extra protection it would provide but also because I was hoping Loch would return if I gave him more time. He did not.

So now I was on my own. I'd try to meet him at our original house if I made it out. If he didn't show, I'd have to find out if he got caught and by whom.

I needed to check the front. With the back door watched, it was unlikely they'd left the front open, but I didn't have to dodge a fence in the front. I crept back through the hallway. I'd like to think that I would hear anyone who had breached the house, but highly trained men and women could be alarmingly quiet.

The front window showed a deserted street. And though I watched for five minutes, I couldn't catch a hint of movement. Doubt crept in. Had I really seen someone on the roof in the back?

I took Loch's cloak out of the bag and put it on over my own. It was less cumbersome to wear than to carry. I tied the bag of clothes I'd bought around my waist. Both hands needed to be free if I was going to have to fight.

I *so* did not want to fight.

I opened the front door and stepped out as if I was going for an afternoon stroll. Make something of that, you bastards.

Nothing moved and I finally realized what bothered me

about this planet—there were no animals. No birds singing or dogs barking. It was eerily still except for the sound of the wind.

I turned left, back toward the main part of town. No one tried to stop me, but I had an itch between my shoulder blades like someone watched my progress. I took a meandering path but I couldn't shake the tail. Whoever tracked me was good, because I couldn't catch a hint of them, even when I doubled back on my path.

I would have to risk the central district to try to lose the tail in the meager crowd. I angled back toward the spaceport. Hopefully I could catch a glimpse of the Rockhurst ship while I was out.

As the number of people in the streets picked up, I dropped into my invisible persona, subtly altering my gait and posture. I also picked up the pace until I was just another harassed underling off to do an urgent task for a demanding boss.

I slipped down alleys and through a busy trading street. I looped back and changed course at random, until the watched feeling faded away. I kept at it for another twenty minutes, even pausing to stop in a tea shop and then exiting out the back.

When I was completely sure that I'd lost any tail, I started working my way back toward our original house. I was on the edge of the central district when Richard Rockhurst stepped out of a restaurant with a com to his ear.

Richard wore a traditional mercenary outfit, complete with cloak, but the hood was thrown back. He was tall and fit, with the blond hair and blue eyes I'd so envied as a young girl. I'd recognize him anywhere.

He was in the middle of the block I'd just entered. There was nowhere to go without drawing attention to myself and it took everything I had not to freeze and give myself away.

"And the man with Loch?" Richard asked with deceptive calm.

Someone on the other end must have responded, but I wasn't close enough to catch it.

"So you're telling me that you have neither Loch nor his contact on this godforsaken planet. You had one job and you failed."

Another pause as the person on the other end tried to save their life. Now I was within a meter of Richard. I ducked my head, dropped my eyes, and thought invisible thoughts. I passed him close enough that our cloaks brushed.

"Find Ada," he said. "That is priority one. Loch is our only lead right now, so that makes him priority two. We know he's here in the city. Now it's just a matter of finding where he's stashed her."

I didn't breathe until I turned the next corner. I kept my pace even and continued on my way. Whoever had been following me thought I was Loch's contact, unless Loch had *another* contact somewhere else. Either way, Loch had also avoided capture.

Ten minutes later I stopped in the darkness between two buildings and scanned myself for trackers. I came up clean. My tail had been following me the old-fashioned way, which begged the question: Why?

It was clear they'd arrived after us, but not by too much if Loch left the house while I was scanning for bugs. Maybe

Loch had drawn off the main set of men, leaving behind a skeleton crew to watch what they thought was Loch's contact's house. If so, we'd gotten extremely lucky.

Luck was a fickle bitch, though, and I'd used up my monthly allotment in the last two days. I needed to be more careful.

# CHAPTER 8

It took me over an hour to return to the house. I could've covered the distance in ten minutes if I took a direct path, but after the scare with Richard I wanted to be absolutely sure I didn't have a tagalong.

Entering a potentially compromised building with only a knife was stupid. But I'd checked the perimeter twice and no one else lurked in the shadows. Stationing your entire team in the compromised house was equally stupid. We'd see whose stupid won.

The back door was unlocked. I slipped inside. "Loch?" I called. It gave me away, but it also meant I wasn't sneaking up on the Devil of Fornax Zero in the dark. And if it wasn't Loch waiting for me, I'd rather know that while I still had an easy exit at my back.

"In here."

"We really should've had a secret 'I promise there isn't a roomful of mercs in here' keyword," I muttered to myself.

"I promise there isn't a roomful of mercs in here," Loch called back. I could hear the grin in his voice.

I locked the back door and approached the room we'd used before. The door was open and the light was on. Loch sat on a barstool that hadn't been in the room before. He clutched a bloody rag to his upper left arm.

"Holy hell, are you okay?"

"Energy bolt grazed me," he said. "Just deep enough that it didn't cauterize. It looks worse than it is."

"That's good because it looks terrible," I said. "Why didn't you get the first aid kit?"

"Didn't know we had one," Loch said. "I'll be fine by tomorrow. Can't say the same for the bastard who shot me."

"What happened?" I asked. I pulled out my com and checked him for trackers and bugs. He was clean, as was the room, and our packs from the ship. The two trackers I'd attached to his cloak didn't set off the alarm since they were mine now. Assuming neither of us had been tracked the old-fashioned way, we wouldn't have to leave tonight.

I rummaged around in my pack from the ship until I dug out the first aid kit. Loch grimaced but didn't object. He was right, the wound looked worse than it was. It was shallow, but as wide and long as my finger. I bet it stung like nobody's business. I cleaned the wound and put a healing bandage on it.

"I went to look for heat only to realize the heater was missing. I'd been feeling twitchy, so I went outside to check the perimeter. Rockhurst's men are sneaky fuckers, I'll give them that. They moved in before I could warn you, so I did what I could to draw them away." He shrugged his bad shoulder. "It worked a little too well."

"If the crew is from the *Santa Celestia*—and I don't know why they wouldn't be—they are some of the most highly trained troops in House Rockhurst. I can't believe they didn't hit you worse than that if they had time to get a shot off."

"He was preoccupied with the direction of my blade," Loch said.

I'd seen Loch in action. I knew he had to have been military at one point because he was part of the team suppressing the Fornax Rebellion. But to know he'd gone toe-to-toe with one or more of Rockhurst's elite soldiers and come out relatively unscathed . . . well, that was just plain scary.

"So who sold us out?" I asked. I shrugged off the extra cloak and untied the bag of clothes from around my waist. I should've grabbed some real food while I was out. Another energy bar held the appeal of eating dirt, but I needed the calories. And I needed to drink more water. I could feel the first signs of dehydration creeping in.

"The punk who tried to shake us down. I found his rat right before Rockhurst closed on us. Said he heard a new crew was looking for a big guy and thought he'd take care of the problem for his boss. He didn't mention you to Rockhurst because he was afraid they wouldn't come if there were two of us."

"I got tagged on my way out. Managed to lose him in the central district. Did you know Richard is on-planet?"

Loch's gaze sharpened and he sat straighter. "How do you know?"

That was a clever dodge of the question. "I nearly ran into him on the street. How did *you* know?"

"I doubled back on the soldiers. Heard them talking about how Richard was going to have their asses if they didn't find me."

Plausible, but not entirely true. I'd been reading people for a long time. Loch lied better than most, but I'd bet anything that he was lying now. So what did he gain by lying? Was he trying to work a double-cross with Richard?

"Did Rockhurst see you?" Loch asked. His own suspicion was obvious now. Clearly our road to trust was progressing not-at-all.

"I don't think so. He didn't stop me and no one followed me. But we're going to need to move fast or they'll catch us again. How many do you think are guarding the ship?"

"At least two. Even with the ship's security they'll leave a couple men behind. But I wouldn't be surprised if it was a six-man team, to give them rotating shifts and backup."

I sat on the bed and dug out an energy bar. This one was blueberry flavored. At least it was less objectionable than the mango one from this morning. I drank the last of the water from the ship. "Any idea if the tap water is drinkable?"

"Should be. These houses are still on the main water system. I'd let it run for a while first."

That was a project for tomorrow, along with a laundry solution and a shower. Tonight I needed to contact one of my siblings and sweet-talk them into giving up prized family intel over only moderately secure channels.

We were all close, as if making up for our parents' distance, but I was closest to my sisters. I could ask them for the moon and they'd do their damnedest to deliver. Just as

I would do anything for them. So they were the most likely candidates for a huge, dangerous favor.

It would have to be Bianca. She had moved back to House von Hasenberg after her husband's death, and she always seemed to have information that no one else could find. Plus, I was closest to her. Even among family we all played the game, though not as ruthlessly.

I activated my true identity chip and held the new com up to it.

"Verify," a computer voice demanded.

"Ada von Hasenberg, smartest of all the von Hasenbergs." Yeah, we got to pick our own verification phrases. I held the camera up to my eye for a retina scan. The com beeped.

"What are you doing?" Loch asked.

"I'm setting up this com to be able to send and receive on the secure House channels. Then I'm going to ask my sister for a huge favor and hope she comes through. Then I'm stealing a ship and leaving this freezing rock behind. What are you doing?"

"Trying not to bleed to death." I glanced up sharply to find him staring at his com and not bleeding at all. He looked up and laughed. "I'm kidding. But if you don't let me in on the plan, that might as well be what I'm doing."

"I just told you the plan. When and if you need to know more, I'll let you know. If you have a better plan, I'd love to hear it." It was somewhat gratifying to see that Loch liked giving up control just about as much as I had when we were landing—that is, not at all.

I quickly typed a message to Bianca letting her know in as much detail as I dared what was happening and what

I needed. I didn't think she'd rat me out to Father, but if she thought my plan was too dangerous, she would send our brother Benedict in to save the day. And Benedict was exactly what this situation did not need.

I sent it priority, but even so, I didn't expect a response until tomorrow morning at the earliest. I checked the rest of the family chatter. There were a few rumbles of trouble with Rockhurst over some planet in the distant Antlia sector.

Nothing overt in the family chatter indicated that Rockhurst was on the brink of war, but the very lack of such information and speculation was telling. Any posts about Rockhurst were carefully neutral. What was going on?

It would be so much easier if I could just call Richard up and ask. But he'd track the signal before the first word was spoken. If I could just get him alone for two minutes, I could ask him in person.

*Hmm.*

I set that thought aside to let it simmer in my subconscious. Getting him alone for a chat would be dangerous, but it might be necessary. If I could figure out his motivation, it would help me and House von Hasenberg.

My thoughts kept circling. I needed sleep. There wasn't anything else I could do tonight, except give my body the rest it required. "Do you know if there are any other beds in the house?" I asked.

Loch looked up from his com with a lascivious grin. "Afraid not. But don't worry, I don't mind sharing."

Sharing a bed with Marcus Loch when I wasn't near death was a recipe for disaster. Hot, sweaty, naked disaster. Heat spread across my face and lower. Definitely lower.

Lord help me.

Loch's grin was just knowing enough to make me want to punch him. It tempted me to play with a fire that I knew would burn. I removed my boots while I fought the desire.

I crossed the room and closed the door. I dragged the broken dresser in front of it. It was harder than Loch had made it look yesterday.

Loch snagged my wrist as I walked past him. With him sitting on the barstool, we were the same height. He usually moved so quickly and quietly that it was easy to overlook his size, but standing next to him, he was a solid wall of muscle.

"Will you give me a judgment-free minute?" I asked him softly.

His expression went guarded but finally he nodded. I stepped closer until I was standing between his legs. Desire lit his eyes. I felt it, too, but he was about to be disappointed. I needed this more right now.

Slowly I wrapped my arms around him and rested my head against his shoulder. He froze. After a few seconds, I whispered, "You're supposed to hug me back."

His arms came around me like I was made of spun glass. I gave him a little squeeze. "I'm not that fragile," I said. "Give me a real hug."

He crushed me to his chest. I sighed in contentment and fought the ridiculous urge to cry. Mother and Father might be as distant and untouchable as the moon, but my sisters and I were always physically affectionate. With them, hugs were frequent and touch always conveyed love and comfort. It helped to balance out some of Father's more merciless training programs.

As we got older, hugs were often replaced by cheek kisses and handshakes, but they were busted out in cases of extra stress or emotional turmoil. I'd say this week counted. Sometimes a simple sign of affection was more powerful than a whole host of words.

Even the illusion of affection from a man I barely trusted was enough to ease my heart.

I straightened and met Loch's eyes. True to his word, I didn't see any judgment in them. "Thank you," I said.

Loch's arms remained around me, though they'd loosened enough that I could step out of his embrace if I wanted to. "You're welcome," he said.

His head tilted and I knew he was going to kiss me. It was my turn to freeze, torn between staying and going. His thumb caressed my lower back. "Easy," he murmured. "Just a kiss and nothing more."

I stood my ground even as logic dictated that I was emotionally vulnerable and this was a terrible idea. Then his lips ghosted over mine and logic lost.

A second pass as light and teasing as the first and I'd had enough. I wrapped a hand around the back of his head and pulled his mouth to mine. He groaned and obliged as if it was the sign he'd been waiting for all along.

His lips were warm and firm. The hot slide of his tongue against mine caused my hand to clench against the back of his head. Lust slammed through me and I stepped closer, trying to meld my body into his.

We were both breathing hard when he gently pushed me back. "I promised you just a kiss," he growled.

My hormones begged me to convince him that I wanted

more than a kiss. So much more. But with distance came a minute spark of clarity and I was glad for his control.

"Go to bed," he said. "I'm going to do a perimeter check." He paused then muttered very quietly, "And stand in the icy cold wind until I'm not acting like a fucking idiot."

I refused to feel hurt that he thought kissing me was idiotic. "You're injured," I said. "You go to bed and I'll do the perimeter check." Honor made me offer. And maybe the tiniest desire to run and hide.

His gaze was scorching. "If I get into that bed right now, there's only one thing I'm going to be doing, and it's not sleeping."

My nipples pebbled under my shirt as renewed lust blazed through my system. Okay, maybe it wasn't the kissing he thought was dumb. Warmth bloomed in my chest even as I told myself that being happy just because he hadn't insulted me was no way to act.

He ran a hand down his face. "But I made you a promise, and I'm keeping it, which means I'm leaving."

He moved the dresser with much less effort than I'd used and slipped out the door into the darkened hallway without another word. The door clicked closed behind him.

I sank down on the edge of the bed and touched my lips. That just happened. And I would've happily climbed into bed with him, consequences and tomorrows be damned. The thought sobered me. I hadn't had this much trouble controlling myself since I was first allowed into Consortium events as a green girl.

Marcus Loch was dangerous for more reasons than I'd initially thought.

I decided to go to bed fully clothed. It was safer for both of us that way. I wrapped the cloak around me, crawled between the emergency blankets, and huddled on one side of the bed.

It took a long time to fall asleep.

ONCE AGAIN I AWOKE ALONE. I HAD VAGUE MEMORIES of Marcus in the night, but I wasn't sure if they were real or imaginary. My dreams had been fraught, I knew that much. The emotional turmoil of the day had followed me into sleep.

I sat up and checked my com. Bianca had responded. Her response involved a lot of sentences in all caps and threats of death and dismemberment, but in the end, she said she'd find the codes for me, though it would take a day or two.

She also dropped some veiled hints that things with Rockhurst were not as they seemed, but the message required a lot of reading between the lines. If she was being this careful even on the secure House accounts, then things were bad. I needed to be extra cautious.

Then she proved once again that she was two steps ahead of everyone else by including the following: *Locks can be good protection but shouldn't be trusted completely.* I stared at the screen for a solid minute in wonder. I hadn't mentioned Loch in my message, so was she fishing or did she know?

Either way, she had felt it necessary to warn me not to trust Loch. But why? The problem with all of the reading between the lines was that it was difficult to communicate effectively, but this was vague even for Bianca.

I had no doubt she was frantically trying to find my location, but I'd bounced the message through several different systems to obfuscate the trail. It wouldn't stump her for long, but maybe it would be long enough for me to escape without her sending in the cavalry.

With that in mind, I decided to see what I could do about a shower and laundry. I would need to hit a shop first. From what I saw yesterday during my wander about the downtown area, there were only two or three general goods shops left. And if I was Richard, I'd have a man watching each of them. Everyone needed food and supplies sooner or later.

I changed into the clothes I'd bought yesterday. A long-sleeved pale blue tunic went on over narrow dull gold pants. A blue and gold scarf wrapped around my head and neck until just my eyes were visible. It was a risk going out dressed as a woman, but I'd seen several women out on the busier commercial streets. My outfit wouldn't attract undue attention.

The slit in the side of the tunic allowed plenty of movement and also allowed me to attach a knife to my belt and still access it relatively easily. The hard credits went in a pouch with my com. I attached the pouch on the opposite hip from the knife.

"What are you wearing?" Loch asked.

I'd heard him a bare second before he spoke, so I managed not to jump into next week in fright. My heart rate still needed a second to recover, however. It needed quite a bit longer when I saw he'd showered and shaved.

"Did you buy soap or shampoo yesterday?" That would solve one problem.

Loch looked at me like I was crazy. Okay, then. I guess I was the only one who cared that my shower involved actual cleansers.

"I'm going out. I need shampoo, even if you don't. And laundry detergent. And food."

"And you're going dressed like *that*?"

"Yes. With the cloak, of course. What's wrong with this? I saw several women dressed similarly to this yesterday and everyone left them alone."

"That's because the men all know those women belong to Mr. Goswami, who will break any man's face who so much as looks at one of his wives or daughters wrong. You, however, are neither wife nor daughter. And before you try it, no. You're much too tall to pass for either."

"How could you possibly know that?"

"I was warned," he said, "when it appeared I'd been staring at the lady in question for too long. In fact I was watching the door behind her, but the merc who warned me didn't know that."

"Well, then I guess the men will have to learn that I, too, will break any man's face who tries to start shit with me."

"And you think a random woman wearing a full face veil and kicking ass is just going to fly right past Rockhurst? He'll snatch you up before you set foot wherever you're going."

"Very well," I said. "With the understanding that I *will* buy shampoo, laundry detergent, and food today, what would you suggest instead?"

"I suggest you eat an energy bar and give up on soap," Loch said. "The more often we're out, the more dangerous it is."

He was right, dammit. But if I had to sit and dawdle in this room all day, I'd go crazy. And while I could think of one delicious way we could pass the time, that would complicate matters even more, especially with Bianca's warning fresh in my mind.

I changed back into the clothes I'd taken from the escape ship. I was frustrated enough that I didn't even care that Loch was in the room, though I changed my pants under the cover of the tunic and turned my back on him to change my shirt.

The drab camo and black mocked the beauty of my former outfit. Impatience and annoyance nipped at me. I needed to recenter myself before I did something stupid. And while seated meditation was always an option, I needed movement.

I moved to the center of the room, closed my eyes, and inhaled deeply through my nose. I held the breath for a few beats then released it through my mouth. Five more deep breaths and I fell into the beginning stance of my short, meditative martial arts form.

Solo, weaponless martial arts forms could be done anywhere with no equipment, so it was something all the von Hasenberg children were taught from a young age. We'd had thirty minutes of practice in various styles before class every day. It helped to build strength and flexibility, but it also helped to calm and center the mind.

I focused on the movements and let the rest of the world fade away. Tension faded, replaced with strength and calm. I finished the sequence and closed my eyes. When I opened them again, Loch stood in front of me.

"Care to spar?" he asked.

# CHAPTER 9

There are moments in your life when you absolutely know what you should do and then you absolutely choose to do something else entirely.

This was one of those moments.

"I would love to spar," I said. "No face, no eyes, no balls, and, for the love of God, pull your punches. Agreed?"

"Agreed," he said. He dropped into a typical mixed martial arts stance. I mirrored his stance and nodded my readiness.

Even obviously slowed down he moved like lightning. I went defensive, dancing out of his reach and deflecting the blows I couldn't avoid. His form was tight and he didn't leave openings in his guard. My self-defense tutor would've loved him.

"You gonna hit me, darling, or you just gonna dance around?" he asked a few minutes later.

I dodged a slow jab at my side. "Hand-to-hand fighting is a last resort for me, and I generally learned how to do it just long enough to make an opportunity to run." I blocked a stomach blow then flowed away from a right cross that would've clipped my shoulder. "Which means I fight dirty then run away. Since neither of those is an option right now, I'm biding my time."

Loch stopped attacking and stepped back into a defensive stance. "Your time is now," he said with a grin. "Bring it on."

I feinted a right then got through his guard low with my left fist.

"That was well done," he said. "You didn't telegraph your intentions at all."

"My self-defense tutor could be a bitch, but she had my best interest at heart. She taught me well. It's not her fault that I didn't take to fighting."

I jabbed at him a few more times, both straight punches and feints, but now he was on guard and blocked or dodged all my attempts. That was why, in a real fight, the first feint would be followed by the hardest punch I could throw. You only had one chance to surprise an opponent with skill.

Loch struck out with his left fist. I saw the blow too late to do more than tense my ab muscles. Even pulled it landed hard enough to smart. I backed away into a defensive stance.

"Don't run away," Loch said.

"I just told you that running away is one of the core pillars of my fighting strategy."

"Okay," he allowed, "run away in a real fight, but don't run away from me. I promised to pull my punches."

"Yeah, but I didn't promise to stand around as a human punching bag," I said as I dodged yet another attempt at my midsection.

"You're quick," Loch said, "and good at reading your opponent. With a little more training you wouldn't have to worry about running."

I laughed. "Don't think my tutor didn't try. I have the knowledge but not the desire. I will fight viciously to save my life or rescue a friend, but most other situations can just as easily be solved by evasion."

"How are you at grappling?"

"Worse than terrible," I said. I watched him closely, because I had a feeling he wasn't asking just for the fun of it. I wasn't lying; if he caught me, it was over.

I avoided him for a minute, but then he snagged my arm and used my own momentum to spin me around until I was trapped with my back against his chest. My arms crossed in front of me and he had a hand clamped around each of my wrists.

"How do you get out of this hold?"

"First, I head-butt you," I said while I mimed doing it. "Then I stomp on your toes if you're not wearing boots. Then I hook my foot here," I said, wrapping my foot around his lower right leg, "and throw my weight back while you're off-balance."

"That would probably work, though then you'd be on the ground. How about this one?" He spun me around until my back was against the wall then pressed close.

I hit him with my sexiest smoldering glance. "First," I said, "I look at you like this. Then I run my hand up your chest like this." I demonstrated, but kept going until my hand rested on the back of his head.

"Then I pull your head down to mine," I said. I licked my lips and his eyes dropped half-closed. "And head-butt your nose, gouge your eyes, and knee you in the balls," I whispered a centimeter from his mouth.

Loch froze then burst out laughing. "That definitely would work." He let me go and backed away. I fought the urge to pull him back and kiss him for real.

I changed the subject to safer topics. "So now you know why running is the core tenet of my defense," I said.

"You don't give yourself enough credit," Loch said. "I was moving slower than my normal speed, but I've sparred at that speed with many trained soldiers who couldn't dodge and deflect as well as you did."

I smiled at the compliment but shook my head. "It's because the mind-set is different," I said. "Soldiers don't retreat by default. I do."

Between the martial arts warm-up and sparring, I was feeling nearly relaxed. My muscles were warm and pliant with none of the residual soreness I'd been carrying for the last couple days. Even my mind was clear and focused.

"So the fence yesterday did not carry any ranged weapons," I said. "Any idea why?"

"Supply is locked down. Mr. Goswami—of the wives and daughters fame—has the only shop in town. And he prefers it that way. Even the fences won't cross him. Those who do disappear."

"Security?"

"Guards twenty-four-seven. Electronic locks and surveillance equipment with redundant fail-safes. All with internal battery backups."

"And you know that how?" Sometimes I wondered if Loch just made shit up to see if I'd believe him.

"You aren't the only person in this group who'd like to have a gun," he said. "I checked out the situation yesterday morning. The door I was watching was the one to Mr. Goswami's shop."

"Okay, so the shop is out. Surely some merc on this planet is stupid enough to have both guns and bad security. We just need to find one."

Loch held out his com. "The address of one Vance Burnam and his boss, August Chisholm. Both of whom are currently in the medbay."

"No!" I said with a disbelieving gasp.

"Indeed yes," Loch said. "Even better, it's nowhere near the central district."

"Why didn't you just lead with that? We could be there already!"

"Even in the shadier districts, it's generally frowned on to break into someone else's house at high noon."

Personally, high noon seemed like an excellent time. The shadier elements were probably fast asleep from their late-night shenanigans. But maybe if people were out causing trouble they wouldn't be home to see us sneaking into their neighbor's house.

For now I needed water, food, and a shower. Definitely water first, though, if I had to choke down another energy bar. I collected my empty bottles and made my way to the kitchen. The hallway was dark but dim light spilled through the frosted glass front window. The endless twilight was starting to get to me. How did people live here?

Unfortunately, I knew better than to turn on a light that could be visible from outside and since the kitchen opened to the dining room window, I had to feel my way around until my eyes adjusted.

I turned on the sink full-blast and let it run for five minutes. We were lucky that frontier towns like this generally didn't meter water or power and didn't shut them off when the occupants left. Yamado owned the whole town—both buildings and infrastructure—so it was easier to just leave everything hooked up for the next tenant.

I filled the bottles and carried them back into the bedroom to check the clarity before I risked a drink. The nanobots in my blood would knock out any waterborne pathogens before they had a chance to take root, but I still didn't relish the thought of drinking dirty water.

The light revealed clear water, so I drank a bottle while choking down two energy bars. They did not improve with familiarity. I had enough to last me a few more days but I wasn't exactly relishing the prospect.

Next up: shower. My delight at a real water shower dimmed significantly when I realized there was no hot water. Someone had probably scavenged parts off of the water heater. The lack of soap worked in my favor, though, because I didn't have to stay in the frigid water long enough to rinse away soapy residue.

Even with the brief shower I was shivering violently by the time I was done. I dried quickly then draped the heated cloak around me while I dressed in the black pants and long-sleeved black shirt I'd bought from the fence. The chill settled into my bones.

This sucked.

Admitting it helped. There was a lot to be said for pushing

on without complaint, but sometimes it was nice to just stop and admit things were terrible. Embracing the terrible made it more manageable, at least for me.

**I SPENT THE REST OF THE DAY CATCHING UP ON NEWS.** There was no mention of the *Mayport.* The SOS beacon should've activated as soon as the emergency ship undocked, so it was unlikely that it hadn't been found. Unless the override Richard's soldiers had used to disable the ship's computer had also disabled the SOS beacon.

The *Mayport* wasn't due at the next jump point for another couple days, so Father wouldn't be searching for me yet, which gave Richard time to act. I'd thought he'd been in the area and I had been a convenient political target, but with everything I'd learned from Bianca, I wasn't so sure.

I checked my accounts to see if Richard had reached out. He hadn't, not even to my personal account, which he knew was secure from the rest of the House.

With nothing else to do, I settled in for a few hours of sleep. It was still early, but I'd learned to catch sleep where I could. I was nearly out when Loch joined me, a wall of warmth against my back that I could feel through our clothes. I hummed in appreciation and snuggled back against him. The man was better than a heat field.

"Go back to sleep, Ada," he murmured. And I did.

**HOURS LATER, LOCH AND I SLIPPED INTO THE TWILIGHT** and skirted around the central district. We headed for the same seedy area we'd visited the first day but we took a much longer route.

We kept to the shadows and darkened alleys when possible. Because we were at the inflection point between late and early, only a handful of people were out. As we got into the more residential areas, even those few people disappeared.

No witnesses was nice, but it also made us stand out. "Is there a curfew?" I whispered to Loch at the next corner.

"Not that I know about," he whispered back. "But I'm avoiding the lawmen just the same."

"Good plan."

We wound through shabbier and shabbier neighborhoods until the plastech buildings were more boards and mud than plastech.

We circled the same block twice before Loch stopped behind the middle house on the block. He checked his com. "This is it," he said. The house was dark, as were the two beside it. Either luck was with us or the occupants knew better than to let light escape.

I peered into the twilight while Loch opened the door. Nothing moved, but I couldn't shake the feeling of being watched.

"I think we should abort," I whispered as soon as we were inside. Loch was a dark shape against the deeper darkness of the room.

"Why?" he asked.

"Just a feeling."

To his credit, Loch didn't scoff. "Five minutes?" he asked.

I nodded reluctantly. If someone was watching us, I doubted five minutes would make a ton of difference. But for us it could mean the difference between finding guns or going home empty-handed.

We moved quickly through the house. I set my com flashlight to the lowest setting and turned it on. It was hard to tell if the house had already been ransacked or if the people living here were just slobs.

Once we checked the house for occupants, Loch and I split up. I searched one bedroom while he searched the other. I found two well-used blaster pistols in the top of the closet, as well as a small cache of energy cells. No holsters, though, so I shoved one gun in my pocket and left the other out for Loch.

I was shoving energy cells into my other pockets when Loch entered the room. "Trouble," he said. "You were right."

I handed him the gun and ammo. "How bad?"

"Rockhurst's men, at least a squad of six. We'll have to split their attention. You should take your hood down."

"They'll never leave me alone if they know who I am." I pulled out the pistol and loaded it. I had a feeling I was going to need it before the night was over. I tucked it back in my pocket. It wasn't the safest way to carry it, but a better option didn't present itself, so I went with what I had.

"But they also won't shoot you in the back," Loch said. It was hard to argue with that logic. "We'll make it seem like you escaped from me. If they capture you, I'll come for you," he said. "You still owe me. Don't do anything stupid."

"You should've taken the money and run," I said. "I tried to warn you."

"Why? This is the most fun I've had in years," Loch said. His eyes gleamed in the dark and I almost believed him. "We both go left then split at the next corner. You go right. You're not going to be able to lose them in the crowd. Run hard and fast."

"Be careful," I said. "Your bounty doesn't specify that they need to keep you alive."

"But they will," Loch said arrogantly. "Rockhurst won't be able to resist parading me in front of the Consortium before he kills me. Ready?"

I wasn't, not even close, but giving Richard time to move more men over here was not going to improve matters, so I nodded.

"Look like you're fighting me without actually slowing us down," Loch said. "Remember: left then right. Run like hell."

"I got it. I'll meet you back at the house or nearby." I left my hood down and followed Loch when he grabbed my wrist and pulled me through the door.

Two men were in the alley across the street. One on the roof. Probably more I couldn't spot. Two pistol blasts slammed into the side of our building close enough to heat the air before I heard my name shouted. The blasts stopped.

The men across the street moved to intercept, but Loch was already sprinting. I tugged on my arm and did my best to appear terrified. It wasn't too difficult.

At the corner I realized that if I split from him, Loch would lose his human shield. I tried to follow him, but he hissed "Right!" at me and then darted left before the soldiers knew we were separating.

I swiped my left hand across the cuff around my right wrist, first inside to outside, then the opposite. I held my hand over the cuff for two seconds. It buzzed once.

My lungs burned and the cold air stabbed at my throat. The cuff pulsed and a wall to my left danced with a shower of electric sparks. These men hadn't forgotten their stun pistols. And the cuff could only repel two more shots.

At the next corner, I pulled the gun from my pocket and spun. The man behind me was nearly a block away. I aimed and fired in one motion. The energy bolt went clean through his thigh. It wasn't exactly what I was expecting to hit, but he went down, so good enough.

I ducked behind the corner just before the second man could hit me with a stun pulse. I had to put distance between us then go to ground. I didn't know how many men Richard had on-planet, but it couldn't be enough to sweep an entire section of city or even the oblivious mercs living here would know something was up.

I kept my turns erratic so they couldn't radio ahead for men to intercept me. These soldiers weren't encumbered with heavy armor and they were in excellent physical shape. Outrunning them proved difficult.

Picking them off one at a time worked, but every time I stopped to aim at one, the others surged closer and I risked getting stunned. Since I'd surprised the first, I'd had a much more difficult time with the other three. I wounded one enough that he dropped back, but the final two were persistent as hell.

I hoped Loch was having better results.

It took nearly an hour of hard running before I lost them. I ran flat-out for another thirty minutes then stopped to check myself for trackers. I didn't find any. The cuff's repulsive field had done its job.

I pushed my exhausted body into a jog and looked for a place to hunker down for the night. I was at least an hour away from the house, even at a jog. And after that run, I needed rest more than I needed to return to base.

The next block revealed more cookie-cutter houses. I randomly chose the third one down as my palace for the night. I made sure I hadn't left any tracks, then picked the lock and eased inside, gun first. The house was cold, dark, and empty. None of the rooms had any furniture, so I selected a bedroom and stationed myself inside against the door.

The constant wind whistled eerily around the abandoned buildings. I was alone in a vast, abandoned city. I pulled out my com and checked on Loch's location.

His trackers were offline, but the last known location was near the edge of the central commercial district. The log showed they'd stayed in that same location for fifteen minutes before being disabled.

Dread twisted my gut. I went further back in the log. His path out of the house had started erratic, dodging around corners at random, but then he stopped entirely for five minutes before making a straight line to downtown. He stopped smack in the middle of the central district for ten minutes, then continued to his final location.

Several possibilities arose, none of them great. Most likely, Loch had been captured by Richard's team. And damn if I didn't feel responsible. I should've been more adamant about leaving when I'd felt something was off to begin with.

I had to be careful, though, because it was also possible that Loch was working with Richard to double-cross me. It absolutely fit his personality, but it just didn't ring true.

However, that could have been my own selfish desire for him to be honorable clouding my judgment.

There was nothing I could do about it tonight. Tomorrow I'd go back to our house and pray Loch showed up. After all, a double-cross was much easier to deal with than a rescue mission.

# CHAPTER 10

T he perpetual gloom had one upside: it made sneaking around in the afternoon infinitely easier. I'd returned to the house to find it exactly as we'd left it—and with no signs of Loch. So now I was positioned on a rooftop three blocks down from the building where Loch's tracker had first stopped, playing a game of Spot the Spotter.

The building had probably once been the home of the Yamado diplomat in charge of the planet. It was made from real wood with delicate sliding doors and a beautifully curved tile roof. The fact that it was still in pristine condition was not terribly surprising—you crossed a High House at your own peril. Even when you thought they were gone, they weren't really gone.

If Richard had taken up residence, he either had permission or enormous balls. If he had permission, then this whole situation was far worse than I realized. One House potentially planning a war with us was bad, but if two Houses were colluding . . . I would have to set aside my personal desires and contact Father immediately—the warning I'd given Bianca would no longer be sufficient.

It took three hours, but eventually my patience was rewarded. Richard Rockhurst emerged from the house flanked by two men. They turned left—toward the spaceport and Loch's final location—and walked with purpose.

The urge to follow them was nearly irresistible. I vibrated with the need to move, but my training hadn't been for nothing. I stayed put. Less than a minute later a shadow detached itself from an alley a block down. Another minute and a new man had taken up the position. Definitely Rockhurst's men and definitely watching for anyone approaching the house.

I needed information and equipment. And I knew just who to call.

AFTER I'D CAREFULLY EXTRACTED MYSELF FROM THE central district, I headed away from home base. I had no doubt that the call would be tracked and I didn't want to lead them back to where I slept.

I pulled out the embossed card the fence, Veronica, had given me as well as the original, insecure com Loch had purchased. I connected voice-only.

"Hello, Irena," Veronica answered on the second ring, "frustrated already?"

The fact that she'd connected my identity to my com just proved that she was the right lady for the job. "Something like that," I said. "Can we meet?"

A long pause followed. I let the silence linger. "I should not," Veronica said at last, "but I find myself intrigued. I will send you the location. Be there in twenty."

The line went dead.

A few seconds later an encrypted message arrived with an address at the edge of the central district nearest to her shop. I'd have to hustle to make it early enough to scope out the location.

With no time to waste, I headed straight for the meeting point. Enough people were on the streets that I could blend into the normal hustle and bustle. I stopped two blocks away. Our meeting place appeared to be a tiny tea shop tucked between two boarded-up buildings. The shop had a steady stream of business.

I activated my cuff into the same defensive mode I'd used yesterday. If I got close to someone they might feel an odd sensation, like the air before a storm, but it wouldn't activate unless someone shot at me.

It was a paltry defense, but it was the best I had.

I approached the shop with unhurried steps. Nothing appeared out of place and I didn't feel watched. A bell over the door announced my entrance. A lovely older lady stood behind the counter taking orders. An older gentleman—her husband, perhaps—prepared each order.

Veronica was not in the store.

It was dinnertime, so I ordered a pot of jasmine green tea, a lemon scone, and a plate of tea sandwiches. I considered paying with the currency chips I had, but Veronica knew I would be here. I'd save the chips for when I truly needed to be anonymous.

After I paid, the old woman peered up at me then nodded. "She is waiting in the back," she said with a wave. "Go on, I will bring your food and tea."

"Thank you," I said.

I pushed through the curtained door, not entirely sure what to expect. Veronica sat on a floor cushion next to a low table. A cup of tea steamed softly in the cool air of the room. She was dressed much the same as I was, except her hood was thrown back.

"Join me," she said. Her voice was just as lovely as I remembered.

I knelt on the cushion that put my back to the wall. It put me adjacent to Veronica instead of across from her. She smiled into her cup but didn't comment.

The woman from the front brought my pot of tea and a delicate porcelain cup. She poured the first cup then went back to get my food. She placed it on the table, bowed, and returned to the counter.

I swiped my identity chip over the tabletop reader and added a generous tip to my order. I'd recently spent four months as a waitress and bartender. It was one of the longest times I'd been able to stay in one place, hiding in plain sight. After all, no one expected Lady Ada von Hasenberg to be running plates and dealing with drunks.

I hadn't needed the money, but after more than a year on the run, I had needed the companionship. The ladies I worked with were amazing, and unlike my experience with the merc squad, I enjoyed their company. But it had been eye-opening just how little a full-time job could pay, so now I was even more conscious about tipping well.

Veronica set a circular device on the table and clicked the middle. I took a sip of tea and pretended ignorance. I didn't know where she'd gotten her hands on a silencer, but

I would dearly love to. All communications from inside a six-foot radius from the silencer would not transmit outside that radius—voices, coms, bugs, nothing. Yet we could still hear the faint murmurs from the front of the shop.

They were so illegal that I hadn't even bothered to steal one when I'd left home. Because while Ada von Hasenberg had permission to carry one, neither Irena Hasan nor Maria Franco did. And getting caught with one was an automatic ten-year sentence.

"You may lower your hood, if you like. It's safe here. And would you prefer Irena or . . ." She paused delicately.

If it was meant to shock me, it worked. I pulled myself together and refocused on my purpose. I lowered my hood. "Irena is fine. Thank you for agreeing to meet," I said after another sip of tea. At least the tea was good.

I picked up one of the delicate triangle tea sandwiches and was transported back to my mother's afternoon tea parties. The women of the Consortium were just as bloodthirsty and power-hungry as the men, perhaps more so, and entering a ladies' tea always struck me as entering a nest of pretty vipers.

"I am still not sure it was a good idea," she said, breaking me from my thoughts.

"Probably not," I agreed. She grinned. The expression made her look years younger. Perhaps she was not that much older than me after all. "But all the same, I'm glad you did," I said. "I need . . . assistance. I am willing to pay."

"Money is only an incentive if I'm alive to enjoy it," she said. "And considering I have an idea of the trouble hounding you, that's a pretty big if."

"I'm not asking for involvement. Just a little information and perhaps an item or two, if you happen to have them sitting around."

She took a sip of her tea. I let the silence settle around us. I'd said all I was willing to at this point. The rest was up to her.

Finally, she said, "And if I want to be involved?"

"I would strongly discourage it," I said immediately. I paused, reconsidered. "Unless you are special ops," I said. "Then I could use the help."

Her laugh was even more entrancing than her voice. "You are not what I expected," she said. "Let us discuss details. As I'm sure you're aware, the silencer will keep our conversation private. I will begin: I want off this planet."

Warning bells went off. "What is preventing you from doing that now?" I asked. From the look of her shop she was highly successful. Successful fences were not poor.

Shadows darkened her eyes. "No one will take me. Even new visitors are warned off before I can book passage."

"Okay," I said slowly. "If I take you, do I need to worry about an angry husband hunting us? It won't affect my decision, but I need to be able to prepare for it."

"He is not my husband, and he is off-planet now, so we should not have to worry about him. But, yes, he will follow me if I leave a trail, so I will not leave a trail. And when I am safe, I will deal with him." She smiled with vicious intent.

I finished the last of the tiny sandwiches and broke off a piece of scone. "I am not opposed to taking you off-planet, but my own escape plan is shaky at best. There are many things that can go wrong. Most probably will. And even if it goes off perfectly, we won't be safe. You should know that before you commit."

She tilted her head and studied me for a few seconds before her eyes widened. "You're stealing a ship," she breathed. "You're stealing *Rockhurst's* ship."

I neither confirmed nor denied the claim.

She laughed, caught between delight and astonishment. "What do you need to pull this off?"

"First, I have reason to believe my companion has been captured. I need to know his location, as well as the building blueprints. Guard locations would be helpful, too."

"Do you know who he is?" she asked. I gave her a pointed look. She smiled, then sobered. "He is being held at the detention center the mercs use before they ship out their bounties," she said. "News travels fast here. So far his identity remains secret but it won't for long. Same for you."

"I am hoping to be gone before it becomes a problem. I also need these items," I said. I held up my com display so she could see the list.

Her eyebrows climbed her forehead as she read but she didn't balk. "I can get most of those today. The last two will take a bit longer. Maybe by tomorrow."

I nodded. "Good. I'd like to be ready by tomorrow night if possible. The longer I stay, the worse the danger becomes." I let frost creep into my expression. "And if you betray me, your not-husband will be the least of your worries."

She remained unruffled. "I would not have met with you if I hadn't already decided to throw my lot in with yours. We succeed or fail together, now. Do not let me down."

The weight of responsibility settled around me. Now I

had two people counting on me. And while I was sure both of them would be fine without me, I always felt responsible for those in my care. According to my father, it made me a terrible von Hasenberg.

WE SEPARATED AND LEFT THROUGH DIFFERENT ENtrances. Veronica promised to contact me tomorrow when she had all of the items I'd requested. That left me the rest of the day to do my initial prep work.

I turned off the insecure com Loch had bought for me. It wasn't that I didn't trust Veronica; it was that I didn't trust anyone. Leaving the com off meant it couldn't be tracked. It also meant she couldn't contact me in an emergency, but the tradeoff was worth it. I wouldn't sleep if I had to worry about a sneak attack.

The detention center was at the edge of the central commercial district near the spaceport. It also matched up with where Loch's tracker went silent. So either they were being super careful to make it look like Loch was being held, or he actually *was* being held. The trick was figuring out which before I barged in and got myself killed.

I cut through the opposite side of the central district from where I needed to be, using the same invisible walk I'd used to walk within a meter of Richard. No one paid me any mind.

I came at the detention center from a diagonal. Without a clear line of sight down the streets, I could get closer before I risked discovery. Six blocks away, I slipped into a narrow alley. It had been wider until some enterprising soul had extended their business.

The close walls worked for me, though, and I climbed to the

roof without breaking a sweat. I kept the chimney between me and the detention center. I didn't think Richard's team would be surveying this far out, but underestimating them was a one-way ticket to Captureville.

I'd never been a quitter—it wasn't in my DNA—but I was looking forward to the days when I wouldn't be stuck on a cold, dark roof trying to figure out if my current favorite fugitive was being held captive inside the building in the distance, all while avoiding an entire city of mercenaries.

For now, I had to be careful. Because if I could see the detention center, anyone there could see me, too. I flattened myself to the roof and crawled around the chimney. With the chimney behind me, my silhouette wouldn't be as noticeable. Probably. Hopefully.

The buildings in this area were all originally single-story, so only chimneys and creative mud-block additions obscured my view of the detention center. The center took up an entire block and had a wide-open plaza around it. It offered no cover and no reason to approach.

I pulled out the digital scope Veronica had given me as we left—it was the first item on my list. Staying as low as possible, I quickly scanned the detention center's roof. I didn't see anyone, but I did see a shit-ton of cameras. There would be no access from the roof unless I wanted the whole city to know when I'd arrived.

Until I got the blueprints, there was no way to know if underground access was a possibility, but based on everything I saw, I would assume not. So I'd have to waltz up to the front door, break in, break Loch out, and waltz back out again before reinforcements arrived.

Right. No problem.

The spotters here were either too well hidden, nonexistent (unlikely), or hidden behind some of the surrounding roof adornments that blocked my view, because I couldn't find any of them, even after watching for two hours.

I stretched sore muscles and crept back around the chimney. Climbing down was way more difficult than climbing up. Luckily foot traffic in this area was low and no one wanted to risk the dark, narrow alley.

I took a fairly straight path out of the central district. I wasn't headed in the direction of the house, so I was not concerned about covering my path just yet. I had nearly made it when three men stumbled out of a building in front of me. They weren't Rockhurst soldiers, so I ignored them.

They did not return the favor.

"Hey, buddy, got any creds?" the one in front slurred. "Help a brother out. That bastard kicked us out." He was stocky, with dark hair, and he reeked of the distinctive chemical odor of cheap synthol and tobacco. His two lankier buddies were in even worse shape, leaning against each other just to stay vertical.

Whoever "that bastard" was, he or she should've kicked them out a long time ago, even though the night was still young. They were all six sheets to the wind and it wouldn't take much to push them over the edge into violence. Especially if they got kicked out because they were broke. Nothing made a drunk meaner than taking away the booze.

I kept my head down and stepped around the men. Stocky didn't appreciate my lack of enthusiasm. "Hey, buddy, I'm talking to you!"

"Sorry," I said gruffly.

"If you're not going to help us out, I guess we'll just have to help ourselves," he said. He pulled a wicked-looking blade and suddenly his companions looked a whole lot more sober. *Fantastic.*

I backed away but Lackey One flashed a blast pistol. Running just became a non-option. "Hey," I said, "I don't want any trouble."

Stocky squinted at me. "You a woman?" A lecherous grin spread across his face. "Looks like our luck's changed, boys."

I stood straight, throwing off my invisible persona. It hadn't protected me, so I needed a new plan. "I do not have time to deal with you right now. Move," I said in my most commanding tone.

Stocky took a half step back before straightening his own spine and closing the distance between us, waving the knife in his right hand. It would've been more threatening if he came up higher than my chin. Still, I could work with this.

I ignored what his mouth was saying—it was hardly polite—and watched his body language. The next time the knife came my way, I struck. I clamped my left hand onto the wrist of his knife hand and pulled it across my body to the right. Without releasing his wrist, I used my right hand to deliver a fast, sharp blow to the back of his hand. He dropped the knife.

The synthol reek must not have been entirely fake, because his reflexes were slow. I pulled him the rest of the way between me and his lackeys, then transferred my grip to the back of his collar. I drew my pistol and jabbed him in the kidney with it.

It took less than five seconds.

The lackey with the pistol gaped at me. He tentatively raised the pistol, but lowered it again when Stocky frantically shook his head.

"Now you've made me late," I said, "and I *hate* being late."

"We didn't mean nothing," Stocky whimpered.

"Oh, I think we both know that's a lie. And you know what else I hate? Liars. So, this is your last chance to get in my good graces. Tell your friends to drop their weapons."

I could tell by the way he stiffened that he had a plan that didn't involve dropping the weapons. I mourned in the second before he moved. Then I let him go as he dropped down toward the knife on the ground. Lackey One brought his blaster up, but not fast enough. I shot him through the chest.

Lackey Two broke and ran. I let him go. It was a bad tactical decision, but I just couldn't shoot him in cold blood. And unless he had reinforcements in the next block, I'd be gone before he returned.

Stocky lunged at me with the knife. I shot him point-blank. The energy bolt punched a hole through his head.

I scanned for new threats. No one had come to investigate, but that luck wouldn't hold for long. I steeled my emotions and quickly searched both men, being careful not to leave fingerprints. I took the blaster and extra energy cells from the lackey. Nothing else was worth stealing.

I left the two men sprawled on the ground and faded into the shadows.

# CHAPTER 11

After checking myself for trackers and coming up clean, I slid down the wall. I was in a hidden alcove far into the abandoned section of the city. Control slipped away and hot tears flooded my eyes. I bowed my head to my knees and let them flow.

Those two weren't the first people I'd killed, but it was cold comfort. And while it was tempting to push the pain away, to bury it deep, I knew that way lay demons. Taking another person's life, even in self-defense, was an event worth mourning. If I lost the ability to feel that pain, then I lost myself.

I poured the pain out one tear at a time until I was empty inside. Then I dried my eyes and pieced myself back together. By the time I stood, I had myself under control. Sadness still pulsed in time with my heart, but my outer armor gave away none of my inner turmoil.

In a High House only the facade mattered, so we each became experts, in our own ways, of hiding behind serene faces and sharp eyes. It was a skill that served me well now.

I worked my way home, being extra careful. The little bedroom was just how I'd left it, but tonight it felt especially empty. I mentally went through rescue scenarios. None were great and all depended heavily on information from Veronica. If she double-crossed me, I was sunk.

When I could no longer keep my eyes open, I gave up and dropped into a fitful sleep.

BIANCA'S MESSAGE HAD ARRIVED OVERNIGHT. IT ONCE again came with many sentences in all caps and dire warnings about my future health if she got her hands on me. But she'd gotten the information I needed and had not told Father.

She had, however, passed along my concerns about a looming war. Based on her oblique references, it was not the first warning they had received, but they were keeping it off the family systems. If they were worried about a spy at that level, things were dire indeed.

I decrypted the files she sent with our personal shared key: *pegasaurus*. It was a magical creature we'd made up as children, a cross between a dinosaur and a Pegasus. It looked like a winged, scaly horse with an extra-long neck and extra-sharp teeth.

Each family member had a secret key shared with one other family member. It kept our communications safe even from the family. Because sometimes a meddling family member was worse than an enemy.

The list she'd sent me contained six potential override codes. Richard was known to use his own codes and change them with some frequency. The latest codes in the list had been changed less than a month ago.

My entire plan rested on these sixty digits. If one of these keys didn't work, I didn't have a backup, and that was a problem. Today I would scope out the spaceport, see what other ships were available for commandeering at a moment's notice. Another ship wouldn't get us very far, but if we found one with a little offensive weaponry, we could at least slow Richard down enough to escape to a busier planet. Hopefully.

I ate two energy bars and drank a bottle and a half of water. If everything went according to plan, I wouldn't be back here tonight. I raided Loch's bag and shoved all of the extra energy bars and clothes into mine. I would leave the pack with Veronica when I busted Loch out. He might appreciate a spare set of clothes.

With everything ready, I set off. Ten minutes out, I turned on the insecure com. I had an encrypted message from Veronica with meeting instructions. She had managed to acquire all but one of the items I requested and she was working on the last item.

Traveling with a pack made it harder to blend in, so I decided to head to Veronica's before checking the spaceport. Plus, if she was going to double-cross me, it was better to know now.

Her house was on the edge of the central district. It was a nicer area, where the plastech buildings were well maintained and not augmented with mud bricks. Most of the buildings on this street were two-story houses. Lights were on in several houses and a few people were out on the street. Nothing set off any alarm bells, but I kept my guard up.

I walked the block, then turned and came up behind the house. I knocked on the back door. A few minutes later, it cracked open to reveal Veronica. "I should've known you wouldn't use the front door like a normal person," she said. "Never mind that this is more suspicious-looking." She stepped back and gestured me in.

"Just be glad I didn't pick the lock," I said.

The house was a minimalist's wet dream, with white walls, faux wood floors, and just enough furniture to prove someone lived here. One look and I knew this was not her house, not with the way her shop was arranged.

"I found the blueprints to the detention center. There weren't any surprises, so if you were hoping for a secret entrance, you're going to be disappointed. I did have a few little birdies report on men loitering around the center, though, so I know the location of two of the outside guards."

"Any info on whether Loch is actually inside?"

"A big man with a shaved head was dragged inside by four of 'those new guys.' He hasn't come back out, but the men come and go."

Well, damn. I had half hoped Loch had betrayed me, because then I wouldn't feel responsible for rescuing him. And while it was still possible I was walking straight into a trap, I just couldn't leave without trying.

"Your little birdies say how many of 'those new guys' are floating around?"

"At least a dozen," she said, "but nobody can get a good enough look at them for an accurate count. Even the working ladies haven't seen them and that's unusual for a merc squad on-planet."

Richard was keeping his troops on a tight leash.

"You have a plan?" she asked.

"I have a plan," I confirmed. A crazy, ridiculous, outlandish plan, but a plan nonetheless. Now I just had to pull it off without getting myself or either of the people counting on me killed. No problem.

"I have all of your stuff in the study," she said. "If you want to take a look."

I nodded and followed her, just to ensure that someone wasn't going to pop out and shoot me. Luckily for me, there was nowhere to hide in the study. A lone desk made from wood and glass held the place of honor across from the door. An uncomfortable-looking white chair sat behind it.

Someone had pulled in a folding table and loaded it down with the supplies I'd need for tonight. It was an unsightly blemish on the pristine minimalism of the room. The contrast jarred, but I'd take the messy clutter over the sterile desk any day.

Looking through the items on the table, I had to give Veronica credit—she had pulled in a lot of strange items on very short notice. Perhaps I'd offer her a House job after all, assuming we made it off-planet.

I shrugged off the pack. "I'll need you to bring this to our meeting point because I can't carry it while I'm rescuing Loch."

Veronica nodded. "I'll make sure it gets put with my stuff."

"For now, I'm going to scope out the spaceport."

JESSIE MIHALIK

"I will go with you." She held up a hand when I would've protested. "I am frequently at the spaceport, either to meet traders or to attempt to find passage. And I often bring a companion. If I go, you are much less likely to be found."

I dug the holster I'd requested out of the pile on the table and strapped it around my waist, then slid in my original blast pistol. The new pistol I'd picked up last night I kept hidden in my off-hand pocket. It wasn't the safest or most convenient, but the element of surprise would be worth it.

"Let's go," I said.

TRUE TO HER WORD, PEOPLE NODDED AT VERONICA BUT few stopped to question her. Those who did ignored me entirely. My fingers remained clenched around my pistol grip, sure every time that *this time* would be when she would point at me and announce me to the world.

When we entered the spaceport terminal, I finally hissed at her, "What are you doing?"

"Trust me," she murmured.

She headed straight for the exit out to the ships. The older man in a security guard uniform looked up and smiled, then remembered to frown.

"Veronica," he said softly, "you know no one will take you."

"Come on, Tabo, I just want a look. Let a woman dream, won't you?"

He sighed, but nodded. "Don't cause any trouble."

Veronica's smile was brittle. "Do I ever?" she asked.

Tabo opened the door and waved us through. Once we were out of earshot I whispered, "I can't believe that worked."

"I told you, I come here often." Her voice was wistful.

146

"Tabo is too nice for his own good. He can't stand to see a woman in pain. He told me once that if he had a ship, he'd take me off-planet in a heartbeat. If there is *any way* to avoid hurting him, please do so."

"I will do my best," I said.

The launch pads were arrayed in a set of three arcs leading away from the terminal. A wide road split each arc in two and allowed ships farther out to have a safe passageway for ground travel.

In total, a dozen ships could land at once. Today, three were berthed, and it seemed like that might be an unusually high number, based on the state of disrepair most of the pads were in.

Larger ships docked on the farthest arc and Richard's ship was the only one out there. It wasn't big enough to require the extra space, so they'd docked it for privacy. The ship practically glowed with good maintenance and money. I'd seen maybe three mercenary ships *ever* that looked that good. No wonder Loch immediately picked up on it being one of Richard's ships. The cargo ramp was lowered, but the door was closed.

Two small ships, both older and in dire need of exterior maintenance, sat in the closest arc, one on each side. If we had to abandon Richard's ship, we would need to run back toward the terminal to take one of these two ships. That was less than ideal, but I couldn't see a way around it.

The ship on the left was a Yamado ship. It was impossible to tell its age just by looking, but I guessed at least fifty. Meant for short-range jumps only, it would truly be our last resort.

The right ship was a von Hasenberg ship that we'd stopped producing before I was born. It was marginally newer than the Yamado ship, but that wasn't saying much. It was equipped with a long-range FTL drive, but it took *forever* to charge. If they jumped it on the way here, it was likely still charging.

*Fuck.*

Based on these two backups, it was imperative that we take Richard's ship. There was no way I could take on six or more elite soldiers on my own, even if my harebrained scheme worked. If Loch wasn't in fighting shape then we would have to abort and settle for the von Hasenberg ship.

"I've seen enough," I said.

Veronica cast one more wistful glance at the ships then turned and headed back to the terminal. I followed.

"We need to walk by the detention center," I said. "The side farthest away from everything else. Then you need to find a reason for why we walked by, even if it's to stop for tea."

"I regularly shop in the market nearby. The detention center isn't exactly on the way, but I often stalk through this district after a visit to the spaceport."

We exited the terminal and turned right. A two-meter plastech fence marked the edge of spaceport property. The holes were too small to use for climbing, so we'd have to go through. That would be the least of our problems.

Five minutes later we walked past the detention center. It was just as bad as I feared: no cover, cameras everywhere, and only two main access points. This would have to be a quick and dirty rescue.

We stopped in the street market while Veronica bartered with a few vendors. I reined in my impatience. Diverting suspicion was worth the extra few minutes, but I breathed a sigh of relief when we headed back to the house.

Once we were inside, I went straight for the desk. A hand wave brought up the display and the flat keyboard embedded into the desk surface lit up. "Is this secure?" I asked Veronica.

"No."

I bounced my connection through a variety of universal servers until I was happy that, while not secure, it would at least be difficult to track the connection back to this address. Then, I got down to work.

The detention center server was easy to find. It was harder to breach. I kicked off my cracking scripts while I manually poked around. It took longer than I would've liked, but the scripts finally found an overlooked, vulnerable service. I set up a back door and then I was in.

I pulled up the various video streams. The outside of the building showed from all angles. No blind spots. The inside was the same story.

I flipped through the cameras until I found Loch. He was in a solid-sided holding cell in the middle of the building. Shackles connected his spread arms to the wall and his ankles were attached to a short chain and leg shackle. By the way he slumped, he was sleeping, passed out, or dead. Blood ran down his arms from his wrists. Bruises and swelling marred his face.

Richard had not been kind. Rage burned hot and my decision to rescue Loch cemented.

I pushed the rage back and focused on the other cameras. The lack of interior guards was an unexpected surprise. The house Richard was staying at was less than five minutes away at a flat run, so they must figure they could get there before any escape attempt succeeded.

I would have to prove them wrong.

Loch shifted. Still alive, then, but I didn't know how hurt. If he couldn't walk then we were royally fucked. I could only deal with one problem at a time, so I prayed he looked worse than he felt and moved on.

Veronica poked her head in the room. "I received word that the last of your supplies just arrived. They were not cheap and I didn't have room to bargain."

"They're worth it," I said without looking up. "I'll reimburse you."

She lingered. "Is this really going to work?"

I met her gaze. "I don't know. But I'm going to do my damnedest to make sure it does. And I need you to do the same. You good?"

"I'd be better if I knew what you were planning."

"All in good time. Are you packed and ready?"

"Nearly."

"Good. We're going tonight."

She sucked in a breath. "I'm almost afraid to hope," she said very quietly.

"Then I'll hope enough for both of us."

I STRAPPED ON THE THIN BALLISTIC ARMOR DESIGNED to deflect energy bolts. It only worked about half the time, but with the backup of my necklace and cuff, I hoped it was good enough to keep me alive. Ideally, it wouldn't even be needed, but I'd never be that lucky.

Pistols went in holsters on each hip. A pair of flash-bang grenades went next to them, along with two modified smoke grenades and a set of six mini vaporizers. A knife and a plasma cutter rounded out my easily accessible equipment. Each had a distinct shape so I wouldn't grab the wrong one by accident.

A backup battery snugged against my low back and connected via inductive charger to my cuff. With the extra boost, the cuff should protect against six or seven glancing shots and two or three direct hits. Loch would not be protected, and I couldn't afford to be slowed down by an extra set of armor. I'd just have to stay between him and any shooters.

A small pack with the rest of my supplies went on, then my cloak would go over the whole lot. Veronica would be responsible for my big pack, as well as her things. Loch and I would meet her two blocks from the detention center.

I picked up the control tablet of the first drone. The drones were the last items on my list and the most expensive and difficult to find. I had no doubt that Veronica reached out to contacts on the smuggler side of the planet to purchase them, because they weren't something that normal people had just sitting around. The fact that she hadn't needed me to transfer money to pay for them said a lot about her financial situation.

The size of a shoebox, these drones were flying EMP bombs used by police and military forces to shut down the electronics of a single building or small block. Depending on the layout and shielding of the target building, either the electronics inside would go down permanently until replacement parts were ordered, or they would experience a temporary hiccup that could be corrected in a matter of minutes. I hoped for the former and planned for the latter.

And there was a sort of beautiful irony in the fact that these were Rockhurst drones.

I logged in to the control tablet, changed all of the default codes, and set the mode and target. I watched as it took off and circled high away from the city. I did the same with the second drone, except I set it to attack fifteen seconds later. The first would hit Richard's house. The second would hit the detention center. Both control tablets went into my pockets.

I now had an hour to get in position. Adrenaline blitzed through my system. My fingers trembled as I set up the last of my scripts on the detention center's server.

My backup plans had backup plans. I patted all of my gear one last time. I was as ready as I was going to be. I pulled on my cloak and settled the smart glasses over my eyes. The glasses synced to my com and could overlay info on the transparent screen. The time ticked away in the upper left corner of the display, along with a countdown timer.

"You know where we are meeting," I said to Veronica. She nodded, but she was pale and sweating, with a hunted expression. "Are you okay?"

Her throat moved as she swallowed. "I'm worried you won't show. That this is all for nothing."

"And I'm worried that you're going to double-cross me at the last minute," I said bluntly. She looked appalled. It was better than the stark fear she'd worn before. I continued, "So we're both worried. But I *will* be there." *If I don't die first.* I didn't say that aloud because it wouldn't help her.

"Okay," she said. "I will be there, too. And I will not betray you."

"See you in an hour," I said.

I slipped into the alley and prayed for success.

# CHAPTER 12

It took forever to work my way around the city to the sentries, but I had planned that time into my schedule. It was late enough that the streets were deserted. This sentry was trying to pass as homeless, but he was too clean, his gear too nice.

At five minutes to the first attack, I palmed a vaporizer and stumbled down his alley. I hummed a bawdy song in my lowest tone. The soldier glanced at me then dismissed me to continue watching the detention center.

It would be his last mistake of the evening. I stumbled into him then activated the vaporizer under his nose. Even training was no use against human nature—he inhaled in surprise. His eyes rolled back and he slumped against the wall. Depending on his metabolism, he'd be out for twenty to forty minutes.

One minute until the first EMP drone hit.

I moved as close as I could while still being in the shadows of the surrounding buildings. I'd already taken the other sentry out. He would be waking up in as little as ten minutes, but a stronger dose would've likely killed him, so I'd just have to work with the time I had.

My com vibrated as the displayed countdown timer hit zero. Drone strike one should have just happened. A new timer popped up on the display, counting up. This was our escape timer. At fifteen seconds, a loud *pop* came from the detention center roof. Now that the danger to my own electronics had passed, I sprinted across the plaza to the back door.

The electronic keypad was dead and the door was unlocked. I sent up a fervent prayer of thanks that the server scripts had done their job in the fifteen seconds between attacks. The breaching charges in my backpack might not be needed after all.

I drew my pistol and eased inside. The glasses immediately adjusted to the darkness, and I could see down the hallway. It was empty. Based on the video feeds and the blueprints, Loch's cell was about halfway down on the left.

I didn't have time to clear all of the rooms. The video feeds had shown them empty, so I would just have to trust that they'd stayed that way. I passed several sets of offices, then large, open-barred cells. The solid cells were clustered together in the center of the building.

When I reached the block of solid cells, I confirmed all of the doors were open. I stopped at the first one in case I needed quick cover. "Loch," I whispered, "the cavalry has arrived. Time to go."

Marcus stepped out of a cell that was definitely not his. He clutched a length of metal and moved with obvious pain.

"I must say, Ada darling, I did not expect to see you again. I figured you'd be long gone by now."

"Would've been the smart move," I agreed. "We have three minutes, more or less, to vacate this building before the backup arrives. Then we're meeting a friend and stealing a ship. Can you do it? I have a single dose of foxy if you need it."

A mix of stimulants and painkillers, amphoxy—street-named foxy—was a common battlefield panacea. It wasn't very good for the soldiers taking it, though, because they'd be more likely to hurt themselves further while they were hyped up and feeling invincible. But if it got Loch from here to the ship, it would be worth it.

He walked over with only a slight limp. "I don't need it. Nice glasses. You got a spare gun?"

Thanks to the high-tech lenses, I had forgotten that it was completely dark in here. But watching Loch, I'd never know it. I vowed to get a closer look at his ocular implants before we parted ways.

I handed over the spare pistol, a knife, and a radio ear-piece, then turned and ran back down the long hallway. Loch kept up without even a grunt of pain. It had been two and a half minutes since the first drone strike.

I stopped by the door and peeked out. No obvious snipers and no one took a potshot at me. Loch tried to stop me before I stepped outside, but I darted out of reach. "I'm wearing ballistic armor," I said. "And we need to move."

No one shot at us as we crossed the plaza to the shelter of the nearby buildings. "We're meeting Veronica the fence," I said. "Don't shoot her unless she has betrayed us."

"I heard that," Veronica's quiet voice said through my earpiece.

Another minute and I slowed. Veronica should be just around the corner. Now was the time of truth: either she'd be there alone, or Richard and his crew would be waiting.

"You think she'll betray you?" Loch asked.

"It's a possibility," I said at the same time she said, "No." A quick glance around the corner revealed Veronica. An overloaded, tarp-covered sled floated beside her. She saw me immediately and smiled a huge, relieved smile. "Told you," she said.

The three of us made our way to the wall around the spaceport. I pulled out my portable plasma cutter. "Will your sled go over the wall?"

"Yes," Veronica said.

That made things easier. Portable cutters didn't have as much power as their full-sized counterparts. Precious seconds ticked by as I cut a hole big enough for the three of us to squeeze through one at a time.

The timer had climbed past five minutes by the time we made it through the fence. Richard would be at the detention center and he would likely guess our next target. Not to mention the spaceport security forces.

"Can you fight the soldiers on board Richard's ship or do we need to take the von Hasenberg ship instead?" I asked Loch.

"I can fight," he said. His heaving chest and pinched brow threatened to undermine his words, but the resolution in his expression said that come hell or high water, he could get it done. I took him at his word.

We arrived at Richard's ship just as the spaceport alarm sounded. "Stay here," I said. I climbed the cargo ramp and slid open the control panel. On a whim, I hit the door-open button.

When the door actually started opening, I stared at it in shock. Was the door unlocked because of hubris or because I was about to face a platoon of men? As soon as the door cleared ten centimeters, I pulled a flash-bang grenade and rolled it into the cargo bay. I followed it with one of my modified smoke bombs.

"Masks!"

Veronica handed us each a nose and mouth mask from her bag.

"Give me the foxy," Loch said. I handed him the injector and he jabbed it in his thigh. The rush would hit in thirty seconds and last for twenty minutes.

"I will need cover," I said. "I'll be stuck at the access panel in the cargo bay until I override the ship's control. Don't take your mask off even if the smoke clears. If we need to retreat, give me warning."

He nodded then ducked under the door and disappeared. I took a deep breath, threw back my hood, and followed him. It was time to do or die.

**THE CARGO HOLD WAS PILED WITH VARIOUS PIECES OF** equipment lashed to the floor. Loch was nowhere to be seen and neither were any Rockhurst soldiers. I heard an occasional shot through the earpiece, but Loch was eerily silent.

Once Veronica and her sled cleared the door, I hit the manual close button. "When that closes," I said, "lock it." I pointed to the lock control. It wouldn't keep out someone with the access codes, but it would prevent spaceport security from opening the door as easily as we had.

I dropped my backpack by the door, then found the internal access panel and slid it open to reveal the control terminal. While I had access to the door functions, everything else was locked down. I pulled up the diagnostic screen and started entering the override codes from memory.

The standard Rockhurst code failed. Richard had changed the default codes, which made my job infinitely harder. I kept trying.

I had just entered the third unsuccessful code when my bracelet pulsed and sparks flew from a deflected stun shot. *Shit.* I turned to find the assailant, but he'd already ducked back into cover.

"Can you shoot?" I asked Veronica. She nodded, so I handed her the gun. "Stand close to me and keep him pinned down for another couple minutes." She was also wearing ballistic armor and if she stayed close, the soldier wasn't likely to switch to deadly ammo because he'd risk hitting me.

The fourth code failed and Veronica fired on the soldier. Angry butterflies took flight in my stomach and my heart rate picked up. Only two codes left. *Come on, come on.*

"Shit!" Veronica yelled. I heard her hit the deck at the same time my cuff pulsed and another shot bounced away. One or two more shots like that and I'd be done.

I steadied my hands and typed in the fifth code. *Failure.* Veronica fired on the soldier's position, but everything felt distant and fuzzy.

I typed in the sixth code—the last code Bianca had included. If this code didn't work, I had no backup. We'd have to haul ass to the von Hasenberg ship, assuming security didn't already have us surrounded.

I entered each digit with extreme care. Veronica shouted something but I didn't have time to bother with her. My cuff pulsed weakly and an energy shot exploded near my head. Had they moved to deadly force?

After entering the last digit, the world paused for an eternal moment.

Then I was in and everything snapped back into real time. I immediately set up new override codes and wiped the ones Richard had set. I did not use my preferred codes because I had no doubt House Rockhurst's spies knew what they were, and I didn't want Richard to be able to take the ship back as easily as I'd taken it from him. I deleted all authorized users and added myself as captain, but voice command authorization would have to wait until we weren't under attack.

I locked the ship down and retracted the cargo ramp. If Richard wanted in now, he'd have to take a plasma cutter to the cargo bay door. Even with a heavy-duty system it would take hours.

Unusual movement in my peripheral vision caused me to spin around. A Rockhurst soldier was valiantly trying to lift a stunstick in my direction, but it appeared my smoke grenade was finally getting to him because he blinked blearily and wove on his feet.

Veronica was down, but she appeared stunned instead of dead. I wrestled the stunstick away from the soldier and hit him with it. Yeah, it was low, but the bastard had shot at me. I didn't feel too bad.

"Loch, I'm in the system. Are you okay? How many are left?"

"I'm busy," Loch growled. "Just stay put."

"No can do, I'm afraid. I have to get us in the air. Keep your mask on." I stepped back to the access terminal, turned on the internal ventilation systems, and turned *off* the filtration. Then I found an air intake vent and cracked my last smoke grenade in front of it. "Don't kill the downed soldiers. We'll dump them before takeoff."

Loch didn't respond.

I checked on Veronica. She was starting to come around. She must've gotten stunned. "Keep your mask on," I said. "I'm heading to the flight deck. I'll let you know when it's safe." She nodded weakly.

Once all of the Rockhurst soldiers were knocked out, I'd have to purge and replace all of the air before we left the atmosphere, but it was safer than fighting the soldiers outright.

I picked up the discarded pistol and kept the stunstick. This was a Rockhurst ship. I had a basic idea of the layout, but unlike Yamado, Rockhurst frequently tweaked their ship designs. Still, the flight deck was generally in the same place. I headed out of the cargo deck toward the front of the ship.

Two more disorientated soldiers met the business end of the stunstick before I made it to the flight deck. The door was locked, but thanks to my newly minted captain status, I overrode the lock.

The room was empty. I entered and locked the door behind me—no reason to let someone sneak up on me. I dropped into the captain's chair and logged in. First, I added myself to the ship's voice authorization. "*Infineon,* this is Ada von Hasenberg, authorize."

"Welcome, Captain von Hasenberg. You are authorized."

"Thank you. Show me the outside cameras."

The screens in the walls came on with a 360-degree view of the surroundings. Two security guards stood behind the ship, talking on handheld coms. The rest of Richard's team had not shown up yet, which meant his communications must still be down.

"*Infineon,* sweep the ship and show me the locations of all life-forms on board."

A translucent 3-D model of the ship appeared above the captain's console. More than a dozen red dots appeared, indicating people. Holy shit. Four were in the cargo bay alone.

"Veronica, are you okay?" I asked. "I see two extra people in the cargo bay. Are you under attack?"

"I am not under attack," she said. That was a dodge of the question, but the two extras weren't moving, so I focused on the only moving dot. I assumed it was Loch, but one of the red dots near him blinked out.

"Loch, what are you doing?" He didn't respond. Shit. "*Infineon,* transfer this map to my com and prepare for takeoff."

"Yes, Captain," the computer responded.

The map overlay came up on my glasses display. The moving dot was down a level near the crew quarters. I slid down the nearest access ladder. Two soldiers—dead, not sleeping—slumped in the hall. I stepped around them and closed on the moving dot.

Loch spun and crouched as I came around the corner. His pistol came up but he paused before firing. He was not wearing his mask. He should not still be awake, but I could tell by his expression that the foxy had a deep grip on him.

"*Infineon*," I said under my breath, "turn on air filtration. Purge and replace all of the ship's breathable air." A chime confirmed my command, then the ventilation system turned on high enough to produce a draft in the hallway.

I held my arms out in a careful gesture. "Loch, it's me," I said. "Put down the blaster. We won."

He stood up but didn't put away the pistol. He frowned at me as if I was someone he distantly recognized. Foxy generally made the user more focused and able to ignore pain. There had been a few reports of odd side effects, but since the results couldn't be reliably reproduced, it hadn't been enough to prevent its use.

I had a feeling I was seeing a new side effect firsthand. I took a step closer but Loch brought the pistol up in a defensive move. Okay, then, no closer. I would have to talk my way out of this one, or wait out the effects.

"Loch, it's me, Ada. You remember me, right? I need your help, but you have to put the pistol down first."

"Ada," he murmured, testing the word. He blinked, holstered his gun, and closed the distance between us in two long strides.

He backed me up against the wall and pressed his big body up against mine. He lifted me slightly and slid a thigh between my own. I settled with delicious friction against the hard muscles of his leg. I bit back a moan.

Foxy did have one well-known side effect: in the right dosage, it was a strong aphrodisiac. It was one of the reasons it was such a popular street drug. The military doses were designed to work around the flaw, but it appeared that Veronica had procured a street dose.

When I wouldn't let him remove my mask, Loch trailed burning kisses across my jaw and down my throat. I arched into him with a hiss before I could stop myself. I had to focus, dammit.

"Loch, you're high as a kite," I said. "The foxy is fucking with your head. You're going to crash and burn in about ten minutes and before you do, ahhh–" I moaned as his hand slid up my ribs and settled under my breast. His thumb traced a tantalizing line over my nipple and it took all of my control not to just say fuck it and go with the flow.

"Before you crash, I need help," I said. My voice wavered.

"I'll help you," he murmured against my neck. He shifted and I felt him, hot and hard, against my thigh. I was going to be nominated for sainthood after this.

"Not *that* kind of help, though, trust me, if you weren't high as hell, I'd consider it." A neglected libido could only be suppressed for so long, and I'd passed the point of no return three kisses ago. I struggled to keep my thoughts on target. I pushed against his chest. "I need you to help me move all of these soldiers to the cargo bay."

I grabbed his head when he would've bent back to my neck. "Loch, *focus*. Richard is going to be here any second and you are slowing us down. If Richard catches us, we're done. He'll kill us."

"He won't kill me," he said. "And I'll protect you."

"That's sweet, but does not help me right now. I just hope you're high enough to forget this," I said. Then I hit him with the stunstick.

He snarled at me and batted the stick out of my hand. I was so surprised that I let it go. I'd never seen anyone *not go down* when directly hit. Even the toughest von Hasenberg soldiers hit their knees. Loch just looked pissed.

"You better have a damn good reason for attacking me, sweetheart."

I smiled in relief. "You're back?"

He scowled at me but then paused to take in our positions. His face went completely blank, then he backed away like I was diseased. Okay, that stung a bit.

"I need you to help haul soldiers," I said. If my voice was icier than usual, he didn't call me on it. "We'll put them out the cargo door before we take off. We have to hurry."

"Or we could purge them," Loch said.

"No. Help carry or get out of the way." I moved to the closest soldier. He outweighed me by at least forty pounds, but he wasn't going to move himself.

I pulled him up to a seated position, then squatted down and wrapped my arms around his waist. A heave up and he was standing enough for me to duck down and get a shoulder under his waist. I gritted my teeth and wobbled to my feet with him balanced in a fireman's carry.

One down, a dozen to go. I would never make it through all of them like this, but I'd at least dump this guy in the cargo bay while I thought of an alternative.

Loch cursed behind me.

"Veronica, if you're up, get a sled out," I said. "We'll pile these gentlemen on it then toss the beacon out the door." Sleds were designed for hands-free operation, so they followed a paired beacon. If the beacon went out the door, the sled would follow. And as long as we were close to the ground, it would deal with the altitude adjustment without dumping the cargo.

"On it," Veronica said.

The cargo bay stairs presented a challenge, but I still said a prayer of thanks that I didn't have to maneuver down a ladder carrying this much dead weight. True to her word, Veronica had a sled out when I walked up, sweating and trembling.

I dumped the soldier on the sled and turned to retrieve another. Instead, I nearly ran into Loch. "You stack them," he said. "I'll carry them." He dumped the two men he was carrying with less care than I would have liked, but he carried two at once and didn't look close to death, so I kept my mouth shut.

Veronica and I sat the first two men with their backs against the vertical back of the sled. The rest we sat in front of them, between their legs, leaning back. It was the only way I thought we could fit them all and also not accidentally suffocate one of them.

Once they were all on the sled, we strapped them down as best we could. A peek at the cargo bay display showed that Richard had arrived and had spread his men out in a wide arc around the cargo bay doors.

He was in for a surprise.

"*Infineon,* take us up six meters and hold." A chime answered me and the engines roared to life. Richard's shocked face stared out of the display. Once we were at altitude, I partially opened the cargo bay door then chucked the beacon out through the opening. The sled sailed after it and landed softly in front of Richard.

Fury darkened his expression and he shouted orders I could almost hear. I blew him a kiss on the display, closed the cargo door, and ordered the ship to take us up to fifteen kilometers.

That done, I turned to Veronica and drew my pistol, but kept it pointed at the ground. "Now," I said, "would you care to explain why there are two extra people in here?"

# CHAPTER 13

V eronica's chin tilted up to a stubborn angle, but she didn't deny the accusation. When I continued to stare at her, waiting, she sighed and went to her sled. She pulled off various bags and boxes until the top of a perforated box appeared.

"It's okay, Imma," she said. "Open up."

The click of a lock, then the top of the box swung open. A young boy of four or five with straight black hair and huge, dark eyes peeped over the top of the box. He had on a mask identical to the ones Veronica had procured for us.

On seeing Veronica, he smiled and reached for her. "Momma!" he cried. "I was very quiet for Imma, just like I promised. Wasn't I, Imma?"

An older woman in a mask stood stiffly and looked around with suspicion. She put herself between a scowling Loch and the kid in an unconscious gesture of protection. "You were very good, baba," she said.

The little boy beamed. "See, Momma?"

Veronica blinked away tears and reached for her son. "Yes, pumpkin, you were very good. I'll get your surprise in a little while, okay? We have to unpack first, and I have some friends for you to meet."

Veronica helped Imma out of the box then led the little boy over to me. I holstered my gun before they reached me. Veronica said, "Lin, this is Lady Ada."

Lin swept into a respectable bow for a youngster and the suspicion growing in my mind solidified. Veronica and I would be having a very long discussion once the kiddo was asleep.

But the kid wasn't at fault, so I dropped into my most formal curtsy. It looked a little ridiculous in pants, but Lin smiled shyly at me. I inclined my head. "Lord Lin, it is a pleasure to meet you."

He giggled and pressed against Veronica's leg. She turned him toward Loch. "That is Mr. Loch." Lin slipped from her grasp and darted over to the larger man. Veronica's jaw clenched but she didn't call him back. Lin held out his tiny hand. "It is a pleasure to meet you, Mr. Loch," he said, carefully mimicking my earlier words.

Loch uncrossed his arms and shook Lin's hand. "Nice to meet you, too, squirt."

"Will I grow up big as you?" Lin asked in awe.

"You might. If you eat your vegetables and listen to your mother."

Lin raced back to Veronica. "Can we have vegetables for dinner?"

She smiled and ruffled his hair. "We can have whatever

you want, pumpkin. But I don't want you to bother Mr. Loch, okay? He's very busy."

Lin's face fell. He kicked a toe at the floor. "Yes, Momma."

Now that I knew Veronica wasn't planning a mutiny, I needed to get us off-planet stat. "I'll leave you to unpack and settle in. I'm going to get us out of here before Richard regroups."

Loch followed me to the flight deck. "The kid is going to be a problem."

"I know," I said.

"But you're not leaving them."

"No," I said.

"Didn't figure you would," Loch said. "Wouldn't let you, anyway," he muttered.

A quick glance confirmed the foxy had finally run its course. Loch wavered on his feet. I pulled him over to an empty chair and he slid bonelessly into it. I needed to grab a med scanner to make sure he didn't have any hidden injuries, but it would have to wait until I'd plotted our course.

I dropped into the captain's chair and pulled up the navigation control. The FTL drive was fully charged and would be able to jump as soon as we cleared the atmosphere. Now for the moment of truth—how far could we go?

I pulled up a list of reachable locations. The list included the space station I'd started at, the closest gate, and a few planets up to three thousand light-years away. This ship definitely had House internals, and good ones at that. Richard would be foaming at the mouth to get it back.

The gate was the obvious choice. I had no doubt Richard

had an array of tracking devices attached to this ship, and I'd never find them all. But if I could get far enough away, the tracking beacons would take so long to reach him that they would essentially become useless.

I plotted a course to Earth, just to see how long the computer thought we'd have to wait at the gate while the FTL drive reset. I frowned at the estimate and changed the destination. But no matter how many different locations I tried, the estimated wait time was the same: one hour. I plotted a course with two jumps and each jump was only going to require an hour's wait.

An hour turnaround on an FTL drive was impossible. House von Hasenberg scientists were shaving minutes off of six hours and calling it a breakthrough. What we'd heard from the other Houses was the same. And, as far as I knew, even if you had the power stored for a second jump, there was no way to cool the FTL drive sufficiently in so little time without damaging it.

So.

*Crap.*

Either the estimate was wrong, which would make us sitting ducks for an indeterminate amount of time, or, more worryingly, the estimate was *right,* which meant Richard would blow us out of the sky at the first opportunity rather than letting me steal the secret.

"Incoming communication," the computer chimed. The screen showed it originated from ground control, but I would bet good money that it was Richard. I weighed the pros and cons, then pressed the answer key on my console. It would keep the video on me rather than the entire room.

Richard wiped the fury from his face, but not fast enough. "Hello, Richard," I said. My aristocratic persona was firmly in place.

"Ada, what are you doing?"

"I am leaving. What are *you* doing?"

He ran a hand down his face and suddenly he looked more tired than I'd ever seen him. "I'm trying to stop a war. You are not helping."

"You have an interesting way of going about it."

"I didn't want it to come to this, but you're the one who ran away. If we were already married, this wouldn't be happening. If we marry quickly, we may still be able to prevent it. If not, well, you would make an excellent bargaining piece."

I ignored the last part because that was just standard House policy. The first part was more intriguing. "We are both far down the House hierarchy. What does our marriage have to do with anything?"

Richard's expression closed. *Ah.* Something about that was important. What did he stand to gain from our marriage? He would gain the contents of my dowry. But I didn't know what all it entailed or how it would prevent war. I made a mental note to look into it.

"I will tell you the same thing I told Father: I will not be forced into marriage. He did not believe me. He thought I would bow to his wishes if he applied enough pressure. He was wrong. I suggest you learn from his mistake."

"You would rather send your House to war than marry me? We were friends once." Richard seemed genuinely hurt.

"I refuse to believe that the only two solutions are our marriage or war. I do not understand why our marriage is so important, and until I do, I will not be marrying you. If you would clarify, perhaps I could help you find another solution."

"Then let me be clear: if you leave in that ship, it will mean war."

"You mean this *mercenary* ship that I found on a Yamado planet? This ship? The one I had to borrow after my transport was attacked unprovoked by House Rockhurst? I think the Consortium will be more than happy to hear the entire story from the beginning, along with the surveillance footage from the *Mayport*. I can call them up now, if you like."

Richard's eyes narrowed. "You always were spoiled. If you have no concern for your people, then I don't see why I should."

"I am not the one threatening war, Richard. You know how to contact me if you want to discuss a mutually beneficial solution." I closed the link before he could respond.

If the *Santa Celestia* was in orbit or at least nearby, then Richard could call down a new transport ship in as little as fifteen minutes. I had to clear the atmosphere and jump before he made it back to his ship or we would be in deep trouble.

"Will you marry him?" Loch growled.

I spun around. Loch still lounged in the chair where I'd left him, but he was clearly awake and more alert than he'd been. How much had he heard? Enough to know that Richard wanted to marry. Would I? That was the million-dollar question, wasn't it?

I sighed. "I don't know. I do care about our people. If it really would prevent a war, I would have to trade my happiness for theirs. What's one person compared to the 'verse, huh?" The words were more bitter than I had anticipated.

"You know it won't be that easy."

"I know. That's why I'm still running. I'll run until I can't, then I'll either stand and fight or resign myself to my fate." I shook off the bitterness and refocused. "For now, I have to get us moving before Richard decides to blow us up for the fun of it."

"Do you have a destination in mind?"

"I was thinking Alpha Phoenicis Dwarf Zero." APD Zero was a large, well-known black market in planet form. Anything that could be bought resided on APD Zero—and everything could be purchased for the right money. The Houses turned a blind eye to the less-than-legal dealings because they all got a cut. And while I normally would choose a space station to disappear, with the addition of Veronica, Lin, and Imma, my contact on APD Zero might come in handy.

"That would be my choice as well. There are plenty of smaller options, but it will be easier to get lost on APD Zero."

I punched in the destination but routed us through two gates. The engines ramped up as we prepared to exit the atmosphere. As soon as we were clear, the FTL would engage to jump us to the first gate. "I shouldn't have any difficulty withdrawing your money when we get there," I said. "Then you'll have your choice of destinations." I'd gotten used to having Marcus around. When he was gone, I would miss him.

A few minutes later my stomach dropped as the FTL drive engaged. The transition was butter-smooth, though. The lights didn't even flicker. *Infineon* requested a jump point from the gate. Once given, a gate jump point was reliable for two hours. We were eightieth in the queue. With the FTL cooldown showing an hour, it would be a race to see if the drive would be ready before the gate gave us the endpoint.

"There's nothing else we can do here for now. Let's get you down to the medbay, so I can run a scan on you."

"I'm fine," Loch grumbled.

"You had a very odd reaction to the foxy and you looked like hell when I came to get you at the detention center. Let's just make sure everything is okay. It'll only take a second. Please?"

"Fine, but don't think I've forgotten how you tried to stun me."

That gave me pause. "You remember that?"

He smiled a slow, heated smile. "I remember *everything*."

"But you were acting so strangely. At first it was like you didn't even recognize me. Then . . ." I trailed off with a blush.

"I'll admit I was out of it at the time, but my memories are fine. If I'd known it was a street dose of foxy, I would've been more careful."

"Sorry, I didn't know, either. Veronica got it for me at the last second after I saw you on the surveillance camera. I thought I might need it just to get you out of the detention center."

"I heal fast," Loch said. "Richard was just toying with me, trying to get me to give up your location. He hadn't started getting creative."

"Why didn't you? Give up the location?"

"Because I figured you'd go back there looking for me. And I made a promise to help you escape. And because Richard would've beaten me anyway."

I skipped the ladder and led him down the stairs. The main part of the ship consisted of three levels. The upper level contained the flight deck and captain's quarters. The middle level included the crew quarters and mess hall. The bottom level was the medbay, exercise room, and the maintenance access for the engine and life support systems.

The medbay door slid open. As modern as the rest of the ship, the medbay glowed with polished metal and white plastech. It barely looked used.

Loch eased himself up on the diagnostic table without being asked. He might put on a strong front, but by the way he moved, something hurt. He lay down gingerly. I set the scanner to run a full-body diagnostic.

"Is there anywhere in particular that hurts?" I asked while I waited for the scan to finish.

"Well, Doctor," he growled in that deep, sexy voice. "I do have one area that's giving me a hard time. Think you could give me a hand?"

It took a supreme effort of will to keep my eyes glued to his face. "I think that perhaps the foxy isn't out of your system yet."

The scanner beeped, saving me from further comment. My eyes widened at the list of injuries, listed from most to least severe. I had to scroll to see the entire list.

Bones in various stages of healing were scattered throughout his body, with many in his hands and feet. Both legs had been broken and were still healing, along with a set of cracked ribs. His kidneys had deep bruising around them. Cuts on his sides and back needed to be cleaned and bandaged. And a knife wound to his shoulder still seemed to be bleeding. I looked for the hole, but it was concealed under his torn and dirty black shirt.

"How are you moving?" I whispered to myself. Even if he

had nanobots and they were operating at full capacity, most of these wounds wouldn't be this healed unless they were days older. But he'd been fine on the ship. Hadn't he? Something didn't add up.

"Am I going to live, Doc?" he asked as he sat up.

"Of course. But first you need to take off your shirt so I can bandage the worst of it. Then you need eight hours of downtime, minimum."

"The shirt I can do." He pulled the tattered shirt off over his head with a grunt. Even his killer abs couldn't distract from the extensive, dark purple bruising that covered most of his torso. I made a pained sound and reached out to touch him. He caught my hand. "It looks worse than it is."

I mutely shook my head. There was no way he could brush this off. Someone had beaten him savagely, most likely while he was shackled and unable to defend himself. "You should've told them where I was."

He tilted my chin up until I was forced to look away from the bruises. "It wouldn't have mattered. This is not your fault."

I pushed my emotions down behind a wall of icy calm. "Of course it is," I said briskly. I stepped around him and opened drawers and cabinets until I'd found the supplies I needed to bandage him.

The knife wound in his shoulder oozed blood as I dabbed at it with disinfectant. "Now you've helped me escape twice, so I shall pay you twice. As soon as we land on APD Zero, I'll make the transfer. Or get hard credits, if you prefer. Then you can disappear before Richard shows up."

"You seem awfully keen on getting rid of me. Why?"

"I don't want you to get hurt again because of me. And the longer you stay, the more likely you'll get caught. I have at least two Houses and a host of mercenaries after me. And if it really is going to come to war, I'll have to return home. As one of the expendables, I'll be expected on the front to bolster morale if nothing else."

Something shifted in his expression. He went from teasing to predator in the blink of an eye. I stilled, my hand frozen halfway to his shoulder.

"Do not mistake me for a little lost lamb. I've been dodging mercs for a very long time. I am here because I want to be. I will leave when I'm ready. Nothing you can do will change that. And if you call yourself expendable again"—his voice dropped into a deep, dangerous rumble—"you won't like the consequences. We clear?"

I swallowed and nodded. I *had* treated him too familiarly. Somewhere along the way I had started to see the man and had forgotten about the Devil. I finished cleaning and bandaging his wounds with quick, clinical detachment.

If only I could rein in my emotions as easily. The wall was harder to build after you already knew someone. I retreated into my public persona. "I have done what I can," I said. "Would you like a shot for the pain?"

Loch slid off the table and invaded my space. I straightened and stood my ground. His fingers slid along my jaw in the softest caress. "Don't hide from me, Ada," he said quietly.

"It is better this way," I said. "Help yourself to whatever." I waved a hand at the cabinets behind him, then beat a hasty retreat.

I stopped to check in on Veronica on the way up to the

flight deck. She and Lin and Imma had settled into two side-by-side rooms. Veronica cast nervous glances my way, but I was too tired to deal with her tonight. Tomorrow would be soon enough.

The flight deck was quiet. Thirty minutes and we could jump. We'd moved up to tenth in the gate queue. The first jump was to a busy gate on the opposite side of the universe from our destination. Two jumps was a risk, but I needed time to scrub the ship's registration to leave a false trail, especially before we landed on APD Zero.

While we waited, I kicked off a full system diagnostics test. It might reveal some of the trackers Richard was no doubt using. I also pulled out my com and searched for bugs the old-fashioned way. I found two: a location tracker and an audio bug. I'd have to go through the ship one room at a time if I intended to keep it.

I checked the captain's quarters while waiting for the diagnostic results. The com didn't find any bugs. I guess Richard valued his privacy.

The diagnostic came back with a few questionable items. None were critical, so I disabled them all until I could dig deeper into their functions. A chime announced the gate had given us a location. Five minutes until the FTL drive was ready.

I dozed until the jump woke me. I checked our location and surroundings. We were exactly where I'd requested. I rubbed my eyes and got to work on the first registration change.

BY THE TIME WE LANDED IN SEDITION, THE LARGEST city on APD Zero, *Infineon* had been renamed and reregistered twice. Now named *Polaris,* it was registered to one of the many dummy corporations I owned. It wouldn't pass a deep dive, but no one was likely to look that closely. And because it was supposedly a merc ship, the name wasn't written on the outside. Bonus.

The name changes would make tracking us a little more difficult, but I doubted they would slow Richard that much. Much more interestingly, each FTL jump actually had required just one hour of downtime, even with two jumps back-to-back. That would require looking into, but not tonight. I just didn't have the mental capacity to dive into an unknown engine system tonight.

I locked the ship down tight. In Universal Time it was morning and I'd been up all night. On APD Zero it was just after eleven at night, so no one would expect us to leave the ship tonight. I'd already paid the docking fee for a week. Now I needed at least a few hours of sleep or I was going to fall on my face at the first opportunity.

I stumbled toward the captain's quarters with a jaw-cracking yawn. I closed and locked the door. I didn't really think anyone on the ship would attempt to take me out, but you never know how a scared mother will react to a situation where her kid could be at risk.

I continued through the sitting room into the bedroom, only to stop in the doorway. Marcus Loch lay sprawled across my bed, wearing only black boxer briefs and barely covered by the sheet. He hadn't been here earlier when I checked for bugs.

My eyes were gritty with lack of sleep. I was entirely too tired to deal with this shit. The urge to kick him out was nearly overwhelming, but he was injured. I sighed softly. The sofa would have to do for tonight because I didn't think I could make it downstairs to a crew bed.

"Come on," Loch said. "The bed is big enough to share. Sleeping only." His teeth flashed white in the dark. "Unless you have other ideas."

I entered the room. "Why are you here?"

"I wanted to talk to you, but you were so deep in whatever you were doing you didn't even notice me enter the flight deck. So I waited here. Then when you still didn't show, I decided if I was here anyway, I should sleep. Doctor's orders."

"We already said all that needed to be said."

"No, we didn't," Loch said quietly. "But that is a discussion for later. Get in bed before you fall down. If you want, I'll sleep on the sofa."

Spite and hurt almost had me blurting the demand. Only the memory of the livid bruises stilled my tongue. "No funny business," I said.

I stripped down to my T-shirt and underwear, put my smart glasses on the nightstand, then crawled into bed. Loch hauled me close when I would've hugged my edge. I protested and tried to wiggle away. "Just sleep, Ada," he murmured against the back of my neck. "I've got you."

I focused on relaxing each muscle, one at a time. I had only made it halfway before the warmth and security of Loch's body at my back lulled me into sleep.

# CHAPTER 14

I awoke with the pleasant stiffness that meant I had slept deep and long. I had forgotten to set an alarm, so no telling what time it was. An arm tightened around my middle when I would've rolled over, and Loch nuzzled the back of my neck.

"Morning," he murmured.

I stiffened. I could count on one hand the number of times I'd woken up with a man. As the daughter of a High House, I had to be careful, both because I was completely defenseless during sex and because many men thought they could use my body to win my heart—and therefore my name. My hookups had been with men I'd trusted, but even then it wasn't usually a stay-the-night kind of event.

Loch's thumb drew a distracting little circle on my waist and all thoughts of being careful scattered. He slid his hand under my shirt, and his palm blazed a trail of heat up my body. When he stopped at my ribs, I arched in invitation. His hand remained where it was.

I huffed in annoyance and he chuckled. "Did you want something?"

I wanted his hands on my breasts, his mouth on my nipples. I wanted him inside of me. The sheer force of my desire shocked me. I took a deep breath and reined in my wayward body. "I want many things," I said honestly, "but I should get up."

Loch pulled me over onto my back and pressed up against my right side. His hand slid out from under my shirt and I shivered from the loss. His grin told me that I wasn't playing it as cool as I thought. It also made him unbearably sexy. *Down, girl.*

"What is your plan for the day?" he asked.

I shoved aside my desire and mentally sorted through all of the things that needed to happen today. "The bank first, I think. Then I can decide if it's worth renting a room or if I should just keep running. Plus it'll be done if I get caught."

"I will go with you," Loch said. "What else?"

"Talk to Veronica, scan the ship for trackers, figure out what supplies I'll need and purchase them, update my sister . . . really, the list goes on forever. What time is it?"

"Almost ten, local time," Loch said.

Shit, no wonder I felt like I'd slept hard—I'd been asleep for nearly eleven hours. That was plenty of time for Richard to catch up with us if he'd managed to track me straight here. I pushed myself up and out of the bed.

Shower first, but for that, I needed my bag of clothes. While I stood thinking, Loch rolled out of bed. All of that gloriously exposed skin drew my eye, but the bandages refocused my attention. His abs were barely bruised this morning; just a faint yellow hinted at what had been.

Even with nanobots, healing that fast was incredible. Maybe he'd spent some extra time in the medbay before he came up to talk last night?

My eyes dropped lower. His boxer briefs did very little to conceal the impressive erection tenting the fabric.

"Sweetheart, you keep looking at me like that and we're going to be back in the bed in two seconds flat."

I lingered for a long second, torn between keeping my distance and gobbling him up. It was already going to hurt when he left. What was a little more pain?

He must've sensed my hesitation, though, because he turned away with a growl. "I put your clothes bag in the bathroom. After you get dressed, I'll meet you in the mess."

I showered—with hot water, soap, *and* shampoo—then put on the pale blue tunic and dull gold pants I'd tried to wear on TSD Nine. I draped the blue and gold scarf over my shoulders. Before I went out, I'd wrap it around my head and neck until just my eyes were visible as extra insurance against recognition.

The mess hall was half dining room, half galley. Two long tables that each sat eight took up most of the room. They were upgraded models with plastech tops modeled to look like wood.

A gleaming industrial kitchen lined the back wall. A state-of-the-art commercial food synthesizer was placed next to an old-fashioned fridge and stove. The extra weight alone proved that this was Richard's personal ship—no merc captain would bother with real food prep when a synthesizer could do it for a fraction of the cost and weight.

Loch sat at the end of the first table and gestured me to a seat with a covered plate. I sat and removed the thermal cover. I was greeted with steaming eggs, bacon, and toast. I looked up in awe. "Thank you," I said.

The corner of Loch's mouth tipped up. "While I appreciate the fact that you think I can cook, you should thank Veronica. I just saved you a plate before Tiny ate it all."

I took my time and savored the first real food I'd had since the *Mayport*. Though simple, the eggs and bacon were delicious.

"Where is Veronica?" I asked when I was finished.

"Last I heard, she was planning to let the kid burn off some energy in the fitness room."

"Okay. I need to stop by and see how much I owe her and how she'd like the money, then I'm ready. You?"

"I'm ready."

I could hear the shrieking laughter even before I made it all the way downstairs. Veronica's voice came from the fitness room, artificially low. "I'm gonna get you!" By the time I made it to the door, Veronica had Lin pinned on the sparring mats and was tickling him breathless.

"Sorry to interrupt," I said after Veronica had helped her son up, "but I'm getting ready to go out and need to talk to you for a second."

Veronica pushed her messy hair behind her ears and came over, expression wary. "Should I get Imma to watch Lin?" she asked quietly.

"No, this is not *that* talk. I'm headed to the bank. How

much do I owe you for the supplies and how would you like to be paid?"

Shock, surprise, then mild offense chased each other across her face. "You don't owe me anything," she said. "If anything, I owe you."

"But—"

"No," she snapped, low and fierce. "I would've paid *anything* to get off that planet. I would've given up every last penny. Paying for the supplies that allowed my escape is the least I can do." She looked like an avenging angel and it transformed her from pretty into stunning.

I bowed low. "Thank you," I said. "I accept your gift with gratitude."

She smiled and the stunning goddess was once again a pretty woman. "I should've known you would understand." She returned my bow.

I did understand. Knowing whether to accept a gift on first offer or to refuse once or more was part of my lessons so I didn't embarrass our House. And if I had refused her generosity, it would've been an insult. But not only that, I also knew about the burning desire to be the master of your own future.

"Do you need anything while I am out?" I asked. "Or do you want to go with us?"

She thought about it then shook her head. "No, I will stay here with Lin and Imma." She paused. "Unless you need protection. I may not be special ops as you requested, but I am not unskilled."

"I've got it covered," Loch rumbled from behind me. "Stay, play with your kid."

"We'll talk when I get back. Figure out what the plan is,

what I can do to help," I said. "I've shut down the ship's external communications, so if you need to contact me, use your com. You have one, right?"

"I do."

"Okay, see you in a little while."

I WRAPPED THE SCARF AROUND MY HEAD WHILE WE waited for the cargo door to open. It was a bit tricky without a mirror, and I fiddled with it until Loch grabbed my wrist. "It is fine," he said. "When we get out, I'll be playing your bodyguard." He pulled on a dark cloak he'd found.

"You'll roast in that," I said. Heat already poured in from the narrow opening in the cargo door. I dreaded going out in long sleeves.

"It's temperature regulated," he said. "Rockhurst kitted this ship with only the best."

"Damn, now I'm jealous. Maybe I'll buy myself one while we're out. Maybe one in blue," I mused to myself.

"I like you in blue," Loch said.

I hoped the scarf covered my blush. "Today, I'm Irene while in company. What should I call you?"

He shrugged. "Guards don't have names. Just call me 'guard' or, better yet, just point at whatever you want me to do."

"My guards always had names. I suppose Marcus will have to do. It's common enough that people shouldn't immediately associate it with the bounty."

I straightened my shoulders, tipped my head up just a bit, and settled firmly into my public persona.

"It's scary how easily you do that," Marcus said. I raised one imperious eyebrow at him and looked faintly bored. He grinned. "That's the whole Consortium in a single expression," he said.

"I had years of practice," I said. "We wield expressions like soldiers wield weapons. One disdainful sniff from a House representative to a lower noble and the whole room will turn on the recipient. But we have to be careful, too. Wars have been started over unintentional insults."

"Sounds tedious," Marcus said.

"Incredibly. Are you ready?" At his nod, I stepped out into the bright midday sun. Stifling heat seared my face. It would be better on the city streets where a combination of building shades and thermoregulators would be hard at work to keep the heat tolerable.

The transport I'd called waited at the bottom of the ramp. I made sure the cargo door closed and locked then slipped into the transport's cool interior. Loch followed me in and sat across from me. I touched my right thumb and middle finger, then ran my secondary identity chip over the reader. "Take me to the nearest von Hasenberg bank," I requested. A location popped up on-screen, five minutes away. I confirmed and the transport glided away from *Polaris*.

The spaceport I'd chosen was tiny, with just a single berth perched on top of a middling building. Hundreds or thousands of such ports existed across the city, and ports for the larger ships ringed the outskirts. Buildings towered around us, protecting our little port from all but the most eagle-eyed spotters.

Once we glided off the edge of the two-hundred-story building, the glass panel in the floor of the transport—ostensibly for tourists but used most frequently to make sure no one was tracking you from below—revealed the chaos inherent in a city of over a hundred million crammed into an area just under eight square kilometers.

Sedition was the largest city on APD Zero by population, but one of the smallest by size. Situated on an island, it had grown vertically when the land ran out. Transport traffic was constant and mind-boggling at every level. Our transport slid into the flow heading down.

In Sedition, the closer you were to the ground, the better off. Only the highest-end luxury brands and the most world-class smugglers and privateers could afford ground-floor rent. The reason was simple—the lower you went, the better shielded you were from the ferocious sun. It also meant that if you tossed so much as a drop of water over the side of your balcony you faced up to a year in prison. The rich didn't appreciate dodging detritus from the sky.

We were headed to the largest von Hasenberg bank in Sedition. It took up an entire ground-floor block. The rent would've been astronomical if the House didn't own the entire building. The other Houses also owned their own blocks for similar reasons. APD Zero might be a smugglers' haven, but the Houses wanted everyone to know that the black market flourished only because of their benevolence.

The transport settled onto a wide, tree-lined avenue. Men and women in expensive clothes strolled sedately along the shops. If you wanted to see and be seen, this was the place, which was a little tricky for someone who wanted to remain anonymous.

Luckily, I wasn't the first person reluctant to show my face on a street full of wolves.

We rounded the corner and entered the private garage reserved for bank customers. And Irene Marie was quite a long-standing customer. Once the transport stopped, I told it to wait for us to return then moved to exit. Loch—*Marcus*—blocked my way. "Bodyguard first," he said.

He climbed out, all dark clothes and radiating danger. After a few seconds he reached in to help me out. He fell in behind me as I headed for the VIP doors. I hit the doorman with my mother's stare before he could embarrass us both by asking for my credentials. He turned magenta and opened the door so quickly it hit him in the face.

Inside, the VIP lobby was done in tasteful shades of cream, brown, and gilt. The whole place screamed old money, including the man moving to meet me. A middle-aged gentleman in a suit that cost more than most people made in a year, he would be easy to dismiss if you didn't notice his shark-like eyes.

Those eyes took in my simple clothes in a single glance. "Madam, I am Mr. Stanley. How may I be of service today?" he asked. "Perhaps I could direct you to our regular lobby?" He all but oozed false obsequiousness.

Unfortunately, I knew his type. If I let him help me, he would poke his nose so far into my affairs that I'd never escape the bank. I settled more firmly into my aristocratic persona. Nothing got bankers moving like an angry aristocrat.

"No, you will not do," I said with a sniff. I looked around. A harassed-looking young man walked by carrying a stack of papers. "Him," I said, pointing.

"But madam—" Mr. Stanley started.

"Now," I said. When he didn't move, I let my expression, mostly hidden by the scarf, go glacial. "Perhaps you did not hear me," I said in a saccharine voice. "Guard"—I snapped my fingers at Marcus—"do you think he has gone deaf? Help him with his hearing."

"With pleasure, my lady," Marcus rumbled. He stepped out from behind me, a towering wall of muscle covered by a dark cloak.

"There's no need, madam," Mr. Stanley said nervously. "I'll go get him and be right back."

I inclined my head a fraction. Sometimes playing a bitch was *awesome*.

"Having fun, are you?" Marcus murmured to me.

"Oh, yes," I said. My smile was hidden by the scarf, but he could probably see it in my eyes. "Excellent work, by the way."

He nodded once and returned to his position behind my right shoulder.

Mr. Stanley returned with the younger man in tow. "This is Mr. Rochester. How may we help you?"

"Mr. Rochester, take me to a private room."

The young man looked a little bewildered, but he knew an order when he heard one. The older man tried to follow us. "You are not needed," I said. I turned away without another word and followed Mr. Rochester to one of the rooms set aside to conduct sensitive business.

"Um, here is the room, madam," Mr. Rochester said. He held the door open while I swept inside. Once we sat, I checked the room for bugs and found none. *Excellent.*

I sat in one of the plush chairs facing the desk. "How long have you been with the bank?"

He moved to sit behind the desk. "Four years, madam.

I assure you, even though I am a junior banker, I can assist with whatever you need."

"Very good. I need to make several large withdrawals from a private account. Please set up the terminal for an immediate withdrawal from a numbered account and then wait outside."

The young man's eyes widened but he started typing on the terminal in front of him.

FTL communication was expensive and finicky. Only financial institutions and Houses had enough at stake to make it worthwhile. Everyone else waited for their messages to bounce through gates, carried by passing ships and communication drones. But it meant that in order to move large amounts of money, you had to physically be at a bank or wait for up to two weeks for the transaction to be confirmed.

I didn't have two weeks.

Accessing my House account would alert Father to my location. And if he happened to be near an FTL com terminal, he could order the bank employees to detain me until a retrieval team arrived. So that account was out, even though it was the one with the most money.

Fortunately, I had more than one account, including several numbered accounts. Not tied to any identity chip, numbered accounts were anonymous but also dangerous. If you forgot the account number or access code, the money was gone forever.

Luckily, I was very good with numbers.

"The terminal is ready, madam. Are you transferring between accounts or do you need credit chips?"

"I will take it from here. My guard will alert you once I am finished."

Mr. Rochester turned the terminal toward me, bobbed a half bow, then exited the room and closed the door behind him. That was the nice thing about junior bankers, they knew how to follow orders and not be a nuisance.

I laid two anonymous credit chips on the desk then pulled up the privacy screen. The other problem with numbered accounts is that anyone with the number could access them. And while I didn't *think* Marcus would rob me, better safe than sorry.

I typed in the account number and access code. A second of delay and then my balance appeared. This account had just under a million credits. I withdrew two hundred thousand and fitted the first credit chip into the reader. A pleasant *beep* confirmed the transaction.

With Marcus taken care of, I considered how much money to withdraw for myself. The account linked to the identity I had chosen for this planet had nearly a hundred thousand credits in it. It was unlikely that I would need more, but another trip to the bank would be additional risk. I withdrew another hundred thousand credits onto the second chip.

Numbered accounts did not keep transaction records. Oh, they kept the running balance and showed when money had been added or removed, but they kept no records of *where* that money came from or went to.

Because anonymous money transfers were so ripe for abuse, opening a numbered account required a House ID. You didn't have to give the banker your name or let them scan your ID chip, but if you couldn't produce a House seal then you couldn't open the account.

The lack of transactional records meant that when these credit chips were used, the money couldn't be tied back to my numbered account. So I could transfer the money from the credit chip to Irene's account without compromising the secrecy of the numbered account. It was the same way I got money into the numbered account in the first place.

I logged out of the account and carefully wiped the terminal screen clean of fingerprints. I lowered the privacy screen and placed the two credit chips in internal zippered pockets, keeping them separate. "Time to go," I said.

Marcus opened the door and stepped out. At his signal that it was clear, I followed him. Mr. Rochester snapped to attention. "Madam, is there anything else you need?"

"No, thank you for your assistance. I am leaving."

Mr. Rochester bowed and escorted us to the door. Marcus and I entered the waiting transport without incident.

I sighed and let my public persona fall away. "Do you need anything while we're out?" I asked. "I was thinking about buying some new clothes, but I can drop you at the ship first if you'd like to head out early."

"I go where you go," he said. "I could use some more clothes, too, assuming you're not shopping down here."

The thought of Marcus Loch in a suit derailed my thought process for a solid minute. All of that muscle and menace hidden beneath a bespoke suit would be a sight to see. *Yum.*

I shook myself out of thoughts of getting Loch *out* of said suit and handed him the credit chip with his money on it.

"This is what I owe you," I said. "There's no transaction history, so don't lose it."

Loch pocketed the chip without comment.

Handing the money over was bittersweet. My obligation was finished, but now he had no reason to stick around. "I guess today is our last day together," I said, hoping he would deny my words.

He did not.

# CHAPTER 15

I pushed aside my hurt and directed our transport to a shopping district in the two hundreds: high enough to be cheap, but not so high as to be poor quality. Most of the middle class shopped in this district. And around the periphery was a thriving black market where you could buy anything from jewelry to weapons to pleasure.

The transport dropped us on a landing pad on floor 215. I ended our ride and confirmed the fare deduction. Once we were out, the transport glided away to pick up the next passenger. I'd order a new transport when we were done shopping.

This was not my first trip to Sedition, but even so, the sheer *scale* boggled the mind on every visit. Looking around, it was easy to forget that we were hundreds of meters in the air. Even the harsh sun was partially blocked thanks to the higher levels.

Shops opened out to wide walkways bustling with pedestrians. Plazas dotted with small trees connected adjacent buildings, both on our level and above and below us. With the exception of the tall plastech and glass wall that prevented accidental falls, this could be a shopping street on any planet.

I moved away from the transport pad. The better deals were found when you had to walk more than two meters to get to the store. Loch followed me, just off my right shoulder. "You don't have to play bodyguard here," I said. "I can look after myself, and we can meet up later. You can shop for whatever you need."

"I'm not playing," Loch said. "That bastard is still after you and I am looking forward to meeting him again." Loch's expression filled with so much predatory anticipation that I almost felt bad for Richard. Almost.

"Yes, but *that bastard* will likely be after me forever. You can't protect me forever. And despite what it looked like when we met, I do a decent job of keeping a low profile."

Loch remained stubbornly silent and glued to my shoulder.

"At least walk beside me," I said. "In case you haven't noticed, bodyguards are not plentiful at this level. We'll draw *more* attention if you keep stalking along behind me."

Loch grumbled something unpleasant but moved up next to me. Other pedestrians still gave us a wide berth.

I purchased a temperature-regulating cloak at the first shop we stopped at. Cream with blue trim, it was in no way practical. But it was beautiful and it kept the sun from making me sweat, so I bought it. It would be destroyed the first time I took it anywhere near a dirty ship, so I also bought a dark gray cloak as a backup.

We crossed over a pedestrian bridge to the next building. I passed all of the little boutiques with their bright colors and cute outfits with barely a glance until a red dress in a display caught my attention and wouldn't let go. I wandered over to the window.

The dress had a fitted bodice with short cap sleeves and a V-neck. A full skirt hit the mannequin just above the knees. I loved it, but if a cream cloak was impractical, this dress was wildly unsuitable.

"You should try it on," Loch said.

"Where would I wear it? In the engine room? It's just something I'll eventually have to leave behind." I suppressed the sigh that tried to escape. One day I would wear dresses like this whenever I wanted; it just wasn't today.

I walked away from the dress without looking back.

On the next block, I found the store I was looking for. It carried both men's and women's styles in simple cuts of sturdy fabric. I wouldn't win any fashion awards, but the clothes would stand up to whatever I threw at them.

Loch wandered off to the men's section while I dug through the women's options. I found a few shirts in my size in various sleeve lengths. The pants I needed to actually try on because it was difficult to find something that fit without sagging. I grabbed a few pairs and headed for the dressing room.

After a frustrating ten minutes, I found one pair of pants that weren't horrible. I went back to see if they had more of that style, and of course they didn't. So I settled for what I had and went to find Marcus.

He lounged by the door, package already in hand. I paid for my purchases and joined him. We exited the shop and kept going, drifting farther and farther from the good parts of the district.

"You looking for something or just trying to find trouble?" Loch finally asked.

"Can't it be both?" I asked. He didn't even grin. "If you must know, I'm looking for a weapons dealer that used to be around here, but he must've moved. I don't know what's on the ship, but I'd like a new blast pistol and some more ammo."

"In that case, we'll need a transport. I've been here before."

I ordered a transport to meet us at the next landing. We climbed in and Loch set the destination. We crossed the city then descended to the ground. I raised an eyebrow.

"Rhys has done very well for himself in the last few years," Loch said.

I only knew of one Rhys who sold weapons in Sedition, but I kept the knowledge to myself. "An old friend?" I asked.

"Something like that. Let me do the talking and try to look inconspicuous. What kind of blaster do you want?"

"Small. A Mosey or Ketchum if he has one, otherwise anything that is small enough to be easily concealable. I don't need any fancy extras, but I won't turn them down as long as they don't make the gun bigger."

"Anything else?"

"Nothing specific, but I'm not opposed to buying more. Really depends on what he has."

The transport rolled to a stop in an alley. A single steel door broke up the expanse of wall. Yeah, this seemed like an ideal place to get murdered. If I wasn't pretty sure we were meeting Rhys Sebastian, I would've bailed.

"I'll go first, you stick close. If anyone gives you shit, let me deal with it."

I paid for the transport then touched my thumb and

pinky, reverting to the likely compromised identity of Irena Hasan, just in case. No reason to burn a perfectly good identity, because while scanning identity chips without notice was against the law, I doubted a black-market arms dealer much cared.

Loch stepped out but didn't offer me a hand. I pulled up the hood of my cloak and climbed out on my own. The transport slid away. Loch pounded on the door.

"Wha'da'ya want?" a rough voice asked from a hidden speaker.

"Tell Rhys that Loch is here to see him."

We waited in silence. Finally the door swung inward to reveal a long, dim hallway and nothing else. We stepped inside and the door slammed shut behind us. Loch didn't even pause.

We climbed two flights of stairs then came out in a small foyer. A beautiful brunette sat behind a gleaming, spotless desk. "Please sit," she said, indicating the leather chairs behind us. "Mr. Sebastian will see you shortly."

Loch crossed his arms and didn't move. The receptionist shrugged a delicate shoulder and turned back to her com terminal. Time ticked past in tiny, frozen increments. Standing behind Loch, I settled in for a long wait.

Perhaps twenty minutes later, the brunette looked up from her com terminal. "Mr. Sebastian will see you now," she said. She indicated the door to her right.

I trailed Loch through the door into a richly appointed office. Real wood floors covered by antique Persian rugs led to a wall of windows looking down on the main avenue through Sedition.

And between us and the windows sat Rhys Sebastian. Rhys and I had started off as friendly acquaintances and had slowly morphed into true friends.

Rhys had acquired a few hard-to-find items for me back when I worked for House von Hasenberg. Thanks to that acquaintance and my knowledge of his skill and discretion, he was one of the first people I'd turned to when I escaped. But back then, he'd been operating from up in the two hundreds.

Rhys had definitely done well for himself. We'd kept in touch regularly over the last two years. He had mentioned his business was doing well, but he had failed to mention *how* well.

And he knew Marcus.

I smiled under my scarf. This would be interesting.

Rhys stood. He was as tall and nearly as broad as Loch, with the same sense of contained violence that his expensive suit did little to hide. His hair was blond and cut close to his skull. But where Loch was roughly attractive, Rhys was perfectly, classically handsome—a statue of an ancient god brought to life.

"Loch, what brings you to my piece of the world?" Rhys asked as he came out from behind his desk. Rhys's age had always been difficult for me to estimate, but after seeing him with Marcus, I guessed they were the same age—mid- to late-twenties.

"My friend needs a little something for personal protection," Loch said. "I figured you could help out."

Rhys flicked a dismissive glance at me, then paused and looked again. He pulled a blaster seemingly from thin air and pointed it at Loch. "Move away from the lady."

Loch crossed his arms and stepped closer to me, blocking Rhys from view. "No."

"It was not a request. Move or I will shoot you, and I won't be aiming for a limb."

"You can try," Loch said.

I peeked around Loch's shoulder. "Gentlemen, while this is all very amusing, perhaps we could get to the business at hand. Rhys, put the gun away unless you're planning to shoot *me,* in which case, Marcus, you have my permission to shoot back."

Rhys nodded and the gun disappeared as quickly as it had appeared. "Lady Ada, I had to be sure you weren't being held against your will."

"You two know each other," Loch said, something strange in his voice.

"Surprise," I said. I stepped up beside him. "In my defense, you didn't specify *which* Rhys we were going to see, and these are new digs. Very nice, by the way."

"It was your money that helped me get here, so you have my thanks."

I tilted my head. "Does that mean you won't alert the authorities now that I have a substantial price on my head?"

Loch cursed quietly but Rhys just grinned. "I'm rich as hell now. I don't need your father's money. And that would be a poor way to show my gratitude. But, in return, I insist you have dinner with me tonight." A pointed glance at Loch. "Alone."

"Like hell she will!" Loch growled.

I pushed back my own urge to accept just because Loch refused to let me make my own decisions. It was clear Rhys had added the "alone" stipulation just to yank Loch's chain. Meeting Rhys again for dinner would be a risk, but he'd helped me before and nothing indicated he would betray me now. Plus he wouldn't have offered if he didn't have a reason.

"I'd be delighted," I said, "as long as I can bring a guest." Loch settled slightly, correctly guessing that he would be my guest. I continued, "And as long as you understand that my wardrobe is lacking. What you see is what you get."

"You look lovely as always," Rhys said, "but I would be honored to send over some dresses for you to choose from, if you desire. I still have your sizes from last time." A world of insinuation saturated his tone.

Loch went stone cold. Rhys noticed it as well, because he half turned into a defensive position. I hooked my hand around Loch's bicep, just above his elbow, like he was escorting me on a walk. His arm felt like touching sun-heated granite. I wasn't sure what I could do if he decided to attack, but for all of his needling, Rhys was a friend and I didn't want to see him killed.

"Thank you for the kind offer, but I must decline," I said. "I happen to *like* these clothes." I felt like I was wading through a Consortium gathering where one wrong step could mean war. The last time I'd talked to Rhys in person, he'd been at turns aloof and amusing. I narrowed my eyes at him. This new persona was annoying and unwelcome.

Rhys watched the entire interaction with sharp eyes and a half grin. When it was clear neither of us would comment further, he sighed and smiled. "Loch, you know you're always welcome at my table, I'm just messing with you. And it was quite . . . *illuminating*."

"I thought you'd gotten smarter over the years, Rhys," Loch rumbled. "Don't make me kick your ass, because I won't hesitate to do it."

Dinner with both of them seemed like torture. Perhaps I could bow out and the two of them and their egos could dine?

"Do you have a gun for the lady or are you all talk?" Loch asked, exasperated.

"What happened to the last one?" Rhys asked me.

"I had it until Father dropped the bounty on my head. Then I had to leave it when mercs started sniffing around. Been traveling light ever since." I shrugged off the pain. Leaving things behind bothered me. I could live a nomadic life, but I didn't enjoy it. I was more of a home and hearth kind of woman.

"My offer still stands, you know," Rhys said, almost gently.

Loch's arm, which had started to relax under my hand, returned to granite. It would be a miracle if these two didn't come to blows. I squeezed Loch's arm slightly.

"I know," I said. "And it means a lot, but my answer remains the same."

"In that case, let's see what I have in the armory."

WE MANAGED TO LEAVE WITHOUT BLOODSHED. I PICKED up two tiny blast pistols and Loch bought a few bigger guns, including a shotgun. He seemed to be loading for war.

As the transport slid away from Rhys's door, Loch asked, "What did Rhys offer you?"

"Just let it go, Marcus," I said.

"What. Did. He. Offer. You," he demanded.

I huffed out a frustrated breath. "He offered me a home,"

I said. Loch's jaw clenched. "But not what you're thinking. He offered to make me a silent partner in his business, which he had just started to rapidly expand. He offered me a place to stay—*not* his house—and vowed to misdirect anyone following me. He was entirely honorable."

Loch grunted. If he thought he was getting off that easy, he was so, so wrong. "Care to explain what all that was about? And how do you know Rhys in the first place?"

Loch's expression shuttered. "We've known each other for years," he said.

I waited for him to continue and when he didn't, I pointed a finger at him. "No. You don't get to demand answers from me then blow off my questions."

He hit me with a cold stare and remained silent. It felt like an unexpected dagger between the ribs. I blinked hard and retreated into my public persona where nothing could get close enough to hurt.

It took a lifetime, but the transport finally dropped us at the ship. I activated the correct ID chip and waved it over the reader, then I stepped out into the afternoon sunshine. Thanks to the cloak the heat was no longer stifling, so I enjoyed the sun on my partially covered face.

The urge to get in the ship and fly off to the ass-end of nowhere rode me hard. Maybe Veronica would like to go with me. It would be a lot of work, but the two of us could manage a ship this size.

Then the current bane of my existence stepped out of the transport and snapped me out of my dreams. I moved ahead of him up the cargo ramp. "*Polaris,* status report," I said as I approached the door.

"No one has entered or left the ship, Captain. Currently there are three souls on board," the computer responded from the speaker near the keypad.

"Open the cargo door," I said.

The door slid upward, revealing the cool, dim, *empty* interior. It wasn't until then that I realized I was gripping my blaster with white knuckles, as if I thought a horde of mercs—or worse, Rockhurst soldiers—would be waiting.

I stepped inside and Loch followed me. But when I stopped at the door control panel, he disappeared deeper into the ship. While I waited for the cargo door to close, I remotely locked the captain's quarters. Loch could find a new place to sleep.

We had a few hours until we needed to leave for dinner. Rhys had tried to persuade me to stay, but I needed to talk to Veronica, and I'd put it off long enough. After all, why stop now when I could make this the grand slam of terrible days?

I found Veronica in her room frowning at a com. The door was open, so I knocked on the jamb. "Hey, you have a minute to talk?"

"Yes, come in. Let me tell Imma that I'll be busy for a little while." She stepped next door and murmured to the other woman.

I swept the room for bugs and trackers and found one. I destroyed it then sat in the guest chair and ordered my thoughts. Veronica returned and closed the door. She sat cross-legged on the bed. "Ask, and I will answer what I can."

"You are running from Lin's father," I said. She nodded warily. "Which Yamado is it?" She looked unhappy but not surprised that I'd guessed.

House Yamado had just three heirs in my generation—

two sons and a daughter. None had children of their own yet, so if Lin was the firstborn's son, even a bastard, it would be very, very bad.

She ran a hand down her face. "It is Hitoshi," she said quietly.

I half expected it, but the confirmation landed like a punch to the gut. Hitoshi was the eldest Yamado heir, and if I was honest, the one most likely to keep a woman hidden on a backwater planet.

"Hitoshi was so sweet at first," Veronica continued. "It was perfect. And, naturally, I was thrilled to have caught his attention. But once it became clear that I was pregnant and going to keep the baby, he went insane."

I sat back and tried to tamp down the tension her confession had caused. It reminded me of my own disastrous dating experience. Did anyone in the Consortium have a normal relationship?

"How did he get you to TSD Nine?" I asked.

"He kidnapped me from my apartment. My parents had kicked me out when they found out I was pregnant. We were well off, and I had been saving my allowance in a private account. It's all I had. Hitoshi dumped me on TSD Nine and since House Yamado controlled it, he prohibited anyone from removing me from the planet on pain of death. When I finally contacted my parents, they didn't care." She spread her hands in an unconscious helpless gesture. Her parents' decision had hurt.

"So how did you become a fence?"

"It took a while. Hitoshi sent me a pittance every month, but it was barely enough to feed myself. I knew once the baby was born I'd burn through my savings. So I started working. I started with legitimate goods, but with so few people and the other stores, it was hard to make money. Moving stolen items was much more profitable. I had some close calls, especially early on, but I learned as I went."

I knew something about learning as I went. The first few months after I left home, I'd found that theoretical knowledge didn't always translate into practical ability. I couldn't imagine having to learn that lesson while also pregnant.

She continued, "After a couple years, I'd built enough of a reputation that smugglers from the dark side of the planet started using my shop to sell to the very men who hunted them. That's when my business truly became profitable."

"What about Imma? Do you trust her?" If I was Hitoshi, I'd be keeping an eye on Veronica and Lin by any means possible. And a nanny would be a perfect opportunity.

"She was my nanny growing up. We kept in touch over the years. When my parents kicked me out, she was the one who helped me find an apartment. She's like my mother. I asked her to come to Gamamine and she did, even though I could barely pay her."

She took a deep breath, sighed, and looked down. "But even so, I looked into her communications, family, and finances. I'm not proud of it, but Lin's life was on the line. She's clean. I trust her completely."

I nodded. "What's your plan now? And how can I help?"

She leaned forward, her face wary. "I need to stay mobile for a while before we settle or Hitoshi will be able to pick up the trail. I was hoping you would allow me to book passage with you."

"That's a really bad idea"—I felt obligated to point it out— "as I already have two Houses after me and this is a stolen ship. It's not safe."

"No, but nowhere is safe for me right now. You know better than most the reach a High House has. Hitoshi can find me wherever I go unless I obscure the trail completely. And you have reason to stay hidden, too."

"I'm not saying no. But you should think about it for a while longer. I have a contact on this planet who could likely whisk you away to safety." A brilliant idea occurred. "In fact, why don't you come to dinner with us?"

"I don't—"

"No, this is perfect. You can meet Rhys and see if he offers a safer alternative to traveling with me. I don't want you to feel trapped into this decision."

Veronica raised an eyebrow with a cool look, and she was once again the capable businesswoman, leaving the scared mother behind. "This is not a decision I made lightly," she said. "I had planned to take this route as soon as I agreed to help you."

"Just because you planned it doesn't mean you won't feel trapped," I said gently. "I know what I'm talking about. Just come to dinner and see if Rhys can help. You don't have to agree to anything or even tell him who you are."

"Very well, I will attend. What should I wear?"

She had on dark pants and a pretty green blouse. "Your current outfit is perfect. I already told Rhys I'd be wearing this," I said, indicating my clothes. I stood. "We leave at seven."

# CHAPTER 16

I messaged Rhys that we'd have an extra for dinner from one of my burner accounts, then made my way to the mess hall. I almost stopped short at the door when I saw Marcus sitting inside, but then I remembered this was my ship, dammit. I gave him a shallow nod of acknowledgment then made my way to the food synth. I didn't feel up to real cooking, even if we had the ingredients.

The synthesizer could produce just about any food under the sun. I punched in an order for grilled cheese and french fries with a glass of sweet iced coffee—comfort food at its best. My stomach rumbled at the thought.

A small rectangular box, the food synth ran off the ship's power and converted energy into matter. Another, larger synthesizer should be somewhere down in the maintenance area to produce spare parts for the ship or anything else we might need. Synth technology and formulas were both strictly controlled by the Consortium.

A happy *ding* announced my food was ready. I opened the

door and pulled out a perfectly toasted sandwich and crispy fries. Simple foods almost always came out perfect. Complicated foods were trickier because there were a limited number of formulas available and everyone expected a slightly different taste. Many people raised on freshly prepared food thought the synth food tasted off.

I pulled my food and drink from the synth then ran into another problem—where to sit. Loch sat at the first table facing the door. Sitting at the second table would put me behind him and out of his view, but it also reeked of cowardice.

Before I could decide, Loch pushed out the chair next to him and tilted his head in invitation. I sat, hyperaware of him next to me. He shifted in his seat, and I snuck a glance. He stared at the table as if it held all of life's answers.

I ignored him and dove into the carb-laden goodness on my plate. I promised myself I'd be healthy tomorrow.

After a few minutes, he broke the silence. "Rhys and I have known each other for nearly a decade, but it's not my story to tell. If you want to know how, you'll have to ask him."

Some of my anger drained away. "Okay," I said slowly, "why not just say that before?"

Loch ran his hands over his shaved head with a frustrated noise. "Rhys knows me well enough to get under my skin, and he loves meddling. I lost my temper with you, when he was the one who pushed me to the edge."

I made a noncommittal sound. I could feel the heat of his gaze but I steadily finished my food. When I placed my napkin on my plate, Loch turned toward me. He cupped my jaw and turned my head so he could meet my eyes.

"I was a jerk," he murmured. "I saw you retreat behind

your mask, and I didn't like knowing that I was the cause of it. I'm sorry."

I'd never been one to hold grudges, so the last of my anger dissolved with his apology. His thumb traced a blazing path across my lips. Heat spiraled through my system. The man was dangerously attractive, especially when he wholly focused on me.

"Rhys and I are just friends," I said. "That's all we've ever been. But even if that wasn't the case, your behavior was unacceptable. You *were* a jerk. And for what? Because I asked a question that didn't have an easy answer?"

Loch growled and dropped his hand. "Because I didn't want to admit I was jealous." His eyes flashed in defiance, as if he expected me to throw the words back in his face.

Now we were getting somewhere. Jealousy hinted at a depth of feeling I hadn't been sure he had. And if he got to be jealous, then I ought to be able to stake a claim as well. A tiny voice at the back of my mind screamed a warning, afraid I was getting in too deep, but I reminded myself that he would be gone tomorrow. One day of possibilities was safe enough—this would not be a repeat of my first season.

"You have no reason to be jealous," I said as I pivoted toward him and leaned in.

I gave him plenty of time to back away, but he held his ground, his gaze hot. I took that as permission and closed the gap, ghosting my lips across his in a featherlight caress. Sparks of lust shivered along my nerves. I pressed deeper, sucking on his bottom lip, then I slid my tongue into the heat of his mouth.

He made a rumbling sound and dragged me closer with

a hand on my hip and one buried in my hair. I slid forward until I was clutched against him, straddling his strong thigh. My breasts rubbed against the muscles of his chest and I moaned low.

His tongue thrust into my mouth and I welcomed the invasion. Loch's hands clenched and he pulled me closer, molding our bodies together. I rocked against him, mindless with pleasure. He pulled back and I chased him, pressing kisses against his lips and jaw.

I ran my hands over his head, relishing the scrape of barely there stubble against my palms. He groaned and the hand on my hip slid up to cup my breast. I hissed out a breath when his thumb brushed over my pebbled nipple. He reclaimed my mouth at the same time he rolled my nipple between his finger and thumb. Pleasure lanced through me and I arched into him.

"Loch," I gasped.

"I've got you," he murmured against my mouth. He trailed burning kisses down to the sensitive spot on my neck. The scrape of his stubbled jaw made my skin hypersensitive.

Then, with disorienting speed, he slid me into my chair and backed away. I stared at him stupidly for a few seconds before I heard Lin's voice just outside the door. Heat flooded my face as I realized I'd been so lost in the moment that I'd forgotten my surroundings.

Loch watched me with smoldering, predatory stillness, his hands fisted on the table. Lin entered the mess hall, talking a mile a minute. Veronica trailed behind. She took one look at us and grinned. *Busted.*

Lin climbed up in a seat across the table from us and

started questioning me about the different components in a ship while Veronica fixed his afternoon snack. Loch listened for a little while, then stood. On his way up he paused to murmur in my ear, "We are not finished, sweetheart."

He took both our dishes and put them into the recycler. The recycler was the counterpart to the synthesizer—it broke items down into energy that could be used by the ship or synth. He nodded a farewell to Veronica and Lin, then left the mess hall.

I entertained Lin for a few more minutes, but when Veronica looked like she was almost done cooking, I escaped before she could corner me and demand details. I didn't have any details to share. I just knew that Loch drew me in like a magnet and the more time I spent with him, the more I liked him.

I told myself that it was for the best that today was his last day. It was a pretty lie.

I SETTLED INTO THE CAPTAIN'S STATION OF THE FLIGHT deck and set an alarm on my com so I wouldn't miss dinner. I needed to do a deep dive in the ship's system processes to find out where the rest of the trackers were hiding. And I needed something completely mind-numbing to focus on so my body would calm down.

I pulled up a log of every onboard process that had accessed the communication array before I had shut it down after our second jump. It was a long list. Navigation alone accounted for nearly half of the calls. The navigation computers tried to access the communication array for additional information each time the plotted course updated.

It took a couple hours, but I finally started to see an access pattern emerge. And in that pattern of normal processes, the tracking processes stood out. Well, at least a few of them. I disabled the trackers I found and set the diagnostic to run again now that I knew what to look for.

"*Polaris,* sweep the ship and show me the locations of all transmitting devices," I said. A 3-D model of the ship appeared over the console with red dots in most of the rooms on the lower two floors. *Great.* The room-by-room sweep would have to happen before I turned external communications back on. Otherwise Rockhurst would know our location as soon as the signal reached him.

I had completed the sweep of the main floor by the time my com's alarm went off. It was tedious work but I felt better with it done. After dinner I would do the lowest level and the maintenance areas.

Fifteen minutes until we had to leave, I climbed up to the top level and entered the captain's quarters. I washed my face and ran a brush through my hair. I didn't have any makeup, nor any desire to wear it. Thankfully it wasn't required—this was not a Consortium dinner, no matter how much it might feel like one.

At five minutes to seven, I went down to meet Veronica and Loch. Both were waiting for me in the cargo hold. Veronica had her face covered with a scarf, much like my own. I loaned her the extra cloak I'd bought. With the sun setting it would be getting quite cool.

Loch wore the dark clothes and cloak he'd worn earlier, and he wasn't exactly looking excited about dinner. If Veronica's presence surprised him, he didn't show it. I opened the door then locked it behind us. We slid into the transport for the short trip.

Rhys's house was separate from his business, so we didn't have to use the creepy, unmarked door. Instead, the transport dropped us off at one of the few blocks that wasn't dominated by a skyscraper. Individual stone houses—complete with yards!—lined the street. All were four or five stories tall, but they were clearly houses. The lot alone had to be worth two fortunes. Rhys had done very, *very* well for himself indeed.

Loch climbed the steps first and knocked on the door. A gray-haired gentleman in a butler's uniform let us in. "Mr. Sebastian is expecting you. He's in the family drawing room. Right this way, please."

The butler led us through an opulent foyer and past a wide, real wood staircase. The drawing room doors were closed, to better show off their delicate stained-glass insets. The butler slid them open, revealing a warm room with comfortable furniture and cozy conversational seating. It was a stark contrast from the rest of the house.

"Welcome, welcome. I figured we'd all be more comfortable in here than in the formal sitting room," Rhys said. He'd dressed for dinner in a dark, formal suit and he looked damn good in it.

I pulled the scarf from my face. "Thank you for the invitation," I said. "Rhys, this is Yasmin," I said, pulling a slightly dazed-looking Veronica along with me. We'd agreed to use her middle name tonight. "Yasmin, meet Rhys Sebastian."

Rhys bowed over her hand. "Ms. Yasmin, it is a pleasure to meet you," he said.

She dipped into a curtsy. "The pleasure is mine, Mr. Sebastian," she said.

"Please, call me Rhys. Come, ladies, sit," he said. He offered each of us an elbow with the grace of a Consortium gentleman. I wondered, not for the first time, about his past.

Loch growled something too low to hear as he followed us. The ghost of a smile touched Rhys's mouth.

Rhys led us to a pair of settees. He settled Veronica on one, then settled me on the second. Rhys's eyes danced with a devilish light as he made to sit next to me. Loch closed the distance and hauled Rhys up, then turned and dropped him next to Veronica.

Loch sat beside me, close enough that his body pressed against mine from knee to shoulder. He sprawled, letting his arm drape behind me on the settee. His fingers played idly with the edge of my scarf. I hid a grin. Loch was very clearly sending a message.

Rhys sat next to Veronica with a tiny, satisfied smile. He knew he was playing with fire, but he didn't care. And Loch's glower did nothing but make Rhys's smile grow.

Interesting.

Rhys turned to Veronica, who still looked a little shellshocked. "So tell me, Ms. Yasmin, what do you do?"

"It's just Yasmin," she said. "Currently, I'm between jobs. But I help people find what they're looking for."

"Ah, a lady after my own heart," Rhys said. He smiled a devastating smile but Veronica was getting her feet under her. Her expression turned knowing. She'd figured out he was blinding her with his beauty and from the way her eyes crinkled at the corners, she was about to turn the tables on him.

"I find myself in a sensitive situation," Veronica said. "Lady Ada assured me you are a friend who can be trusted. Can I trust you to keep my confidence?" she asked.

Rhys's expression turned serious. "Of course. Ada's friends are my friends, and even if that were not the case, I try not to throw women or children to the wolves if at all possible. It's bad publicity."

Veronica unwrapped her scarf. Now it was Rhys's turn to look dazed. Veronica's makeup was stellar and she looked stunning. "I am running from a House," she said simply. "I have asked Lady Ada to take me with her when she leaves, but she suggested I talk to you first. She thinks I'll feel trapped by my decision to throw in with her. What do you think?"

Rhys blinked twice then shook himself out of the daze. "Running from a House is a tricky proposition," he said finally. "How is your financial situation?"

"It is of little concern."

"In that case, you have two, maybe three options." He ticked them off on his fingers. "One, if your face isn't well known, you can hide in plain sight with a new identity. It is very expensive, but quality work can be had for the right price. Two, you can run and keep running. Or, for the third option, you can disappear into the farthest reaches of the 'verse and hope you're never found."

"And which do you recommend?"

"Depends on the person. I can help you with one and three, but two works better for some, our lovely Ada included—despite my best efforts." Rhys tossed a suggestive smile at me.

I rolled my eyes, but Loch rumbled. I felt the vibration more than heard it and my nipples tightened in response.

Thank God for lined bras. I nudged his shoulder with mine and he quit, but his hand flexed around my other shoulder and pulled me closer.

Even though Loch had to know Rhys was just messing with him, he seemed incapable of shrugging it off. Rhys knew exactly how to get under his skin.

A knock on the door prevented further discussion. "Enter," Rhys said.

The butler slid the doors open. "Dinner is ready, sir," he said.

"Excellent," Rhys said. He stood and helped Veronica to her feet. Loch stood as well. After a pointed look from Rhys, Loch offered me a hand. I accepted his help up, then hooked a hand through his elbow before he could walk off. It was obvious that Loch was unfamiliar with the social niceties the rest of us understood without thought. And by the scowl on his face, either the knowledge gap or the niceties themselves pissed him off.

The dining room was just as ostentatious as the rest of the house. A beautifully carved wooden table big enough for fourteen sat under a brilliant chandelier that glittered with cut crystals. Four place settings were centered in the middle of the table.

Rhys led Veronica to the near side, then rounded the table and sat across from her. Loch followed his lead and deposited me next to Veronica. When he sat across from me, I gave him my best wicked smile. His eyes darkened, and I decided: I would have this man tonight, if he would have me.

I tabled my dirty thoughts. Rhys, Veronica, and I chatted lightly about a wide range of topics. Both Rhys and Veronica were excellent conversationalists, so I found myself enjoying their company. Loch occasionally chimed in, but he seemed content to let the conversation flow around him. Rhys threw the occasional flirtatious remark my way, mostly to annoy Loch, but it was clear to me that he was focused on Veronica.

The food was exquisite and the wine flowed freely. I allowed myself two glasses, then switched to sparkling water. A gentle buzz was fine, but getting hammered was not in the plan.

After dinner, Rhys turned to Loch. "Please escort Ms. Yasmin back to the drawing room. Ada and I will join you momentarily."

Loch did not move. Veronica glanced at me and I nodded slightly. She stood with a pointed stare at Loch. He settled more firmly into his chair.

I rolled my eyes. "Did you already forget our earlier conversation?" I asked him.

His eyes dropped half-closed and he grinned lazily. "I believe that conversation was unfinished."

Heat flushed through my body. I kept my voice even through sheer force of will. "Well, if you want any chance of *finishing* that conversation, I suggest you trust me now."

Loch held my gaze for a long moment, then nodded and stood. He and Veronica left the room.

Rhys cast me an appraising look. "You're playing with fire," he said without preamble.

I didn't pretend ignorance. "He's leaving tomorrow."

Rhys seemed surprised. "Are you sure?"

"Very," I said.

Rhys idly swirled the wine in his glass. "I've known Loch

for a long time," he finally said. "And I've only seen him like this once before. It ended poorly."

Jealously stabbed deep. "Oh?" I asked in what I hoped passed for a casual tone.

Rhys's expression turned knowing. "Pretend indifference all you like, but I know you, Ada von Hasenberg. Just be careful. I don't want either of you to get hurt. And Loch guards those he thinks of as his like a dragon guards gold."

"We just have good chemistry," I said. "He doesn't think I'm his." Just the thought made me twitchy, but underneath that, warmth tried to bloom. Damn my soft, traitorous heart.

Rhys merely raised an eyebrow and stood. "Let's join them before he proves you wrong," he said.

We returned to the drawing room to find Veronica grinning and Marcus scowling, but neither would say why. Rhys poured a round of brandy. The alcohol burned on its way down, leaving me pleasantly warm and languid, but Loch apparently did not share my feelings. "Care to spar?" he asked Rhys with studied casualness. "Or have you gone soft?"

Well, that was one way to throw down a gauntlet. "You're going to ruin a perfectly good meal with exercise?" I asked, trying to give Rhys an exit.

"It appears so," Rhys said with an exaggerated sigh. "Ladies, if you'll excuse us."

Veronica and I stood with the men. "If you think we're going to sit down here while you two beat yourselves bloody, you think wrong," I said. "Someone has to be there to knock some sense into you once your egos take over." Veronica nodded in agreement.

Rhys led us upstairs to a large open room with a padded

floor. He and Loch stepped into a side room. They both came out wearing loose pants and no shirts. Veronica and I shared an appreciative glance. Both men were built with defined abs and heavy musculature. Loch was the slightly bulkier of the two, but it was a near thing.

Loch's stomach was no longer bruised. He must've spent the afternoon in the medbay.

The men began taping their knuckles with a single-minded determination. Even Rhys's easygoing charm had morphed into careful concentration. "If you kill each other," I said, "I'm not cleaning up the mess."

"I'm not going to kill him, I'm just going to rough him up enough that he remembers why he shouldn't mess with me," Loch said. "It shouldn't take long."

Rhys grunted. "I'm not going to kill him, either. I'm just going to beat some manners into his thick skull. Feel free to thank me later, Ada, in any way you'd like," he said with a sly grin. Loch lunged at him, but Rhys expected it and flowed out of the way.

Then it was *on*.

Both men moved faster than anyone I'd ever seen. Arms and legs blurred as hits landed with solid *thud*s. They were not pulling punches and they used both hands and feet in some style of mixed martial arts. It also became clear that this was not the first time they had sparred. While they were not pulling punches, they also weren't aiming for maximum damage.

When I realized they weren't actually going to kill each other, I focused on the fight itself. All of that exposed skin and honed flesh working with such obvious strength and skill . . .

JESSIE MIHALIK

I hated to admit it because it was violent and uncivilized, but it was *hot*. A quick glance at Veronica proved I wasn't the only one who thought so.

They'd been fighting for a solid fifteen minutes when Loch caught the edge of Rhys's jaw with a hard cross. Rhys landed a solid kick to Loch's ribs on the way down. Then it was a grappling game, with each man rolling, throwing punches, and attempting to pin the other. They were both battered and bloody by the time Loch pinned Rhys in a choke hold. Rhys struggled for a few seconds then tapped out.

Loch stood and spat blood, then he helped Rhys up. Rhys slapped his back and said, "I forgot how hard you hit, old man." He grinned and dodged as Loch threw another lightning-fast punch at him.

Loch turned and met my eyes. Everything in me went still and tense at the naked desire in his gaze. My body responded, tightening as lust blazed through my system. He tilted his head in silent invitation and I nodded once.

"Which way to a spare room for me to clean up?" Loch asked.

Rhys grinned and rolled his eyes. "Go up a level and pick whichever room you want," he said.

Loch strode over and offered his hand to me. He stood still, a conquering warrior waiting for his lady's favor. His scorching gaze locked on my face. Tingles spread throughout my body even before I slid my hand into his. He pulled me to my feet with effortless strength and the arousal I'd been feeling all day ignited into burning desire.

Loch took the stairs two at a time. I laughed and kept pace, driven by the same urgency. Once upstairs, he stopped

222

at the first door on the right and clicked on the light to reveal a bedroom in shades of blue. He stepped inside and closed the door behind us. He backed away a few steps, leaving me next to the exit.

"If you stay in this room, we're going to fuck," he said plainly. "If that's not what you want, you should leave now."

He was asking for consent and doing it without trying to coerce me. He might not know how to escort a lady to dinner or which fork to use for salad, but at his core he was more of a gentleman than a good chunk of the Consortium.

So long as I remembered it was *just sex,* I would be fine. My body throbbed in need. Opportunities for what I hoped would be mind-blowing sex didn't happen every day, so I would guard my heart and have a night of fun. Tomorrow he would be gone and I'd go back to being alone. I refused to dwell on why that made my heart ache.

"I'm staying," I said quietly.

"Are you sure, Ada?" he asked again, seeking confirmation. The rumble of his deep, gravelly voice sent a little frisson of lust through my system. I shifted restlessly. "Yes," I said. "Yes, I am."

He stepped close and pressed me against the door. "Good choice," he murmured against my neck. My whole body came to attention. He smelled like warm, sweaty male, but under that was the musty, metallic scent of blood. Conquering warrior or not, the blood had to go.

"You really do need to clean up first," I said. "But if you ask me nicely, I'll wash your back."

Loch groaned. "You're going to kill me, darling," he said. "Hold on." He hooked my legs around his waist then picked me up with strong hands under my ass. He carried me to the en suite bathroom. He set me down and turned to start the shower. "Get naked," he said over his shoulder, "unless you don't like those clothes and want me to help."

I shucked my clothes with economical motions, but from Loch's expression you'd think I was performing a striptease. Anticipation tightened my stomach. It had taken a number of years, but these days I was comfortable in my own skin. I knew that I was slender and toned, and if my breasts were on the small side, well, they went with my body.

Then Loch dropped his pants and it was my turn to ogle him. His jutting erection was an obvious clue to his state of arousal, but it was his smoldering stare that had me crossing the room to kiss him.

His mouth fused to mine and the hot, hard length of him pressed into my belly. "Shower," I growled, "now."

We fumbled into the shower stall, and I sighed in bliss at the cascade of warm water from every direction. Trust Rhys to have guest room showers with more heads than any one person could ever need.

I ran my hand under the soap dispenser then smoothed it over Loch's chest, grazing his nipple. He sucked in air. I liked that reaction, so I repeated the motion on the other side. His hands clenched on my waist.

I washed away the blood from his chest and back, and made note of the cuts and bruises, checking to ensure nothing needed immediate attention. He would be bruised to hell in the morning, but nothing looked serious. "You'll live," I told him.

"Not if you keep this up," he muttered. "Turn around."

I turned and he pulled me back against his chest. His left hand flattened on my lower belly to hold me in place while the other glided across my chest with soapy slickness. He circled both breasts while ignoring my nipples. I whimpered and ground back against him.

His right hand slid down my front while his left traveled upward. He glided a finger over my clit at the same time he pinched my left nipple and that was all it took. I'd been on edge for so long that I fell into the orgasm without any warning.

I moaned and shivered as he held me through it. Then he scooped me up, turned off the shower, and headed for the bedroom. I clung to his neck when he would've dropped me on the bed. "Not the bedspread!" I said.

He snarled and ripped the bedspread and part of the sheets off of the bed then dropped me in the middle of the remaining mess. I didn't mind. He climbed over me, all bronzed flesh and wicked intent. He claimed my mouth in a fierce kiss and I moaned as I sucked on his tongue.

I spread my legs in welcome and reached down to caress him once, twice. He groaned, his eyes glowed, and then nothing mattered except where our two bodies met. He rubbed against me, then slid inside, centimeter by delicious centimeter. He was big and he hit nerves I didn't even know I had. I flexed around him and he slammed forward with a growl.

I wrapped my legs around him and tried to press closer. He retreated then slid back with a measured stroke. Another and another until he hit somewhere that caused stars to explode behind my eyes. "Yes," I hissed. "Do that."

As if my words had unleashed him, he drove into me with

abandon. Every stroke wound me tighter until I was clutching at his back just to stay anchored.

"Ada, what do you need?" he demanded.

"I don't know," I whined. I slid a hand between our bodies and ghosted a finger over my still-sensitive clit. Close, but not quite there. I whimpered.

Loch bent down and told me all of the things he wanted to do to me next. Between his filthy language and his guttural voice, he sent me sailing over the edge screaming his name.

He groaned against my throat and his thrusts became hard and erratic until he collapsed on me, breathing hard.

"So, that was marvelous," I said once I could talk.

"That was just round one, sweetheart," Loch said with a grin that threatened my guarded heart. "It only gets better from here."

He proved himself right.

# CHAPTER 17

**B**etween rounds two and three I'd sent Loch to check on Veronica. I hadn't exactly asked when she wanted to leave, so I'd needed to know if we should go so she could get back to Lin. He'd come back with an amused expression and told me that she would be fine until morning or perhaps late afternoon.

Now, in the light of day, I saw what he meant. She looked like she hadn't gotten any more sleep than I had, which wouldn't be too suspicious, except she had a bad case of stubble-burn reddening her jaw and down her neck. That plus the cat-that-got-the-cream expression led me to believe she and Rhys had had an interesting night of their own.

I caught her eye, tipped my head toward Rhys, who was deep in conversation with Marcus, and raised an eyebrow. She blushed then grinned. "And I told him who I am," she whispered, "so you don't have to call me Yasmin anymore. You and Loch?" She raised her own eyebrow. I nodded and grinned, though in truth, I was uneasy.

The sex had been beyond amazing, but I'd expected Loch to be gone when I woke. When he wasn't, Rhys's warning had come back to me with a vengeance. One-night stands I was comfortable with, relationships I was not. It was a lesson I'd learned the hard way during my first season.

At seventeen I'd been allowed to join the adult Consortium events for the first time. James had been a decade older and handsome as sin. He was from a small house of no importance, but he showered me with the attention and affection that I secretly craved. I'd thought myself in love.

My parents refused to let me see him, which only made him more tempting. He wooed me with all the skill and cunning of an apex predator. He was my first, and it was only thanks to my older sisters that I didn't end up pregnant—they had taken me to get a birth control implant a month before my debut.

No one could deter me from James, and when he asked me to marry him, it was the happiest day of my life. I accepted and broke the news to Father. Father laughed until he saw I was serious, then he told me that I was free to marry "that bounder" but that I would be cut from the House if I did. I didn't care—it was true love.

James had a different reaction. I told him that Father would disown me if we married, but I would sacrifice my House for him. I'll never forget his sneer and his response: "You are worthless to me without your name. I can't believe I wasted months on you." Then he turned and walked away, just like that. At the very next event he had showered attention on Elizabeth Rockhurst while the Consortium ladies twittered behind their fans at "that poor von Hasenberg girl."

It wasn't until years later that I realized exactly how lucky I'd been, but by then the damage was done. I'd become just as cynical and jaded as the rest of the Consortium, especially about relationships, which I avoided like the plague.

But no matter how cynical I became, I couldn't escape my younger self, the girl who just wanted someone to love me for myself and not because I was a daughter of High House von Hasenberg. It was a personal failing, so I armored over the weakness and kept people at arm's distance. If I didn't give them an opening, then they couldn't use me.

Loch's continued presence was a gigantic opening. Why would he decide to stick around? Did he realize how vulnerable I was to him? Doubts assailed me.

But while my mind had concerns, my body had no such qualms. Loch brushed a casual kiss across my mouth on the way to the dining room and I nearly hummed in pleasure. This was bad, so very bad.

Rhys fed us breakfast, and it was over delicate crepes that my com exploded with messages from all of my sisters. I read the first one and my heart sank. House Rockhurst was now overtly threatening war over my broken non-engagement and demanding my dowry in exchange for peace. Father was having none of it because we didn't have any official agreements in place.

"What's wrong?" Loch asked.

"House Rockhurst is rattling their sabers at us and demanding my dowry, with or without me. And Father doubled my bounty in an 'excess of caution,' so I'm now worth more than some planets."

"What is so special about your dowry?" Veronica asked.

I opened my mouth to tell her I didn't know, then paused. Richard had demanded marriage when I'd talked to him on TSD Nine, too. I had meant to look into why he wanted my dowry, but I'd forgotten to do it. "That's a really good question," I said. Bianca, bless her completionist heart, had attached a list of what my dowry included. Money, land, ships, planets, and mineral rights were all included, mostly for planets I'd never heard of.

But one rang a bell: a tiny frozen planet in the heart of the Antlia sector. Hadn't I heard something about Rockhurst and that planet already? I pulled up the planet's info on my com but it was listed as barren. So why would Rockhurst want a frozen, barren planet?

I widened my search and found Rockhurst controlled several planets in that sector already. All were mining planets, but none listed what they were mining. That was unusual but not completely unheard of. It usually meant they were mining something they wanted to keep under the radar.

So, if they'd found a new resource, they wanted to corner the market before they released any info. And our planet threatened that monopoly. But what would be worth starting a war over?

None of the reasons I came up with made any sense, except one: faster FTL drives. If the resource needed to produce faster drives was only available in the Antlia sector, that would absolutely be worth war, or at least the threat of it.

"What's the fastest you've ever heard of an FTL drive being able to recharge?" I asked the table.

"I've heard rumors that Yamado's got it down to five hours and change for moderately sized ships," Rhys said.

"Five or six hours is what I've heard, too," Veronica said. "Why?"

I considered everyone at the table and how much I trusted them. I sighed. At least if they betrayed me, someone besides myself would know the secret. "Because the ship I stole from Richard can jump in an hour. I plotted it up to four jumps and they were all going to take an hour each."

Loch and Veronica looked only mildly surprised. They must've guessed we were jumping faster than normal from our travel time. Rhys, however, looked stunned.

"Do you know what this means?" he asked.

"Yeah, it means you're all likely to betray me and try to steal my ship," I said drily.

Rhys shot me a reproving glare. "It means you're sitting on a piece of information worth unimaginable wealth. Your father would drop the bounty in an instant in exchange for the ship. Yamado would grant you safe passage and set you up like a queen. And Rockhurst will kill to keep it a secret."

"I know," I said. "It's why I plan to leave today after I stock up on supplies. I've shut down communications and the trackers I've found are all short-range and dependent on the ship's communication array, but even so, it's not safe to stay in one place for too long. That's why I wanted Veronica to talk to you as soon as possible."

"Rhys and I talked last night," Veronica said. She almost managed it without a blush but faint color stained her cheeks when I grinned knowingly at her. "I still think joining you for a while is my best option. I know it will be dangerous, but if we're in a ship that can out-jump everything else out there, the danger should be manageable."

"That would be true if I planned to keep running, but if it comes to war then I can't. I might not care for Father or his policies, but I'm still a von Hasenberg. Plus, I do care about my siblings and want to be there for them."

"Could you bring me in as part of your Cabinet?" Veronica asked.

"I could," I said slowly, thinking it through, "but I would have very little power to protect you. I'm the fifth of six children. Father only cares about me insofar as what my marriage will gain him. But it is possible that I could make your safety and position a condition of giving up the ship."

Veronica nodded as if that settled it.

"However," I said, "I'm planning to go check out a hunch first. It'll take me deep into Rockhurst territory, very likely territory they don't want looked at."

"Why not have your father send someone?" Loch asked.

"Because we're already teetering on the brink of war. If one of our House ships goes and starts poking around it could be enough to start the fight. And, yes, I know Father could send someone more low-key, but he wouldn't—that's not how he rolls. I might be able to persuade Bianca to send someone to check it out on the sly, but by then I could've just gone myself."

I did not mention that it was possible we had a high-level spy in our House. I trusted them, but only so far. Either way, my concerns were valid. If Father thought Rockhurst was hiding something valuable, he'd send in a fleet and that would be that. And with as fast as *Polaris* jumped, I could be in and out before Rockhurst even knew I was in the area.

But I also wouldn't go without letting my sister Bianca know exactly what was happening—I wasn't stupid. If I didn't return in a few days, she would share the information with Father. And if anything changed while I was away, I trusted her judgment. If Father needed to know sooner, she would update him.

"If you are intent upon this madness, I will go with you," Rhys said.

I looked at him like he was crazy. "I'm trying to talk people *off* of my ship, not on it, you dummy."

Rhys shrugged. "War might be good for business in the short term, but it's bad for everyone eventually. And while you would get picked up immediately, I happen to be a well-respected businessman-slash-smuggler. People expect me to show up in strange places."

I rubbed my temples and prayed for patience. The hell of it was, he was right. Having him along would be better for me, but I tried not to use my friends like pawns, especially when it put them in danger.

"Plus, I'm dying to get a look at the ship," Rhys said with a grin.

"I'm in," Veronica said.

"Well, if you all are going to get yourselves killed, I'll go, too. You're going to need someone to bail you out. And I am quite looking forward to my next meeting with one particular Rockhurst," Loch said with a feral smile.

Pleasure and panic thrummed through my system. I couldn't decide if I was happy or terrified at the thought of Loch's continued presence. My mind was very much against it, but my heart danced in joy. I was in trouble.

I sighed. "You all need to think very carefully about what you're doing. We will be flying a stolen ship into a potential war zone where we are very much unwanted." Rhys started to protest and I cut him off. "Just take a few hours to think about it. Anyone who still wants to go can meet me at the ship at sunset. For now, I have to get back, assess what supplies I'll need to purchase, and update my sister."

VERONICA AND LOCH RETURNED TO THE SHIP WITH ME. Rhys promised he'd meet us at sunset. I half hoped he'd change his mind. I wasn't used to feeling responsible for anyone but myself and now I had a whole group of people counting on me.

I swept the bottom level of the ship for trackers and cleared the ones I found. Then I dove into the result of yesterday's diagnostic. The search with the new pattern for input had caught a couple more trackers deep in the ship's system software, but I assumed that *still* wasn't all of them. Richard was thorough, the jerk.

After I'd done as much as I could with the trackers, I started going through the ship's manifest, looking for anything that needed to be resupplied. Nothing was terribly low, but I would need to stock up on more real food if Veronica wanted to cook. Otherwise, more ammo was always a good thing. I sent an encrypted request to Rhys along with promise of payment.

Next, I tracked down Veronica and tried to get her to give me a list of food she wanted. She changed it so many times while I was standing there that we decided it would be best if she just came with me when I went shopping.

Loch was in the fitness room when I found him. He was throwing punches at a heavy bag. He'd removed his shirt and sweat beaded across his back. I got lost in the mesmerizing movement of his muscles.

"Did you need something or did you just come down to watch?" he asked without stopping or turning around.

I shook myself out of my daze. I didn't want to make things awkward between us. We would be stuck together on the ship for a few days while we checked out the Antlia system. I'd assumed last night was a one-time thing, but now that today hadn't brought farewell, I was unsure how to proceed.

"Veronica and I are going shopping," I said. "Do you need anything while we're out?"

"I'll go with you," Loch said.

"There's no nee—" I started.

"I will go with you," he said again. "That way I can pick up a few things, too."

I was pretty sure he was using that as a thin excuse just to keep an eye on us, but I let it go. "How long until you're ready?"

He shrugged on a shirt that clung to his damp chest and arms. *Yum.* "I'm ready now," he said. "Unless you keep looking at me like that."

Heat burned through my checks. So much for not making it awkward. "Veronica is waiting in the cargo bay," I said.

"Too bad," he said.

Too bad, indeed, but I made myself turn and head up to meet her.

SHOPPING TOOK MOST OF THE AFTERNOON. I BOUGHT enough supplies to last a month even if the food synth went down. It wasn't typical, but I felt better with the backup, especially with all the extra people on board.

After we returned to the ship, I wrote a lengthy message to Bianca. I laid out all of my suspicions about the FTL drive and the Antlia sector, as well as my exact plan. If something went wrong and I was captured or killed, House von Hasenberg had to know what happened. With Rockhurst threatening war, it was more than just my life on the line.

The sun had just kissed the horizon when the proximity alarm alerted me that someone approached the cargo door. I pulled up a visual and found Rhys standing with three sleds piled high with various boxes and bags.

"*Polaris,* scan the immediate surroundings for life-forms."

"One person detected in the cargo ramp quadrant," the ship responded.

He wasn't trying to smuggle someone else on board—I'd had enough of that, thanks—but he was bringing far more stuff than I expected. "Rhys is here," I announced over the ship's intercom. "I'm going to go let him in."

By the time I made it to the cargo hold, Marcus lounged against the wall next to the door. He looked relaxed on first glance, but something in the way he held himself spoke of hidden tension.

"You okay?" I asked.

He straightened. "I'm fine."

I refrained from rolling my eyes—barely—and opened the cargo door. Rhys ducked inside as soon as the door was high enough. He said, "Rumor has it that you're on-planet. I don't know if Richard is spreading it or if someone caught sight of you. Either way, it's time to go."

"Unless he wants to flush us out and catch us in orbit," Loch said darkly.

"It's possible," Rhys agreed. "We should be ready to jump as soon as we take off. We're close enough to the gate to request a jump point now and wait here until we make it through the queue."

"I'll request our jump after we secure the supplies. What *is* all of this?" I asked Rhys as he arranged his three sleds in the cargo bay.

"Just a few things I pulled together," he said. "My personal pack is on top," he waved a hand at a smallish rucksack, "the rest of this is for our journey. I brought the ammo you wanted, then decided if we were heading into hostile territory, we shouldn't go unprepared."

"Is there anything in there that I need to worry about blowing a hole in my ship?" I asked warily.

"*You* don't need to worry," Rhys said with a grin. "It's the other guys who need to worry."

"Fantastic," I muttered. "Well, lash it all down in case we need to make extreme evasive maneuvers, then go find yourself a bunk. Crew quarters are on the middle level." I remembered Lin. "And remember, *anything* you see on my ship is confidential." I let a hint of icy warning creep into my tone. "Do not break my trust."

Rhys lost his veneer of easygoing charm. He looked more like I remembered him from when we first met. He also looked more like Loch. "I owe you a great deal, Lady Ada," he said softly. "And I respect you in equal measure. I will not betray you or your secrets. But do not threaten me again."

I nodded once. "I apologize," I said. Hopefully when he saw Lin, he would understand my caution. "And you owe me nothing," I added. "Our debt has long been settled. If anything, I owe you."

"We will have to agree to disagree," Rhys said.

I'd tried before to tell Rhys he didn't owe me anything, but the man was nearly as stubborn as me. The first time I'd met him, I happened to be in the right place at the right time. I'd spent months tracking him down on a rumor that he had an inside line on Yamado's newest weapons. House von Hasenberg very much wanted to examine them but we hadn't been able to break into the supply chain. Even after I found him it took weeks of careful negotiation to set up an in-person meeting.

But Rhys, never content to do only *one* illegal activity, was also an expert forger. And it turns out that he'd forged documents for a person of interest to House von Hasenberg who had folded under questioning and given Rhys up. So while I was there undercover, trying to negotiate for the weapons, my own freaking House had raided his warehouse.

I wasn't about to trash months of work for a little forgery, plus by then I'd gotten to know Rhys enough to like and respect him. I broke cover and bailed his ass out of trouble. After that I funneled as much House business his way as I could, and when he talked about expanding his business, I gave him the loan the bank wouldn't.

In return, Rhys had never betrayed me, even after I left the House. He set up my new burner identities and forwarded me any info he had on where Father's security forces were searching. He repaid my loan with interest, which gave me a tidy little off-the-books profit. I trusted him almost as much as I trusted my sisters and that was no small thing.

Rhys grinned and the moment passed. His mask fell back into place, as seamless as my own. "Loch and I will take care of securing this stuff. You get us a jump point."

I mock saluted him then headed to the flight deck to do as he requested. If Richard did know we were here then it made sense to leave as soon as possible. Of course, turning on external communications could let any remaining trackers lead him straight to us. It was a risk, but one we'd have to take.

I brought the ship to flight readiness then requested a jump point in the Antlia sector near the supposedly empty von Hasenberg planet. Because it was so close to APD Nine, the gate was busy and we were deep in the queue. Even with the constant upgrades busy gates received, it would be at least two hours before we'd get our jump coordinates.

Two hours as sitting ducks.

I set the ship's computer to alert me as soon as we hit tenth in line, then returned to my quarters to change into workout clothes. Watching as we slowly crept through the queue would drive me crazy. I needed to burn off some energy.

I took my blasters just in case of trouble, then slid down the ladder to the fitness room. The room was empty so I cranked up the music and set a brutal pace on the treadmill. It took longer than usual, but I finally found the zen point where my body worked hard but my mind drifted freely.

With an entire ship of people counting on me, I needed to execute my plan flawlessly. First, I would check out the von Hasenberg planet. According to our records it didn't even have an outpost, so risk of discovery should be low. And if there was something there, then I'd know both sides were obfuscating the truth.

Once I'd ascertained that the records were correct, I'd head to the Rockhurst planets. The size of the mining operation would give me a good idea if I was on the right track about the planets being linked to faster FTL drives—if I was, they'd be stripping the planet bare as fast as possible.

Then I would have to reassure my sister I was alive and negotiate with Father—*Polaris* for my freedom.

I ran until my legs ached and my lungs sawed the air. Sweat dripped down my arms and soaked through my clothes. I increased the incline until I was sprinting uphill. My heart rate skyrocketed, and I felt my pulse pound through my body. I kept it up until I thought I'd collapse if I took another step, then I did another five minutes. When running was your best defense, you learned to run like hell.

By the time I was done with cooldown, my legs had picked up a fine tremble that I couldn't control. I wobbled as I stepped off the treadmill. It was only then that I realized I wasn't alone. Loch smoothly bench-pressed a bar loaded with weights. A quick calculation proved he was benching over 150 kilograms as easily as if it was the bar alone.

He could bench-press more than two of me without breaking a sweat. No wonder he had no trouble carting me around.

He racked the weight and sat up. "You done?" he asked.

"I should probably do some upper body work but I'm wiped," I said. "And I need to be able to climb back to the flight deck when the alarm goes off." Already the stairs were daunting.

Loch put the weights back and wiped down the bench.

"I'll follow you up." His expression went flat. "I need to get my bag out of your room, since I'm locked out."

Right, I'd locked him out after he was a jerk at our first meeting with Rhys and before we'd slept together. I rubbed a tired hand over my face. We needed to talk anyway. "Okay," I said.

The trip upstairs was slow but Loch didn't rush me or offer to help. I gripped the handrail with white knuckles but I didn't fall. I pressed a hand to the access panel and the door to my quarters slid open. Loch followed me in.

The door slid closed. I had already half turned to him when he grabbed me and spun me around. The blaster appeared in my hand without conscious thought. He casually knocked it aside then his tongue slid into my mouth and my thoughts scattered.

Several minutes later he pulled back. "If you're not going to shoot me," he said, "you might want to put the gun away."

Oh, this was bad. Bad, bad, bad. I took a large step away from him. He let me go but watched me with predatory stillness. I holstered the blaster, unnerved at how easily he had knocked it aside and distracted me. Even now my body burned for him.

"We need to talk," I said.

"That's never a good start."

"No, probably not," I said. I sighed. "I thought last night was the last time I'd see you," I said, opting for honesty. "I figured you would be gone this morning. I don't mean to offend"—I rushed on when I saw thunderclouds gathering in his expression—"it's what I expected. In fact, if I'd known you were planning to stick around, I might've made a different decision." I shook my head. The world ended in what-ifs and might-have-beens.

"You wouldn't have fucked me, is that what you're saying?" he growled, scowling.

"Yes. No. I don't know," I said. I shook my head in frustration. "I know how to have one-night stands. I don't know how to have a relationship. Relationships require a level of trust I've never felt comfortable with. As daughter of a High House, no matter how far down the hierarchy, I've always been seen as a means to an end rather than a real person."

His scowl deepened. "You think I fucked you because of your name?"

I hadn't, not at the time, but I hadn't been doing much thinking at all. "Did you not?" I challenged. I was a bastard for asking, but now that the possibility was there, I had to know. Tentative hope bloomed. Maybe he really had just seen Ada and not Lady von Hasenberg.

He turned away from me in an explosive move, a caged tiger with nowhere to escape. He turned back, furious. "You've tied my hands neatly, haven't you?" He continued without waiting for my answer, "Deny it and you'll think I'm lying. Agree and I'm an evil bastard."

My hope died. I wanted him to deny it, emphatically and unequivocally. He didn't and it *hurt*. He'd wormed his way under my skin, past my barriers. I liked him without meaning to—perhaps more than was wise.

"I should've seen this coming from a Consortium bitch," he continued with a sneer. "You only care about your precious House. I'm good enough to fuck but not good enough for anything else. Did you enjoy slumming it with the most wanted man in the 'verse? Because I didn't hear any complaints while my cock was inside of you."

Shock and hurt slapped me. My emotional shields snapped up and I retreated into my public persona. I lashed out, wanting to hurt him as much as he was hurting me. "I. Have. Had. Better," I said, enunciating each word with cold relish. It was a lie, of course, but he would never know. "Get your stuff and get the fuck off of my ship."

Loch went stone cold, his expression wiped clean. "I said I will go on this trip, and so I will. And I dare you to try to stop me, Lady von Hasenberg," he said, his voice soft with menace.

The title was a knife to the chest, and I only kept my expression placid through long practice. I very nearly picked up the gauntlet he'd thrown down. But if he didn't leave soon, I was going to break down in front of him, and I couldn't allow that to happen. "Very well. Retrieve your stuff and choose a new bunk on deck two."

Loch stalked into the bedroom and came out a few minutes later carrying his bag. He let himself out without a word or glance.

The world went watery, but I refused to let the tears fall.

# CHAPTER 18

We made the jump to Nu Antliae Dwarf Seven with no signs of Richard. Either he hadn't caught up to us on APD Zero or he was biding his time, waiting for me to appear in a less populated sector. If it was the latter, then I'd just handed him his golden opportunity.

To ease our transition back to Universal Time, Veronica cooked breakfast for dinner and announced it was ready over the intercom. I would've preferred to grab something from the synthesizer and retreat to my room, but I refused to hide.

I was the last to arrive and sat at the end of the table facing the door. The table was piled high with a platter of pancakes, a large frittata, and a bowl of fresh fruit. I'd told Veronica she didn't need to cook for everyone, but she said she enjoyed it—and I wasn't going to turn down real food if she felt like making it.

Loch was pleasant to everyone around him but ignored me as thoroughly as if my chair was empty. Veronica shot me a questioning look but I just shook my head slightly. I ate without tasting the food and retreated as soon as I could without looking like I was running away.

I allowed myself an hour's power nap, though I hardly slept, then I got to work. I would go to bed early tonight and by tomorrow my internal clock would once again match Universal Time.

Today would be long, though.

Because the Antlia sector was so sparsely populated, we had jumped in close to NAD Seven and by the time I made it to the flight deck, we were five minutes out from orbit. Scanners picked up no transmissions or signs of life.

The planet visible through the windows was larger than I expected, covered in white with sheer black cliffs breaking up the landscape. The ship confirmed the planet had atmosphere, but not one breathable by humans. It was close enough it could be terraformed, but no one had decided it was worth the trouble.

I settled us in a polar orbit and watched the planet slide beneath the window. The scanners kept searching but found nothing. Whatever it was that House Rockhurst wanted with this planet—if, indeed, this was the planet they wanted—our House hadn't found it.

Perhaps I was on a snipe hunt, chasing after a reason that wasn't a reason at all. Maybe House Rockhurst really was just upset that I'd thrown over their golden son, even if nothing had been made official. If they were willing to go to war over the marriage, I'd have to marry him, my own desires be damned.

I set the scanners and defense systems to alert me at the first sign of anything unusual. The FTL drive was ready to send us to our next destination, just as soon as we were finished with this one. The Rockhurst planets might orbit the next nearest star, but it was still several light-years away. That might make them next-door neighbors in space terms, but only because the scale of space was so mind-numbingly gigantic.

I dozed lightly, trying to snatch rest where I could. The *swish* of the flight deck door woke me some time later. A time check confirmed I'd been asleep for less than half an hour.

Rhys flopped into the navigator's chair slightly in front of me on the right. He watched the planet through the window, then spun around to face me. For all of his studied casualness, something in his posture alerted me that he wasn't as chill as he seemed.

"What's up?" I asked.

"Did you know that Loch and I were in the RCDF together?" he asked.

The Royal Consortium Defense Force was the combined military arm of the Consortium. While each House maintained its own fully operational military, those forces masqueraded as solely defensive units. The RCDF deployed when Consortium interests were threatened, even if it was just against a single House, because they were the only military units authorized for offensive maneuvers. But the RCDF would not intervene in wars between Houses.

"I didn't know," I said. "Loch refused to say how he knew you. He said I'd have to ask you." Burning curiosity warred with guilt—I desperately wanted to know more about Loch but I felt slightly dirty getting the information from Rhys instead.

"I'm not surprised," Rhys said. "It wasn't exactly the highlight of either of our lives."

I put two and two together and came up with seven. Still, I couldn't resist testing my theory. "You were at Fornax," I said. Another realization struck when he didn't deny it. "You're part of the missing squad."

Rhys nodded once. The world tilted, then snapped back into a strange new form. The Consortium blamed Marcus for the death of his commanding officers and the unit with him. But the bodies of his squad had never been recovered, supposedly burned to dust in a massive explosion.

"There were eight of us," Rhys said. "Loch was our squad leader. He bought our freedom with his."

I frowned at the phrasing. "What do you mean?"

Rhys's grin was sly. "You'll have to ask him."

"In that case, I'll go to my grave never knowing," I said. "He's decided I no longer exist. I'd have better luck questioning the door."

"You were both fine this morning. What happened?" he asked.

"I happened," I said with a sigh. "I freaked out because he appeared to be sticking around and my relationship experience thus far has been shit. He was too angry to understand my concerns, so we fought. And now I am persona non grata."

"Do you want him to stick around?" Rhys asked.

"Yes," I said, "and that's the problem. How do I know he's sticking around for me and not because I'm a von Hasenberg?"

"Loch can be as manipulative and conniving as they come," Rhys said. He held up a hand to prevent me from interrupting. "But he's also one of the most honorable men I know.

And honorable men don't take advantage of women, no matter what their name is." He paused and gave me a hard stare. "And honorable women don't pursue a relationship they have no intention of committing to. Get your head straight."

I nodded my understanding. "Thank you, Rhys."

"If you need an opening, ask him about the Genesis Project." He stood. "Tell him I told you to." With those cryptic words, he left.

I tried searching for anything related to the Genesis Project but we were too far from a net node to get live data, so I had to make do with the cache on the ship's computer. Nothing came up, but it was hard to target such a generic search term.

Rhys knew me well. The curiosity would eat me alive until I had to talk to Loch. It was a genius plan on Rhys's part, but I vowed to hold off as long as I could because he was also right that I needed to get my head straight.

A glance at the commander's console showed our orbit had covered 75 percent of the planet's surface. I decided to wait to jump until the ship scanned the final 25 percent. It was unlikely anything would be found, but if I didn't know for sure, I'd wonder about it later on.

I drifted in the realm between awake and asleep until the gentle beeping of the ship's alarm pulled me fully alert. The planet's entire surface had been scanned and no life-forms were found. No radio transmissions or signs of human settlement were found, either. As far as the ship was concerned, nothing man-made existed on this planet.

The feeling of defeat was unexpected. I'd known this planet was a long shot, but subconsciously I must've been hoping to find something that would allow me to stop here. Without that find, I had to move on to more dangerous waters and drag the rest of my passengers along with me.

The door slid open again and Lin's excited chatter entered with him. He went silent when he caught sight of the planet through the window. Veronica nudged him forward.

"I hope you don't mind," she said, "but this is his first space voyage. Rhys said we were over a planet, so I hoped it would be okay for Lin to look."

"Of course it's okay. I'm sorry, I should've offered. Lin, if you'd like to sit in the navigator's chair, I'll stream over the data we're getting from the planet."

He looked at me with wide eyes, then a grin split his face. He looked up to his mama for permission and she nodded solemnly at him. She smiled when he turned and raced to the chair. I duplicated my display on his console but locked him out of input.

Veronica came to stand on my left while Lin marveled at the console and window in turns. "How are you?" she asked quietly.

The simple, genuine concern almost unraveled me. "I've been better," I allowed. "But I've been worse, too."

"I know we are not close, but if you need to talk," she said, "I've been told I am a good listener."

"Thank you," I said. "Same thing goes for you. And if Loch bothers you or if you decide you're done with Rhys and he won't take a hint, definitely let me know."

Color rose on her face. "I don't think that is going to be a problem," she said. "I didn't expect to see Rhys again, but now that he's here . . ." She trailed off, her expression going warm and distant. She had it bad, but from the heated glances Rhys had been throwing her at dinner, he was in the same boat. Maybe she'd end up settling down after all.

While I continued on alone.

I turned back to my console to hide the pain I couldn't keep off of my face. I knew it was better that everyone was getting settled, especially if House von Hasenberg was going to war, but I envied her future.

Sensitive to my mood, Veronica called Lin away from the navigator's chair. "Time for bed, pumpkin," she said.

He cast one more awed glance out the window then moved to her side. "Thank you, Lady Ada, for letting me visit," he said in carefully formal tones.

"You are welcome to come back anytime," I said. "When we have more time, I can teach you about the various console displays."

Joy suffused his face, so bright I had to smile back. "Thank you!" he said. Veronica mouthed the same words then ushered Lin out of the flight deck.

I pulled up the list of reachable locations. Xi Antliae Dwarf Six, Rockhurst's closest planet in this sector, was first on the list. Two more Rockhurst planets and the gate completed the main list.

I could dig deeper to find planets without human occupation, but most of the time pilots never bothered unless they were specifically looking for a place to disappear or had a dire emergency. Most of those planets were unsettled because they were inhospitable to life.

I plotted our course to XAD Six, then, in an abundance of caution, plotted the continuing jump to the gate. I needed to be sure we would only be stuck in Rockhurst territory for a little over an hour.

A red warning flashed on-screen: *insufficient alcubium*. The second jump required a six-hour cooldown. I plotted a third jump. The same warning appeared and the third jump required a forty-eight-hour cooldown.

My pulse quickened. I'd never heard of alcubium, but it seemed to be responsible for the faster FTL jumps. Originally, I'd thought House Rockhurst was mining a resource needed to *manufacture* the faster FTL drives. But if alcubium was instead used on a per-jump basis, Rockhurst would absolutely go to war to corner the market on it.

I checked the ship's manifest, but alcubium was not listed. Did we not have any extra? I looked more closely, checking each line against what was normal. I found the most likely option buried deep in the engineering section: a hundred units of copper. It wasn't strange enough to raise flags, but with synthesizers on board, ships usually didn't carry raw minerals.

I would have to go down to the engine room and look for it, but for now I needed to see if I could disable the faster jump. If I could disable it *now*, I'd wait the six hours and save the fast jump until we needed to leave Rockhurst's territory. Plus, even if we had extra, Father's scientists would need as much alcubium as I could provide to figure out how the drive worked.

IT TOOK TWENTY MINUTES OF PERSISTENT POKING through the ship's various settings, but I finally figured out how to turn off the alcubium drive and rely on the standard FTL for our next jump. The cooldown had started after our previous jump, but even so, we had over four hours to wait until we could jump again.

I could've spent the time sleeping, but I was trying to be a little more productive. And it was possible I didn't want to be alone with only my thoughts for company.

I knew just enough about FTL drives and ship engines to get myself into trouble, so it was with some trepidation that I breached the maintenance tunnels. But the alcubium wasn't going to find itself and if I needed it resupplied in a hurry, I had to know how to do it.

The maintenance tunnels were narrow and warmer than the rest of the ship, but they were spotlessly clean and perfectly illuminated. I wondered if Richard had even used this ship before he came after me. Perhaps it had been kept in the *Santa Celestia*'s hangar to use as an escape ship. Or maybe Richard was testing it as a prototype. That would be best because if their entire fleet was already equipped with fast FTL drives, they would slaughter us if it came to war.

The maintenance tunnel ended in a ladder down and a crawl space that continued on. Luckily, I'd retrieved the smart glasses Veronica had procured for me on TSD Nine. "*Polaris,* show me a map of the ship and my current location."

The map overlaid the display of my glasses, automatically oriented in the direction I faced. The crawl space led to several life-support systems, but the ladder led down to the engine compartment. I waved the map away and slid down the ladder.

A couple meters farther on, the narrow tunnel widened into a workshop. Lined in cabinets with pristine plastech counters, it looked brand-new. Neither dirt nor grease had the audacity to cling to a single surface. A large industrial synthesizer took up most of the far wall, while a sizable lift platform in the floor could be raised through the doors in the ceiling to retrieve parts directly from the cargo bay overhead.

Two wide catwalks led toward the back of the ship, flanking the FTL drive. Ladders linked to catwalks above and below this main level, allowing all parts of the drive to be accessed. Mostly self-contained, FTL drives had very few parts that could be swapped while in space. But if something did go wrong, the whole damn thing had to be taken apart, so the walkways were a necessary evil.

Another wide tunnel led off to the main engine. Used to power the ship's life-support systems as well as the traditional propulsion, it, too, was a highly contained, redundantly backed-up system. Engine troubles were rare unless you got in a pissing contest with someone who shot holes in your hull. And then you generally had bigger problems.

So if I was going to hide a secret material needed for the FTL drive, where would I hide it? I spun around slowly, looking at all of the cabinets. The problem was that I had no idea how big a hundred units *was,* since the units weren't specified. It could be a spoonful or a roomful.

I decided to look for where it interfaced with the drive, because that would give me an idea of its size. "*Polaris,* show me the manual entry for alcubium replacement."

The technical document showed up on my glasses, complete with detailed diagrams. I tilted my head, trying to decipher what it was showing me.

"What are you doing?" Loch asked from behind me.

"Ah!" I spun and pressed a hand to my heart. I hadn't heard him at all, even on the metal floors, and he'd scared the bejeezus out of me. I breathed through the adrenaline spike. "I'm looking for the secret FTL drive," I said when I was sure my voice would be steady. "Did you need something?"

He looked the same, like we hadn't just stomped all over each other's feelings. He didn't even look any worse for wear, the bastard.

He shrugged. "Saw you come down here. Since we haven't jumped yet, I figured I'd see if the drive was damaged."

I stared at him for a few seconds, trying to see past my hurt and judge him fairly. He'd come this far. Maybe he would betray me the second the opportunity presented itself, but he deserved the truth, or at least part of it. "The drive seems to use a specific resource. Supposedly there are a hundred units stashed somewhere on board. I'm reading the manual, trying to find where it is, because we only have one fast jump left. That's why we haven't jumped, I'm waiting out a standard FTL cooldown."

"You want to be able to jump out of Rockhurst space quickly," he said.

I nodded and went back to the document. It seemed to be showing the right side of the FTL. I started down the catwalk, looking for anything that resembled the diagram. I found it about a quarter of the way down: a small, round hatch marked ALC with an inset handle. To access the hatch, the diagram indicated rotating the handle ninety degrees left and then pulling out a cylindrical container.

I read the rest of the instructions. The drive needed to be put in standby before the hatch would open and allow access to the alcubium. When I returned to the control panel in the workshop, Loch still lounged against the wall of the tunnel leading to the main part of the ship.

He didn't look threatening exactly, but there was something off about his stance. I still had both blasters and my necklace and cuff, so I pushed away the fear. If he tried to take me, he'd come out sorry.

I put the FTL drive in manual standby then returned to the alcubium hatch. I reread the instructions, then turned the hatch handle ninety degrees and pulled. An illuminated plastech cylinder a little less than a meter long slid from the hole. Nestled inside was a smaller cylinder filled less than a quarter with a glowing, viscous pink fluid.

That seemed ... bad.

"*Polaris,* is this stuff radioactive?"

"Minimal levels of radiation detected. Levels remain well below the safety threshold for humans."

Well, that was a relief. My nanobots could probably handle some radiation damage, as long as it wasn't extreme, but I didn't relish the thought of testing their capability.

I slid the alcubium container back into place and locked it in, then returned the FTL drive to active. Now I just had to find a meter-long tube of glowing pink liquid. No problem.

It took another consultation of the manual, but I finally found the locked cabinet where the spare containers were stored, in the wall across the catwalk from the hatch. It had room for ten cylinders, but currently held only one faintly glowing pink tube.

This setup, more than anything else I'd seen so far, indicated that this was a prototype ship. In a fully functional production model, the entire process would be automated. Either this was an early model and they'd moved to automation in newer models, or they were not as far along in production as I feared.

One thing was clear: if alcubium tubes were being manufactured on XAD Six or Seven, I had a duty to my House to try to secure as many as possible. Of course, if I got blown up in the process, that would be counterproductive, so I'd have to weigh the risks once I saw what sort of defense they had.

When I returned to the workshop, Loch still hadn't moved. I'd have to squeeze by him to return to the passenger section of the ship. "Did you need something else?" I asked from across the room. "Or did Rhys talk to you, tell you what he told me? I wasn't planning to ask you about it, if that's what has you worried."

He straightened and narrowed his eyes. "What did he say?"

"He said a lot of things, actually. *He* is still speaking to me." It was a mistake to expose the wound, but I couldn't help myself. "He was meddling, trying to use my curiosity against me." I waved a negligent hand. "He knows me too well."

That barb struck home. I watched Loch's expression turn furious before being wiped clean. "That fucker needs to keep his mouth shut and stay out of my business," he growled.

I sighed, abruptly bone-weary with the whole thing. "Look, I'm sorry about the things I said, and I'm sorry Rhys is meddling. If you want to talk about your past, I'm here. If not, that's fine, too. In a few more days we can each go our own way and that'll be that. Can we at least try to be civil until then?"

Loch's expression was inscrutable, but finally he nodded once.

"Thanks," I said. "Now I need to get back to the flight deck and see if this heap has any offensive ability before I decide to do something potentially stupid." I slid past him, careful not to touch. Loch followed me back to the passenger area, silent as a ghost.

It did not escape my notice that he had not apologized.

# CHAPTER 19

The deeper I dug into *Polaris*'s systems, the more I fell in love. House Rockhurst had spared no expense. Not only did it have the offensive and defensive prowess of a small corvette-class warship, but it also had exceptional stealth and cloaking ability.

I knew House von Hasenberg had ships that could match it—at least, if you took out the alcubium FTL drive—but I'd never captained one. It would be hard to turn *Polaris* over and let our scientists dismantle it. During negotiations, I would have to ensure that I received the ship back in perfect working order—or that I received an early prototype to match it. Father would *love* that.

I catnapped as I waited for the FTL drive to cool down. It was strange how quickly I'd gotten accustomed to fast jumps and how waiting six hours—a very short wait by conventional standards—was agony. It was no wonder House Rockhurst was willing to go to war to corner this market. They'd make enough money to *buy* the rest of the Houses.

Once the drive was nearly ready, I sent an announcement over the intercom. "We're getting ready to jump into Rockhurst space. We're going in cloaked, but things may get rocky. You have fifteen minutes to secure loose objects and yourself. I'll sound a warning at one minute. Let me know if you need more time."

I started a countdown on my com and went to check my quarters. Hopefully the ship's compensators would counteract any maneuvers we had to make, but it wasn't always guaranteed, especially if we had to fight. Nothing that I'd left out would take damage from falling, but I went ahead and put away my clothes and bag.

By the time I returned to the flight deck, Rhys and Loch were seated in the navigation and tactical stations, respectively. I dropped into the commander's station and clicked in the harness. The timer went off, and I sounded the one-minute alarm.

"You think we're going to hit trouble so soon?" Rhys asked.

"I hope not. I'm going to jump us a few hours out from XAD Six to give the FTL time to recharge before we get close enough for them to notice us. But if we run into a patrol it might get tricky. Better to be prepared."

I plotted our course then brought us into full stealth. The visual cloaking wouldn't hold through the FTL jump but the lack of external communications would. Full stealth hobbled our own ability to locate foreign ships, but it prevented our ship from sending out enough signals that anyone in the sector could spot us. Once I'd surveyed our exit point, I'd lower the stealth level enough to see who else was out there.

After waiting another minute to be sure no one needed extra time, I pressed the jump confirmation button. The lights flickered and my stomach dropped, just as it would on any conventional FTL jump. Interesting. The alcubium FTL must use a lot less of the ship's energy in order to be so smooth.

The ship lurched then punched back into normal space with a shudder that was in no way normal. Warnings flashed red across my screen. The FTL was critically overheated, so I put it into emergency shutdown and cooling. I dealt with the fallout from the various connected systems as fast as I could. We skated a hairsbreadth from catastrophic system failure.

My hands shook as the warnings dwindled, then disappeared. We'd made it.

*We'd made it.*

"What was that?" Rhys asked.

"Conventional jump with the FTL. Even though the system said it was good to go, once we jumped, the drive overheated." I headed off his next question. "I have no idea why, but I intend to find out."

"Are we dead in the water?" Loch asked.

I shook my head. "Not totally. The main engine wasn't damaged and I shut the FTL down before it took damage. But I have no idea how long the FTL drive will need to cool before it's ready to jump again, even if we add back the alcubium."

"The what?" Rhys asked.

The jump had shaken me to the point where I wasn't watching my words. "Alcubium seems to be the element that allows the FTL to jump faster than normal. I suspect Rockhurst is mining it on the planet we're going to check out."

I watched him make the mental connections. "If they own the drives and the resource that powers them, they'll be unstoppable," Rhys said.

"Yes. They'll certainly outfit their military ships first, once they scale it up. They can jump in, attack, and jump out before our reinforcements can arrive. It'll be the fall of House von Hasenberg and likely House Yamado. It may already be too late to stop them, but I have to try."

"The Consortium may be far from perfect, but I'd take it over a single House dictatorship any day," Rhys said.

I turned back to my console. "Let's see who else is out there," I said. I tweaked our stealth level so the scanners could check surrounding space. When the results started streaming in, I frowned at the screen and tweaked the settings again.

"What's wrong?" Rhys asked.

"I'm picking up a whole lot of empty space," I said. "Getting faint signals from the planet, but nothing in orbit or in a wider patrol."

"A trap?" Loch asked, finally joining the conversation.

"Possibly. Or I'm completely wrong about the importance of this planet."

"Or Rockhurst doesn't want to call undue attention to their little project by having a flotilla guarding it," Rhys said.

I rubbed my face, feeling the weight of responsibility and divided loyalties. I had a kid on board, but that kid would have a shitty future if Rockhurst steamrolled the other Houses, not to mention most of my siblings would be on the front lines if it came to war, the first to die.

And, more selfishly, if I found enough information, I

could bargain with Father for the freedom to choose my own path in life.

"I have to get a closer look," I said finally, "trap or not. But first the FTL must be functional. After the emergency shutdown, I'll have to go down and manually start it up again."

"Loch and I can handle that," Rhys said. Loch didn't seem super enthused to be volunteered, but he didn't disagree.

"Thanks. While you do that, I'll go through the logs and see if I can figure out what happened."

They left and I dove into the diagnostics. It took a bit of backtracking but I finally found the root of the problem: the drive had been much too hot at the beginning of the jump. Turning off the alcubium had also turned off some sort of accelerated cooling.

Adding alcubium made the drive operate at a higher temperature but with better cooling. And because the engineers who built the ship had bolted the alcubium on a standard FTL, the safety coding was a mess—the fail-safes hadn't caught the fact that the drive was too hot for a standard jump because it was within spec for an alcubium-boosted jump.

I disabled the six-hour jump. Conventional jumps would have to wait the full two days for the drive to cool sufficiently. Until the safety coding was fixed, we'd be taking conventional jumps slowly. It was overly cautious, but we'd come close enough to disaster that I didn't want to risk it a second time.

After Rhys and Loch went through the manual startup for the FTL, I enabled the alcubium again to help bring the drive temperature down. Plotting a jump course showed a fifty-five-minute cooldown. With the alcubium once again in use, I had to believe it was within spec. If I started doubting every command, I'd drive myself crazy.

We were three hours out from XAD Six and still flying stealthed. I set us on a course that would put us into orbit if I didn't alter it, set the sensors to maximum sensitivity, then went to grab a snack.

Veronica sat facing the door, staring into a steaming mug, when I entered the mess hall. Lin and Imma sat across from her. Lin was talking a mile a minute between bites of a grilled cheese sandwich, but Veronica's smile was wan.

I waved her over, and Lin turned around when she stood up. "Lady Ada!" he said.

"Hello, Lord Lin," I said. "Is that grilled cheese? Grilled cheese is my favorite."

He beamed at me. "It's my favorite, too!"

"Don't talk with your mouth full," Imma said gently. "And finish your lunch." Lin pouted but turned back to his food without complaint. It was clear Imma adored the kid and Lin returned her affection.

I led Veronica over to the galley to give us a bit of privacy. "You okay?" I asked quietly.

"Yeah," she said. "Just trying to revert to Universal. Lin barely slept, so we're all tired." She waved her mug. "Caffeine helps."

So did adrenaline, but I didn't think she'd appreciate the option. "You're welcome on the flight deck, you know. Rhys and Loch were up there."

"If we're going to be blown out of the sky, I'd rather not know in advance," she said with another wan smile.

"I hope it doesn't come to that, but we are going to have to get closer. Looks empty, but it could be a trap."

"I knew it was dangerous when I decided to come along. Imma and I are both armed. We won't go quietly."

I pulled an orange out of the fridge and peeled it slowly. The bright citrus scent lifted my mood and steadied my resolve. "None of us will go quietly. I'll get you out," I said, "whatever the cost."

She met my eyes. "Don't forget to get yourself out, too."

"Of course," I said easily. I popped the last piece of orange into my mouth before she could question me again. I waved goodbye to Lin and returned to the flight deck. Rhys and Loch were back in their seats. Rhys studied the navigation console.

"You're taking us into orbit?" he asked.

"Probably not, but it was easy to plot. If the surroundings remain empty, I'm headed for the surface. If we meet a fleet of warships, I'm going to run like hell."

I kept us cloaked and in stealth as we approached the planet. The sensors didn't detect any other ships, but they were picking up various signals from the surface. Once we were in range, I scanned the surface. XAD Six was just as frozen as the von Hasenberg planet we'd left, but it teemed with radio activity.

"There's a lot of something going on down there," Rhys said, looking at the sensor data.

"Yes. Most of it seems to originate from a single point, at least on this side of the planet. Let me see if I can get a visual." I pointed the ship's long-range cameras at the most likely origination point for the signals. I piped the resulting images to the flight deck's video screens.

A large spaceport surrounded by white landscape came into view. A single squat building sat off to one side.

"They're underground," Loch said.

"Of course they are," I muttered. Infiltrating a warehouse on the surface wasn't terribly difficult; infiltrating an unknown underground facility *was*.

"They didn't bother to terraform the planet," Rhys said. "If they're mining, they'll be underground anyway. Makes sense to just put all their buildings there."

"I would've preferred an obvious, unguarded pile of alcubium sitting out in the open," I said.

"Where's the fun in that?" Loch drawled.

Rhys grinned at him. "I have to agree."

I huffed out a laugh. "I'm glad you feel that way because if our path remains clear, we'll be planetside in a little under an hour. Rhys, I don't suppose you brought anything useful for this, did you?"

"Why, Lady Ada, I thought you'd never ask!" he said with a melodramatic flourish. He sobered. "I didn't pack rebreathers or space suits, though. Didn't think we'd be visiting an unterraformed planet."

"The ship has plenty of suits," Loch said. "Found them when I went looking for clothes."

"I need a codebreaker to get me through the door and something to keep me alive on the other side. And, ideally, a distraction to let me slip back out again."

"You seem to be under the mistaken impression that you're going in alone," Rhys said.

"It's not a mistake," I said sweetly, "I *am* going in alone."

"The hell you are," Loch said.

"I need you two to keep the ship secure and make sure I have a way out. In the event that I'm caught, I want you to promise to take the ship to Father. My sister Bianca knows all about this trip and she will let Father know if I don't check in. He'll expect you," I said. It was as much threat as warning. "I don't care how much you bend him over a barrel in negotiations, but the House von Hasenberg scientists and engineers need this ship."

"All the more reason for me and Loch to enter the building while you stay with the ship," Rhys argued.

"I agreed to bring you along. I didn't agree to let you risk your neck more than necessary. If I am caught, they will keep me alive and eventually I'll escape or be traded back to the House. If they catch you, they'll kill you."

"But—"

"No buts. My ship, my rules. If you no longer wish to supply me with gear, I won't hold it against you."

"Of course I'm still going to give you gear!" Rhys exploded. "Damn, woman, you'd try the patience of a saint. I don't know how you deal with her," he said to Loch.

We all froze for an instant as his words sank in. "He doesn't," I quipped lightly, as if the knife-sharp pain in my chest didn't exist. "I'm going to get suited up."

"Ada—" Rhys started, but I ignored him and fled the flight deck.

DESPITE MY PROTESTS THAT IT WASN'T NECESSARY, both Rhys and Loch donned space suits. They pointed out that if they had to fight outside the ship, they needed to be prepared. And we'd be able to communicate over the headset radio.

I knew a losing argument when I saw one, so I capitulated as gracefully as I could.

These space suits were top-of-the-line models, designed to be worn next to the skin. The fabric was millimeter-thin but strong enough to deflect small physical projectiles. Even the gloves didn't dull tactile sensation.

I could move as easily as if I wore workout clothes, but the suit lacked any pockets. Luckily, it was thin enough I could wear it as a base layer under normal clothes. I pulled on a pair of cargo pants and a long-sleeved T-shirt. The extra layer also helped to hide some of the blinding white suit fabric.

I wondered if Richard had told the rest of his House that he'd lost this ship and everything in it. And, if so, if he'd survived the conversation. If I was him, I'd be waiting until the last possible second in hopes of recovering the ship before anyone noticed it went missing.

XAD Six loomed large in the window. It was nearly time to make a course correction if I wanted to enter the atmosphere and land at the spaceport. I checked the sensors. They still showed vast, empty space. Results also streamed in for XAD Seven, the other Rockhurst planet in this solar system, and it wasn't any better protected.

The lack of ships made me twitchy. I debated aborting and returning to House von Hasenberg with *Polaris*. There was enough alcubium that the scientists could at least get started, especially if I used conventional jumps all the way home.

But my reckless side, the side that had prompted me to run away from the only home I'd ever known rather than marry a practical stranger for political power, that side knew I would land on the planet. I had to know if my hunch was correct.

So I'd prepare for a trap and hope for the best. With Loch and Rhys on the ship and the FTL ready to go, they should be able to make it out either way. And if I could confirm Rockhurst mined alcubium here, they could take that info to Father along with the ship, even if I had to be left behind.

I turned to Rhys and Loch, both of whom had been subdued since Rhys's verbal slip. "I need you both to swear that if things get rough, you'll prioritize getting the ship to my father over rescuing me," I said.

"No," Rhys said flatly.

"You don't swear, we don't land. We don't land, House Rockhurst goes to war unimpeded and becomes your new dictator. You okay with that?"

"I'll do it," Loch said. The knife in my chest dug a little deeper, but I nodded.

"I need you to back him up," I told Rhys quietly. *I need you to make sure he doesn't double-cross me and steal my ship,* is what I didn't say. "Please."

Rhys stared hard at Loch. A wealth of nonverbal communication passed between them. Rhys sighed. "Very well," he said. "But if we leave you behind, your father is not going to appreciate the negotiation."

"I hope you all become wealthy beyond compare. Father can afford it. Don't forget to get a share for Veronica, too."

For a second, Rhys's charming mask slipped and his eyes flashed with fury. "How can you discuss being left behind so casually?"

"This is what I do." I paused. "Well, what I *did,* at any rate. Did you think I just sat around wearing pretty dresses and going to balls all the time? It doesn't work that way in a High House. I was groomed from birth to spy on my future husband, to infiltrate his deepest secrets and report back. And nothing teaches faster than experience."

I tamped down the memories. "I've been caught before. At some point, I'll be caught again. I know *exactly* what I'm risking." At best, a slap on the wrist and the humiliation of being traded back to Father like chattel. At worst . . . well, there were things worse than death.

Rhys stared me down but I didn't flinch. "Okay," he said at last, "then let's discuss the plan. Why do you want to land? You could jump from the upper atmosphere and parachute in. If we keep the ship stealthed, you might escape detection until you breached the facility."

I shuddered. I wasn't afraid of heights. I'd been known to perform dangerous stunts at height just for the thrill. But I'd never enjoyed skydiving. "If I jump out of this ship, it's only because it's on fire. And having the ship on the ground gives me a solid retreat option if I run into more trouble than I can handle," I said.

"If this is a trap, it also gives Rockhurst a solid target," Loch said. "We'll be sitting ducks."

"You think he'll blow up a prototype ship when he has a chance to recover it?" I asked.

"If he's sure you're not on board? Yeah, I think he'll blow us up and not bat an eye," he said. If I didn't know better, I'd think he was arguing just for the sake of arguing.

"Fine," I said, addressing both men. "You can drop me off and return to orbit. We'll still be able to communicate and you can jump at the first sign of danger. In fact, if I find that this is the planet where they're mining alcubium, you can go ahead and jump to the gate. I'll find my own way back. I'll write down my demands from Father before I go—I'd appreciate it if you included them in the negotiations."

If anything, Loch looked *less* pleased by that option. I threw up my hands. "I'm done arguing. You will drop me off and return to orbit. If it's a trap, jump out at the first opportunity. If it's not, you can pick me up when I'm done poking around."

Neither Loch nor Rhys looked happy, but both nodded begrudgingly. I changed the flight plan to land us at the spaceport. The ship estimated arrival in twenty minutes.

"*Polaris*, make Rhys Sebastian and Marcus Loch temporary first officers," I said. The ship prompted them to confirm their identities and voice imprints. As temporary first officers, they would be able to pilot the ship but not add or remove crew—notably me. So they couldn't remove me from the captain's position and take us into safer space.

They also wouldn't be able to assign anyone else as captain, so Father would still need me in order to completely secure control over the ship. I hadn't sent my sister the ship's override codes and they were not codes I had used before. So if I died, Father would have to spend a great deal of time and effort cracking the codes by brute force. I decided it was an acceptable risk.

"Time to gear up," I said. "Rhys, let's see if that giant pile of stuff you brought is actually useful."

"I have the codebreaker you need," he said, "plus a few extra items that will come in handy."

I led the way down to the cargo bay. The flight got a little rougher as the ship entered the atmosphere, but the compensators on this ship were much better than those in the escape shuttle we'd landed on TSD Nine.

Rhys sorted through his gear while Loch leaned against the wall with crossed arms and a distant expression. His posture screamed disinterest, but his eyes were sharp. I could almost see the wheels turning in his head.

While Rhys dug, I typed out my ideal concessions from Father on my spare com. I doubted Rhys would be able to get them all, but even one or two would make my life easier. I sent the list to Rhys, hesitated, then sent it to Loch as well. There wasn't anything too surprising on the list and having a backup wasn't a bad idea.

At five minutes to touchdown, Rhys called me over. He handed me a backpack and started loading it and my cargo pockets with the gear he thought I'd need—a backup com, grenades, ammo, a stunstick, breaching charges, door stops, and small charges with remote detonators. Smaller items went in my pockets while the larger things like the breaching charges had to be in the backpack.

On the belt around my waist he clipped the codebreaker that would hopefully get me through the doors without need for the explosives. A pistol blaster went on my right hip with extra ammo clipped to the belt. A stun pistol went on my left hip. A long blaster with a beam that could be adjusted from shotgun to rifle strapped across the backpack with a quick-release buckle.

"And now, for the pièce de résistance," Rhys murmured. He pulled a silver disk the size of a hockey puck from a locking storage box.

"Is that what I think it is?" I said.

"It depends. Do you think this is the very latest prototype of von Hasenberg shielding technology?"

"How?" I whispered in awe. Realizing what I'd asked, I held up a hand. "Wait, I want to remain friends, so don't tell me." This prototype was so new I'd never seen one exactly like it. It was like the tech built into my cuff, only much more powerful. The last time I'd seen one, they were the size of a dinner plate, but the shape and markings were unmistakable.

"I've been told this will stop up to a dozen close-range blaster shots," Rhys said. "When it starts beeping and the light flashes red you know it's about to fail. You activate it by clicking the button in the middle. A long press deactivates it. It uses power while active even if it's not deflecting shots, so use it wisely." He attached it to the front of my belt.

The one-minute warning sounded. A storm of bees took flight throughout my system as adrenaline began flowing. "Thank you, Rhys. Take good care of my ship."

He nodded and pulled me into a hug. "Come back safe, Lady Ada," he murmured against my temple.

I moved to Loch. "I'm sorry we're not parting on better terms," I said. I drank him in with my eyes, aware that this could be the last time I'd ever see him. I let him see the regret and sadness, the longing and desire that I would never be brave enough to admit to aloud. "Look after everyone, okay?"

He could've been carved from ice and I would've received more acknowledgment. Okay, then.

I snapped on my helmet and my suit powered up. "Testing coms," I said.

Rhys already had his helmet on. "I hear you," he said.

"With the ship in stealth, you won't be able to communicate with me, but you should receive my signals. You don't need to respond unless I specifically ask for transmission confirmation. I'll leave my com open for as long as I can so you can monitor my progress."

Eventually Rockhurst troops on the ground would realize the outgoing transmission wasn't one of theirs and start listening in. When that happened, I'd have to shut it down or risk broadcasting my location and plans. I couldn't risk an active tracker or video feed for the same reason.

I waved to Rhys then sealed myself inside the docking bay airlock built into the side of *Polaris*'s cargo bay. This ship wasn't big enough to bother with an atmospheric containment field over the cargo bay door, so I couldn't open the cargo bay directly without admitting the foreign atmosphere.

The airlock hissed then the outer door opened. A short, steep ramp led down to the ground and I realized Rhys must've extended it. As soon as I was clear, the ship lifted into the sky and disappeared.

Loneliness tweaked my heart, but I shook it off and headed for the low bunker at the edge of the spaceport.

I had a job to do.

# CHAPTER 20

The bunker was larger than it appeared from a distance. The opening was nearly eight meters tall by ten meters wide. It was curtained from the outside air with the faint shimmer of an atmospheric field. Hopefully that meant the air inside the building was breathable and I wouldn't have to make my way through an airlock.

If anyone occupied this base, they likely knew I was here by now, since landing a ship was hard to miss, but the inside of the bunker was empty. Railings surrounded a wide, circular platform set into the floor with a control panel on the far side. If they had an industrial lift, they definitely transported large quantities of *something*.

A square room occupied the far back corner of the bunker. Solid concrete and concealed by a heavy, sealed door with a control pad on the wall, it probably contained the stairwell and elevator.

Time to see if Rhys's codebreaker was any good.

I attached the com-sized device to the door's control

panel and hit the override button. While not as rare as the prototype shield on my belt, codebreakers still were not easy to come by. Thirty seconds later, the door popped open with a *click*. I put away the codebreaker and unholstered a blaster.

"I'm heading inside," I murmured into the helmet's microphone. I didn't know if Rhys and Loch were still in range or if they'd already taken the ship and disappeared, but I wasn't going to ask them to drop stealth just to reassure me.

A quick peek revealed an empty room. A specialty airlock elevator took up the left half of the room and another heavy door lead to a stairwell on the right. The elevator had too many potential failure points. If the security forces overrode the commands from the codebreaker, I'd be trapped in a metal box.

I put a door stop on the room door. A piece of metal that clamped around the edge of the door, it prevented the door from closing and locking behind me. The part that touched the door was coated in an insta-weld compound that permanently secured it to the door.

The door stop would have to be cut off to be removed. Using them was kind of a dick move on an unterraformed planet, because if the atmospheric field fell, the intermediate doors wouldn't seal properly and would allow unbreathable air to seep inside.

I hoped the people inside practiced their contingency plans.

The codebreaker cracked the stairwell door's unlock code in ten seconds, which told me that either it was less secure than the previous door or their codes relied on a pattern that the breaker had picked up on.

I eased the door open. The landing was clear. Where *was* everyone? I put a door stop on the door then peeked over the side of the banister. The stairwell was square. The stairs hugged the wall, leaving a hole in the middle. It had to be at least ten stories down to the distant floor.

"Too bad I didn't bring rappelling gear. Would've made this faster," I muttered. I resigned myself to spiraling down the steps as quickly as possible. And I was not looking forward to hauling ass back up these steps.

There were no other exits on the way down. At the bottom, a closed door greeted me. It was on the same side of the stairwell as the door at the top, leading out under the rest of the bunker. The industrial lift should be just out and off to my left. The codebreaker made quick work of the lock.

I crouched down and barely cracked the door open to reveal a large, brightly lit warehouse. Farther in the distance, separated from the warehouse by a wall full of windows and a wide door, large tanks were connected to a production line with thick plastech pipes.

Nothing glowed pink.

And, more worryingly, the vast room waited in silence.

"I've found the warehouse entrance, but I haven't confirmed they're mining. Setup looks right, but no material is visible. And the whole place is dead. Watch your backs," I said softly.

I put a door stop on the door. No one moved in the warehouse and nothing disturbed the silence. The amount of radio traffic from this location was too high for it to be abandoned. So were they working in another section of the building or had they fled when they spotted me?

Or, perhaps, they were drawing me in, luring me deeper, until the trap sprang closed.

On this end of the room there were no hiding places. The warehouse was empty and from what I could see, there weren't any other rooms off of the main one. The production line room was another story. It had desks and lab tables scattered throughout, plus the low wall between the two rooms would allow an entire platoon to hide behind it.

"I'm going to check the next room. Be prepared to run," I said, still talking to people who might've already left me.

Either way, I needed to get a closer look at the production room, so I opened the door and sauntered out into the warehouse. The rubber soles of my boots squeaked against the hard floor and my pulse pounded in my ears.

Nothing moved and I slipped through the door into the production room without getting jumped. Based on the setup, this was a research area. I brought up the nearest console, but it was locked. Snooping in desks was easier than cracking passwords because scientists liked to jot down notes while they worked.

"I'm seeing references to the element," I said into my headset. "This planet is at least involved in the research."

I crept deeper into the production facility. A low hum from the tanks on my left caused me to freeze. Perhaps they weren't empty after all. I climbed the ladder of the nearest one. On the top, a circular observation window was covered by a sliding panel. I slid the panel aside to reveal a tank of glowing pink liquid.

Jackpot.

I whispered to Rhys and Loch, "They have vats of the element here. This is definitely—"

"Come down, Lady Ada. Slowly, if you please," Richard said from behind me.

I nearly fell off the tank in shock. I clutched the ladder and waited for my heart to steady.

"Richard is here—abort, abort now!" I whispered frantically while making enough noise on the ladder to cover my conversation. "Get out of the system!"

I clicked on the shield generator and palmed a flash-bang grenade in my left hand while I descended. Once on solid ground, I turned to face Richard. He was in a space suit, but he had removed his helmet. He was flanked by four guards still in full space suits. The fact that I hadn't heard them approach meant either I was losing my touch or they were using a silencer. I hoped it was the latter.

I pulled on my public persona like armor. "Hello, Richard," I said.

"My wayward fiancée returns," Richard said. "And you were kind enough to bring back my ship as a wedding present."

"Richard, we were never engaged," I said with exaggerated patience, as if explaining to a small child for the umpteenth time.

His mouth pressed into a flat line, but he recovered quickly. "Nevertheless, you will marry me. When you do, I'll let your friends go and even give them a shuttle to get back to populated space," he said. "Except for Loch. He's mine."

Because he hadn't included specifics when he mentioned my "friends," I doubted he had the ship. And even if he had, he wouldn't be offering to let them go so easily if he'd gotten a glimpse of Lin. So there was hope, however slim, that they had escaped. Now I had to focus on my own escape.

"I do not think Loch swings that way, Richard. And planning an affair so soon after our wedding?" I tutted and shook my head.

Richard took an abrupt, furious step toward me before he pulled himself together. I'd pushed him close to the end of his patience, so I double clicked the button on the end of the flash-bang grenade. A subtle vibration counted down the seconds.

"Drop your weapons, Lady Ada," Richard said.

"Why?"

"Because they'll stun you if you don't," Richard said, waving an arm at his guards.

"Not man enough to do it yourself?" I asked, as the grenade's pulsing sped up.

"For the love of—" Richard growled, but the grenade had reached constant vibration.

"Catch!" I yelled, launching the grenade at them and darting left, farther into the room. I heard the explosion behind me. It wouldn't cause much damage, even if he was stupid enough to catch it, but it bought me precious seconds.

I dodged through the desks and tables, trying to prevent the soldiers following me from getting a clear shot. I slammed through the doors at the end of the room into a wide hallway.

And my shield promptly took hits from multiple stun rounds. I shot both Rockhurst soldiers blocking the hall, but I could see another squad in the next room. I turned to go back the way I'd come, but Richard's soldiers were already there. The shield took more hits and started beeping a low-power warning. I fired back and they retreated through the doors.

I couldn't let House Rockhurst have our shielding technology. I'd left my cuff and necklace hidden in the ship for the same reason. Before the shield completely ran out of power, I clicked the middle button in a seemingly random pattern. Rhys hadn't mentioned it because he likely didn't know, but all House von Hasenberg advanced tech had self-destruct options built-in. A small vibration confirmed I'd gotten the code correct.

I now had ten seconds before the shield self-destructed. I had at least five people between me and the hangar and eight or more if I kept moving deeper into the facility. I decided retreat was the best option. I slung the long gun off of my back and set it to shotgun mode.

Time for shock and awe.

I hit the doors at a run and fired before I had a clear sight line. My firearms tutor would be extremely disappointed, but one of Richard's guards went down and another had been clipped. I fired again and missed, blowing a hole in a lab table. At least it made the remaining guards wary of leaving cover.

I kept firing, but, unfortunately, I was still badly outnumbered and no longer protected by the shield. A stun round narrowly missed me on the left. I swung the shotgun around and blasted the table the soldier was using for cover.

The shield's vibration pattern went steady at the same time Richard stuck his head up, so I unclipped it and threw it at him as hard as I could. The shield generator self-destructed midair in a burst of white-hot flames. I didn't get to enjoy the surprise on Richard's face for long because stun rounds hit me from two different directions.

I screamed as little bolts of agony licked through my

system, causing my muscles to contract and twitch. I caught a glimpse of soldiers in space suits as I fell. The world went distant, and I didn't feel the floor that rushed up to meet my helmeted face.

When I came back to myself, a blurry Richard stood over me. Someone had removed my helmet. I blinked to clear my vision, but it helped only marginally.

Blood caked the side of Richard's face from a cut over his eye. With the blood, his handsome face had taken a sinister turn. "It didn't have to be like this, Ada," he said. He sounded sincere.

"Then let me go," I gritted out.

"I'm afraid not," Richard said. "You know too much, as evidenced by your search. You must not be allowed to alert the other Houses before we are ready. So, you can marry me, save your friends, and live in relative comfort, or you can rot in a cell while your friends die. You have until *Santa Celestia* returns to decide. Take her to the holding cell."

I was lifted by two soldiers and placed on a stretcher. They strapped me down, then picked up the stretcher and moved deeper into the building. I tried to keep track of our movements, but the ceiling kept dipping and swirling in my vision.

I couldn't feel the backpack under me, so they must've stripped me of gear while I was out. On the bright side, they hadn't stripped my clothes. If I could find my helmet or another like it, I'd have a working space suit.

The soldiers maneuvered me through a doorway into a small room. They lowered the stretcher to the ground. The restraints loosened but didn't fall away completely, then the soldiers left. The door closed and locked behind them.

I forced my neck to work. It looked like I was in an office that had been stripped of furniture. There was a large window next to the door, and a helmeted guard faced me through the glass. Another guard faced out into the larger room.

So much for escaping unnoticed.

It was much more interesting that all of the soldiers I'd seen so far were wearing space suits. Either Richard expected me to blow the atmospheric field or he had only just arrived and they hadn't had time to change.

It took a few minutes, but I finally made my arms functional enough to pull the restraint strap off of my chest. I sat up with a groan. My abs trembled with the effort. I pulled the restraint from my legs and wobbled to my feet. I would need a few minutes of recovery before the ass-kicking started. I staggered to the window and tapped on the glass in front of the soldier facing me.

He did not react.

Looking past him, I could see a few more soldiers milling around in what appeared to be an office area. Desks sat in neat rows with a cleared space in the middle where a grouping of couches surrounded by a low wall made an informal meeting spot.

Richard stood next to one of the couches, close to another man who had also removed his helmet. The man nodded while Richard talked. By the deferential way he stood, even though he towered over Richard, he was likely the guard commander.

In fact, all of the guards were on the tall and bulky side— not a lanky guy or gal among them. My plan to play guard would go nowhere fast; they'd take one look at me and realize I wasn't one of them.

I turned around and leaned against the window to better assess the room. Solid plastech walls and ceiling meant I wasn't escaping unless I found a plasma cutter stashed conveniently nearby. I looked around, but the room failed to deliver. Even the air vent was a tiny rectangle that no human could fit through.

Richard had chosen my prison well.

My only chance of escape would be the window or when the soldiers entered the room to move me. And with a dozen guards standing outside the door, the chance of success rested at approximately zero.

It would help if I knew what Richard had planned for me. We were waiting for Richard's battle cruiser, the *Santa Celestia,* to return, which meant it wasn't here. Telling me that information was a slip on his part because it meant he had no backup except the soldiers with him. And while I worried that the *Santa Celestia* had followed Rhys to the gate, even if it had, space was vast and the stealth on the smaller, nimbler *Polaris* was second to none.

It meant that *Polaris* wasn't caught yet.

It also meant that I had two hours or so to escape, assuming the *Santa Celestia* jumped with an alcubium FTL. Escaping from Richard's ship would be orders of magnitude more difficult than escaping from this barely secured facility.

I just had to get out of this room.

I walked to the back wall. When that was successful, I paced back and forth. The soldier watching me didn't move his head, but I had the sense that he carefully tracked my movements nonetheless.

I had a stretcher, a glass window, and a locked door, plus a roomful of soldiers waiting outside. These were not the ideal circumstances for escape.

I kept pacing, stretching the muscles that had tensed into knots under the onslaught of the stun rounds. Once pacing no longer hurt, I boxed an invisible foe. My arms felt heavy and slow, but I kept at it until the muscles warmed and softened.

Richard walked out of sight, the commander trailing behind him. The rest of the guards stayed, though they lounged around more with their superiors gone. Plans flitted through my head, but I discarded them as fast as I thought them up. Richard had been thorough and I didn't have much to work with. Only one option presented itself and it was guaranteed to get me stunned again.

Yay.

With nothing to lose, I picked up the stretcher and slammed it into the window in one smooth motion. The handles penetrated the window and glass shattered into a million tiny pieces. I kept pushing, ramming the guard who watched me. Before the other guard could react, I'd caught him by the belt and pulled his blaster from the holster, using him as a human shield.

The room froze, as if they couldn't quite believe their eyes. I did not waste time. I'd hit three soldiers with incapacitating shots by the time they regrouped and took cover.

The guard I held tried to pull away. I jammed the blaster in his kidney. "Move and die," I said.

"You won't shoot your shield," he said. His voice came out muffled thanks to his helmet.

"Oh, but I will. I have this nice wall to hide behind. And

if you don't quit squirming, you'll see how serious I am." I jabbed him again with the gun.

"What the fuck is going on here?" Richard demanded. He walked into sight, his face furious.

The man should know better than to walk into a combat zone. But perhaps he hadn't heard the blaster shots, just the shouting.

"My lord, get—" an anonymous soldier tried to warn him.

I took a potshot at Richard. It went wide, but it forced him into cover. The guard in my grasp spun, trying to pull me off-balance. Instead, I let him go and shot him point-blank.

I mentally boxed up the revulsion caused by my actions. I would mourn him later. I would mourn them all. But for now, I was still trapped. A half-full blaster was the only thing standing between me and a stint aboard Richard's ship.

It would not be enough. I knew it even as Richard yelled for the soldiers with stun pistols to pin me down. Stun bolts slammed into both the wall I hid behind and the back wall of the room, sending sparks flying everywhere.

A quick glance out the window proved the guard commander was back and issuing silent orders via hand signals. The remaining soldiers fanned out. I jerked my head back as a barrage of blasts plowed into the wall.

There was no substantial cover between me and the soldiers. The second I went over the wall, they would stun me into next week. But the longer I stayed here, the more prepared they became.

"Richard," I yelled, "call your men off. I do not want to have to keep killing them."

"You have a single blaster and are trapped in that room.

Give up now and I won't let them beat you to death," he yelled back.

It wasn't a bad deal, all things considered, but if I was going down, I was going down in a blaze of glory. It might be a near-zero chance of success, but I'd been lucky before. Another glance showed me two soldiers on my left and three on my right. Both Richard and the commander were also on my left but they were now tucked out of sight. I pulled back before they shot at me again.

I took a deep breath, held it, then released it slowly as I mentally prepared myself to do something that I knew was going to hurt—*a lot.* Success rested on surprise and speed. Any hesitation due to fear of pain would guarantee failure.

I transferred the gun to my left hand. I wouldn't be able to shoot worth shit but I needed my right hand to help me vault the window ledge. Without stopping to think too much, I launched myself out of the window while shooting at the locations I'd last seen the guards.

I made it far enough that I began to hope.

Then the pain hit in vicious waves as stun bolts slammed into my sides and back. I think I must've screamed but the pain was so intense my brain shut down for an indeterminate amount of time.

I slowly came back to myself. Several people nearby cursed angrily in loud voices. My sides from my shoulders to my ankles throbbed with a deep, bruising pain. Maybe they had tried to beat me to death after all?

"Enough!" Richard shouted over the general ruckus. "Sedate her then scan her for internal injuries. I want her loaded up and ready to go as soon as the ship returns. I do *not* want her awake causing trouble. She is valuable to the House. The next person who hits her dies."

Something cool pressed against my neck with a short hiss. I didn't fight the fall into blissful oblivion.

# CHAPTER 21

I felt a hundred years old. My bones creaked as I rolled over and nearly fell out of the bed. I caught myself just in time, balancing precariously on my side in the narrow cot. Both my mouth and my head felt stuffed with cotton.

What the hell had happened?

It came back in bits and pieces. Richard had captured me; I'd become a liability to House von Hasenberg. *Fuck.* I only hoped Rhys and Loch had made it back to Father with *Polaris* so he would feel like rescuing my sorry ass.

I caught my balance and pushed myself up. The change in position sent shards of pain racing down my neck and back. I carefully tilted my head, working out the kinks. I felt like I'd gone a few rounds with my self-defense tutor on a particularly bad day.

My space suit was gone, as were my outer layers of clothes, but they'd left my undergarments on. The cot I sat on was not luxurious, exactly, but it had real sheets and blankets. I looked around. My room was rather large, as far as such cells went. It was wide enough that the cot spanned the back wall instead of the more usual location of lengthwise in the room. There was also a tiny, curtained-off en suite bathroom where I could shower and use the facilities in pretend privacy.

The cell walls were steel but they'd been painted a warm cream. A small white round table with two orange plastech chairs sat in the middle of the right half of the cell. The table was secured to the floor. The chairs' honeycomb construction meant they wouldn't have enough mass to be used as an effective weapon, so they were not bolted down.

My pants and shirt were folded neatly atop the table. If it wasn't for the door with no handle or control panel on this side, the room could be mistaken for a normal—if spartan— room on any ship. Richard was playing nice. I had no doubt that if I proved too uncooperative, my lodgings would deteriorate rapidly.

I pushed myself up and pulled on my clothes. I felt better with another barrier between me and the world. I sat on the edge of the cot and contemplated where my life had gone wrong. Perhaps it was when Lady Louisa had thrown mud on me at a Consortium event when we were six.

Or, more likely, when I had retaliated by making her *eat* mud.

How was I supposed to know she was heir to one of the lower houses? She was a bully and I'd put her in her place. Only, because I was the child of a High House, it looked to everyone else like *I* was the bully.

And clearly whatever they had given me to knock me out was not entirely out of my system. I tried to pull my thoughts into some semblance of order, with only mild success.

A short while later the room's only door opened and a soldier entered with a tray of food. He set it on the table without a word and left. The insistent growling of my stomach told me that more than a few hours had passed while I was unconscious. I got up to take a look. The food—waffles with fresh strawberries, eggs, and sausage—smelled divine.

It didn't make sense to keep me alive just to poison me with food, so I shrugged and dug in. Besides, Richard knew I had House-level nanobots that would take care of most toxins. Unless House Rockhurst had cooked up some radical new poison, I would be okay. And while a hunger strike might make a nice political statement, hunger led to weakness, which meant a smaller chance of escape.

I could be practical when it suited me.

Once I'd finished with the meal, I rebuilt the walls of my public persona. It was an act I'd have to carry off for weeks or months, potentially. I hadn't had to be *on* that much since I'd left home. And like a muscle, my ability to maintain the illusion for long periods had atrophied. Hopefully I wouldn't be forced to endure Richard for more than a couple hours a day.

As if summoned by my thoughts, Richard waltzed into the room without warning. A different guard followed him. The guard took my tray and disappeared. Richard sat across from me.

"Ada," he said, "I'm glad to see you're awake. My soldiers got a little . . . *overzealous* in their anger. You've been unconscious for over sixteen hours."

That explained the breakfast food. I'd lost almost an entire day. I smiled politely. "Thank you for your concern," I said. "I feel much better."

"Are you ready to discuss our upcoming nuptials? Or would you prefer to be moved into the general holding cells while I purge your friends?" he asked, almost casually.

I wasn't sure why he still wanted the marriage. If it was for my dowry, he had to know that House von Hasenberg would not turn it over so easily in light of the new information. But perhaps he didn't know I had worked out the details of the FTL drives.

Or my information was bad, which was far worse for me.

"Very well," I said, "we may discuss it. What is your offer?"

"We marry. Your friends live. You'll be inducted into House Rockhurst. You will prove your loyalty to the House by sharing everything you know about von Hasenberg shielding technology, as well as any other advanced technology. You will then continue to spy on House von Hasenberg as a sign of your ongoing allegiance to our marriage."

I kept my expression placid when I would've liked to tell him where he could shove his proposal. "Will the marriage require consummation?" I asked.

His eyes darkened and his gaze raked down my body. "Yes. I expect you to provide me with several heirs."

I raised an eyebrow. "Is that a part of the agreement? What if I am barren?"

"Are you?"

"I do not have any children, so all available evidence points to yes." That and very good birth control. "How many times will you require sexual intercourse per month?"

"Per month?" he scoffed. "We'll fuck as often as I desire."

I pursed my mouth. "I do not think so. Once per month until I am pregnant, then zero until the baby is born. One year after birth or miscarriage we will resume at once per month until the agreed-upon number of heirs has been produced."

He laughed in my face. I tilted my chin up slightly and hit him with Mother's stare. He went red. He said, "You seem to have the mistaken idea that you have any leverage. You will accept my terms. You should be grateful I'm willing to give you your friends' lives."

"And you seem to forget that you need me to willingly sign my life away before I become your wife. My life does not come cheap. If you are not prepared to pay the price, perhaps we should cease negotiations now."

"I could purge your friends right now," he snarled.

"Could you, though?" I asked thoughtfully. He still had made no mention of Lin or Veronica, or named any of my friends other than Loch. "I want proof of life. And while we are discussing things we *could* do, I sent my House a detailed plan of where I was headed and what my suspicions were, both about the planet and the alcubium FTL drive."

I smiled at him. "If I do not contact them in four days' time, with my personal encryption codes, they will assume I have perished at Rockhurst hands. Father will launch an attack on House Rockhurst. I do not believe your House is ready for war, so it is in House von Hasenberg's best interest for me to do nothing."

He recovered quickly, but not quickly enough. His flinch led me to believe I was on the right track with the importance these planets had to their new drives. "I could get the codes from you," he tossed out idly, as if torturing me was of no more importance than the day's weather.

I let arctic ice frost my expression. "No, you could not," I promised softly. I let the words hang in silence for a few seconds, then continued, "If all you bring are threats and demands with no willingness to compromise, you can leave. We will not find a mutually acceptable solution today. Come back tomorrow and we will try again."

He exploded out of his chair. "I will not be ordered around on my own ship!" He got in my face. "We will marry in the next three days or your friends will fucking die. Then I will personally hunt down your siblings one by one."

White-hot rage burned through my veins at the threat to my friends and family but I kept my expression serene. "Your crude language is unbecoming. Until tomorrow, Richard," I said. I turned my chair away from the table, effectively giving him my back. I wanted him off-balance, but I had to be careful that I didn't push him into rash action. Of course, if he completely lost his head then it would be an opportunity for me.

"I will enjoy destroying that ice shell you wear like a shield," Richard said.

I still had trouble believing that this cold, cruel man was the same person I'd played with as a child. He had invited me to play with the older kids at Consortium events, even though I was two years younger. He had been my hero.

In fact, it was because of that early friendship that our parents had started discussing marriage in the first place. It was supposed to ease the tension between our Houses.

Friends were liabilities to a member of a High House. They could be used against you, as Richard was so aptly demonstrating. As we grew out of childhood, perhaps someone in House Rockhurst thought Richard and I were getting too close or maybe I was deemed a bad influence, but whatever the reason, Richard disappeared from Consortium events for nearly four years.

He returned when I was in my early teens, but he'd changed. He was colder and he seemed to have no time for me. The flame I'd carried for him faded and winked out completely during that season. As the years wore on and stories of the *Santa Celestia*'s exploits came in, my feelings morphed into distaste and finally disgust.

Our marriage talks were not called off, even though I pleaded with Father. Left with no other choice, I had fled what I knew would be a horrible match. Unfortunately, my actions did not improve relations between our Houses.

I glanced over my shoulder and met Richard's eyes. "What happened to you, Richard?" I asked gently.

His face shuttered completely. Oh yes, there was definitely something there worth exploring. Today wouldn't be the day, though, because he swept out of the room without a word.

Without a clock it was impossible to know the time and trying to figure it out would slowly drive me insane. I stood and stretched. I still felt like I'd been used as a human punching bag. And, from Richard's words, I had.

I moved the chairs against the wall. The table was on the right side of the cell, leaving a clear path from the door to the cot. That gave me just enough space to lie on the floor if I wanted to do push-ups. Which I did *not*.

But I did want to go through a slow movement-based meditation routine. It would waste time while also gently working my muscles. I'd asked a lot of my body over the last few days, especially with the lack of sleep. Thanks to my forced nap, sleep was no longer a problem, but another day of rest would do me good.

And it might lull my guards into a false sense of security. Lord knew I needed every advantage I could get if I wanted to escape.

I eased into the first form and let my mind drift. I could always plot later. For now I needed to focus on my body and just *be*.

I FELT CALMER AFTER COMPLETING THE ROUTINE. THE residual muscle stiffness from being knocked out for sixteen hours had faded. I remained stuck in an untenable position aboard an enemy's ship, but I was ready to tackle the challenge of finding a way out.

I propped my pillow against the wall to cushion my back and sat crosswise on the narrow cot. Looking at my bare feet, I realized I hadn't seen my boots since I'd woken. Unless they were hiding in the bathroom, Richard had confiscated them.

Those were my favorite boots, dammit.

If he thought missing footwear was going to keep me from breaking out, he was sadly mistaken. With that in mind, I focused on recalling everything I knew about the *Santa Celestia*. It was not a lot.

The huge ship was newly built and freshly christened when Richard took command six years ago. And while House von Hasenberg had acquired a full set of blueprints and schematics, we'd never managed to get anyone on board long enough to verify their accuracy. I had a basic understanding of the ship's layout but unfortunately didn't know of any weaknesses in the holding cells.

I tried to mentally place where this cell would be in the ship. I couldn't hear or feel the engines, so we had to be toward the front. The fact that this cell was nicer than most meant it was designed to hold high-value hostages and political prisoners.

My mental map was fuzzy, but I thought I was on the second deck in the front quarter of the ship. If House Rockhurst would do us all the favor of using the same ship designs for hundreds or thousands of years like House Yamado, it would be much easier to memorize their ship layouts.

The crew quarters would be on decks two through four in the front quarter of the ship, while the two battalions of shock troopers and their air support personnel would be quartered on the same decks in the rear half. All of the common areas— galley, mess hall, medbay—would be on the bottom midship decks to better serve both crew and troops. The middle midship decks would house the hangars and landing bays.

The landing bays were precisely where I needed to be, if I could just get out of this damned cell.

Richard had not been obviously armed when he visited. He didn't carry a blaster or knife I could steal and use against him. And in a straight battle of strength, he would trounce me, even with surprise on my side. The soldier who brought my food was similarly unarmed. I suppose they weren't risking me taking a hostage. It was smart—and annoying.

I turned escape possibilities over and over until the door clicked. A half a beat later, it slid open to reveal a new soldier carrying a food tray. The door closed silently behind him, giving me no chance for escape. And not only was each soldier unarmed, but they were sending a different person every time, so I wouldn't be able to build a rapport with any of them.

He set the tray on the table and turned to leave. The door clicked again then slid open. It stayed open for three seconds, then closed behind him. I caught a glimpse of at least one other person in the hall and he or she *was* armed.

So I had half a second's worth of notice in order to rush the door, push out the soldier who was either entering or leaving, disarm the other soldier, and disappear into the maintenance tunnels. It was technically *possible*. It just wasn't very *probable*.

But if that remained my only option in a few days, I'd likely be crazy enough to try it.

Lunch consisted of a roast beef sandwich, a steaming cup of French onion soup, and a glass of iced tea. All of the dishes and the tray itself were made out of either flimsy plastech or sturdy paper. I would not be turning any of it into a shiv.

I pushed the tray away but stayed seated at the table. I wanted to see if the soldier would return while I remained within reach. I sat statue-still while I waited. It was a skill my deportment tutor had despaired of me ever learning, but eventually I'd fallen in line. And I had to agree, it was a useful skill—it never failed to unnerve the other people in the room.

It was also the perfect way to disguise plotting. Or thinking.

My mind drifted to Loch. I missed him. He and Rhys were hopefully already negotiating with Father. I might never see him again. My heart twisted and realization struck—I cared for him, but I had let fear rule me.

The admission hurt because it revealed flaws I preferred not to think about. My first relationship had scarred me deeply, but I was no longer the girl I had been. While I still wanted love and affection, I was experienced enough to spot manipulation; I just had to trust in myself.

And everything in me said Loch hadn't been interested because of my name.

If I escaped, *when* I escaped, I would find him. We might not work out, but it wasn't going to be because I was a coward.

The door clicked then slid open, interrupting my thoughts. I kept my expression serene as the guard in the hall stepped into the doorway, a blaster held loosely at her side. The other guard retrieved the tray then backed out of the room. I raised an eyebrow but otherwise didn't move.

So they would retrieve the tray with me close, but only with backup. *Armed* backup. There might be a way to turn it into an advantage if I looked hard enough.

I glanced around my cell. The worst part of being a political prisoner was the crashing boredom. It was part of the process, of course. Because when Richard finally offered me entertainment, I would be grateful. A few more tiny interactions along those lines and I would think that perhaps he wasn't such a bad guy after all. The pull was so strong that even awareness, training, and vigilance weren't always enough to overcome it.

But being a political prisoner still beat the hell out of being in the general cells. I wouldn't be eating waffles and iced tea down there. I'd be lucky to be eating at all.

I sighed internally, careful to keep my outward appearance calm. They would be waiting for signs of weakness. They would have to keep waiting.

With nothing better to do, I lay down on the cot. I wasn't sleepy, but it was more comfortable than the honeycomb chairs. It was also easier to feign sleep while continuing to think.

RICHARD DID NOT RETURN FOR THE REST OF THE DAY. I told time based on the meals they brought but I had no way to know if the timing was correct. They could be bringing me food every two hours for all I knew.

I slept surprisingly well. The cot wasn't the most comfortable bed I'd ever had, but it was far from the worst. Overall, I was bored and frustrated by my lack of a solid escape plan, but well-rested and healthy.

I was sitting at the table when Richard arrived with breakfast.

"Good morning, Ada," he said, "I trust you are well this morning." He set the tray with two plates of food on the table. He also had a tablet tucked under his arm. He slid it under the tray.

"Good morning, Richard," I said. I summoned a smile. "I am well, thank you for asking. Yourself?"

"I am quite well," he said. "I decided to dine with you this morning. I hope you do not mind."

"It is your ship," I said drily.

His grin was sly. He had something up his sleeve. But all he said was, "So it is. Let's eat."

The breakfast soufflé was excellent. He had either a high-end food synthesizer or a fabulous personal chef. The fruit salad was equally delicious. My life might be misery if I married him, but at least the food would be good.

When we were finished, he waved a hand and the door opened. Yet another new soldier removed our dishes. With a complement of close to a thousand—not including the three-thousand-strong fighting force—he could send in a new person every meal for almost a year.

"I've brought your proof of life," he said. "Consider it an early wedding present." He picked up the tablet and tapped on it. He turned it around so I could see the screen, but pulled back when I reached for it. "As much as I'd like to be bashed in the head with this, I think I'll hold on to it instead, if you don't mind," he said with a glimmer of humor.

I grinned at him, my first true expression since I'd been captured. "If you insist," I said. I focused on the screen. Sure enough, *Polaris* sat in the landing bay. The cargo ramp opened. Rhys and Veronica were marched out at gunpoint by a squad of soldiers, cuffed and hobbled.

Son. Of. A. Bitch.

I waited, but no one else appeared out of the ship. The video jumped location and Rhys and Veronica were shown moving around in separate cells. I kept my expression perfectly flat, even as hope warred with rage. There was no sign of Loch, Imma, or Lin. If I had to guess, I'd guess this was a screwed-up rescue attempt, never mind the fact that I had *very specifically* asked Rhys to deliver *Polaris* to Father.

As soon as I was out of this cell, I would find Rhys and Veronica and wring their necks.

"Where did you catch them?" I asked, more out of curiosity than anything else.

"We found them waiting at the gate," Richard said. "We caught them before they got a jump endpoint."

This sector was nearly deserted. The gate was probably ancient, but even so, it wouldn't take more than half an hour to get through the queue and get a jump point. With the alcubium left in the first cylinder, they could've jumped straight to the gate. Swap the cylinders, which I'd shown them how to do, and they would be on their way again in an hour.

Unless Richard caught them waiting at the gate on purpose, after they'd already jumped out, dropped off the others, and jumped back.

"Oh, did they run out of alcubium?" I asked, subtly fishing. "I know we were getting close. I burned through a lot before I realized how the drive worked. That is why I wanted to explore XAD Six."

"They had half a cylinder left," Richard said. "But they seemed to be having trouble plotting a course. I'm surprised you left two inexperienced pilots in charge of your ship. What happened to Loch?" Now he was the one fishing.

I shrugged as if he hadn't given me a key piece of information. "Loch disappeared on APD Zero, so leaving the ship with those two was the only option. Neither was equipped to infiltrate the facility. At least on the ship they had a chance of success."

And it had worked. If they only had half a cylinder, then they'd made multiple jumps before Richard caught them, which would explain the missing people. They'd gotten Loch, Lin, and Imma to safety.

Loch's abandonment stung. But I'd told them to run. I should not be upset that he'd followed my advice. I just wish we'd parted on better terms, because I had no doubt that I'd never see Marcus Loch again.

"We will be married tomorrow," Richard said with a triumphant smile. "That will give a synthesizer time to prepare your dress. The purser is a licensed minister. After our marriage, I will give your friends a shuttle and enough supplies to get them to populated space."

"I will have that in writing in our marriage contract," I said. "In fact, bring me the entire contract today, and I will review and amend it as necessary."

This time, his smile was full of teeth. "Do not press me, Ada."

"If you think I will marry you with only your word protecting my friends, you are incorrect. Their safety will be a cornerstone of our contract. In fact, I suggest you send an escort with them, because if *anything* were to happen to them en route, it would nullify the only contract I will sign."

I didn't know what Rhys and Veronica were thinking, but they'd put me in a damned difficult position. I'd planned for the long game, to wait until someone made a mistake, gave me an opportunity, and then I would strike. Now I had to escape by tomorrow or marry Richard. And Houses did not take divorce lightly—or at all. The only way out of a House marriage was a breach of the marriage contract or death.

*Shit.*

Richard stood. He didn't even try to hide his smug smile.

He had me and he knew it. All I could do was make the best of it. I needed to comb through the marriage contract line by line because I had no doubt he'd try to sneak in whatever he could. I planned to do the same.

"Until tomorrow, Lady Ada," he said with a mocking bow. "I will have someone deliver the marriage contract later today. Take care with your changes—your friends' lives depend on it."

He left, taking the tablet with him. I stared straight ahead, careful not to let my shoulders slump or my head bow. I could only imagine the monstrosity of a contract he would try to force me to sign. I would have to pick my battles wisely.

And then, tonight, I would have to escape.

# CHAPTER 22

The contract came after lunch on a tablet meant for children. With a thick rubber case and no networking components, it was useless both as a weapon and as a communication device. I wondered where Richard had gotten it.

The contract was as bad as I feared. Signing it would be far worse than any marriage Father would've arranged for me. The irony was not lost on me. Fate was a capricious bitch and it was my turn to be hit.

I read through the entire contract then started again at the beginning, highlighting passages in various colors: red for egregious, yellow for bad, blue for livable but not great, and green for favorable.

Green did not get used.

The document was half-red by the time I'd made the first highlighting pass. The rest was yellow with just a smattering of blue. Beneath my calm outer shell I shook with rage and suppressed tears.

The second pass split the red into various shades—the

darker the hue, the worse the passage was for me. At least a quarter of the contract remained dark red, even though I thought I'd been generous in my use of lighter shades.

If I signed this contract, Richard would own me entirely for the next five years. After that probationary period, I might be allowed limited freedom of movement and communication as long as I was always accompanied by a companion of Richard's choice. If I breached the contract, Rhys's and Veronica's lives were forfeit.

In addition, I would be forced to feed my family false information about House Rockhurst, information that would likely cost lives during the war that was sure to come. Using incorrect encryption codes or otherwise tipping them off would be considered breach of contract. So now I was balancing my life, the lives of my family, and the lives of those loyal to House von Hasenberg against the lives of my friends.

It was an impossible situation.

If I signed the contract, my only out would be to escape or kill Richard, warn my friends to go into hiding, and then go into hiding myself. My family would not take me back or protect me. I would truly be on my own for the rest of my life.

It would still be better than the life Richard had planned for me.

I saved a clean copy of the contract then began my revisions. The foundation of my changes would be saving as many people as possible. Not only did I want Rhys and Veronica to escape alive, but I wanted them to *stay* alive and out of Richard's hands. If they died early or were imprisoned in any way, it would breach the contract.

Line by line I subtly massaged the contract language. It

was tedious, painstaking work. I didn't notice the time passing until the door clicked then slid open. It must have been dinnertime already and I hadn't even made it through half of the contract.

I also hadn't come up with a better escape plan than *rush the guard and hope for the best*.

A guard carrying a tray stepped through the door. I would rush him on the way out. A second guard did not step into the room, even though I was sitting at the table, and the door slid closed before I thought to look outside. The guard set the tray on the table and backed up. I tensed.

The door clicked.

I launched myself at the soldier and threw the tablet at his head. The throw didn't have any force behind it, but it brought his arms up to protect his face, and because he'd been backing away, he was off-balance. He didn't have time to fix his stance. I put my shoulder down and plowed him through the open door and into the wall across the hall.

I spun for the armed soldier but instead found a blaster in my face.

"Move, darlin'," a familiar voice drawled.

I looked past the blaster. Loch was dressed in the same uniform the soldier behind me wore. When I remained frozen in shock, he pushed me aside and shot the soldier point-blank.

"I'm happy to see you, too," he said drily.

I opened my mouth but the words were stuck. I finally got out, "What?"

"I'll explain later. Rhys and Veronica are already on their way. Best case scenario, we have about twenty minutes until the next shift takes over and notices something wrong.

We have to move." He picked up the soldier he'd shot, along with another I hadn't noticed, shoved them into my cell, then closed the door. He handed me a blaster. "You good?"

I shook myself out of my daze and focused on the important part—escape. "I'm good. You know where we're going?"

He nodded and started off.

"Wait," I said. "Do you have a com? I'm probably tagged and geofenced. If I leave, it'll set off alarms. And I'd rather not have to strip naked." He grinned but pulled out a com and scanned me for trackers. I only had one, in my back pocket. I took it out and dropped it near the door. "Thanks," I said. "Now I'm ready."

He led me down the hall to an alcove with ladder access to the maintenance tunnels. On a ship this large they would be seemingly infinite. They were also less likely to be empty than on the *Mayport* because ship maintenance was a never-ending job.

Loch slid the access panel closed behind us. The tunnel was sparsely lit, narrow, and short enough we couldn't stand up straight. But at least we didn't have to crawl. "If we make good time, it's eight minutes to the landing bay where *Polaris* is. You okay to run?" He looked me up and down, as if he could see any injuries through my clothes. His gaze snagged on my feet. "You're not wearing boots."

The steel grating of the tunnel floor dug into the soles of my feet, but it was a minor inconvenience in the grand scheme of things. "I don't know what happened to my boots; I woke up without them. But I'm good to run," I said. "I want off this pile of scrap."

Loch took me at my word. He nodded then started off in

a ground-eating jog. After sitting idle in the same six square meters for the last two days, it felt nice to move.

We twisted and turned through the tunnels, sometimes going up or down a level. Loch never hesitated and never slowed down. My feet ached from the abrasion against the grated floor, but they hadn't started to bleed yet so I kept my mouth shut and my body moving.

Loch stopped at the next corner and turned back to me. "We're almost there," he breathed into my ear. "The next part is tricky because it passes a maintenance crew supply room they've converted into a break room. There's no other way unless we want to take twenty minutes to go around. Stick to me. If things go sideways, shoot to kill."

I nodded. The blaster felt heavy in my hands. I hadn't properly mourned for the last people I'd killed and now I was likely going to add to my total.

We rounded the corner into a fully illuminated tunnel. As we approached the door in the middle, I could hear conversation—at least three people. Loch moved silently. I shadowed him. When we reached the door, he held up a hand and crouched down to peek into the room.

He stood and held up four fingers—there were four people in the room. Using hand signals, he relayed that two of them were facing the door. We could either try to cross unnoticed or shoot them now.

The hallway continued uninterrupted for fifteen meters past the door. We would have no cover. But shooting innocent people in cold blood didn't sit well with me, either. I indicated I wanted to cross.

Loch looked like he would argue, but finally he nodded.

We synced our stride and walked past the door, Loch closer to the people inside, me hopefully hidden by his body. We sped up once we were clear of the door.

"Michaels, is that you?" someone called from inside.

"Nah, looked like he was in a hurry. You know Michaels doesn't hurry," someone else said. Everyone laughed. Neither speaker had sounded like seeing someone was cause for concern.

Their voices faded as we moved down the tunnel, but I didn't relax until we turned a corner and put steel between my back and their eyes. "How much farther?" I asked in a whisper.

"We're nearly there," Loch said. "If we're lucky, Rhys and Veronica are ahead of us."

True to his word, a minute or two later we dropped down a ladder into one of the storage rooms off of the landing bay. Through the open door, I saw *Polaris* waiting with the cargo ramp down.

I could also hear a ridiculous amount of blaster fire. Most of it seemed to be getting absorbed by *Polaris*'s shields. Two people in the ship's cargo bay were returning fire, shooting at someone or something I couldn't see from here.

"Seems like we've been noticed," Loch said.

"Tell me that's Rhys and Veronica on the ship," I said.

"With the shield up, that's the most likely case, but I can't see either of them to confirm. I just hope they got some alcubium loaded before they were caught," Loch said. "Or we're going to be dead in the water."

"You know where it's stored?"

"It's down with munitions," Loch said.

"If they didn't get any, I will go," I said.

"Rhys and Veronica were dressed as crew. If they couldn't get it, your chances are nil. And the longer we wait, the more reinforcements Rockhurst is going to call in," he said. I started to reply but he cut me off. "Let's have a little look-see before we do anything rash."

We crept out of the storage room. A few stacks of cargo gave us some cover. We stopped behind a pallet stacked high with emergency water rations. A solid fifty meters of open space separated us and *Polaris*. Without shields, we wouldn't make it without getting shot.

"I don't suppose you have one of Rhys's fancy shields?" I asked.

Loch shook his head. "Rhys only had one. And, if you re-member, you blew it up in Rockhurst's face."

"How could you possibly know that?"

He grinned at me. "I was there," he said.

That left me with more questions than answers, but now was not the time. I peeked around the edge of the cargo. At least six soldiers hid behind similar cargo piles on the far side of the landing bay.

And sitting out in the open between us was a sled full of alcubium tubes in protective triangular covers.

It looked like a few soldiers had tried to retrieve the sled, only to be picked off by shots from the ship. I saw four bodies on the ground. The sled was not hovering, which meant it was either dead or deactivated.

"We have to get that sled," I said. I roughly calculated the weight of each cylinder at a little over five kilograms. There were probably thirty cylinders on the sled. That was a shit-ton of weight to move, not including the busted sled itself. I revised my statement. "Or as many tubes as we can carry."

"We have five minutes max until we're overrun," Loch said.

I edged around the cargo sled we'd crouched behind. The control panel was unlocked with big red and green buttons for ease of use. I hit the green GO button and the sled lifted. The water rations weren't the best shield, but none of the other cargo was any better. Too bad the soldiers had neglected to leave a sled full of ballistic armor sitting around.

"We use this as our shield," I said. "We run for the alcubium. You load, I shoot. We grab as much as we can before the water containers disintegrate, then we make for *Polaris*."

"The soldiers are being careful not to shoot the alcubium. I suggest you do the same," Loch said.

"I'll do my best," I said with a grin. Adrenaline pumped through my veins. "You ready?"

"Let's do this," Loch said.

We grabbed the webbing that strapped the water to the sled and pushed. The stack of water containers was high enough that we could run bent over and still be protected.

We crossed more than half of the distance to the alcubium before the soldiers noticed we weren't on their side and started shooting at us. Water spilled out of the front containers, wetting the floor and putting the nonslip flooring paint to the test. The cool water soothed the abrasions on my feet.

"Give me your blaster," I said as we maneuvered our sled next to the alcubium. Blaster bolts sailed overhead and into the part of our sled not protected behind the alcubium sled.

Loch handed over his blaster. I took a deep breath then stood up and started shooting with a blaster in each hand. It wasn't the smartest thing I'd ever done, but it focused attention on me while Loch transferred alcubium cylinders to our sled.

And with a pallet of alcubium between me and the soldiers, I could almost *feel* their reluctance to shoot at me and miss.

When a bolt sailed close enough to my head that I could feel the passing heat, I ducked back down with a warning to Loch. He'd moved five cylinders.

"Once again?" I asked. The soldiers had blasted through nearly a third of our water containers. If we wanted to make it to *Polaris* with any shield left, we'd have to make this quick.

Loch nodded. I moved over slightly, so I would pop out in a new place, then stood and started firing. The break had given the soldiers time to prepare. They returned fire with furious intensity.

My left arm went white-hot then icily numb. The blaster slipped from fingers I could no longer feel. I shot twice more with the blaster in my right hand, until it clicked empty.

"Down," I called to Loch as I half ducked, half fell back into the protection of the cargo sled. I refused to look at my left arm, happy to leave it in a state of numb unknown until we were safe. "Time for a strategic retreat," I said with a grimace.

We pulled the sled toward *Polaris*. And by *we,* I mean *Loch;* I mostly held on and tried not to fall down as we were forced to walk backward. With flagging support from the ship—they must be low on ammo—the soldiers became bolder. They were trying to disable our sled.

We were four meters from *Polaris*'s cargo ramp when they succeeded. The sled slammed down a mere centimeter from my unprotected toes.

"We're going to have to drag it," Loch said.

I grabbed the webbing, dug in my feet, and *pulled*. Loch strained beside me and the sled creaked into motion. I was so focused on pulling, moving my feet, and ignoring my arm that Rhys's appearance caught me by surprise. He grabbed the webbing and pulled with Loch. The sled rocketed into motion so quickly I had to dance back or risk my toes.

*Show-off.*

We hit the end of the cargo ramp and finally had the protection of *Polaris*'s shield. Of course, if any Rockhurst soldiers got *inside* the shield, they could still shoot us. Rhys handed me a cylinder, then he and Loch grabbed four each.

Veronica covered us with sporadic blaster fire as we made our way up the ramp. As soon as we were inside, she hit the button to close the cargo door and retract the ramp.

"Can someone get us out of here?" I asked. "I'm not sure I'm fit to fly, even if I don't have to go manual." My left arm throbbed with increasingly difficult-to-ignore shards of agony. It felt like crushed glass had been embedded under the skin and the pieces grated together with every movement. "And does anyone have a blaster with ammo left?"

Loch left for the flight deck. Rhys handed me a blaster. "What are you thinking?" he asked.

"I'm going to shoot their alcubium supply," I said.

"Are you sure that's a good idea?"

My smile was full of teeth. "No."

"I'll let Loch know to expect a boom," Rhys said. "Then I

want to see you in the medbay." He turned to Veronica. "Make sure she gets there, okay?"

"She'll get there. We didn't rescue her just to have her die on us now," Veronica said.

Rhys grinned then disappeared behind me.

I went to the control panel and activated the external PA. "Dear Rockhurst soldiers, I'm going to blow up that pile of alcubium. This is your ten-second warning. I suggest you flee," I said. I felt better having given them at least a chance to run.

I flopped down on the deck of the cargo bay with a jolt of pain, but the door opened from the bottom. I didn't want to open it all the way in case the explosion was bigger than I anticipated. "*Polaris,* open the cargo bay door ten centimeters," I said.

A chime indicated that the ship still saw me as its captain. Richard hadn't had time to crack my personal codes with brute force or he hadn't bothered, thinking me safely in his grasp. He likely would've demanded the codes once we were married.

*Ha.*

"Veronica, can you get ready to close the door?" I asked. She nodded and moved to the controls. "It might get a little explody in here," I warned.

The door raised just enough for me to see the alcubium. A line of soldiers frantically tried to move cargo in as a barrier, but they were too late. I checked the charge on the gun then fired two warning shots. The soldiers fled. I waited until I couldn't see them, then fired on the alcubium.

It took three shots.

On the third, the pallet exploded in a bright orange fireball that kept growing as more and more cylinders ruptured. The flames licked against the ship's shield as warning messages blared. Even with the shield, heat seared my face before the cargo door slid closed.

I blinked the black spots from my vision. Okay, that was a little more energetic than I had expected.

At least the inferno was in a landing bay. If all else failed, they could put out the fire by lowering the atmospheric field and letting the vacuum of space work its magic.

It also meant they'd be less likely to close the blast doors and trap us inside.

"Let's get you to the medbay," Veronica said. She helped me to my feet when I wobbled on the way up.

"I should make sure Loch isn't having trouble with the ship," I said.

"He's fine, but you're not going to be in a few more minutes. You're going to get patched up *now*," she said in her best mom voice.

"Triage now, fix it later," I said. "There's a first aid kit on the wall."

Her mouth compressed into a hard line, but when I didn't budge she sighed and grabbed supplies out of the kit.

I risked a glance at my left arm and wished I hadn't.

Blood soaked the sleeve of my shirt and dripped in a sluggish stream from my fingertips. The bolt had caught me on the outside of my arm, halfway between my shoulder and elbow. A large chunk of flesh was missing, leaving a bloody mess.

The hole in my sleeve was singed around the edges, as was my flesh. This was beyond the capability of my nanobots. They'd have their work cut out for them just to stop the bleeding.

I swayed, light-headed, as renewed pain stabbed me with vicious barbs. Veronica returned with a trauma bandage. "You're just lucky that it was an outside hit," she said. "Looks like it missed the bone, which will help with recovery."

I looked away and willed my stomach not to crawl out of my mouth while she applied the compress.

"This bandage buys you fifteen minutes. After that, I expect you in the medbay, even if I have to drag you there myself."

"Thanks," I said.

The stairs up to the flight deck were daunting, but Veronica had given me a shot with the bandage and I felt *awesome*. Which meant it was probably a shot of foxy, and I'd crash hard about the time my bandage was due to be changed. Sneaky woman.

Both Loch and Rhys looked up when I entered the flight deck, but Loch was too busy trying to get us out of the landing bay to yell.

Rhys had no such qualms. "Why aren't you in the medbay?"

"I will be, just as soon as we're clear. Veronica stabilized me." At least I assumed she had because blood no longer dripped from my fingers.

The vid screens were up. We were nearly out of the landing bay, but fire still raged behind us. Gas visibly leaked through the atmospheric field. They were lowering the field slowly, which was smart, as long as they didn't let the landing bay burn down in the process.

In front of us, a handful of fighters offered heavy resistance. Richard must've launched the ships from the other landing bay. The fighters were doing their best to keep us pinned in place. Richard probably wanted them to keep us here until the retrieval ship launched.

Our shields were taking the brunt of the damage, but so were theirs. We couldn't punch an opening in their line, and Loch needed to get us free of the landing bay so we could jump without risking damage to both *Polaris* and *Santa Celestia*.

"Strap in," Loch barked. I sank into a seat and clipped in. Veronica did the same.

The fighters were playing chicken with our ship. They hovered close enough that if Loch kept creeping out of the landing bay, he ran the risk of overlapping our shields and theirs. If he did, the results could range from nothing to explosive failure of both shields.

Loch eased farther out of the bay, centimeters at a time. He was not going to flinch first, but the fighters must have been under orders to stand their ground. His hands flew over the manual control console.

"What are—" I started.

Loch dropped the forward shield, rammed *Polaris* out of the bay before the fighters could take advantage, then engaged the FTL drive practically on top of them.

After the jump, the windows and vid screens showed vast quantities of empty space. I breathed a sigh of relief. No doubt we'd have to do some repairs after Loch's little stunt, but we'd made it.

Loch tapped on the manual control screen then stood up. "Medbay, now," he snapped at me. Fury darkened his face.

I scowled at him. I'd been about to congratulate him on

his piloting, but I changed my mind. People who yelled at me didn't get compliments.

I unclipped from my seat and stood. I wobbled slightly but steadied myself with the back of the chair. Indignation and foxy kept me going for half of the trip downstairs. The second half was powered by sheer will. When I hit the medbay, I admitted defeat.

"I think I need to lie down," I said. My voice sounded funny. I collapsed onto the diagnostic table. My arm lit up in agony at every tiny movement.

If I never moved again it would be too soon.

Loch cut off my shirtsleeve and the trauma bandage. I hissed in pain as black spots danced behind my eyes. He pressed something cool against my shoulder, and I heard the distinctive hiss of an injector.

The pain did not lessen.

Loch prodded at the wound in my arm. I yelped and tried to pull away. "You can still feel that?" he asked.

"Yes, obviously," I said.

"Okay, then this is going to hurt," he warned.

"It hurts now," I said.

"The anesthetic should kick in soon, but I don't want to wait because you're bleeding again. And you're already white as a sheet, so you don't need any more blood loss."

I clenched my good hand. "Do your worst," I said.

He did.

# CHAPTER 23

My arm was cleaned, coated in regeneration gel, and bandaged, then my scraped-up feet were given the same treatment. Only then was I allowed to leave the medbay. I had also been given a large glass of orange juice by Veronica and stern instructions to drink it all.

She also insisted on escorting me up to the flight deck when I listed drunkenly to the right on bandaged feet while trying to walk out of the medbay door. Loch followed silently.

Veronica helped me slump into an empty chair while Loch dropped into the captain's station. "Thank you," I told her, "for everything. I mean it, even when I yell at you later for ignoring my request and risking your life."

"You are welcome. I'm glad your arm is bandaged properly," she said. "You should've let me do it before." She sat beside me. I'd scared her and now she was hovering. I could deal with hovering.

"You'll also have to yell at me," Rhys said cheerfully from the navigator's chair. "And Loch."

"Don't worry; I will," I said. "I'm just saving up my strength. Where are we?"

"Ten light-minutes from the gate," Loch said. "It'll take longer to get a jump point, but Rockhurst will not expect us this far out. We're stealthed. With the exception of the gate frequency, everything else is shut down. And I've matched our trajectory with a large planetoid; you can't see it, but it's below us."

At ten minutes out, our gate communications would take twenty minutes—ten minutes to the gate and ten minutes for a response. But it made the area Richard would need to search in order to find us so vast that he'd have to get extremely lucky to even have a sliver of a chance.

"Thank you," I said. "And nice work getting us out of the *Santa Celestia* in one piece, even if you did yell at me afterwards."

Loch inclined his head. "It was a little risky, but it worked," he said. He might be playing modest, but he'd proven once again that he was a first-rate pilot.

I turned to Rhys and Veronica. "How long does the gate take to give you an endpoint?"

"You figured out that we'd jumped before, huh?" Rhys asked.

"Richard tipped me off when he mentioned how much alcubium you had left. I suppose now would be a good time to yell at you for being crazy, stupid, and reckless, both with yourselves and with my ship?"

"Yell at Loch," Veronica said. "He's the one who decided to jump out of the ship after you. Without his calming influence, Rhys and I were left to our own devices." She said it with a straight face, but her eyes danced with humor.

I rounded on Loch. "You did *what?*"

"I told you I was there when you blew up Rhys's shield in Rockhurst's face. I wasn't on the ground when *Polaris* took off, so how did you think I arrived? *You* might not like jumping out of ships, but I don't mind it."

"Wait, wait, wait . . . back up," Rhys said. "You *blew up* my shield? Do you know how much trouble I had to go through to get that?"

"Hopefully, it was a lot," I said without remorse. "But we're getting sidetracked. We were discussing how Loch jumped out of the perfectly good ship he promised to take to Father."

Loch shrugged. "I never promised anything. You just assumed I did because I made a vaguely agreeing statement."

I glared at him. "You made an agreeing statement *right after* I asked you to promise. Next time I'll get it in writing, in triplicate," I grumbled. "So you jumped out of the ship. Then what?"

"All of the soldiers were wearing Rockhurst space suits. So was I. In the chaos you created, one of them disappeared and I took his place. Once I was on board the *Santa Celestia,* things got dicey a few times, but no one expected a foreign operative on the ship."

*I* certainly hadn't expected it, so I doubt Richard had even given it a moment's thought.

Loch continued, "I knew approximately when Rhys and Veronica were due, so I just had to find your cell. It took longer than I expected; Rockhurst kept your presence quiet. Otherwise, I would've given you warning. Nice escape, by the way."

"I'd spent the day going over my marriage contract. I was getting out of that cell no matter what."

Veronica turned to me. "Rockhurst still wanted to marry you?"

"If you can call it that. He was blackmailing me into a sham of a marriage with a number of threats, including one on your life and Rhys's."

"You wouldn't have gone through with it, right?" Veronica asked.

"I don't know," I said honestly. "The way the contract was originally written—no. Richard wanted me to feed false information to my House, which would've cost hundreds of thousands of lives. I was modifying it when Loch rescued me. If I could've gotten it into a halfway decent state, I would've signed it, only to breach it as soon as an opportunity presented itself. Signing it would've given you and Rhys at least a slim chance of escape."

"But that would me—" she started.

"Trust me, I knew what it meant," I said.

Veronica bowed her head to me. "I am glad we rescued you from that," she said.

I smiled at her. "You and me, both."

"You want to clue in the rest of the room?" Loch asked.

"When two Houses join in marriage, there is a marriage contract that lays out all of the details, like the dowry. The lower houses try to marry into a High House for power and prestige. High Houses marry into lower houses for strategic purposes or because the lower house offered money, territory, or technology as part of the contract."

"Sounds mercenary," Loch said.

"It is and even more so when two High Houses marry. The duty usually falls to younger sons and daughters, those far down the inheritance hierarchy. It pays to have a spy in your enemy's House, as well as a tiny bit of influence. Plus the contracts are dense with concessions from both sides, and sometimes marriage is the only way to get treaties signed. But neither side actually wants the two Houses to combine, so heirs are not married to rival High Houses."

I shrugged and continued, "If I'd signed the marriage contract Richard proposed, I would belong to him, both in his eyes and in the eyes of the Consortium. It wouldn't matter that it was coerced. If I broke the contract, Rhys and Veronica would die. If I killed or escaped him, I would be shunned by the entirety of the Consortium, including my own House."

Loch looked furious but Rhys didn't seem shocked. I wondered again about his background. I decided to pivot the conversation back into safer waters. "Where are we jumping?"

"Back to Sedition on APD Zero," Loch said. "Veronica's kid and nanny are there. Plus we can drop off this worthless bastard." He jerked a thumb at Rhys.

"This worthless bastard managed to get his partner out of the *Santa Celestia* and back to this ship without either of us getting shot," Rhys said. "How did that work out for you?"

Loch scowled at him.

I turned to Veronica. "I saw video of you and Rhys being walked off the ship and again once you were in your cells. How did you get out?" I asked.

"Loch got us out before he went to get you," Veronica said. "We went on ahead, dressed like crew, to try to secure *Polaris* and as much alcubium as we could find. Unfortunately, Rockhurst's actual crew found us out before we could get the alcubium on board. We retreated and prayed you two would make it."

The ship chimed. "We've got a jump point," Loch said.

"How long until the FTL is ready?" I asked.

"Ten minutes." He tapped on the screen. "Looks like it's good we got here when we did, because Rockhurst is trying to overload the gate with requests. That's why it took longer to get a jump point."

"If I sit here and wait for ten minutes, I'll drive myself crazy," I said. "I'm going to see if the soldiers found the stuff I hid." I stood with only a minor wobble. Whatever Loch had given me for the pain was wearing off, which made my balance better but tiny daggers stabbed down my arm when I jostled it.

On top of that, the regeneration gel had started to kick in. I schooled my expression so no one would worry.

"I will help you," Loch said. He followed me out of the room. "How's the arm?" he asked after the door closed behind us.

"Still attached," I said. When he frowned at me, I continued, "It hurts like the devil has decided to jab me with his pitchfork every time I even think about moving."

"Pain meds wearing off?"

"Yeah. If it gets worse, I'll take something." That wasn't technically a lie. It would just take extreme values of *worse* to make it true. Unfortunately, I had a feeling I'd be there before too much longer.

I pressed my right hand against the control panel for the captain's quarters. The door slid open. I stumbled inside. Sweat dotted my brow and trickled down my back. Maybe I'd lie down until the regeneration gel did its thing.

"Are you okay?" Loch asked.

I nodded then immediately shook my head. "It's the regeneration gel," I said. It had been a decade or so since I'd needed to use it, but the side effects remained burned in my memory. True to its name, regeneration gel healed even major wounds quickly. But in return, it was hell while active.

"Shit, I should've brought extra anesthetic," he said. He led me to the bedroom and helped me lie down. "I forgot how some people react to the gel. You probably know this, but you're about to be in for a bad time."

He stood and went to the intercom. "Rhys, I'm going to need you to pilot. Veronica, can you get me some anesthetic, both local and general?"

"Sure thing," Rhys said. "Veronica's on her way down to the medbay. Everything okay?"

"Ada's regeneration gel is kicking in. She's feverish."

"Good luck, friend. Let me know if you need anything. I've got the ship."

I closed my eyes as a wave of nausea rolled over me. I'd like to think that Loch was overreacting, but based on how I felt right now, he might be *under*reacting. My arm burned like liquid fire.

Time stretched. I focused on breathing through each second without screaming. The doorbell broke my concentration, and I whimpered.

"Hold on," Loch said. "Veronica's here with the painkillers."

Loch disappeared and returned with Veronica. She frowned at me. "You should've told us you were in pain earlier," she said.

"It wasn't this bad," I gritted out.

Loch injected me with something that took the fire from an inferno to a smolder. My arm still ached, but now I could think around the pain.

"Remind me not to get shot again anytime soon, okay?" I said. My stomach dropped as the FTL drive kicked in. We would be on Rhys's planet soon. "Any idea how long it'll take until I'm healed enough for my arm to stop feeling like it's burning off?"

"With a small wound like that, probably half a day," Loch said.

The fact that a missing chunk of my arm was something Loch considered a "small wound" was telling. "Any reason I shouldn't move around?"

"You're not feeling it, but you're still feverish. Your body will be weaker than you expect. And you'll be loopy from the anesthetic. So long as you don't try anything crazy while feeling invincible, you should be okay."

"Does that sound like something I would do?"

"Yes," Loch and Veronica replied at the same time.

"Ada, if you're awake, I'm going to land us in one of my hangars," Rhys said over the intercom. "It's more secure than a public spaceport and you know Richard is going to look here."

"Thank you," I said. "How long until we're on the ground?"

"Looks like about forty minutes," he said. "I'll give you a heads-up before we enter the atmosphere, but it should be a smooth ride—this ship is fantastic." I beamed like a proud parent. I may've stolen *Polaris* from Richard, but the ship was mine now.

I sat up. My arm burned, but it was a distant pain. The

painkillers had worked their magic. I stood up and my pain didn't increase, but I was a little shaky.

I opened the closet and got a nice surprise—my extra clothes were still inside. Hopefully that meant my com, necklace, and cuff were safe. I'd hidden them in a concealed drawer in the top of the closet. I'd only found it on accident while looking for a hiding place, then it had taken me five minutes to figure out how to open it.

"Could one of you help me?" I asked. "There's a hidden drawer, but it requires two hands to open. There's a button in the far back corner that you can barely feel. You have to press it and pull on the front at the same time."

Loch popped the drawer open then handed me the contents. I put on the cuff and necklace, though I didn't bother arming them; I'd wait until I was alone.

I'd locked the com before I stored it, which meant it needed my real identity chip to activate—the chip in my left arm. I made it through the series of hand motions required to activate it with barely an additional twinge of pain. Whatever painkiller Loch had given me was *good*.

I held the com to my identity chip then went through the verification process. I immediately sent my sister a quick update. I hadn't been lying to Richard about the consequences of failing to contact her.

It was only after I'd sent the update that I checked the news.

House Rockhurst had declared war on House von Hasenberg. Father had responded in kind. House Yamado remained neutral for now, but the various lower houses were already choosing sides.

"We're at war," I said, as if voicing the words would make them feel real. The last full-scale war between High Houses spanned two decades, claimed nearly ten million lives, and resulted in one less High House in the Consortium. Since then, we'd been at peace for more than five generations.

"Who declared?" Veronica asked.

"Rockhurst, against us, yesterday," I said. I shook my head. I had been planning to send *Polaris* to Father through an intermediary after we negotiated terms. That plan was dead. I would have to return home as soon as possible.

I met Veronica's eyes. "I need you to think very seriously about your future. I can still try to take you with me as a Cabinet member, but only if that is what you want. Houses at war are not the safest places. I will likely be sent to the front lines. If you don't travel with me, my protection will be limited."

She nodded. "I will consider it carefully. I will also go tell Rhys the news in case he hasn't heard."

# CHAPTER 24

After Veronica left, I sank down on the edge of the bed. Worry pressed on my shoulders. There hadn't been any news of outright attack, but it would only be a matter of time.

Loch leaned against the wall across from me. "What will you do?" he asked.

I sighed and rubbed my eyes. "I have to go home. I need to be there for my siblings. I'll still negotiate with Father before I go, but it'll be rushed. We'll both have to settle for less than we wanted. What about you?"

"I don't know. I thought I might try my hand at private security. You know anyone headed to a war zone who might need a little backup?"

I looked up in shock. He met my gaze calmly. "I might know someone," I said, fighting a smile. "What are your qualifications?"

"I was trained in the military. I'm tough. I heal fast." He gave me a smoldering look. "And I've been told I'm fantastic in bed."

"Hmm, I'm not sure my brother much cares about that last one, but I'll be sure to pass it along," I said with a straight face. Loch laughed and the sound loosened some of the tension I carried.

His expression turned serious. He sat next to me and rested his elbows on his knees. I couldn't see his face. "I joined the RCDF when I was seventeen," he said. "I was the perfect candidate—strong, smart, and eager to fight—except that I had a difficult time taking orders."

I sucked in a breath when I realized what he was doing.

"But I still managed to toe the line enough to rise quickly through the ranks. So when my commander approached me about a new project, one where I would command my own elite unit, I jumped at it."

He shook his head. "I was still just a kid. When they told me they wanted to make us supersoldiers, I thought it sounded awesome. They called it the Genesis Project. There were four squads of eight that started the project, broken into groups based on DNA similarities. I was the squad leader for my group."

I wanted so badly to ask questions, but I kept silent, afraid if I moved or made a sound, he would stop talking.

"We signed away our rights without reading the contracts because our supervisors told us everything was on the up-and-up. The scientists tinkered with our DNA. My eyes are not ocular implants, they're genetically engineered."

I gaped at him. The sanctity of DNA was one of the foundational principles of the Consortium. We might introduce nanobots into our blood or augment ourselves with biomechanical implants, but our DNA, the core of who we were, was strictly off-limits. It had been that way from the beginning of the Royal Consortium. Genetic engineering could still be found, of course, deep in the black market, but only the most desperate would risk it, because it carried a Consortium death sentence for both provider and patient.

"Soldiers started dropping right from the beginning, but they didn't cancel the project. It was hell. My squad was the only one that made it through, and only just," he said. Old pain laced his voice.

I wrapped my arm around his back and squeezed him in a half hug.

He continued, "We spent months in training missions. The conditions were brutal. The scientists wanted to see what we could do, how much damage we could take, and how quickly we would spring back. Requests for reassignment went nowhere. Fornax was our first real mission."

"Rhys was there with you?" I asked quietly.

"Yeah, he was in my squad. We were elated to be sent on a real mission, thinking the worst of it was over. We were wrong. The people of Fornax Zero were starving because House Rockhurst was taxing them to death. They were rebelling against the price of food."

He took a deep breath. "Because it was a Rockhurst planet, House Rockhurst sent Richard to oversee the operation. I think it was his very first assignment and he was eager to prove himself by whatever means necessary."

"But he couldn't have been in the *Santa Celestia*," I said. "I distinctly remember that was after Fornax. And there was no mention of him being at Fornax at all."

"No, at the time he was in an older ship. He had a passel of military advisors with him, but he ignored their advice and ordered us to attack. We were sent in to quell the rebellion by killing women and kids, which is probably why House Rockhurst didn't proclaim his involvement."

Loch shook his head in disgust at the memory. "At that point, we all knew the only way out for us was death. As the squad leader, it was my responsibility, so I 'killed' them. Then I really did kill the bastards in charge, and I'd do it again in a heartbeat. If I could get my hands on Richard, I'd kill him, too. Unfortunately, the fucker seems to know about my abilities and has taken precautions every time I've gotten close."

"Why didn't you go to the Consortium?"

Loch laughed without humor. "Who do you think funded the entire thing, sweetheart? And who increases my bounty year after year? House Rockhurst might've owned Fornax Zero, but all three High Houses approved the Genesis Project."

I wasn't so naive as to believe the Consortium was all rainbows and puppies, but I'd never truly been exposed to the darkest parts, either. "How did the others in your squad escape notice?"

"The Consortium wiped all external record of us once we went into the program. A minor name change and a new black-market ID and they were good to go. Even their prints and DNA don't have matches in the system."

I had to be careful about my fingerprints and DNA when using a false identity because either could lead someone straight back to my real name. Not having to worry about it would relieve a huge burden.

"So your eyes are not implants? But you can still see in the dark?" I asked. I'd been fascinated by his eyes from the beginning and knowing they were genetically engineered didn't detract from their allure.

"Yes, I can see in the dark. And heal from major wounds in hours or days. And break bones with my bare hands." He glanced over his shoulder at me. "I tell you everything and that's all you have to say?"

The reminder wiped the humor from my face. "No, I have plenty to say, most of it to Father and the rest of the Consortium. I'm sorry about what happened to you and your squad. So very sorry. It must've been devastating to realize you were stuck with a House daughter on *Mayport*."

"Actually, I planned to use it to my advantage. But then you turned out to be so damned *nice,* even when you were trying to manipulate me. I thought it was another act. It wasn't until you risked your life coming to get me that I started to think that maybe you weren't like the rest."

"I am exactly like the rest," I said. "I just hide it better."

Loch met my eyes again. "You may think so, but you're wrong. Every House member I've ever met would've sent me to investigate the bunker on XAD Six while they stayed safely with the ship. They wouldn't have thought twice about it."

"It was my responsibility," I said. I looked away. "You were so cold to me when I said goodbye. I thought you were still mad and expected you to try to steal the ship."

Loch turned to face me. "I was furious that you insisted on going alone. I kept imagining all the things that could go wrong for you before I'd even hit the ground. I should've handled it better," he said, running a hand down his face. "I meant to talk to you sooner—that's why I followed you into the maintenance area. But I bailed at the last second."

His fists clenched. "You're not the only one with history. I jumped to conclusions and said things I regret. I'm sorry."

Someday I would get the story from him, but for now, I let it go. "Apology accepted."

"I want you," he said bluntly. "I know we're too different and I don't care. We can make a relationship work."

Warmth and nerves fluttered in my belly. Loch had rescued me from Richard's ship when he stood to gain a great deal more by taking *Polaris* to Father and leaving me to rot. I trusted him.

"I want you, too," I said with a smile. "And I want to make it work." I blew out a breath. "But I *have* to go home. It's not just about duty and honor, it's about love."

"And I can't go with you," he said. He made to stand up.

I put a hand on his arm before he could retreat. "Wait. Talk to me. If we're going to make a relationship work, we have to get better at communication. I want you to go, but not if it means risking your life. Help me think of a solution that works for both of us."

"I've tried. Short of the Consortium pardoning me, there's no way visiting House von Hasenberg would be safe, even if old Albrecht let me in—which he won't."

I was pretty sure I could get him in, but he was right, it wouldn't be safe. But a full pardon . . . that had potential. "I might be able to get you a pardon," I said.

"You've got to be kidding."

I shook my head. "While the Consortium thrives on scandal, it only likes internal scandal. Public scandal is to be avoided at all cost. DNA experiments that killed RCDF soldiers would be a huge public scandal. I might be able to twist enough arms to get a vote for clemency passed. It'll be harder with the war with Rockhurst, but I think I can swing Father and Yamado. The vote doesn't have to be unanimous."

"And what prevents them from killing you to keep the secret?"

That surprised a laugh out of me. "The same thing that always has: luck, skill, and the reams of documents that will be publicly released upon my death. It's how the game is played."

# CHAPTER 25

Rhys landed in Sedition without any trouble. The enclosed hangar made me a little nervous, but I knew it was better than sitting out in the open. He and Veronica immediately departed for his house. They promised to return in the morning for breakfast, even if Veronica decided not to continue with me.

I watched their transport slide away from the cargo ramp. Loch stood beside me. "What do you think she'll choose?" I asked.

"Rhys will push hard for her to stay," he said. "But she is tougher than she looks. She'll make him work for it, whatever she decides. What do you want her to choose?"

"The selfish part of me wants her to stay with me because I enjoy her company. But I know she'll be safer if she stays here, especially if Rhys can talk her into staying at his house."

The hangar door closed behind their vehicle, blocking out the sun and leaving us in twilight. Weariness pressed in. It might be late morning on this planet, but I'd reverted to Universal Time and it was past time for me to sleep. Maybe by the time I woke up my arm wouldn't feel like I was getting jabbed with a hot poker every time I moved.

"I'm going to bed," I said. "I'll message Father in the morning. He's on Universal Time, so if I stay up to do it tonight, he won't see it until the morning anyway." I knew I was making excuses, but I really didn't have the brain capacity to do it justice tonight. Tomorrow would be soon enough.

"How's the arm?" Loch asked as he followed me upstairs.

"It hurts, but I'll live. The painkiller is still keeping the worst of it at bay. It only really hurts when I move." After I'd answered, another reason for the question occurred to me. "I'm going to bed to sleep, I'm afraid. You're welcome to join me but I might not be good company."

"I'll take my chances," Loch said.

Once we'd made it to the bedroom, I shucked my pants with weary motions. I instinctively reached back for my bra closure and hissed in pain.

"Let me," Loch said. He reached under my shirt and unhooked it as easily as I would've. He helped me ease it off while keeping my shirt on.

"I see you know your way around women's undergarments," I said, trying to break the weird tension that gripped me. I felt unaccountably shy considering I'd already slept with him.

"I live to serve," he murmured against the nape of my neck. I shivered. "Now stop stalling and get in bed."

I set my com to wake me up in seven hours then climbed into the bed still wearing my shirt and underwear. Loch stripped down to his boxer briefs. All of that warm bronze skin tempted me to play with fire, but I yawned in spite of myself. He climbed into bed and curled around my right side, being careful of my injured left arm.

Sleep hit me like a frigate.

THE ALARM CAME TOO EARLY AND TOO LOUD. I GROANED and tried to burrow deeper into my pillow.

"I don't think that's going to work," Loch said drowsily. His voice rumbled through me. "I'm all for sleeping more, but you have to turn off that racket first."

"I can't," I grumbled. "I have work to do. And Rhys and Veronica will be back soon." I threw the covers off before I was tempted to stay. I sat up and turned the alarm off. Shower first, then coffee, then maybe I'd feel like facing the rest of the day.

My left arm almost felt normal again. The bandage would have to stay on for another day or two, but it was waterproof, so I enjoyed a long shower. By the time I had gotten dressed, I almost felt human again. Human except for the lack of boots. I'd have to do something about that because I couldn't return home in socks.

Loch was still sprawled in bed when I came out of the bathroom. He cracked one eye. "I see you were serious about getting up."

"Yeah, but you don't have to. I'm going to be writing a message to Father for the next few hours."

He blinked in surprise. "That long?"

"It's going to be a legally binding contract, so yeah, that long. I want to make sure there aren't any loopholes for him to exploit."

"I'll be down in a little while," he said.

I grabbed my com then headed down to the mess hall. After fortifying myself with a tall glass of iced coffee, I went through the complicated ritual necessary to authorize my necklace and cuff. When I didn't have anything left to prolong my procrastination, I pulled out my com and got to work.

I started with our basic House contract. I added the things I wanted. First up was the ability to pick my own spouse, the freedom to come and go at will and without supervision, and the immediate cancellation of my bounty. All three of those things were hard requirements. I loved my family but I wasn't returning if it meant a prison sentence or a forced marriage.

I added the ability to choose my own staff and security detail because if I didn't, I might as well count on having Father's spies following me everywhere. I also added diplomatic immunity for my staff and five people of my choosing. It probably wouldn't survive the cuts, but it was worth the ask.

Next, I required the return of *Polaris* in working order within three months. Father would balk, but I wanted my ship back. Three months would give the scientists and engineers enough time to study the alcubium FTL drive and get started on their research.

Lastly, I asked for Father to vote yes in a clemency hearing of my choice. I doubted the request would survive the negotiations, but it worked as an opening salvo. Father would know I was serious when I later came to him about the Genesis Project.

In return, I would let his people pick over *Polaris* for three months, hand over all the alcubium I had on board, and submit to no more than a week of debriefings about everything I'd learned about the alcubium FTL and while on XAD Six and the *Santa Celestia*.

With the rough draft complete, I began revising, tweaking the language until it was ironclad. Loch came down sometime during the first pass, but when I muttered something vaguely intelligible at him after he questioned me for the third time, he laughed and left.

I didn't make any changes on the fourth pass, so I figured it was as good as it was getting. I'd dealt with enough contracts to at least be familiar with the common pitfalls.

With the contract done, I began working on the accompanying note. It had to strike the right balance between friendly and threatening or he'd gut my contract without a second thought. By the time I was happy with it, my back ached from hunching over the table for so long.

I signed the message with my personal key, encrypted it with our House key, and sent it highest priority. Because APD Zero was within minutes of the gate, Father should receive the message in the next twenty minutes.

I also sent a copy to Bianca. Perhaps she could be the voice of reason if Father got carried away.

My stomach twisted as anxiety dumped adrenaline into my system. I stood and stretched. I needed to move and not just because I'd been sitting for hours. Fight or flight rode me hard even though the danger was likely sitting behind a desk a million light-years away.

I slid down the ladder to the bottom deck. My arm stung just enough to remind me to take it easy. I heard the rattle of weights before I entered the exercise room. Either I'd found Loch or the ship was haunted.

Loch was doing deadlifts with some ridiculous amount of weight. He wore a pair of low-slung athletic shorts and no shirt. Watching the muscles play across his body as he lifted the weight was a thing of beauty.

"Hey," I said once he was done with the set, "I sent my message and need a distraction. Care to spar?"

"You going to run away?" he asked.

I grinned at him. "Probably."

"What do I get if I catch you?"

"I'll give you a pat on the back and permission to feel smug for a whole thirty seconds."

He chuckled. "With an offer like that, how can I refuse?" He turned serious. "How's your arm?"

"Mostly fine, but still a little tender. Try not to directly hit it if possible." I moved to the sparring mats and dropped into an alternate stance with my right side forward. It was my weaker stance, but it kept my left arm farther out of harm's way.

Loch mirrored my stance. It didn't surprise me that he could fight reversed. He threw a slow right jab at me. I danced back, out of range of the left cross I knew would follow.

Unfortunately, I'd forgotten how quick he was when he wasn't purposefully slowing down.

Instead of the left cross I expected, he closed the distance between us, changed his stance, and threw a *right* cross at me. I deflected it—barely—but it cost me. His left hand connected with stinging force to my right side. If he'd been hitting me at full strength, he would've broken ribs.

"Do I get my pat on the back yet?" he asked. He retreated to let me regroup.

"Sure," I said with a grimace. "Come closer and I'll give it to you."

A flash of a grin was all the warning I got before Loch tackled me to the mats. He held his upper body so that his chest just barely brushed my breasts, but his hips were wedged firmly between my thighs, pinning me in place. "Is this close enough?" he asked. His deep voice was huskier than usual. I shivered as lust blazed hot and fast.

I patted him on the back before his growing erection destroyed my ability to think. "There you go. Shall I count for you?"

"I have a better idea," he murmured against my jaw. He trailed kisses up to the corner of my lips. I clutched his head when he would've moved on and slid my tongue into his mouth. He groaned and kissed me deeply.

I spread my legs wide, planted my feet, and lifted my hips to rub against him. We both hissed in pleasure. Loch helped me shimmy out of my clothes, and I pushed his shorts down to reveal he was commando underneath. I reached for him, but he backed away with a wicked gleam in his eyes.

He ran his hands from my ankles up to my knees, then pressed a kiss to my inner thigh just above my right knee. His hands inched higher and kisses followed their path. Anticipation tightened my stomach as I fought the conflicting desires for him to linger and to hurry. When his breath ghosted over my clit, I moaned and tilted my hips in invitation.

His lips closed around me and two fingers pressed inside. I clutched his head and rocked against his mouth, desperate to come, desperate to prolong the pleasure. Release roared toward me, driven by his clever lips and fingers and tongue. His name was a chant and a prayer as I tipped into bliss.

Loch barely gave me time to recover before he rolled me over onto my hands and knees. "Is this okay for your arm?" he asked, his voice tight.

Truth be told, I couldn't feel my arm over the pleasure still pulsing through my system, so I nodded. He groaned and rubbed against me. I shifted, impatient. He gripped my hips and entered me with one smooth thrust. He felt huge from this angle and hit every still-sensitive nerve I had. "Yes," I hissed.

He thrust slowly, once, twice, then froze. "Ah, fuck," he growled. "I need—" His control shattered, and he set a frantic pace that ratcheted my desire higher with every stroke. I dropped my chest to the floor and he felt even bigger. The pleasure nearly blinded me.

When he reached under me to pinch a stiff nipple while he continued to thrust, I hurtled into another orgasm with a gasp. He followed with a muttered curse and a groan. He pulled us over onto our right sides, still buried inside of me. He pressed a kiss to my shoulder and I sighed in bliss.

"For future reference, I like your ideas," I said.

He chuckled. "I'll keep that in mind," he said. "How are you feeling?"

"Better. Calmer. I don't feel like I'm going to crawl out of my skin," I said. "But it'll only last until I check my com. If Father has responded, expect me to go neurotic again. If he hasn't, well, same result really."

The proximity alarm went off. "*Polaris,* show me the location of the alarm," I said. A vid screen in the wall showed Rhys and Veronica on the cargo ramp. Veronica held a shopping bag, but my heart sank. If she was planning to go with me, she would've brought Lin and Imma. "Scan the immediate vicinity for life-forms."

"Two people detected in the cargo ramp quadrant," the ship replied.

"Open the cargo door and tell them we'll meet them in the mess."

**BY THE TIME WE CLEANED UP AND REDRESSED, RHYS** and Veronica had beat us to the mess hall. Rhys grinned when we walked in. "It's good to see you two getting along again," he said. "I thought I was going to have to knock your heads together."

"You're welcome to try," Loch growled at him, but there was no heat behind the words.

It had been nearly an hour since I messaged Father, so I checked my com. No response yet. I set it faceup on the table and tried to ignore it.

"Ada, I brought you boots," Veronica said. "I didn't know if you planned to go shopping, but I noticed you came out of Richard's *care*"—the word was heavy with sarcasm—"without any. I got a few different sizes."

"Thank you so much. Richard confiscated my only pair."

"I think this is the brand you wear," she said. She pulled four different sizes of my exact brand and style boot out of her bag. She had a brilliant eye for detail and noticed things that would slip past me.

I found the right size, pulled them on, and laced them up. They fit perfectly. "You're my hero," I said seriously.

She blushed and ducked her head. "Think nothing of it," she said.

My com vibrated against the table. I snatched it up. The breath whooshed out of me. Father had responded. I tapped the message with a trembling finger. This was the first direct communication we'd had in nearly two years.

"Is it from Albrecht?" Loch asked.

I nodded as I read. The message was mostly bluster, going on about how I should bring the ship in because it was my duty as a von Hasenberg and not because I wanted something from him. But under the bluster was a thread of reluctant respect—he was impressed that I'd captured an enemy ship.

I opened the contract. He'd modified a few minor wording issues but largely left it unchanged. He'd signed the contract with every request I'd asked for, even the ones I thought I wouldn't get. I double-checked that it truly was his signature, both physical and electronic. Both checked out.

He must be desperate to get his hands on *Polaris*.

"He agreed to everything I asked," I said. "I can get you all diplomatic immunity. He'll let me choose my own spouse and come and go freely." I looked up and met Loch's eyes. "He'll vote however I ask on one case of clemency."

"What did you agree to in return?" Rhys asked.

"Access to the ship for three months. All the alcubium on board. Which reminds me . . . could you store four containers of it for me? I'll swing back by and pick it up in about three months."

"Oh, that's clever," Rhys said. "And here I was starting to think you weren't living up to your House roots. Of course I will. What else?"

"I also promised him a week of debriefings on everything I know about the drive, XAD Six, and alcubium."

"That's it?" he asked.

"I know, right? It's unlike him not to at least try to negotiate terms. But the contract is legally binding and will stand up in the Consortium courts. I'd like you all to look it over, see if I'm missing something obvious."

I brought up the vid screen in the wall and transferred the contract to it, large enough that everyone could read it at once. They read in silence while I looked for anything that would invalidate the contract. Father was sneaky, after all.

"Everything looks fine to me," Rhys said.

"Me, too," Loch and Veronica agreed.

I turned to Veronica. She met my eyes and then glanced away. "Did Rhys persuade you to stay?" I asked gently.

"I can be *very* persuasive when I put my mind to it," Rhys said with a grin.

Veronica's face flushed with color. "Yes, I've decided to stay. However, when your father sends you to war, I want to go with you." She cut me off before I could do more than utter a syllable. "I know it will be dangerous. But I owe you. I know you say I don't, but I do. And besides that, I like you and don't want you to die. So I will go with you and keep you out of trouble."

"Good luck," Loch muttered. I elbowed him in the side.

"And I'm going, too," Rhys said. "So don't think about leaving me out of the loop. And if Albrecht even *thinks* about going back on his word, you know we'll bust you out."

Loch sighed and ran a hand over his head. "Rhys is right; your father better not try any shit. And I suppose I won't mind sharing a ship with these two again."

"You don't know how much your support means to me," I

said. I hugged each of them. "I'm going to miss you. I will try to visit even before I get my ship back."

Rhys and Veronica left a little while later. They were trying to convert back to local time and it was already deep into the night. Loch stayed but we both knew our time was limited.

I signed the contract and sent it to Father, along with a note that I would arrive tomorrow, barring any trouble. Postponing my departure would just make it harder. Besides, the sooner I left, the sooner I could return.

I found Loch on the flight deck, going through the maintenance records for the ship. "Find anything interesting?" I asked.

"Just ensuring everything is ready for you," he said. "I know it's only one jump, but I won't be there if anything goes wrong. It's making me crazy."

I bent down and pressed a kiss to his neck. "How about I distract you?"

He made a sound low in his chest. "I could be persuaded," he said.

I swung his chair away from the console and straddled his lap, facing him. Then, with a grin, I proceeded to show him just how persuasive I could be.

# CHAPTER 26

The next morning I found Loch back on the flight deck, staring moodily into a steaming cup of coffee. As far as I could tell, neither of us had slept well.

Loch met my gaze and his jaw clenched. He looked like a man getting ready to impart bad news. Nervousness settled into my belly as I imagined what he was going to say. Had he decided I was too much trouble for a relationship after all? What if this was truly goodbye?

"I'm going with you," he said, his voice hard.

I blinked, sure I'd heard him wrong.

"If you won't take me on *Polaris,* I'll follow on my own. But either way, I'm going with you. I know it's not safe and I don't care."

Relief and joy surprised a laugh out of me. "Okay," I said.

Now he was the one who looked blindsided. "You're going to agree, just like that?"

"Yes. In fact, I was going to ask you to come. I couldn't sleep last night, so I spent the night thinking. I have a plan, but it's dangerous."

His smirk was sharp enough to cut. "*I'm* dangerous," he said. "It's time the Consortium figured that out firsthand."

I shook my head. "If you go in as a threat, they'll treat you like one and eliminate you. This is my area of expertise. You have to be willing to trust me and follow my lead, even when it seems what I'm doing is counterintuitive."

I held my breath as his eyes raked over my face. Finally, he sighed and nodded. "I'll defer to your expertise. But if things get dicey, I'll get us out by whatever means necessary. Let's hear your plan."

"I'll bring you with me as my bodyguard. Thanks to the contract with Father, I can get you diplomatic immunity. It won't prevent the other Houses from attempting to capture you if they realize who you truly are, but it will give you some cover. Do you have a secondary identity chip and a clean identity?"

Loch nodded. "I contacted Rhys this morning to make sure it was still good."

"That will make things easier. I'm going to have to let my sister Bianca know your real identity because I need her help. We'll use your secondary identity for everyone else." I sighed. "It's still going to be risky. It would be much safer for you to stay here."

"I'm going. And going as your bodyguard is a lot less risky than sneaking in, which was my other plan."

I stared. "You're kidding, right?"

His grin did not reassure me.

**I SENT BIANCA A PRIORITY MESSAGE WHILE WE WAITED** for a jump point. I'd need her help as soon as I landed, so it was better to give her at least a little warning. Loch had clipped into the navigator's chair while I wrote the message. I slid into the captain's chair and tried to ignore my nerves.

After we received the jump point, I triggered the hangar's roof door to open, then let *Polaris* take off under autopilot. The route to Earth was already programmed.

I was going home.

The thought didn't fill me with the warmth I thought it would. I felt vaguely uneasy. I'd changed a lot in the last two years. I wasn't as naive or trusting, and while I was still loyal to House von Hasenberg, I'd lost the rose-colored glasses. I wasn't sure my family would appreciate the changes, especially when they arrived along with a convicted murderer/bodyguard and a lot of uncomfortable questions about the Genesis Project.

APD Zero dropped away and the sky opened up. As soon as we'd cleared the atmosphere and put enough distance between us and the other ships in the area, the FTL kicked in and we jumped.

I hadn't swapped out the alcubium, so this was a conventional FTL jump. I kept an eye on the systems as we popped out the other side, but the time in Sedition meant the drive had had plenty of time to cool down. The ship slid neatly back into normal space and Earth glowed blue in front of us.

"Beautiful, isn't it?" Loch asked.

"Yes," I whispered. It was hard to imagine that the entirety of the Consortium's vast power flowed from this little sphere of blue and green.

Because of its importance, everything within a light-year of Earth was neutral territory. That neutrality was fiercely defended by the most seasoned of the RCDF forces. No matter what happened between Houses out in the greater universe, Earth remained peaceful.

That meant I had a good chance of seeing Richard in person at the next Consortium event, and I couldn't even punch him in his pretty face. And I had no idea how I was going to prevent Loch from going after him.

No one challenged us as we approached. I'd added my House seal to the ship's registration. The RCDF would verify the validity of the seal, but once it proved genuine, they wouldn't even log our passing—only non-House ships were logged.

The House designation also meant that I'd been able to request a jump point much closer to the planet. We'd be on the surface in less than thirty minutes. My fingers trembled with anxiety.

I began pulling on my public persona. The spaceport might be in von Hasenberg territory, but it was still public. My father would expect me to act above reproach until I was safely in our private residence. And if I was going to bluff Loch's presence in, I'd need to be as cold as ice.

I pushed my anxiety deep, until I was a still lake. I could do this. I *would* do this. We entered the atmosphere and my calm barely rippled.

*Polaris* dropped toward Serenity, the only city on Earth and the heart of the Royal Consortium. Thousands of years after Earth was abandoned, the Consortium had worked for decades to make it habitable once again. Then they turned it into the seat of their power and a natural museum to human history. Anyone was welcome to visit, but few were invited to stay.

The city itself formed a circle, with the Consortium common buildings in the center and the three remaining High Houses each in their own quarter. The last quarter used to belong to the fourth High House, but after its fall, the lower houses took over, moving in from the outer sectors.

Each quarter operated independently, with its own utilities, amenities, and security. The quarters were divided into sectors starting from the middle and moving outward. Sector One, the innermost sector, contained the family residence for House members. Access was restricted to family and high-ranking staff.

Sectors Two through Ten contained various extended family and staff residences, as well as offices, shops, and all of the other things found in a large city. The sector numbers were used mainly for addresses and directions—sectors weren't divided by functionality. Travel between the various quarters and sectors was encouraged and frequent.

The von Hasenberg family spaceport was on the outer edge of Sector One. There was a larger spaceport out past Sector Ten, but *Polaris* was small enough not to need the extra room.

Serenity was spectacular on approach, a beautiful city carved out of a lush green jungle. The ocean sparkled in the distance, a shining blue jewel.

Each quarter's architecture reflected the High House who claimed it for its own, especially in the inner sectors. The outer sectors tended to be high-rises, as the need for housing outstripped the need for design.

But the family residences were works of architectural art.

House Rockhurst's residence was a gleaming metal and glass building with clean lines and simple, elegant design details. House Yamado's residence was a beautiful natural wood building with a stunning curved tile roof. And House von Hasenberg's residence was a stone building with tiny, intricate details carved into each of the various facades. I'd stared at our house for hours and discovered new details each time.

*Polaris* settled into a hangar at the family spaceport with a barely perceptible bump and anxiety tried to break through my control. I took a deep breath and held it until I no longer felt like I would vomit the instant I moved.

Loch unclipped and bent down to peek at my face. "You okay?"

"I will be," I said. Loch nodded and pulled on the hooded cloak we'd decided was his best defense against recognition. I took a deep breath and stood. Loch shouldered both of our bags. Showtime.

No one came out to greet us, so I locked up the ship and headed to the house. I used my real identity chip to let us in. This was a side door, so the foyer wasn't as grand as the main entrance, but the marble floors and plaster walls were just as I remembered them. A passing staffer gave us a curious glance, but other than that, no one noticed our arrival.

Disappointment stabbed deep.

I don't know why I expected Father to be waiting with open

arms, but I guess childhood dreams are the slowest to die. I stiffened my spine and decided to beard the lion in his den.

"Stay close," I murmured to Loch.

I found Albrecht in his study, consulting with three of his military advisors. The room was filled with rich wood paneling and heavy, ornate furniture. It was a room designed to intimidate, and when I was younger, it had worked. Looking at it now, though, it appeared hollowly ostentatious.

"Hello, Father," I said, not bothering to wait until he acknowledged me. The three advisors darted startled glances at me but none dared to comment. *Cowards.*

Albrecht was a little older and grayer than the last time I saw him, but he'd lost none of his presence. His gaze pinned me in place. He waved a hand at his advisors without looking at them. "Leave us. Return in ten."

They practically tripped over themselves to exit the room.

"Where is the ship?" Albrecht asked.

"It is nice to see you, too, Father. Yes, I have been well, thank you for asking." At his pointed glare, I continued, "*Polaris* is in the family hangar. The House codes are allowed as first officers." It would allow the scientists and engineers access to the ship without allowing them to remove me as captain.

I'd also geofenced the ship to Earth's orbit, so there would be no long-distance travel without me on board. If Father wanted more access, he'd have to renegotiate our deal or crack my override codes.

"Who is that?" Albrecht asked, gesturing at Loch.

"My bodyguard. He requires diplomatic immunity, as agreed."

Father brushed a nonexistent crumb from his dark suit jacket. "Ian will take care of it. Expect debriefing to start in two hours. You are dismissed." He turned back to the display on his desk.

"Debriefing will begin tomorrow or not at all," I said calmly.

Father looked up with narrowed eyes. That look meant trouble. Anxiety churned through my system, but I kept my face serene. I would not be steamrolled this time. I felt Loch move closer as I stared down one of the three most powerful people in the universe.

When I didn't flinch or look away, Father's lips twitched into a grimace. "You always were the one with the most backbone," he said. "Damned inconvenient, but you did manage to bring me a Rockhurst ship. Debriefing will begin tomorrow at six. Do not push me further."

I inclined my head. "Thank you, Father," I said. I retreated before he could change his mind.

In the safety of the hallway, the adrenaline pumping through my body made me shaky and nauseous. I kept my facade intact and breathed through it. I had too many things to do to have a breakdown. First and foremost, I needed to track down Bianca.

"So that was your father," Loch said quietly. His tone was neutral and his voice was flat. I couldn't guess at what he was thinking.

"That was him in a good mood," I said.

"Are all the councillors of the High Houses like him?"

"In one way or another. Lady Rockhurst is known to be coolly levelheaded and ruthlessly persistent. Lord Yamado has an explosive temper and both the will and the firepower to back up his threats. House von Hasenberg has long been known as the moderate House, but being moderate compared to the extremes isn't exactly moderate."

I led Loch back toward my suite, so he could drop off our stuff before we went looking for Bianca. Walking down the familiar hall to my rooms brought back a million memories. This house was saturated in them. I opened the door, unsure what to expect.

My suite looked exactly the same.

The foyer opened to a large living area with clustered seating areas. Done in shades of cream and blue with dark hardwood floors, my suite had always been an oasis in the heart of the Consortium storm. On the left was a small, fully functional kitchen—though the synthesizer saw more use than the stove. A dining table for fourteen dominated that side of the room.

On the right were the doors leading to the formal sitting room and study. A hallway led deeper into the suite to the guest bath and my private rooms. Just seeing it again, preserved as if I'd never left, was enough to bring tears to my eyes. I blinked them away and ushered Loch in.

"You're late," Bianca called from the sitting room.

I froze for a half a breath, then I ran to greet her. "Bianca!"

Bianca sat on a brown and gold brocade settee, but she stood when I entered the room. She wore a somber gray day dress that still managed to emphasize her delicate figure. Bianca wore the colors of mourning while in public thanks to her bastard husband's death nearly a year ago. In another month or two she could return to her usual bright colors and she would be free of the man once and for all.

She was the shortest member of the family by far, so she made up for it by wearing ridiculous heels. The pair strapped to her feet today seemed to defy gravity. When I hugged her, we were the same height, even though I knew she was more than ten centimeters shorter than me.

She squeezed me tightly. "I'm glad you're back," she said softly. "I worried about you."

Bianca felt almost fragile in my arms. She'd lost weight she couldn't afford to lose. I pulled away to look at her face. Under the carefully applied makeup, she looked tired and worn. "What's going on?" I asked her.

Her smile was quick and rueful. "I should've known you would notice," she said. "I am fine, just tired. I've had a lot on my plate lately."

I looked away. A lot of that stress was due to me. "I'm sorry," I said. "I never meant for you to work yourself to the bone. You should know that."

"It's not your fault," she said. At my disbelieving look she amended, "Okay, it's not *all* your fault." Her eyes darted over my shoulder. "But I would like an introduction to the man who is trying to claim my baby sister."

"Be nice," I warned.

"I'm always nice," she said innocently, but her smile spelled danger.

"I'm assuming you swept for bugs?" I asked. At her nod, I waved Loch into the room from where he was hovering at the door, still cloaked and hooded. "Bianca, meet Marcus Loch," I said when he reached my side. "Marcus, meet my older sister Bianca. You can take off the cloak."

Loch threw back his hood. His face was set in hard, forbidding lines. He crossed his arms over his chest and stared down at Bianca. He looked as welcoming as an arctic tundra.

"If you hurt her," Bianca said softly, her smile still in place, "I will geld you with a rusty fork."

Loch blinked then raised an eyebrow. "Think you can?"

"Absolutely," she said with utter certainty.

Loch laughed, fracturing his badass image. "In that case, it's nice to meet you, Lady Bianca," he said, extending a hand. "And if I hurt her, I'll let you."

She nodded in understanding and shook his hand. "It's just Bianca when we're with family," she said firmly.

"Now that we've gotten the threats portion of our day out of the way, can we get down to business?" I asked. "Loch has a clean identity on a secondary chip. We are going to need Ian to set him up with diplomatic immunity."

Bianca barely flinched at Ian's name, but it was enough for me to catch. She wasn't in public persona mode, so it was easier to read her. Ian Bishop was the director of House von Hasenberg security. He and Bianca had some sort of history, but I'd never been able to pry it out of her.

"How good is the identity?" Bianca asked.

"Rhys set it up," Loch said. "It's solid."

"Okay, then the identity is the least of our worries. But Ian is bound to recognize you," Bianca said, "and you can't go around cloaked all of the time. Even if we figure out how to deal with Ian, someone else will recognize you."

"There's no way around recognition, at least not here," Loch said. "The identity I have lists me as Marcus Loch's cousin. I'll claim familial looks. With a solid identity it should hold, but it forces me to rely on diplomatic immunity more than I'd like." Loch shrugged. "It's the best Rhys and I came up with on short notice."

I didn't love the plan, but between the debriefings and working behind the scenes to get Loch a pardon, I planned to lie low. Loch wouldn't be too exposed until I had to start moving in Consortium society. And I would hold off on that until I was close to a pardon hearing.

Bianca didn't look convinced, either, but she didn't object, which meant she didn't have a better alternative. "What do you need for the pardon?" she asked.

"I need everything you can dig up on the Genesis Project," I said. I briefly filled her in on the details and was gratified to see her get more and more upset. By the time I was done, she practically vibrated with the need to get started.

"Leave it to me," she said.

A huge weight lifted from my shoulders. Bianca was the best at information gathering. If it could be found, she would find it. "Thank you," I said.

"You're welcome," she said. "Send Ian a message and ask him to come here. He'll be easier to deal with here than in the main security office if something goes wrong."

"Didi, ask Director Bishop to come to my suite to add my bodyguard to the diplomatic immunity roster," I said. A chime sounded throughout the room as the suite computer sent my message. "I wasn't sure that would still work," I said.

I'd changed the name of my suite computer to Didi ages ago, but I had expected Father to wipe everything after I left.

Bianca caught the direction of my thoughts. "As far as I know, Father didn't touch your room," Bianca said. "I checked on things a few times, but I don't think anyone else, other than staff, ventured inside."

Another, subtler chime sounded. "Read the message," I said.

"Director Bishop replied that he is on his way," Didi said.

Bianca started fidgeting. Anxiety churned in my gut. Only Loch, the one with the most to lose, looked completely calm. He pulled me into a half hug with an arm around my waist. "It will be fine," he said. "You know Rhys's identities are bulletproof."

"The identity may be bulletproof, but you're not," I reminded him.

He gave me a squeeze and brushed a kiss across my temple. "We've got this. Now, what's my name?"

"Vincent Loch," I said. "Marcus Loch's cousin on his father's side, as far as you can tell." The key to a good identity was the details, and Rhys always sweated the details. Vincent Loch had a family, deceased, of course, but with all the paper trails necessary to throw off all but the most dogged investigators.

The suite doorbell rang. "Director Bishop is at the door," Didi said. I pulled on my public persona and watched Bianca do the same. It was always odd to watch the change on someone else. Bianca's face smoothed out and her expression went cold and distant. Her chin tilted up just slightly, and her eyes were flat and hard.

I moved to the sitting room doorway, then checked if Bianca and Loch were ready. Bianca settled back onto the settee then nodded. Loch lounged against the wall. "I'm ready when you are, darling."

"Let Director Bishop in," I said.

# CHAPTER 27

The suite door opened and Ian Bishop stepped inside. I'd never seen him in anything other than a suit or tuxedo and today was no different. He wore a dark navy suit with a white shirt and pale blue tie. He was a handsome man, with blond hair and blue eyes and just enough rough edges to be interesting.

Ian bowed slightly. "Lady Ada, I heard you had returned. I am glad you are safe." He sounded almost sincere, despite the fact that I'd been *unsafe* for two years thanks to him.

"Thank you, Director Bishop. Please, come in." He stepped past me into the sitting room. He was nearly as tall as Loch, but built a little leaner. In his late twenties, he was incredibly young for the director of security of a High House. He'd climbed through the ranks so fast no one had noticed until he was running the show.

"You already know Lady Bianca," I said with a wave to her. Even watching closely I couldn't see a reaction from either of them. Bianca was well and truly in public mode.

"And this," I said, turning to Loch, "is Vincent Loch, my bodyguard. He needs diplomatic immunity and access to the house. I've already cleared it with Father."

An odd look passed between Loch and Ian, but it was over before I could catch the meaning.

"*Vincent* Loch, you say?" Ian asked.

"In the flesh," Loch said.

"Lady Bianca, Lady Ada, may I speak with you privately?" Ian asked, his gaze laser-focused on Loch.

"No, you may not," I said. "Mr. Loch is in my employ. I vouch for him. Add diplomatic immunity and house access to his identity chip."

"You are making a mistake," Ian said. He met my eyes. "He is dangerous."

"Not to me," I said simply. "And I advise you to keep your theories to yourself. If anything happens to Mr. Loch, I will come after *you* and then you will see who is truly dangerous."

Ian stared at me for a few more seconds as if judging my seriousness, then he smiled. Bianca's eyes widened before she regained her icy control. She had it bad, but he *was* incredibly gorgeous when he smiled. I wondered what would happen if I accidentally locked them in a closet together.

"Very well," Ian said at last. He turned to Loch. "I need to scan your identity chip."

Loch held out his right arm. Ian used his com to scan the chip then tapped on the screen a few times. "Your identity has been tagged with House von Hasenberg diplomatic immunity, but that won't necessarily prevent other Houses from arresting you. Stay out of trouble."

"I'm not here to cause trouble. I'm just here to protect

Lady Ada," Loch said. He grinned and continued, "*She's* here to cause trouble."

Ian slanted me a sharp glance. I shrugged. "I am not going to blow up the building, if that is what you are thinking. I am on a diplomatic mission."

"I will ensure Lady Ada stays out of trouble," Bianca said.

Ian did not look reassured. But his gaze had snagged on Bianca and now seemed stuck. *Interesting.*

"If you are finished," Bianca said, "you are free to go." She followed it up with a dismissive sniff. The condescension was so perfectly executed that if I hadn't seen her reaction earlier, I'd buy it—and I was her sister.

Ian didn't stand a chance.

He stiffened as if struck, then his mask slid back in place. He bowed to Bianca and then myself. "Ladies, I am glad to be of service. Please let me know if you need anything else." He didn't wait for dismissal; he just walked from the room and let himself out of the suite.

I rounded on Bianca. "What was that?" I asked, outraged on Ian's behalf. She tried the sniff on me and I laughed at her. "Oh, no, that doesn't work on me. Spill."

Bianca's public persona crumpled and she looked small and frail and sad. "I don't know," she said miserably. "I always say the wrong thing to him, so I've started preemptively striking to end the conversation early. It's less embarrassing for both of us."

I crossed the room and sat next to her. I pulled her into a hug. "Hey, it's okay," I said. "You like him, right?"

"Yes," she whispered. "But it's one-sided."

"You don't know that—" I started.

"I do, actually."

I winced. Okay, that had to sting.

"Just let it go, please," she said quietly.

I nodded my agreement and changed the subject. "What are the odds that Ian will go to Father with his suspicions about Loch?"

"I don't know," she said.

"He'll keep it to himself for now," Loch said. "If not, he wouldn't have warned me about the limits of the diplomatic immunity."

"We'll still have to keep a low profile and hope Rhys's identity holds," I said. "And get the info about the Genesis Project as quickly as possible."

Bianca stood. "I will get started. Will you host dinner tonight?"

I nodded as I rose. It was tradition that whichever sibling was most recently returned from a trip would host a dinner for the others. "Who is around?"

"So far, just Benedict and myself," Bianca said. Benedict was Bianca's twin brother. "With the war, Father called everyone in, but they haven't arrived yet."

I smiled. It was rare for all of us to be together at once. House business usually kept my siblings spread across the universe, with only one or two stationed in Serenity to represent House von Hasenberg's interests. It would be nice to be able to catch up with everyone, even if it was under the threat of war.

Bianca turned to Loch. "Remember my vow," she said.

He inclined his head with a poorly suppressed grin.

**AFTER BIANCA LEFT, I SHOWED LOCH AROUND MY** suite. It was one thing for him to know I was the daughter of a High House but it was entirely different for him to see it. I flushed with embarrassment. My *guest* bathroom was bigger than most of the places I'd stayed in the last two years.

Loch's scowl deepened in each new room. By the time we reached the master bedroom, he'd returned to the chilly, forbidding face he'd used to meet Bianca. When I reached out to touch his arm and he didn't react, I knew we needed to talk.

"Okay, I know I'm hideously embarrassed for you to see how spoiled I was growing up, but what's going on with you?" He tried to shrug me off, but I tightened my grip. "Communication is important, remember?"

He refused to meet my eyes, but finally he said, "How am I supposed to compete with all of this?"

"You're not," I said. "I don't care about any of this stuff. I left it all behind. It's true that I like a little luxury when I can get it, but I have enough money to make that happen—for both of us." I swallowed and looked away. I couldn't preach communication then refuse to follow through. "I care about *you* far more than I care about any of this," I said, waving a hand at the suite.

Heat crept up my cheeks. I held my breath to see what he was going to do with the fragile piece of my heart I'd extended. I peeked up at him to find him staring at me as if he could see the thoughts in my head if only he tried hard enough.

"You mean that," he said.

"Of course—"

His lips slanted across mine, interrupting my words and scrambling my brain. His tongue traced my lips and I opened with a moan. He pulled me closer as his tongue slid into my mouth. I pressed up against him and slipped my hands under his shirt to caress the rippling muscles of his stomach. He made a deep sound of pleasure that sent lust bolting through me.

A few minutes later, I pulled back with a groan. When Loch tried to follow, I pressed a kiss to the corner of his mouth. "I have to put in the dinner order with the kitchen before you distract me and I forget," I said.

He gave me one last squeeze then let me go. "Hurry," he said with a devastating grin.

Stepping away from that grin was nearly impossible, but I forced myself out of the room and to my study. If I stayed in the bedroom with him, dinner would be the last thing on my mind.

The study looked the same as I remembered, with silvery walls and an antique wooden desk that dominated the middle of the room. A mail cart had been added next to the desk. It was piled high with luxury paper invitations to various Consortium events. A large, flat box topped the pile.

I sat down at the desk and pulled up my House account on the terminal. I sent the invite to Benedict and Bianca then put in a food order with the kitchens. I had neither the time nor the energy to cook, and while I could pull everything out of the synthesizer, I'd gotten used to eating freshly prepared food again thanks to Veronica.

As I stood up, the box caught my eye again. Packages were unusual. Curious, I picked it up. It felt light for its size and didn't rattle when I shook it. There was no return address, but it had been sent from APD Zero several days ago, before I'd gone to the Antlia sector. Had Rhys sent me something and not mentioned it?

I opened the box and gently dumped the contents on my desk. A tissue paper-wrapped bundle of red fabric slipped out, along with a folded note. I picked up the note first. Bold script flowed across the page.

*Darling Ada,*
*Not everything has to be left behind.*
*—L*

I carefully unwrapped the tissue paper, revealing the red dress I'd desperately wanted but had talked myself out of buying. Loch had bought it for me while I shopped for practical clothes. Tears pricked my eyes and I blinked rapidly to clear them.

I touched the fabric reverently, almost afraid the dress would disappear. I looked up and caught Loch watching me from the doorway. I knew he must've seen the depth of my emotion, but I couldn't hide it and didn't want to. He'd touched me deeply.

"Marcus, it's perfect. It's the best possible thing you could've given me," I said softly. "How did you know to send it here?"

"I sent it the morning before we left APD Zero to hunt for the Rockhurst planet. With the war looming, I knew you'd find your way home sooner or later. I wanted you to have something to remember me by."

"I prefer having *you* to remember you by," I said with a smile, "but I'm not going to turn down a gorgeous dress."

"Try it on," he said.

"You just want to see me naked," I teased.

"Sweetheart, I never tire of seeing you naked," he rumbled at me. He was *so* getting laid tonight.

I took the dress to the bedroom. I stripped off my practical clothes, then slid the dress over my head. It fit perfectly. I went to the full-length mirror in my closet to see how it looked. The snug bodice and V-neck enhanced my figure without making me look like a twig.

I twirled and the skirt fanned out around my legs. I could conquer the universe in this dress.

I met Loch's eyes in the mirror. "I'm going to wear this dress to your pardon hearing," I said. "And then, when we get home, I'm going to demand you remove the dress. Slowly. With your teeth," I said with a saucy grin.

He stepped up behind me, wrapped his arms around my waist, and nuzzled my neck. "Maybe I should practice now," he murmured against my skin.

I shivered. "I think that is an excellent plan."

He proved just how talented his mouth could be.

AFTER DRAGGING MYSELF OUT OF BED, I'D SHOWERED and redressed in clothes I'd found in my closet. The silver and blue dress I'd chosen was a modest tea length, but I still felt almost naked without the sturdy pants and long-sleeved shirts I'd lived in for the last two years.

"Are you sure you won't join us?" I asked for the tenth time.

Loch reclined on the bed, watching me get ready. He shook his head, as exasperated with me as I was with him.

"*Why* won't you join us? You already met Bianca. I want Benedict to meet you."

"The fewer people who know about me, the better," he said. "I'll meet him after the bounty is lifted."

"My parents may not be the nicest people in the universe"—huge, huge understatement—"but my siblings would never do something to hurt me, and betraying you would hurt me." Our parents had tried to drive us apart, to pit us against one another, but it had massively failed. Everything they tried just drove us closer together.

"What if he thinks it's for your own good? Are you saying your brother wouldn't opt for you to feel a little short-term pain in return for a long-term benefit? Tell me you absolutely believe that and I'll join you for dinner."

I hesitated and the argument was lost. I knew my sisters would stick with me no matter what, even if they had to threaten Loch's balls to make their point, but my brothers were the wild cards. I couldn't say with absolute confidence that Benedict wouldn't think turning Loch in was for my own good.

"Fine," I grumbled. "But I still don't like it."

"Ada, go, enjoy your family. Don't worry about me."

The doorbell rang before I could argue further. "Kitchen runners are at the door," Didi said.

"Let them in and tell them to arrange dinner on the table. I will be there directly." I crossed the room and kissed Loch. "Once they leave, I'll bring you dinner. There's also a synthesizer in my private sitting room if you need anything. Dinner will probably run late. If you change your mind at any time, you're always welcome to join us."

I reluctantly left Marcus in bed and closed the bedroom door behind me. The kitchen staff was nearly done. Each place setting was laid out with stemware and cutlery. The wine had been decanted to breathe and now two staffers transferred food from the cart to the table.

I'd ordered individual dinners because my siblings were a bunch of damn picky eaters. Bianca ate meat, but she preferred fish, while Benedict couldn't stomach "anything with fins." Luckily, the kitchen maintained a list of each person's favorite meals.

Each dinner arrived in an elegant silver thermoregulator. The chefs figured thermoreg time into their cooking schedule, so the meal was hot and ready at the appropriate time. It gave the staff time to set up the meal and leave before guests arrived.

A young woman in a House uniform set a vase of fresh-cut flowers in the middle of the table. "Do you need anything else, Lady Ada?" she asked.

"It looks lovely, thank you."

She bowed and the staff withdrew. My brother and sister would arrive in a little over five minutes, which gave me just enough time to deliver Loch's dinner. I checked the labels but I needn't have bothered—the staff laid out the table exactly as I requested.

I picked up Loch's dinner and place setting. What do you know, waitressing skills came in handy when you had to balance too many things on too few arms.

Loch raised an eyebrow when I eased into the room. "Need a hand?" he asked.

"It'll be easier if you grab the thermoreg, thanks," I said as I neared. He stood and took it, then set it on the nightstand. I put the rest of his cutlery beside it.

"You ordered me dinner," he said, a strange inflection in his voice.

"Oh, well, you don't have to eat it. As I said before–"

He touched my jaw and brushed his thumb over my lips. "Thank you, Ada."

I smiled and kissed his palm. "You're welcome. I hope you enjoy it. Give it fifteen minutes or so to finish cooking."

The doorbell rang before he could respond. Of course Benedict and Bianca were going to be on time. "Your dinner guests are at the door," Didi said.

"Let them in," I said. They knew their way around my suite and would make themselves at home until I joined them.

"Go," Loch said. When I hesitated, he turned me toward the door and smacked my butt with a grin. I blew him a kiss over my shoulder.

Time to face the twins.

BIANCA AND BENEDICT STOOD AT THE KITCHEN BAR. Benedict sniffed a bottle of clear alcohol with a grimace. "Do you think this is still good?" he asked Bianca as he held the bottle up to the light.

"You're the connoisseur, not me," she said with a shrug.

Benedict looked down to frown at her and caught sight of me. "Ada!" he cried.

He and Bianca shared the same long face, sharp nose,

and light brown hair that they'd inherited from Father. Bianca softened her look with careful makeup and hair dye, but Benedict embraced the stamp of familial legacy. Standing together, it would be immediately obvious that they were related, as it would be for any of my four older siblings. I'd felt like an odd duck with the dark hair and golden skin I'd inherited from Mother, at least until my little sister Catarina was born—she looked just like me.

Benedict had let his wavy hair grow out some since the last time I'd seen him. He smiled as he came around the bar. He squeezed me in a tight hug then leaned back until my feet left the ground. He was the tallest sibling, and Bianca constantly grouched that he'd stolen all of her height.

"Hello, Benedict," I said with a laugh. "I missed you, too."

Benedict put me back on my feet, then held me out at arm's length. "Are you okay? We've been worried about you," he said. "I recently heard a crazy rumor that you'd fought off fifteen mercs with a spoon. Can you believe that?"

"Well . . ." I hedged. I hadn't actually *fought* the mercenaries with a spoon. I'd distracted them then ran away, narrowly escaping. It had happened on the station before the one where Captain Pearson had picked me up.

Benedict turned outraged eyes to Bianca. "Did you know about this?"

"Who do you think started the rumor?" she asked with a grin.

"My sisters are going to be the death of me," Benedict muttered to himself. "I don't care if your alcohol has gone bad, I need a drink." He squeezed my shoulders then let me go and moved back to the bar. "Let me know if you want something other than the usual."

"The usual is awesome," I said, and Bianca agreed. Benedict made a mean martini and few of us strayed from it.

"Coming right up!" he said.

Bianca and I settled into the living room couches. She sat across from me, and after Benedict handed me my drink, he joined her. By unspoken agreement, we didn't talk about the impending war. Instead, my brother and sister did their best to catch me up on two years of gossip in an evening. When dinner was ready, we moved to the table and clustered around one end with Benedict sitting at the head.

The food was delicious and wine and cocktails flowed freely. Benedict and Bianca relished telling me about one another's most embarrassing moments, even as the embarrassed person groaned at the telling. Then, without any other siblings here to stop them, they launched into tales of the others' embarrassing moments.

It was perfect.

I'd proven that I could handle myself out in the world alone, but I loved having my siblings around. I'd missed this. However, I also found myself turning to look for Loch, and he wasn't there. The third time I did it, Bianca caught my eye and raised an eyebrow. I tilted my head very slightly toward the bedroom. She nodded.

As the hour grew late, Benedict retired for the night, but Bianca made herself at home on the couch. I sat down next to her.

She turned to me. "So, spill," she said.

"About what?" I asked. I had hoped to avoid an inquisition, but I should've known that Bianca wouldn't waste an opportunity to grill me while we were alone.

"I don't know, why don't we start with the hulking convict you brought home who touches you like you're his." Bianca said it sarcastically, but a thread of true worry lurked in her tone. "Of all the men in the universe, you had to pick the Devil of Fornax Zero?"

I shrugged. "It started out as a business deal, but the more time I spent with him, the more I liked him. Plus, he's hot."

Bianca smiled but she wasn't deterred so easily. "You believe his version of what happened on Fornax Zero?"

"Yes," I said. "His story is corroborated by another friend who has no reason to lie."

"How are you going to use the Genesis Project information to get him pardoned?"

"I have Father's agreement to vote on a clemency hearing of my choice, so I just have to bring Yamado or Rockhurst around to my side. I think enough careful threats about going public with the details might do it."

She thought about it for a moment, then nodded in agreement. "Are you sleeping with him?" she asked abruptly.

Heat spread through my face, which was answer enough.

"You never were one for easy paths," she said at last. "Be careful, Ada. I don't want to see you get hurt." Something old and sad touched her expression before she wiped it away with a raised eyebrow. "Why didn't you invite him to dinner?"

"I did, but he thinks that keeping a low profile is the smarter move until he's cleared. He's probably right."

"Benedict wouldn't betray you," Bianca said, "and I've already met him."

"I know. But old habits die hard, and he's been on the run for a long time." I decided that inquisitions could work both ways. "What's going on with you?" I asked.

Her expression flickered before smoothing into a smile. "I'm not used to the whirl of the Consortium anymore," she said. "And remembering to play the grieving widow in public is taxing." She stood before I could respond. "Speaking of, I have to get up for Lady Yamado's breakfast in the morning," she said, "so I need to get to bed."

I knew a dodge when I heard one, but she looked tired enough that I didn't call her on it. I walked her to the door.

Bianca pulled me into a tight hug. "I never told you this," she said softly, "but Hannah offered me the chance to run, once Father started making noise about my wedding. I couldn't do it. I don't exactly regret my choice, especially because my husband's timely death left me a happy widow, but I'm so proud of you," she said.

It didn't surprise me that Hannah, our oldest sister, had offered Bianca an out. Father had arranged Hannah's marriage without her input. It was not a happy union.

"What about Catarina?" I asked, worried about our youngest sister. "Has Father started on her?"

Bianca's expression turned dark. "Yes," she said. "Cat is playing along for now, and Hannah and I are doing what we can to stall, but it won't be enough. She's like you—independent and not willing to settle for someone of Father's choosing. We may need to get her out."

"Or let her get married then kill her husband," I said, mostly joking.

Bianca smiled a secret smile. "That is one option," she said. Before I could question her about it, she nodded and left.

I breathed a sigh of relief once the quiet settled over my room. I'd gotten used to fewer people and quieter surroundings. It would take me a while to settle into the hustle and bustle of House von Hasenberg again.

That is, assuming my plan didn't get me killed.

# CHAPTER 28

A fter a week of debriefing, I was ready to make a run for freedom. Eighteen-hour days meant at the end of each day Loch and I barely had time to fall into bed before we had to start the process over the next day. I could feel him growing more distant by the day, but I didn't know how to fix it.

Add to that the fact that Bianca was having trouble tracking down information about the Genesis Project, even with Rhys and Veronica's help, and I was ready to snap.

I stood and stretched, trying unsuccessfully to work the knots out of my back. It was nearly midnight. Hunger had hallowed out my stomach hours before but no one had taken the time to order food. The middle-aged scientist who'd been questioning me about alcubium looked up. His name was lost somewhere in the exhausted fog in my brain. "You're not leaving, are you?" he asked.

I'd spent a week wearing my public persona, so Mother's glare came as naturally as breathing. The man flinched back.

"I *am* leaving," I said. "And I am taking tomorrow off. Tell the teams." A week of debriefing fulfilled my contract with Father, so technically I was done, but I knew the scientists still had questions.

"But, my lady," he stammered.

This time my glare was sharp enough to cut. "The only words I want to hear from you right now are 'Yes, Lady Ada.'"

He gulped. "Yes, Lady Ada."

"Very good. The first person tomorrow who messages me, or knocks on my door, or disturbs me *in any way,* dies. The same goes for the second person. And so on. Do I make myself clear?"

His eyes were huge. "But Lord von—"

"Do. I. Make. Myself. Clear?" I asked again, jabbing a finger into the desk with each word and leaning forward until I loomed over him.

"Yes, Lady Ada."

I inclined my head slightly and swept out of the room. By the time we made it to the suite I was ready to crash facedown on whichever horizontal surface happened to be handy. Even the floor looked tempting.

Loch led me to the table when I wanted nothing more than the bed. I nearly cried. He pulled me into his arms. "Shhh," he said. "You need to eat. I've been listening to your stomach growl for hours and it's driving me insane. Let me feed you."

I nodded against his shoulder and slid into a chair. I think I must've dozed off because the next thing I knew, Loch was setting a plate of food in front of me. I ate without tasting anything, half-asleep. Loch helped me get ready for bed and then, finally, I fell into the soft arms of my mattress.

I woke the next morning flat on my back with Loch curled around my right side. I kept still, not sure if he was awake.

"Why do you let them push you so hard?" he asked. He smoothed a hand down my left side and tugged me deeper into his embrace.

"Because this technology is the difference between winning the war and losing it. It's important." I sighed. "I know I haven't done much toward your pardon yet and I'm sorry. Bianca is working on it. I'm planning to meet with her today."

Loch made a frustrated sound. "This isn't about me. You're letting them work you to death."

"I know," I said. "But I have this constant feeling of dread, like something terrible is going to happen. And the longer we're here, the worse it gets. I've put all of my siblings on alert and so far no one has noticed anything unusual, but I can't relax. And if I can't relax, I might as well work. My obligation to Father is finished, so I can set my own hours now. But that doesn't mean you have to stick with me. You're free to come and go."

He kissed my shoulder. "Do you think that's going to happen?"

"No. You are as stubborn as I am. But you seem unhappy," I ventured.

"Fuck yes, I'm unhappy. This place is making me antsy. Plus I've had to sit on my hands and watch you work yourself to exhaustion for a week straight. And I can't even be useful as a bodyguard because there's no one to guard your body *from*."

"Be careful what you wish for. Once I start stirring up the Genesis Project trouble, plenty of people will prefer us both out of the picture."

"You didn't mention that it would be dangerous for you," he said.

"It will be more dangerous for you. My High House status will protect me to some degree."

"I know you want to do this for me, and you don't know how much I appreciate it, but maybe we should forget it."

"Not going to happen," I said as I slid out of bed. "Now get up. I promised Bianca we'd lunch with her and it has to be late already since I don't feel like a zombie."

BIANCA'S SUITE WAS LAID OUT THE SAME AS MINE, EX-cept with light wood floors and dark, delicate furniture. Loch looked like he would crush anything he sat in, but the furniture, like Bianca, had hidden strength. The metal nanocomposite frames could support a transport—I knew it for a fact because Bianca had forced the salesman to back up his claim with a demonstration.

She'd changed her wall color from bright aqua to flat, metallic silver. It made the space look very modern but a little cold. I didn't think that was a coincidence, either.

"I can't believe Father let you have the day off," she said. She wore slim white pants and an orange blouse. She was barefoot, which meant she considered Loch nearly family already.

I grinned at her. "Father didn't. I threatened the scientists with death if they knocked on my door. I've barely slept for the past week so I wasn't doing anyone any good. My brain is mush, but the torture starts again tomorrow. At least I've done enough to fulfill my part of the contract, so Father can't complain if I choose to work normal hours this week."

She led us over to the table that was already set with food, freshly prepared. Bianca actually *liked* to cook. Craziness.

"I'm glad you're free today," she said as we settled down to eat, "because we made some significant progress yesterday. We were cracking archive systems when Veronica found one with a few Genesis Project records. Those led us on a merry chase, but we finally tracked down the genetic reports for a squad of eight."

I took a bite. The delicate salmon fillet drizzled in some sort of dill cream sauce melted in my mouth. Bianca not only liked to cook, but was exceptional at it. Ian Bishop had no idea what he was missing.

"Which squad?" Loch asked.

Bianca shrugged. "We don't know. Names were redacted. We wouldn't have known to look at these records at all if not for the Genesis Project files. They are buried deep in a generic database. We're going through the rest of the records to see if they are related."

"Is it enough to prove the Consortium was experimenting with genetic alterations?" I asked.

"It's no smoking gun," Bianca said. "But it's a start."

"Thank you for helping," Loch said.

"Family sticks together," she said with a smile. "And if I ever need someone intimidated, you'll be the first person I call."

"Would you like me to have a talk with a certain director of security?" Loch asked. "I'd be happy to help."

Bianca beamed at him. I'd never seen that smile directed at anyone other than a sibling. She glanced at me. "You can keep him," she said.

"You're too kind," I deadpanned.

She inclined her head regally before cracking into laughter.

We finished with lunch and moved to the couches for coffee. The conversation turned to lighter subjects for a while before inevitably drifting to the war. "Have you heard anything?" I asked when Bianca brought it up.

"There have been a few minor skirmishes," she said, "but both sides seem to be biding their time. I'm assuming Father is waiting for the report on your ship so he knows what he's up against. I don't know why Lady Rockhurst is hesitating."

"I got the impression from Richard that they were trying to avoid war. Maybe their new fleet isn't ready yet. Or maybe they're waiting to see what Father does with *Polaris*. If he announces the technology, Yamado will likely side with us for a share of the prize."

"Do you think he will?" Loch asked.

"No," Bianca and I said at the same time. I waved her on. She said, "The only way he'll announce it is if we are losing badly. If he defeats Rockhurst, he can corner the market for House von Hasenberg. Even if Rockhurst has the technology, if they don't have the resource then they're dead in the water."

Bianca sighed and continued, "He's waiting and watching to see how far along Rockhurst really is. He knows we have a superior force if they don't have fast FTL drives in the majority of their ships. It's risky, but the reward is too enticing for him to pass up."

"Consortium politics are fucked up," Loch said.

"Yes, pretty much," Bianca said. She turned to me. "Speaking of, are you going to tonight's party?"

"No," I said. One of the benefits of debriefing was I got a free pass to ignore all social obligations.

"Lady Rockhurst is hosting."

I groaned. "Why did you have to tell me that?"

"Why does it matter?" Loch asked. "I thought you all had parties all the time."

"We do," I said. "But High Houses don't actually host evening events all that often. There are four major events per year, once per quarter. The three High Houses each host once and the lower houses all contribute for the fourth event. Otherwise, the lower houses host smaller parties, and those events overlap, which means it's rare for all three High Councillors to be in the same place at once. But when a High House hosts, *everyone* shows up."

"So if Ada wants to speak to Lady Rockhurst and Lord Yamado, tonight is her best chance of catching them both in the same place until House von Hasenberg's gala in four months," Bianca said.

"I don't suppose it's a masquerade?" I asked hopefully.

"No, it's not."

"Nothing's ever easy," I sighed.

"Taking Loch would be a mistake," Bianca warned. "He will be recognized. Diplomatic immunity can only do so much, especially in a foreign House."

She was right, of course. But I doubted very much that Loch was going to be happy to be left behind.

**MOST OF THE DRESSES IN MY CLOSET WERE TWO YEARS** out of style. I flipped through them and tried not to worry about Loch. He'd stormed off in a temper when it became clear he wouldn't be able to talk me out of going. I reminded myself that the Devil of Fornax Zero could take care of himself.

I pulled out a long silk dress in soft gray. A simple sheath dress with a timeless silhouette, it would be as fashionable today as it was two years ago. I tried it on and, miracle of miracles, it still fit beautifully. A slit up to the middle of my right thigh offered a tasteful glimpse of skin and also allowed me to move unhindered. Strappy black heels completed the picture.

Using the bathroom mirror for reference, I twisted my dark hair into an updo. It took a few tries to get it right—I was rusty. I used to be able to put my hair up without needing a mirror at all. For makeup, I decided on deep red lips and subtle eyeshadow that enhanced the blue in my blue-gray eyes. I double-checked the settings, then hit the application button and closed my eyes.

At the beep, I checked my appearance in the mirror. The stunning, elegant woman staring back at me looked like a stranger.

I put on my bracelet and necklace, then found a clutch big enough to hold a small blaster. Members of High Houses weren't searched, which meant nearly everyone carried some type of weapon. The unwritten rule was that it had to be discreet. I'd never been to an event where weapons were needed, but even so, House members liked the additional security.

I paced in the living room while I waited for Bianca, trying to get used to wearing heels again. Nervous energy fluttered through my system. I wished Loch was here to kiss me goodbye and wish me luck. And a small, vain part of me wanted him to see me when I was all dressed up.

When the doorbell rang, I opened the door to reveal a subtly furious Bianca in a gorgeous blue-black dress. Before I could say anything, she jerked a thumb over her shoulder with an irritated huff. Ian Bishop stood a few feet behind her, dressed in a black tuxedo.

"Father believes we need a security detail because of the war. And Director Bishop is apparently the only agent available in the entirety of House von Hasenberg, which seems like a massive security risk," Bianca said with a pointed glare at the man in question.

Ian didn't react. He merely watched Bianca with a predatory stillness that reminded me of Loch.

"If you're worried about Vincent," I said, using Loch's cover identity, "then you shouldn't be. He's indisposed and won't be joining us this evening."

"I know," Ian said.

I blinked at him in surprise. He must've seen Loch storm out because while the private suites weren't under surveillance, the rest of the House definitely *was*.

Ian continued, "I am responsible for both of you. Normally you each would have an agent, but as I explained to Lady Bianca, we are short-staffed this evening. It will make my job easier if you stick together."

Something was going on. House von Hasenberg had never been short-staffed in its history. Bianca caught my eye and nodded very slightly. She sensed it, too. But who was pulling which strings and why?

"Did Albrecht assign you to us?" I asked bluntly. That would at least narrow the players in this little drama.

Ian smiled, a barely there twitch of his lips, as if laughing at an inside joke. "No, Lord von Hasenberg does not concern himself with security details." His expression turned serious. "I mean you no harm, Lady Ada. If you trust nothing else, trust that."

"It is not myself that I am worried about right now," I said. "I've been swimming in the shark-infested waters of the Consortium ballrooms since I was a girl."

Ian inclined his head. He stepped closer and lowered his voice. "He can take care of himself," he said.

I knew it was true, but with Loch missing, the tension that had been riding me for the past week ratcheted higher. We were approaching a breaking point and I couldn't see the cliff coming.

"I hope you are right," I said. I held out an elbow to Bianca. "Shall we, my dear? We don't want to keep Lady Rockhurst waiting."

She linked her arm with mine and we headed toward the nearest transport pickup. "Do you have a plan?" she asked quietly.

"Yes," I said. I didn't elaborate with Ian stalking along behind us.

"Are you armed?" she asked.

"Of course. You?"

She nodded. She also wore her bracelet tonight. It seemed we both expected trouble.

THE TRANSPORT DROPPED US OFF IN FRONT OF HOUSE Rockhurst's public entrance. The gleaming building shared the metal and glass architecture of all of House Rockhurst's buildings. A constant stream of people flowed through the entryway, but we bypassed the line and used the entrance reserved for High House guests. A guard scanned our identity chips then waved us through.

The gigantic ballroom's soaring ceiling dripped with crystal chandeliers, and a wall of glass showcased the beautifully lit balcony and garden. Several panels had been moved aside to allow guests access to the cooler outside air.

Inside, the crush of human bodies threatened to overwhelm the air-conditioning system. Bianca clicked on a personal cooling field and the temperature around us dropped by a few crucial degrees. Ian trailed along behind us, a silent shadow.

"Lady Rockhurst first?" Bianca asked. Even standing beside me she had to raise her voice to be heard over the din.

I nodded and we joined the flow of people moving deeper into the ballroom. Finding Lady Rockhurst wasn't hard—she was in the middle of an adoring group of people. Speaking to her was another matter.

I left Bianca and Ian on the edge of the crowd. "Move," I said to the person in front of me in my most aristocratic tone. The man turned around to glare, then recognized who I was. He nearly tripped over himself to get out of my way. Smart man.

I used the same tactic over and over until I stood in front of Lady Rockhurst herself. She was coldly beautiful, with the signature blond hair and blue eyes the House was known for. She had to be over sixty but she could still easily pass for a woman in her forties. She wore a vibrant green dress that hugged her figure. Lord Rockhurst stood beside her, chatting with a business associate.

I dipped into a shallow curtsey. "Lady Rockhurst," I said. "Thank you for hosting tonight's party. I hope your family is well."

If looks could kill, I would be a dead woman. "You have some nerve, girl," she hissed at me.

I smiled serenely at her. "Indeed. In fact, I would like to set up a private meeting with you."

"I have nothing to say to you," she said.

"That is too bad," I said. "I had hoped to keep this a private matter between Houses, but I suppose I could release it publicly instead."

She stepped closer. "You dare to threaten me?"

I was treading a dangerous path. Push her too far, and she'd eliminate the threat—namely, me. But if I didn't push her far enough, she wouldn't meet with me, which meant Loch's clemency hearing would go nowhere.

"Of course not, my lady," I said. "I am merely offering an opportunity to find a mutually acceptable solution."

"To what problem?"

"*Mayport,*" I said quietly, naming the ship Richard attacked in his attempt to retrieve me. "I have the security footage."

She waved a dismissive hand. "That is not worth my time."

"Lord Richard *has* been something of a disappointment lately, but I never expected you to abandon one of your own, Lady Rockhurst." I shook my head sadly. "I had hoped to resolve this quietly, but now I suppose I must go to the full Consortium."

"Listen here, you little bitch—"

"Lady Rockhurst, I could not care less about what happened on board *Mayport*." It was a lie, but she didn't need to know that. "But not everyone will feel that way. All I want is a private moment of your time to discuss matters."

Her expression turned crafty. "Perhaps we can also discuss how you aided and abetted the universe's most wanted criminal, hmm?"

"I look forward to it," I said honestly.

That threw her. She blinked before the mask slipped back in place. "Very well. You get fifteen minutes to persuade me not to just kill you and be done with it. My assistant will set it up."

"Thank you, my lady," I said. I curtsied again then melted back into the crowd.

One down, one to go.

Bianca met me at the edge of the crowd. She looked drawn even through her public persona. Ian hovered at her shoulder. "Well?" she demanded.

"She agreed to meet, but she's not happy about it. Now let's see if I can piss off another High House tonight."

We made our way through the crowd to Lord Yamado's group. I pressed through the crowd until I stood in front of the man himself. Lord Hitoshi stood next to him. Lady Yamado tired easily and generally avoided evening events unless they were official government events.

Lord Yamado was older than Father, his hair snow white, and his face was lined with age. I curtsied to him and his eyebrows crept up his forehead. Lord Hitoshi did not look pleased to see me.

"Lady Ada," Yamado said, "to what do I owe the pleasure?"

I'd always liked Lord Yamado, but his son Hitoshi was

another matter. "My lord, I am afraid I am here on business,"
I said.

He became guarded. "I cannot help you," he said.

I understood his concern. If he was seen talking business
with me, it could look like he meant to throw in with House
von Hasenberg in the war. Unfortunately, I didn't have time
to play nice, but I took one more stab at it before pulling out
the big guns.

"It is not about the war," I said. "It is of a more personal
nature."

He shook his head. "I should not even be talking to you
now, Lady Ada, as much as I regret it."

I'd spent the ride over here trying to decide the wisest
course of action. Rockhurst knew I left TSD Nine with a
woman. Hitoshi would review the surveillance video as soon
as he found Veronica was missing, so he would know that I'd
helped her. Still, she was my friend and it felt wrong to use
her.

"I recently visited Tau Sagittarii Dwarf Nine," I said in a
seeming non sequitur. "I would like a short private meeting
with you to discuss what I found, nothing more."

Lord Yamado's expression turned faintly puzzled. Was it
possible he didn't know what Hitoshi had done? In any other
House I would bet against it, but House Yamado always had
been a bit of an oddity. Lord Hitoshi, however, knew exactly
what I meant. His glare promised painful, deadly retribution.

"What did you find?" Lord Yamado asked.

"Perhaps you should ask Lord Hitoshi," I said with a wave.

"Father, we should not discuss this here. And definitely
not with *her*."

"What have you done this time, Hitoshi?" Lord Yamado asked quietly.

"Why would you believe this little wh—"

"Watch your mouth, boy," Yamado said sharply, cutting him off. The kindly grandfather look fell away as his temper woke. "Lady Ada is a respected member of House von Hasenberg and will be treated as such."

Lord Yamado turned back to me with a suppressed sigh. "It seems I will be meeting with you after all, Lady Ada. Please call my assistant to set it up, but I would appreciate your discretion."

I curtsied again. "Of course, my lord. I look forward to our meeting." I fled before Hitoshi could make a grab for me. Ian might be up to something, but at least he was paid to protect me from people like Hitoshi.

Ian's eyes narrowed at me. "Should I be concerned?" he asked.

I glanced over my shoulder. I could no longer see Hitoshi, which wasn't as comforting as I hoped. "I *might* have made Hitoshi angry," I said.

"How angry?" Bianca asked.

"Murderous," I said flatly. "Perhaps we should mingle over there," I said, and pointed to the other side of the vast ballroom. Hitoshi would have to be crazy to attack me in a public space policed by RCDF soldiers, but it wasn't a risk I was willing to take.

We worked our way around the edge of the room, stopping to chat with friends and enemies alike. A few brave gentlemen asked Bianca and me to dance, but we turned them down. Getting separated at this point seemed like a bad idea.

We were nearly to the far wall when Bianca stumbled and only Ian's quick reflexes kept her upright. She went chalk white under her makeup and her pupils dilated until the black nearly swallowed her unusual golden hazel irises. "What is wrong?" I asked. I visually searched her for injuries but I couldn't see anything amiss.

"They have Loch," she said with a glance at her com. Ian swore viciously.

"What? Who? How do you know?" I fired off the questions too quickly for her to answer, but I couldn't stop myself. I resisted the urge to shake her only because Ian looked like he might punch me if I tried it.

"Bianca," I said as calmly as I could manage, "who has Loch?"

"Father," she said. She looked up with a devastated expression. "He knows who Loch is. And he's calling a meeting of the High Councillors to hand down the execution order."

# CHAPTER 29

**B**ianca's information proved to be correct. A ripple went through the crowd as Lady Rockhurst and Lord Yamado made for the exit. The buzz of conversation climbed higher as everyone speculated about what was going on.

I turned to Ian. "You have thirty seconds to explain to me why I shouldn't kill you where you stand," I said. My voice sounded eerily calm.

"I didn't know," he said. "I didn't tell Albrecht a damn thing about Loch. And I know it's going to seem a little convenient now, but Loch is the one who asked me to keep an eye on you tonight."

Ian was difficult to read, but I didn't get the sense that he was lying. I nodded, accepting his answer for now. We would definitely be revisiting this conversation at a later point, once I'd hauled Loch out of danger. "I need to return home immediately," I said. "Bianca, can you walk?"

She straightened and Ian reluctantly let her go. "Yes," she

said. She turned and headed for the door. "We'll plan on the way. You won't have much time."

Ian sliced us a path through the crowd with sheer menace. A House von Hasenberg transport sat waiting for us at the entry. Once we were inside, it lifted off toward our House.

"They are holding Loch in the High Chamber," Bianca said, looking at her com. "Father is waiting for Rockhurst and Yamado to arrive. Rockhurst is on her way but Yamado is returning home first, presumably to pick up his seal. What is your plan?"

"I'm going to get Loch back," I said, "even if I have to break into the High Chamber to do it." I rubbed my temples. "Have you learned anything else useful about that thing we talked about?" I asked. I couldn't very well name the Genesis Project with Ian sitting across from us, but Bianca knew what I meant.

She shook her head. "Nothing definitive."

*Fuck.* I closed my eyes and said a silent prayer. I wasn't usually the praying type, but tonight I could use all the help I could get.

"If I don't come back," I said quietly, "I want you to release everything you have to the public. I'll forward you surveillance footage from the *Mayport,* release that, too. And talk to Rhys and Veronica. They'll have more info for you. You have the backup key to my files—it's the same as our personal encryption key. I have a death folder full of relevant information."

Bianca interrupted me. "You're coming back."

"I aim to," I told her.

"You're coming back," she said again, more forcefully.

"Just in case I don't, this is information you need to know. You are my backup plan, Bianca. If you don't hear from me in an hour, release everything. You know information is my only hope."

She looked sick to her stomach but she agreed.

"Are you planning to storm the place single-handedly?" Ian asked.

"Yes," I said.

"Do you think that's going to work?" he asked.

*No.* "Maybe."

He sighed and shook his head. "I can get you to the High Chamber, but I can't be seen," he said. "Once I get you in, you're on your own."

"Why would you help me at all?" I asked.

"I'm repaying a debt."

I didn't have time to question help, so I nodded. I pulled out my com and sent an emergency message to Rhys and Veronica. It should be morning there, so they would get it as soon as it bounced through the gate. I asked them to come to Earth and be prepared for a hot pickup.

I attached an official invite, which would allow them to bypass a lot of the RCDF checkpoints. I kept the details to a minimum because even the extra encryption was no guarantee the message wouldn't be intercepted, but I told them to contact Bianca for more information if they couldn't reach me.

I hoped it wouldn't come to that.

"I will meet you back here in ten minutes," Ian said as the transport dropped us off. "Don't be late."

I nodded, hugged Bianca, and ran for my room.

In my closet, I stripped off my dress and shoes. After a

moment's hesitation, I put on the red dress Loch had bought me. I told him I'd wear it on the day he got pardoned and that day was today, one way or another. My boots didn't exactly go with the dress, but I put them on anyway.

After all, sturdy boots were a must when running for your life.

I slid aside the panel in my bedroom that concealed my armory and picked up two blasters, two stun pistols, a handful of plastech ties that could be used for handcuffs, and two thigh holsters. The full skirt of my dress concealed the weapons and ties. It wasn't the most comfortable, but it would have to do.

I gazed around the room one final time, hoarding memories. I'd barely settled in but it still hurt to leave again. Last time I left, I'd naively thought Father would give up after a year or two. This time I was under no such illusion.

Bianca waited for me in the hallway. She hugged me fiercely. "You don't *have* to do this—you know that, right? Is he worth it?" she asked.

The thought of Loch dying alone while I stood aside and did nothing tore holes in my heart. "He's worth it," I said.

She hugged me tighter. "Please don't die," she breathed.

"I'm not planning to," I said. "And I'll do what I can to keep Director Bishop out of trouble."

That startled a watery laugh out of her. "Good luck," she said. "Let me know how that works out for you." She let me go and stepped back. "I've already set up my scripts to release everything in an hour unless I intervene, so even if they grab me, you'll be protected."

"Thank you," I said. I had my own set of safeguards that

JESSIE MIHALIK

needed to be reset every few days. Nearly everyone in the Consortium did. Mutually assured destruction was one of the reasons so few assassinations were attempted.

I left Bianca and ran for the entrance. Even so, a cloaked man was already waiting for me. I stopped short. Had someone else figured out my plan?

"It's me," Ian said from the depths of the hood.

I squinted at him in the dim light. He wore dark fatigues and a black shirt. I never would've guessed it was Ian Bishop under the cloak, which I guess was the point. I didn't know he owned anything other than a suit. A black balaclava covered the lower part of his face. He looked intent and dangerous. In fact, he reminded me of Loch.

He gestured to the unmarked transport waiting for us. "I'll brief you on the way."

I climbed in and he followed. We set off for a service entrance of the main Consortium building.

"Do not call me by name once we are inside," he said. "I don't have the authority to override their security logs. I can get you as far as the High Chamber door. You're lucky that it's after hours and a special meeting they want to keep secret. There should only be two guards posted outside, but you will have to deal with them on your own."

"I'll take care of it," I said.

"There is an auxiliary guard station just down the hall, so don't linger. But neither security personnel nor surveillance are allowed inside the High Chamber." At my disbelieving look, he continued, "Tell me about it. I've been trying to change it for years, but the councillors don't want their meetings recorded in any way."

He continued, "Once you get inside the High Chamber, there is a panic button on the control panel near the door. Pushing it will lock the room from the inside. Each councillor's seat has its own panic button and override. If you want the room to stay locked, you need to get them away from the buttons. Once the room is locked down, only a councillor's identity chip and the override can unlock it. And once the room goes into lockdown, expect a shit-ton of RCDF troops to be waiting outside when the doors open."

"Any other exits?"

"There is an escape tunnel, but it requires a councillor's identity chip at multiple checkpoints. It's also well-known among the security teams, so expect troops there as well."

"So once I go in and lock down the room, I come out with a pardon or in a body bag?"

Ian nodded grimly. "Do you have a plan on how to procure a pardon?"

"I have a plan," I said. A crazy, stupid, ridiculous plan, but a plan nevertheless.

Ian didn't look convinced, but he didn't press for details. It was for the best.

THE TRANSPORT DROPPED US OFF AND IAN LED ME through a labyrinth of service hallways at a fast walk. He kept his hood up, even with the balaclava, and we didn't speak. I held my breath every time we came to a closed door, but so far no one had noticed us.

Ian did not scan his chip for the door in front of us. Instead, he stepped into my personal space and grabbed my arm when I went to back up. I reached for my blaster, sure that he was betraying me at last. He shook his head, grabbed my other arm, then dragged me closer until his mouth was directly next to my ear.

"This is the final door," he whispered so quietly I could barely make out the words. I realized he didn't want his voice recorded in the security logs and stopped trying to break his hold. "The guards will be directly across from you, slightly to the left. Security in this building is all RCDF elite, so shoot first."

"Is the High Chamber locked?" I whispered back.

"Not usually," Ian said, "but if it is, the guard's identity chip will open it."

I put my mouth right next to his ear. "If I don't make it out, I expect you to watch out for Bianca," I whispered. Something deeply troubled my sister but so far she'd deflected all of my subtle questions. I hadn't had time to force the issue but maybe Ian would have better luck.

"I will keep her safe," Ian said.

I nodded, activated my cuff, then drew my stun pistol. I pulled the pistol up into a ready-to-fire position and met Ian's gaze. He waited a beat then swiped an arm across the door's access panel.

I watched the door slide aside in slow motion. I saw the nearest guard's face flash to surprise, but I was already pulling the trigger. He went down with a shout, stunned and furious. I shot the second guard before his blaster cleared the holster. He, too, went down with a shout. I hoped the High Chamber doors were thick enough to block the sound.

A sweep showed me a clear hallway. I crossed to the chamber door. The first guard was already starting to recover. "Sorry," I said, then stunned him again.

The door was unlocked. I pulled it open and marched into the Consortium meeting as if I owned the place.

The High Chamber was circular. The three councillors sat at elevated desks against the curved far wall. Chairs could be brought in on the floor level for matters that required an audience, but tonight the floor was empty except for a single chair in the middle of the room.

A single chair containing Loch.

Loch slumped against the chains that bound him to the chair. Blood dripped sluggishly from his left arm, forming a small pool on the marble floor beneath him. His head turned fractionally in my direction. Still alive, but for how long?

I blocked out my worry and retreated deep into my public persona.

"What is the meaning of this?" Lady Rockhurst demanded.

I hit the panic button on the control panel next to the door. Metal panels clanged into place, physically blocking the doors while energy shields glowed around the room. Damn, security was intense. I pointed my stun pistol at Lady Rockhurst, Lord Yamado, and Father.

"Raise your hands and move to the floor of the room," I said. None of them moved. I shot a stun bolt over their heads, nearly grazing Father. "Now, if you please."

"Ada—" Father started, thunderclouds in his expression. He hadn't expected me to notice Loch's disappearance, and if not for Bianca, I wouldn't have until it was too late. Father had seized the opportunity to solve all of his problems at once and then deny any involvement. Honestly, I should've expected it, but I thought, for once, that Father would be honorable. *Ha.*

"You have one second to comply," I said. I moved my finger to the trigger, prepared to stun all three of them and drag them away from their desks.

Father raised his hands and stood with a scowl. Lord Yamado followed suit. Lady Rockhurst glared coldly. I smiled and tightened my finger on the trigger. Whatever she saw in my face caused her to raise her hands and flounce down from her desk.

With them on the floor level, I closed the distance to Marcus. I felt for his pulse—it beat strong and sure under my fingers. He was definitely injured, but he wasn't as bad off as he looked.

"You should've left me," Loch murmured. His eyes swept over me before he added, "Nice dress."

I kept an eye on the three most powerful people in the universe while I tried to figure out how to free Loch. Lady Rockhurst inched toward the wall but a stun bolt that passed close enough to nick her green dress stopped her progress. "Keep pressing me and I will stun and tie the lot of you," I warned. "Where is the key to the chains?"

"The only copy is with the guard outside," Lady Rockhurst said with smug satisfaction.

"I can get free," Loch whispered, his lips barely moving. "I need ten seconds of warning."

"I'll do my best," I told him quietly.

"Ada, put down the gun and we can discuss this like civilized adults," Father said.

"You went behind my back and grabbed one of my employees," I said. "That doesn't seem very civilized."

"You mean your fuck toy?" Lady Rockhurst said, contempt dripping from every word. "I should have expected you to lower yourself—"

I shot her with a stun bolt. She went down with a scream. Neither Father nor Lord Yamado moved to help her. "Would anyone else like to comment?" I asked.

"Ada Irena Maria Franziska von Hasenberg, I am your father and you will do as I say," Father barked. "Put down the gun and stop embarrassing yourself." True fury saturated his tone. He really meant I should stop embarrassing *him*—and possibly House von Hasenberg, but I'd bet even it was a distant second right now.

That tone of voice plus the use of my full name used to be enough to shove me back into line, but tonight it was not going to work. "You do realize that I vastly prefer Ferdinand, right?" I asked, naming my oldest brother and heir to House von Hasenberg. "You are in no position to demand anything of me."

"I will disown you for this," he promised.

Even though I knew it would likely come down to this, hurt sliced through my system. Family was everything to a High House, not for sentimental reasons, but in order to maintain a strong, powerful House. I couldn't remember the last time someone was disowned.

As part of a High House, no matter what happened, you knew the House would have your back. So did everyone else. Even when I left home, I knew that if things ever went completely sideways, I could just reveal my identity and House von Hasenberg would do whatever it took to get me out.

By threatening to remove the protection of our House, Father had just promised that everyone who held a grudge against House von Hasenberg in general—or me in particular—would target me because there would be no House retaliation.

I would become the most hunted woman in the 'verse, with or without a bounty.

I kept my expression cool through sheer force of will. "You will do what you have to do, just as I am. Now either we can have a conversation, *like civilized adults,* or I can shoot you all dead and take my chances with the RCDF forces outside."

Lady Rockhurst climbed to her feet. Hatred twisted her features for a few seconds until her mask fell into place. She smoothed her dress with a hand that barely trembled. Stun bolts packed much less of a wallop than stunsticks, but even so, her recovery time was impressive.

"What do you hope to accomplish here?" Lord Yamado asked. Oddly, he seemed like the most rational of the three despite his legendary temper.

"A full pardon for Marcus Loch and myself, including removal of the bounties, plus posthumous pardons and familial restitution for every member of the Genesis Project," I said. Three sets of eyes snapped to me in shock. I had their attention now. "Or I will burn down your world," I vowed.

Lady Rockhurst rallied fastest. "I do not know what you are talking about," she said.

"That is unfortunate considering it was *your* son who was the one directing the only surviving Genesis Project squadron to attack the starving women and children of Fornax Zero. But I suppose if you do not know about it you will not mind when the information is released in"—I checked the time on my com—"forty-three minutes."

"Did this man tell you that?" Lady Rockhurst asked with a wave at Loch. "And you were stupid enough to believe him?"

She sneered. "You deserve to be disowned. In fact, I am going to demand it."

My temper flared but I was encased in the ice of my public persona. I looked down my nose at her and arched a single, imperious eyebrow. She didn't wilt like most whom I hit with the expression, but that had never been my intention. I needed to provoke one of them into making a mistake. "Do I need to shoot you again?" I asked. "Because it would be my pleasure."

Lady Rockhurst flushed red in outrage. If pure hate could kill, I'd be dead.

"Even if it was true, why would anyone care what happened to a military squadron so long ago?" Father asked.

"You think parents who watched their babies die from a simple gene deformity that the Royal Consortium arbitrarily decided cannot be altered are going to stand idly by when it comes out that you used illegal genetic manipulation to create supersoldiers? Especially when those soldiers were used to slaughter starving innocents? There will be riots in the streets of every occupied planet."

"She is bluffing," Lady Rockhurst said. "The information was destroyed. We all agreed."

"I would hope so, since it was your job to destroy the shared data, Anne," Lord Yamado said. "We destroyed our copies."

Lady Rockhurst rounded on him. "You are not pinning this on me, Ren, so do not even try it. The data was destroyed."

They both turned to Father. Albrecht stared them down. "She did not get it from our House," he said. "I personally oversaw the deletion of our files."

Despite their words, they all very likely had offline back-ups of the data because they were all backstabbing bastards. They would want to ensure that they could take down the other Houses if the data ever came to light in a way that was unfavorable to them.

They seemed to silently communicate for a few seconds. "If we give you a pardon, you will turn over all of your data to us," Lady Rockhurst said.

I laughed at her. Even Father looked vaguely insulted that she thought I was that stupid. "The data will stay where it is. If I ever fail to reset the timer, it will automatically be made public."

"For how long?" Lord Yamado asked.

"Forever. When I am old and gray, standing on death's door, I will disable the timer, assuming I have no children to protect. Until then, it stays."

"What if you die young from natural causes?" Lady Rockhurst demanded.

"Well, you had better hope I watch my diet and exercise," I said, "because if I die young from *any* reason you all are screwed. You forget that I know how the Consortium works. One convenient space station 'accident' and I am no longer a threat. It is in my interest to make it in *your* interest to keep me alive. And free, obviously." I tacked on the last bit because their idea of safety was more than likely a cell in the deepest, darkest pit they could find.

"Will she break, Albrecht?" Lady Rockhurst asked.

Loch rumbled next to me. I guess he didn't appreciate them talking about torturing me as if I wasn't here. I was with him on that, actually.

Father gave me an appraising glance, then shook his head. "Not fast enough," he said. "She always was a stubborn one. Corner her and she will fight to the death."

"How sure are you that she is bluffing?" Lord Yamado asked Lady Rockhurst.

"How sure are you that *your* data was destroyed?" she responded with an arched eyebrow. He inclined his head, conceding the point.

"I only need two of you to agree, which makes one of you expendable," I said. "And time is wasting. It will take me at least ten minutes to return to my room or ship in order to reset the timer. Keep arguing and the decision will be made for you. Then you all become expendable."

"As do you," Father pointed out.

"I have always been expendable," I said. "Today is no different."

Loch growled. "Let me kill them and be done with it," he said, weighing in for the first time. His deep voice rolled around the room like thunder. "I can deal with the RCDF."

I tilted my head, considering it. Killing the councillors had never been my intention, but if they refused to negotiate, I would not let them walk away unscathed. Of course, if I killed all of them then there would be no safe place left in the 'verse, no matter what information I held.

"Give me the ship, and I will agree to your terms," Father said.

Lady Rockhurst's eyes widened at the offer. She cut a glance at Lord Yamado, who presumably didn't know about *Polaris* or at least didn't know the details. "Give *me* the ship, girl, and *I* will agree."

"The ship is not up for negotiation," I said. "It is mine and I am keeping it."

It was clear Lady Rockhurst vehemently wanted to argue about who owned the ship, but to do so would be to tip off Lord Yamado. She kept her mouth shut, but her glare burned with hatred.

Lord Yamado, however, was not stupid. "What is so important about this unnamed ship?" he asked.

And with that, he gave me exactly the extra leverage I needed. My smile was bright enough to rival the sun.

Father and Lady Rockhurst shared a glance. They might be at war, but neither of them wanted another entry into their battle at this point. Each was confident they'd crush the other and keep the secrets—and power—of a faster FTL drive for themselves.

"We will give you and Marcus Loch full pardons, as well as remove the bounties," Lady Rockhurst said. "In return, you will disavow all knowledge of the Genesis Project. If the information becomes public, your pardons will be rescinded. You will also be formally disowned from House von Hasenberg."

She did not mention the other members of the Genesis Project, but I hadn't expected to get those pardons anyway. As far as the Consortium was concerned, they were dead. That would have to be good enough. But still, I didn't want to have to look over my shoulder every second. Watching for the Consortium would be exhausting enough without having the rest of the universe after me.

"No," I said. "We have no reason to publicize the information if you keep your side of the bargain, so if it becomes public you are welcome to do your best to try to kill us out of spite, but our pardons stand. And if I am disowned, how long do you think it will be before someone with a grudge grabs me? I cannot reset the timer if I am being tortured to death for House von Hasenberg's crimes."

Father said, "While you will officially remain a member of House von Hasenberg, you will be banned from Earth and all Consortium events. You will have no contact with *any* member of the Consortium. House von Hasenberg will not be responsible for your welfare."

"No," Loch said. He tipped his head up to me. "You can't give up your family for me," he said quietly, correctly reading what Father was trying to do. "I'm not worth it. I won't agree to it."

Loch was worth far more than he thought, but I was not going to let my own Father railroad me into an agreement that prevented me from seeing my siblings. For this brief slice of time, I held all of the cards. I might as well make use of it.

"I will not be kept from my brothers and sisters," I said, "and I am not at fault if a member of the Consortium approaches me. You won't be able to break our agreement just because you sent someone to talk to me. I agree that House von Hasenberg is not responsible for my welfare unless I am taken by an enemy of the House as a political target. Then you'd better send your best and brightest to retrieve me."

"Agreed," Father said.

"Very well, I agree," Lady Rockhurst said.

"I *do not* agree," Lord Yamado said. "Not until someone explains the importance of the ship." But the pardon only needed a simple majority to proceed, so Lord Yamado could complain, but he couldn't stop it.

It took twenty minutes of furious negotiations before the pardon and contract language were deemed acceptable, and only then because I kept pointing to the timer on my com that ticked down the minutes. If Loch or I died or were held against our will, my information would automatically go public. If either of us tried to make the information public on our own, the Consortium would hunt us both down with extreme prejudice.

I would get to see my siblings, it just wouldn't be on Earth. And I could contact Consortium members regarding contract-related issues but otherwise could not interact with them. I'd added the contract stipulation because I knew if I didn't, Father would attempt to steal *Polaris*. I still wouldn't put it past him, but at least now I could fight him in court.

I insisted on signed and sealed hard copies in addition to the electronic copies. They would hopefully never be needed, but an additional layer of security was worth the time it took to print them out and sign them. It also caused no end of grumbling from Lady Rockhurst, which was a win in itself. Lord Yamado refused to sign anything.

Loch remained chained to the chair in the middle of the room. I wasn't sure why he hadn't already escaped. Perhaps he was more hurt than he was letting on. With the hard copies safely in hand, I walked over to check on him.

"Are we done here?" he asked.

"Yes," I said. "I will get the key from the guard. Or I can pick the locks, your choice."

"No need," Loch said. He smirked at the councillors as he gripped the shackle around his left wrist with his right hand. His arms flexed and the lock snapped open. He dropped the blood-slicked shackle to the floor. I stared in shock as he snapped the other side open just as easily.

Just how strong was he?

He removed the chains and stood to his full height. He towered over everyone in the room. Blood coated the left side of his chest and arm, but he ignored the wound. "Come after me again," he said, "and next time Ada will not be there to save you."

I shivered at the lethal promise in his voice. Lady Rockhurst made a dismissive sound, but she didn't take her eyes off of him. He was a threat and she knew it. I didn't undermine that threat by asking if he was okay. I just handed him my spare blaster and stun pistol. Unlike me, he pocketed the stun pistol and pointed the blaster at the councillors.

"Betray us and die," he said. "You know what I am capable of. All of the RCDF forces in the 'verse can't stop me before I've killed the three of you if you try to fuck us over."

"A deal is a deal," Father said stiffly. "The guards have been briefed not to shoot first."

"For your sake, I hope they follow those orders," Loch said. "Open the door."

Lady Rockhurst went back to her seat and swiped an arm across the chip reader. She pressed a series of buttons and the room returned to normal—no shields, no metal panels blocking the door.

Two seconds later, a dozen RCDF soldiers streamed into the room decked out in full combat armor.

# CHAPTER 30

I edged slightly in front of Loch. When he tried to pull me back, I shook my head and flashed the cuff still around my left wrist. It wouldn't do much against a dozen soldiers, but it might give Loch time to get a shot or two off.

"Lady Rockhurst, Lord von Hasenberg, Lord Yamado, are you well?" one of the soldiers asked. With the full-face helmets it was impossible to determine who spoke, but my money was on the squad leader. He stood in the middle with sergeant's insignia on his shoulders.

"We are fine," Lady Rockhurst said coldly, "no thanks to you."

I winced. The problem with saving my own ass was that inevitably someone else got thrown to the wolves in the process. I just hoped the sergeant would survive Lady Rockhurst's wrath.

"Escort these two to the nearest spaceport and ensure they leave Earth immediately," Father said. His face twisted into a superior smirk. "No detours or stops allowed. They are to be on the first ship off-planet, I do not care where it is headed."

Of course he would prevent me from saying goodbye to my brothers and sisters. I should've expected no less from the bastard who raised me. Still, pain and rage flashed through my system. *How dare he.* My hand tightened on the stun pistol. I wished it was a blaster.

Loch placed a warm palm on my lower back. "Easy, darling," he murmured. "No matter how much he deserves it, now is not the time."

"Unless you want the timer to expire, I *will* be stopping by my ship or my room," I said.

"You may use the terminals here," Lady Rockhurst said.

My laugh was not nice. "And have you trace exactly what I access? I think not."

"She may stop by her room for five minutes," Father told the sergeant. "Prevent anyone from speaking to her. You are authorized to use nonlethal force as necessary."

Too angry to speak, I jerked my head toward the door. The squad leader turned as Loch and I approached. The rest of the soldiers fell in around us.

Once we put some distance between us and the High Chamber, I pulled out my com and called Bianca. "I am safe for now," I said. "We are heading off-planet after a very brief stop by my room. Father forbade me from speaking to anyone in person so you might as well save yourself the trip. Have housekeeping pack up all of my stuff and meet me in Sedition when you can."

Even on the encrypted line she knew better than to press for details. "Consider it done," she said. "Your ride contacted me. They are in orbit."

"Ask them to meet me at the public von Hasenberg space-port as soon as they are able."

"Will do. Are you okay?" she asked.

"I am uninjured," I said.

She took that for the "no" that it was. "Be careful," she said. "I will see you soon. And I will let the others know."

I ended the call. After a few more turns down empty corridors, we stepped outside to find a troop transport waiting for us.

The sergeant stopped by the door and offered me a hand up. "After you, Lady Ada," he said flatly. He wasn't offering to help because he wanted to but because it was expected.

"Thank you, Sergeant. What's your name?" I asked. I stepped into the transport, confident Loch had my back if this was some sort of trap. Seats lined the edges of the transport, facing toward the open middle area. I sat across from the door.

"Edwards, my lady," the sergeant said. He followed me in and sat beside me.

"Well, Sergeant Edwards, I know I've put you in an uncomfortable position," I said. I didn't apologize because I would do the exact same thing again. "If Lady Rockhurst or the others make your life too miserable, come find me in Sedition and I'll put you to work."

"I am responsible for the failed security. I will accept whatever punishment is deemed necessary," he said stiffly.

"Of course," I murmured. I couldn't force him to join me, but I'd at least planted the seed. Perhaps his survival instinct would kick in if things became dire.

Another soldier sat on my left. Loch was the last person

to board the transport. He stopped in front of the soldier beside me and glared. "Move," he said.

The soldier glanced at the sergeant for permission then moved to another seat. Loch dropped into the empty seat with a barely audible grunt. His bloody left side was pressed up against the soldier on his other side so I couldn't check his wound.

We made the trip to my room in silence. When I opened the door, Sergeant Edwards tried to follow me in. I blocked his entry. "You may wait here," I said. "I will be out in five minutes as agreed."

"Lady Ada—" he started.

"Father did not give you permission to breach my personal rooms. Wait here," I said. I waved Loch in then closed the door in Sergeant Edwards's face before he could continue arguing.

"Didi, set a timer for four and a half minutes," I said. A chime confirmed the command.

I pulled Loch into the master bedroom, only to stop short at finding Bianca waiting for us with a first aid kit. "Sit," she said to Loch, pointing to the chair she'd pulled over. Loch sat.

"How did you know?" I asked.

"I didn't," she said, "but I wanted to be prepared."

"I have four-ish minutes to dump my accounts," I said. "Unless you need help, I'm going to do that."

"I'm fine," Loch said. "Do what you need to do." Bianca nodded in agreement.

House von Hasenberg was directly linked to the main bank in Serenity, so transferring money would be as instantaneous as if I was at the bank in person. I'd already moved a good deal of my money out of my House accounts, but I had no doubt Father would lock down whatever was left.

I authenticated with the bank then transferred all of the remaining money in my House account into a numbered account. Eventually I would need to make a legitimate named account, but this would work as a temporary solution.

After the transfer completed, I opened another connection and routed it through several secure servers then kicked off a script that did a whole lot of nothing. Oh, it made a bunch of secure tunneled connections and updated various files across a number of servers, but none of it mattered—all of the files I really had on time-release weren't on any of these systems. But the thought of the Consortium trying to track down all of these random connections made me smile.

That done, I disconnected and wiped the session history. Then I opened the armory and started packing weapons into a travel case. I hadn't taken them last time because I had been traveling undercover. This time I would at least have my House name to protect me from being arrested for being a walking arsenal.

Bianca said to Loch, "I've done what I can, but you need to spend some time in the medbay when you get to the ship."

I glanced over my shoulder as he stood. "How bad?" I asked.

He shrugged. "I'm functional. You want me to do that?" he asked.

I nodded and headed for the closet. Bianca followed me. "You're leaving?" she asked.

"Yes," I said. "Father wanted to disown me but since that wouldn't be good for my long-term survivability, he banished me instead."

I waved my arm in front of a random panel in the middle of my closet wall. A small door opened, revealing a safe. I held my left arm next to it and typed in the fifteen-digit code with my other hand. The safe unlocked and I opened it to reveal a small locked case.

"Is that what I think it is?" Bianca asked.

"Yes," I said. This case held hard copies of all of the material I had under time-release, plus all of the documentation that proved I was a member of House von Hasenberg. "I hate to move it, but I have a feeling I will never see this room again."

"Ferdinand will welcome you back, you know that," Bianca chided gently.

"Father has to die first, and that old bastard is mean enough to live forever just to spite me," I said.

A chime sounded throughout the room. "Didi, stop," I said, then I called to Loch, "Thirty seconds!" I grabbed the case and closed the safe. I hugged Bianca tight. "I'm going to miss you," I said. "I expect to see you in Sedition within the month."

"You will," she said. "Stay out of trouble."

I blinked back tears. I hadn't thought I would lose my family again so soon. I let Bianca go, put the case in the bag I'd brought with me a week ago, dumped some random clothes on top, then went to meet Loch.

Bianca stayed in the bedroom. Loch carried the weapon case. I slung my bag over my shoulder and headed for the door. Everything in me wanted to stay with my brothers and sisters. And while I knew they would visit me, it would not be the same.

I sniffled once then walled the tears behind my public

persona. I didn't have time to break down; I still needed to get to Rhys's ship. "Ready?" I asked Loch.

He nodded, so I swept out into the hall. Rather, I attempted to, but Sergeant Edwards blocked the doorway. He stepped back in surprise. The other soldiers stood at attention along the walls.

"It has been five minutes, Sergeant," I reminded him when he didn't move.

He shook his head and I wished I could see his face to read his expression. "I thought I would have to drag you out," he said.

"Over my dead body," Loch rumbled.

"I have to agree," I said. "You try to drag a von Hasenberg anywhere he or she does not want to go and you are going to have a bad time, Sergeant."

He bowed slightly. "You have my thanks for returning on time, Lady Ada," he said.

We returned to the troop transport then headed for the von Hasenberg spaceport. I messaged Rhys and got an instant response. He, Veronica, and a half dozen of his crew were on the ground in *Jester,* one of the more heavily armed and armored smuggling ships in Rhys's fleet. He had taken me seriously when I said it might be a hot extract, but he had come anyway.

I directed the troop transport to drop us at *Jester* and also let Rhys know not to blow us out of the sky. By the time we arrived, *Jester*'s cargo ramp was down. Sergeant Edwards insisted on escorting us out of the transport.

"Thank you for the escort, Sergeant. And remember, I'll be in Sedition if you need anything."

"Make sure you take off as soon as the flight checks are through," he said, ignoring my offer once again.

I bid him farewell and turned toward *Jester*. An unfamiliar woman in fatigues with a long blaster held across her body waited at the top of the cargo ramp. Her eyes flicked over me dismissively, but they snagged on Loch and held. She scowled. "Get to the medbay," she ordered.

"Yes, ma'am," he said.

Jealousy slammed into me. The woman was undeniably beautiful, with long, curly red hair she'd braided down her back. She was tall and fit and looked like she knew what she was doing with that blaster.

I fought the urge to wrap a possessive hand around Loch. He was mine and I didn't doubt him, but jealousy was a hell of a beast.

When I didn't move, Loch ushered me into the ship with a hand on my back. "Ada, meet Captain Scarlett Hargrove," he said.

"Scarlett, this is Ada. She's mine," he said. Something passed between them and the pleasant feeling I'd felt at his possessive words died.

"Welcome aboard," she said to me. Her expression made ice look warm. "Rhys is on the flight deck getting us clearance for takeoff. You should join him."

"I believe Rhys knows how to talk to ground control without my help," I said. I turned away from her in a purposefully dismissive move. "Let's get you patched up," I said to Loch.

He grinned at me. "After you," he said.

*Jester* was a recent von Hasenberg ship, so I didn't have to embarrass myself by asking for directions. Bigger than *Po-*

*laris,* this ship had four levels instead of three. The top level housed the flight deck and captain's quarters. Crew quarters took up the entire second level. The third level included the mess hall and medbay, while the exercise room and maintenance access were on the fourth level.

As soon as we entered the medbay, Loch dropped the weapon case and pulled me into his arms. I frowned at him. He chuckled and took my bag and dropped it next to the case. Then he kissed the corner of my mouth. I turned my head away. He pulled back and met my eyes.

"Ada, don't be jealous," he said. "I'm not interested in Scarlett, not like that. She's like a little sister to me. The only woman I'm interested in is you."

Relief flooded through me, but then I remembered that if Loch claimed Scarlett as family, I'd have to be nice to her. I scowled.

Loch groaned then his mouth slanted over mine. I forgot all about everyone else as I opened in welcome. His tongue plundered my mouth with smooth thrusts and teasing licks. Desire and something deeper, more powerful, fizzed through my blood.

I pressed closer, mindless. Loch picked me up and I wrapped my legs around his waist. I could feel him, hot and hard against me. I grabbed his shoulders and my right hand hit the tackiness of drying blood. That jerked me out of my daze.

His hand traced a dangerous path up my thigh. "Wait, I need to clean and bandage your wound," I managed to gasp out. "I don't even know how badly you're injured. You shouldn't be holding me."

"It'll take more than a couple minor wounds to prevent me from holding you," he growled. "Especially when you're wearing that dress." He tried to capture my mouth again but I evaded him.

"I'm not kissing you while you're dripping blood. Let me look at your wounds and I promise you can peel me out of this dress later," I said.

Loch grumbled but he put me back on my feet. I kissed his jaw. "Thank you," I said. "Now hop up on the diagnostic table and let's see what's going on."

He moved to the table and I set the scanner to run a full body diagnostic. For all I knew, he could be hiding injuries other than his shoulder. "I'm going to have to cut off the rest of your shirt," I said. Bianca had already cut out a section but I needed to see his entire shoulder.

"If you wanted me naked, darling, you just had to ask," Loch drawled with a grin.

I dug around in Rhys's pristine medbay until I found a pair of scissors. Laser cutters could be a little finicky with blood-soaked cloth, so it was easier to do it manually. I cut away most of the shirt, leaving the section that was stuck to his skin.

The scanner beeped and I checked the display. I blinked and read it again. "You have a blaster hole in your shoulder," I said. "*Through* your shoulder."

Loch shrugged. "When the cowards realized their stun bolts didn't work so well, one of them shot me," he said.

"You picked me up when you had a *hole through your shoulder,*" I reiterated.

"Bianca triaged it. It's just a flesh wound and I heal fast."

I counted to ten and prayed for patience. When I could speak without yelling, I said, "From now on, if you get injured, even if it's just a 'flesh wound,' you will get it taken care of immediately. You will not go around aggravating the injury further." Loch looked ready to argue. "Please," I added, "for me."

He grumbled out something that vaguely resembled agreement.

"Thank you," I said. I doused the remaining piece of shirt in saline and gently pulled it away from the wound. Bianca had bandaged over the worst of it, but according to the diagnostic, the whole wound needed to be irrigated and slathered in regeneration gel.

"I'm going to have to remove the bandage," I said, "and clean out the wound. How do you react to regeneration gel?"

"Better than you," he said with a grin.

# CHAPTER 31

Ten minutes later, Loch's shoulder was covered front and back in bandages while the regeneration gel did its thing. I'd used a sterile wipe to clean off some of the blood, but he still needed a shower. And a new shirt—Scarlett was still somewhere on this ship.

"If you two lovebirds are done playing doctor," Rhys's voice said from the overhead speaker, "then get up here and clip in. We're ready to leave."

Loch flipped off the room then slid off the table.

"Are you sure you don't want me to grab some pain meds, just in case?" I asked again.

"Regen gel doesn't incapacitate me," he said. "It's tingling and that's about it."

I nodded and picked up my bag. Loch picked up the weapon case before I could grab it. "Don't even try," he warned.

We stopped by the crew quarters on the way up and Loch found a spare shirt. He shrugged it on without so much as a wince, and his delicious chest disappeared under the fabric. My fingers itched to pull it off of him again.

"Keep looking at me like that and we're not going to make it upstairs," Loch said.

I was tempted, but we needed to leave before the RCDF decided to take drastic measures. I winked at him and left the room. He followed with a growl.

When we entered the flight deck, I wasn't surprised to see Scarlett in the captain's chair. Rhys knew better than to override the captain of the ship, even if he owned said ship. He sat at the navigator's station and Veronica hovered by his shoulder. An unfamiliar dark-haired man sat in the tactical station.

"Clip in," Scarlett said. "Ground control is getting quite insistent that we leave *now*." Her hands moved over the controls with confident familiarity.

Loch and I sat in the extra chairs along the wall. Veronica sat on my other side. She touched my arm. "Are you okay?" she asked.

Unexpected and unwanted tears flooded my eyes. The one-minute-warning chime sounded throughout the ship, which gave me a moment to compose myself. I blinked rapidly then met her gaze and very slightly shook my head. She squeezed my arm in silent support, then turned her attention back toward the control stations.

The ship lifted away from the ground. This was the last time I would be on Earth for a very long time. I closed my eyes and breathed deeply. I refused to break down in front of strangers.

We settled into orbit and Scarlett stood and turned to me.

"We have about six hours before we can jump back to Sedition. How likely are we to be harassed by the RCDF now that you're on board?"

"They will leave us alone," I said. "I'm still a von Hasenberg and I left the planet with permission."

She eyed me for a few seconds longer then nodded. "Okay. In that case, I'm going to grab some shut-eye. Unlike this fool"—she jerked a thumb at Rhys—"I'm on Universal and I've been up forever. Felix, you're off duty, too. Get some sleep."

The dark-haired crewmate stood. "Yes, Captain," he said.

Scarlett turned to Rhys. "Do not let anything happen to my ship," she said. "I expect her to be in one piece when I wake up."

"I'll do my best," Rhys said.

Scarlett narrowed her eyes but didn't comment. She and Felix left the flight deck together. After the door closed behind them, Rhys said, "Ada, while I'm glad we didn't have to bust you out, how bad is it?"

"It's not great," I said. "Thank you for coming. I'm sorry I involved you, I just didn't know who else to ask."

"You can always come to me for help," Rhys said gently.

"And me," Veronica said. "Rhys tried to leave me behind. See how well it worked for him?"

The maelstrom of emotions I'd experienced today all decided that now was an excellent time to make a break for it. Tears escaped faster than I could blink them away. I took a shuddering breath and tried to get myself under control.

Loch picked me up and dragged me into his lap. He wrapped his arms around me. All semblance of control shattered. I hid my tears against his shoulder and gave myself permission to let go for a few minutes. Loch would keep me safe—I knew it down to my bones.

Loch's deep voice rolled over me while he told Rhys and Veronica what happened. I blocked out the words and just listened to the vibrations as I slowly pulled myself together. I wiped my eyes as the tears stopped, but I kept my head where it was.

"News of your pardon is already hitting the net," Rhys said to Loch. "They're spinning it as a reward for protecting Ada from an unnamed threat and returning her to House von Hasenberg."

"Good," I said. "That means they are sticking to the agreement. At least for now."

"What is your plan?" Rhys asked.

I pushed aside the lost, helpless feelings that tried to rise. I was a von Hasenberg, dammit, and we were never helpless, even when the odds were stacked against us. The worse the odds, the harder we fought.

"First, I need to find us a place to stay on Sedition," I said.

"You're welcome to stay with me while you look," Rhys said. "In fact, you're welcome to stay with me indefinitely." Loch rumbled at him. "*Both* of you are welcome, of course," Rhys said with an eye roll.

"Thank you," I said. "I'm not feeling particularly loyal to Father at the moment, but my brothers and sisters will still be dragged into the war. I will do what I can either to help them win it or to make it unnecessary." After all, neither of my agreements prevented me from telling Lord Yamado exactly what Father and Lady Rockhurst were fighting over. I'd have to weigh the pros and cons, but it was at least one option.

"You're not going to war for the son of a bitch who banished you," Loch said.

"No, I'm not," I agreed. "I'm going to war for Bianca and my other siblings."

AFTER SPEAKING TO RHYS AND VERONICA FOR A FEW more minutes, Loch and I returned to the crew quarters where we'd found his shirt. Luckily there were plenty of rooms to go around, so we were alone.

I sighed in relief as the door closed behind us. We had at least five hours until *Jester* could jump and I was bone weary. Without fear and adrenaline driving me, I just wanted to collapse.

"Are you okay?" Loch asked, expression guarded.

"Yes," I said slowly, "are you?"

He paced the short length of the room. "You lost everything because of my stupidity. You should've left me," he said.

It took me a second to follow his thoughts. Anger sparked, chasing away the fatigue, but I took a deep breath and swallowed the furious words that wanted to escape. We both had issues we needed to work through and this was one of his.

"Marcus," I said quietly, "I'm *never* going to leave you to die if I can do something about it. Just the thought of you dying *hurts.*"

"I'm not worth your life," he said.

"No, you're worth so much more. I don't regret my choice tonight and I would make it a thousand times over. I don't want to fight about this, but I will if you force me. This is a battle you cannot win. You will never convince me that you're not worth it."

I caught his wrist and drew him close. I gazed up at his gorgeous face. Once I had his attention, I said, "I want you beside me. Please stay with me, Marcus."

I glanced away and continued, "I mean, I understand if you don't want me or my drama anymore. I am troublesome and I don't see that changing. But please don't leave because you think you'll save me from yourself. You'll break my heart."

A gentle hand tipped my face back up to his. His eyes glowed. "I want you," he said, "more than I've ever wanted anything. Never doubt that. You're so damn loyal and kind and cunning. Watching you slay your foes with that arrogant little tilt of your head makes me hard as a rock. I may not deserve you, but if you stay with me, I'm keeping you."

My smile had to be blinding, but I didn't care. "You're mine," I said. I pulled his head down to mine and brushed a featherlight kiss across his lips. "And I'm yours."

He groaned and his mouth crashed into mine. I licked his bottom lip then slipped my tongue into his mouth. He sucked on my tongue, sending a bolt of lust straight through my body. I moaned and hooked a leg over his hip, trying to climb him before I remembered he was injured.

I tried to pull back, but he was already picking me up. "Your shoulder," I protested between kisses, but I still wrapped my legs around his waist.

"Is fine," he said. "You don't get to escape me twice in one day while wearing my dress."

He backed me into the wall and held me in place with his hips. The hard length of him pressed against me, a tease of what was to come. I tightened my legs and undulated against him, but he pinned me more firmly to the wall, stopping my movement.

"What are you wearing under this?" he asked. My nipples pebbled from the heat in his gaze. "I've been imagining it all night."

"Why don't you find out for yourself?" I challenged.

His right hand slid under my dress and caressed my thigh, then slipped higher to the edge of my underwear. I thanked the stars that I'd worn something sexy for once. His eyes burned hotter as he traced the lacy design with a fingertip. His palm branded my low belly as his fingers dipped under the waistband of my underwear. I tilted my hips in invitation and moaned softly.

He kissed me slow and deep as his fingers slipped a fraction lower. I whined when he stopped just short of where I wanted him. "I will take care of you," he promised, his voice rough.

"Now," I demanded.

"Always," he said. His hand slid down until his fingers glided through the slick heat of my desire. I claimed his mouth in a scorching kiss as he touched me. Desperate to feel his skin, I pulled his shirt up as far as I could and ran my hands over the hard planes of his stomach. His fingers moved faster and I gasped into his mouth, teetering on the brink.

Wanting to bring him with me, I stroked him through his pants. He hissed out a breath. "Take them off," he ordered.

I fumbled the button twice before I got it open. He pulled back enough for me to free him, then he pressed me back into the wall. I could feel his length nudging me through my underwear, even as his fingers continued their maddening circles.

"How much do you like this underwear?" he asked.

"I'll buy more," I said.

"Good answer," he growled. He gripped the delicate lace and pulled it in half. I moaned at the loss of his fingers. I was so close. Then he tilted my hips and buried himself in me.

The world exploded.

He worked me through it, then kept going. Languid delight gave way to building desire. He kissed and licked and petted until I once again hovered at the edge of orgasm. When he hit the place that made me see stars, I was determined to take him with me. I pulled his head down for a kiss and clenched around his length. He tensed and his smooth thrusts became erratic as he, too, tipped over into bliss.

He braced a hand on the wall, breathing hard. "You'll pay for that," he said without an ounce of threat. "I had plans for you." He walked backward to the bed, still buried inside of me. He fell back and took me with him.

I nestled against his chest, sated and content. "Well, I plan to have my wicked way with you just as soon as I can feel my legs," I told him. "So you'll just have to wait."

He smoothed his hands down my back and I sighed in contentment. We basked in the afterglow for a few minutes, then Loch rolled onto his side and met my eyes. "What will you do in Sedition?" he asked.

"After we figure out how to save my siblings from war, I thought we might see if Rhys needed a business partner," I said, subtly emphasizing the *we*. "Unless you have something else in mind. I wasn't kidding when I said I had plenty of money for both of us, but I can't just sit around. I need something to keep me busy or I'll drive us both crazy."

"I've been on the run for so long that I don't even remember how to be normal," Loch said.

"Normal is overrated. If we go into business with Rhys, you would make a kickass smuggler," I said. "Or you would be a fantastic mercenary, though I don't recommend that route so much." I caressed his cheek. "I don't care what we do," I said, "as long as we're doing it together."

Loch pulled me close and tucked me against his chest, under his chin. "I'm afraid you're not getting rid of me now, darling," he said. "You're mine. And I'm all yours."

"Good," I said around a jaw-cracking yawn. "I wouldn't have it any other way."

"Sleep, Ada. I've got you," he said.

As I snuggled safely in Loch's arms, exhaustion crept up on soft feet. Tomorrow I would endeavor to win a war I wanted no part of, but for right now, in this one perfect moment, I was exactly where I wanted to be.

BIANCA AND IAN'S

EPIC ADVENTURE

IS COMING

FALL 2019.

BE PREPARED.

# ABOUT THE AUTHOR

Jessie Mihalik has a degree in computer science and a love of all things geeky. A software engineer by trade, Jessie now writes full time from her home in Texas. When she's not writing, she can be found playing co-op video games with her husband, trying out new board games, or reading books pulled from her overflowing bookshelves. Visit her at www.jessiemihalik.com.